MW00829997

DESTINED
MATE

—⟨ 1 ⟩—

TWISTED FATE TRILOGY

CHAPTER ONE

WOLF HOWLS PIERCED MY EARS, adding more of a chill to the already cold Oregon February breeze blowing across my skin.

The sound was only a mile or two away. The noise had come from behind me, which meant the wolves could stumble upon my scent and track me.

A shiver raced down my spine.

I wasn't supposed to be out here, far from our pack neighborhood in Oxbow, Oregon. This area marked the state line between Idaho and Oregon, where someone in our pack could easily trespass onto Idaho land and cause problems with the neighboring royal adviser. There was no telling who these wolves were.

Coming here to hike Hells Canyon National Recreation Area had been a mistake, but this was one of the safest places for me to walk alone, and I desperately needed time to myself after our alpha, Zeke, had forced me to clean his house and miss my shift at the local coffee shop *again*. I was going to get fired, and my chance to escape the pack was being stolen from me because of my position as the weakest wolf in it.

I tried to push away my concern and admire the shining full moon high in the vast, cloudless night sky. Cloud-free nights were rare here—another reason I'd decided to sneak out for this walk.

The third reason was that I couldn't shift because my wolf was so weak, so when I had a stressful day like today, I came here.

Multiple wolves howled, and they were closer... only about a half mile away.

My chest constricted as the wind picked up, rustling the branches of the surrounding larch, lodge-pole pine, cypress, and true fir trees and adding to the already eerie atmosphere. My wolf stirred within me— or so I suspected. The sensation resembled a churning in my chest rather than in my stomach.

Gods, I wished I could pack link, but that was yet another thing I couldn't do.

Knowing I couldn't head back because I'd run into them, I ran deeper into the woods toward the canyon the Snake River flowed through. I could use the water to cover my scent. If these wolves were part of my pack, I couldn't use the knife strapped to my ankle to defend myself against them, or I'd be in trouble with the alpha. But standing here to take whatever abuse they decided to bestow upon me wouldn't be smart, either. I had to get away.

Hell, the only reason I had the knife was to defend myself against another pack, especially with the king and queen of the Southwest territory making moves to take over Oregon.

I propelled myself into a run. I could hear the

panting of the wolves drawing closer and the pounding of their paws in the forest mulch.

The hair on the nape of my neck rose. With each breath I took, air puffed in front of me like fog. The temperature was close to freezing, but I no longer felt it. Not with adrenaline and fear pumping through my blood.

For each step of mine, the wolves gained two on me, and a prickly sensation washed over me. I was their prey.

I pushed forward, determined to get away. I dodged roots and tree trunks across the forest floor, knowing them almost as well as every beat and cadence of Evanescence's "Bring Me to Life," a song that spoke to me on a level very few did—one that hit me in the gut and defined how beaten down and numb to my future I'd become.

Rocks lay scattered less than a half mile away. Losing focus, I stumbled over a large stone hidden by grass and landed on all fours. Sharp pain jolted through my hands and knees, which had taken the brunt of the tumble. This was nothing compared to what my pursuers could do, so I scrambled back to my feet. Hopefully, I was being overly paranoid and these wolves were merely running and playing and just so happened to be heading toward the Snake River Canyon like me.

Something inside me flinched at my naivety.

Despite my warmer internal wolf temperature, a frigidness settled deep in my bones as the pack drew closer until I could make out five wolves behind me. They'd be on me in minutes, no matter what I did.

I'd been foolish to come out here on a full moon, but

it was forbidden to be in this area in wolf form, or so I'd thought. What the heck? My anger and resentment had made me willing to take the chance, and now I wished I could go back in time and stay home.

Unable to link with anyone in my pack, I reached for my phone in my back pocket. I needed to call Theo. He'd come and help me, and they'd listen to him since he was the alpha's son. I paused, hating to stop, but escape was futile.

As I typed out *help*, the wolves emerged behind me between two larch trees. My eyes widened as I took in who they were, my attention settling on the one that hurt the most, my sister Pearl. It was easy to tell her apart from the others, as her fur was almost solid white.

After hitting send, I stuffed my phone back in my pocket and faced them.

The dark-gray one—Charles, my sister's boyfriend—was in front. He snarled and bared his teeth at me. His minions behind him followed his lead, including my sister.

They wanted to scare me. They wanted me to feel weak. They wanted me to cower.

That was what any *good* weak wolf would do—submit. But I was never able to, not even when it was in my best interest. My parents always scolded me, but something inside me *refused* to show weakness and would rather take the beating.

I straightened my shoulders despite the nausea churning in my stomach. A small but logical voice screamed at me to flee, but my body stood firm and still while I lifted my chin in defiance.

With two wolves flanking Charles, they stopped short of me. Bryson, at the end on the left side, shook his light-gray fur while Josh's beige wolf stood between him and Charles. Pearl was between Charles and Fred, a charcoal wolf whose fur stood on end.

I tried to keep my expression indifferent, showing no fear or anguish. But seeing Pearl here, actively trying to bully me, squeezed my heart like a vise. I didn't know what she had against me, but she was the sibling who'd never accepted me as part of the family, even though I was five when they took me in.

Straightening my shoulders, I said, "I'm just out for a walk. I'm not trying to cause problems, and I won't tell Zeke you were here in your wolf forms if that's what you're concerned about." It wasn't as if our alpha would believe me, anyway, if the five of them called me a liar. He always thought the worst of me, no matter the situation.

Charles bared his teeth, drool dripping from his snout. He pawed at the ground as if he were about to charge.

I needed to submit. They'd still be cruel, but nowhere near as bad as if I didn't. However, I *couldn't* avert my eyes to the ground. I stared into Charles's eyes as if I were challenging him. A lump formed in my throat, and I struggled to breathe around it.

Great.

He crouched, ready to spring at me and prove he was stronger. That was when some logic sank through my thick skull, and I took a step back. He was in wolf form, which was when a shifter's magic was at its strongest, while I was human. There was no way I could win a fight against him. Hell, I didn't want to attempt to fight because I had no doubt how it would end.

I lifted my hands in surrender, but my dumb ass still couldn't break eye contact. "Seriously, I don't want any trouble. I need to be close to nature, and since I can't shift, I come here. Just go run and play, and I'll head back home. You won't see me again."

The breeze picked up, and the temperature dropped several degrees as Charles's hackles rose.

Josh chuckled, which sounded like a wolf choking. The hardening of his ebony eyes and his low tone made the sound as cold as the air. They were going to attack to teach me some fucked-up lesson. I might as well go down with a little bit of dignity.

Inching closer, Charles kept his attention on me. He moved slowly, no doubt to get inside my mind, making me anticipate the attack. The emotional side of abuse was more important to them than the physical— that was just the icing on the cake. Their prize for being so patient and toying with me.

Tensing, I glanced at the huge true fir on my left. I could climb it and wait for Theo to get the message and come help me, but that would be worse in the long run. They would know their advances had frightened me.

They would wait for another opportunity to teach me whatever lesson they thought I needed.

Charles pounced, his front paws aimed at my chest. When his claws ripped into my skin and his momentum pushed me over, I screamed. I landed on my back, my head hitting the trunk of a lodgepole pine. The stinging exploded down my spine while a pounding throb flooded my brain. My chest clenched from the cuts, and my favorite fuchsia shirt was now ripped and stained crimson with blood. My head fogged from a combination of fear and suffering.

He dug his claws deeper into me, and I whimpered loudly. His mouth opened, and his tongue lolled out as if he were smiling and crazed.

I had to get my knife. There was no telling how far he would take this, especially with the other four behind him, pacing and yapping, egging him on.

Letting my instincts take over, I rolled onto my side, catching Charles off guard. He fell off as I got my knees underneath me and jumped to my feet.

Out of the corner of my eye, I saw white fur barreling toward me. Before I could move, Pearl had steamrolled me straight into the tree. I couldn't catch my breath, and my ribs screamed, on the verge of collapsing.

They'd never injured me this badly before. Usually, I got a few bruises or scratches from being shoved or grabbed, but this was far beyond that.

Screaming from my injuries, I grabbed her neck behind her wolfy head and yanked. She faltered a few steps, then swatted at my arm, her claws slashing my skin. The other three wolves surrounded me, caging me in by the tree as Charles got back to his feet.

His icy-green eyes glowed as he linked to the others. They had to be discussing what to do with me.

Pearl took a few steps back, and I swore I saw regret or uncertainty in her hazel eyes, but within a second, they hardened.

All five of them moved toward me. This wasn't just bullying—they were intent on hurting me, possibly worse. I was out here alone and completely at their mercy.

More paws pounded toward us, and I hoped Theo had returned home from his run and seen that I needed him. But when the other five didn't react, my stomach soured.

I swallowed, knowing I had no choice. I had to use the knife...if I could get to it. I wasn't ready to die. I believed there was something more out there waiting for me.

I bent to retrieve the knife from my ankle strap. As soon as I moved, they rushed me, likely because Pearl knew what I was doing. Our parents had given us each a knife.

Josh jumped onto my back, knocking me over. I did a forward roll, his claws tearing the skin along my spine. Torturous agony radiated all over my back, chest, and ribs. My vision blurred, and another scream rang in the air from somewhere...or maybe I was yelling. Not that it would do any good.

As I landed back on my feet, I flailed the knife around, desperate to hit something, anything. I felt it connect, and a wolf whimpered, but I wasn't sure who. I could only hope I'd hit some sort of mark.

My hope was short-lived as Bryson and Fred attacked me from opposite sides.

They nipped at my shoulders, their teeth cutting my flesh, but not so deep that I'd bleed out...at least not quickly.

Whimpers from Charles and Josh hit my ear. Then Fred and Bryson were ripped away from me. I smelled four new shifters, people I'd never met before. I couldn't see what was happening.

My shirt was shredded, so I wrapped my arms around my chest, ignoring the throbbing that ripped through me, and scooted back to the bottom of the tree.

I took in the four newcomers. They radiated even

more power than Zeke did. One had blond fur, while the others were various shades of brown. They definitely weren't from our pack, as most of us were gray and white. We'd gotten another pack involved in our confrontation.

Zeke was going to kill us...especially me.

CHAPTER TWO

BLOOD LEAKED from my shoulders down my arms, the warm liquid coating my fingers as I took in the sight before me.

Pearl had lowered her head to the point it was almost touching the ground. She was cowering as Charles and the others had tried to make me do.

Charles and Bryson swayed on their feet. Josh and Fred were slumped at the bottom of the two trees closest to me where they'd been tossed.

I quivered as the adrenaline wore off and the reality of the situation washed over me.

I wasn't sure how far Charles and the others would've taken this attack. I understood they had wanted to make me cower, and I'd refused. But to what end? My death? And why the hell hadn't I submitted? Why had I fought back, making the problem worse? I had to be a glutton for punishment, but the thought of giving them more power over me didn't sit right.

The blond and the two darkest-furred wolves hunkered down in front of me. They watched Fred and

Josh get back on all fours and kept an eye on Pearl and the others. They bared their teeth, revealing they were fine with attacking again if needed.

The chestnut-furred wolf trotted over to me, his warm and somehow familiar indigo eyes examining me. They captivated me as I struggled to place where I'd seen them, but I came up blank. Despite Zeke leading the Oregon territory, I rarely associated with wolves outside my pack members. Of the few I had met, I would've remembered eyes like those.

He huffed and shook his head as if completely disgusted by what he saw.

Now *that* was a look I recognized. Everyone in my pack looked at me that same way. Like they couldn't believe someone could have such weak magic.

He sniffed me, then gently nudged me with his head. Pain rocketed through my ribs, and I gasped and jerked away.

Flinching, he hurriedly moved back and flicked his head up, trying to communicate with me. He wanted me to stand.

Sitting here all night wasn't an option, so I gritted my teeth and slowly climbed to my feet. More suffering enveloped me, but somehow, someway, I got onto two legs, each breath labored.

I looked down, cataloging the injuries I could see. As I'd suspected, my shirt was in shreds and drenched in crimson. The bites on my shoulders were deeper than I'd imagined and would take a couple days to heal, even with my shifter magic. My body stung and ached, a combination I'd never experienced before, and my suffering increased as the adrenaline wore off.

Charles whimpered and stepped toward me, and

even though I wanted to flinch, my body remained still. I locked eyes with him again. I had to stop doing that, but I physically couldn't force my gaze away. It was as if something inside me had taken control, and I was at its mercy.

Charles emanated a strangled, angry noise—a warning.

The blond wolf sidestepped between us and growled at Charles, forcing him to drop to all fours and submit again.

The chestnut wolf huffed, and now that I wasn't locked in some demented power struggle with Charles, I turned my attention to him. The wolf jerked his head behind us in the direction from which we'd all come.

"Do you want me to head that way?" I asked.

He nodded and jerked his head again.

I wondered if these wolves were from the Southwest pack, but I didn't care. Even if they were, they'd helped me, which was more than my own pack had ever done, and they were trying to communicate with me with growls and barks, showing me some respect.

I would use them for help as long as they were willing, though once I got home, I'd be on my own. But Theo, my best friend and the alpha heir would be there and have some influence, so things might not be quite so dire.

My knife had fallen to the ground during the attack. There was a little blood on the tip, confirming I'd hit someone before they'd teamed up and jumped me. I bent down to retrieve it, and blood rushed to my head, causing the world to spin. My ribs screamed in protest, and bile inched up my throat.

The chestnut wolf grunted as he ran to me and

picked up the knife with his mouth. He then trotted toward our pack neighborhood.

Standing upright, I bit the inside of my cheek, trying to focus so that I wouldn't vomit. Taking a small step forward, I closed my eyes and waited for the discomfort to intensify, but the movement wasn't as bad as bending over. Nothing below my waist hurt, so there was that.

I took slow and steady steps, following the chestnut wolf.

The three strong wolves formed a barricade behind me, growling softly as if they expected Charles and the others to attack. My pack wolves stood in place while I shuffled away, the chestnut wolf slowing to walk by my side.

An owl hooted close by while a larger animal—I guessed a bobcat from the sound—stalked around near us. Nature was back in full swing as if nothing almost life-altering had occurred.

I couldn't deny that things were getting worse between me and my pack. That was why I was determined to maintain a job outside of pack life—so I could save up and get the hell out of there. The more I refused to submit, the more determined they were to break me. The cycle was becoming a self-fulfilling prophecy—as if I had a death wish.

I didn't. I wouldn't fight against them nearly as hard if I did.

The chestnut wolf padded leisurely beside me, keeping my pace and not pushing me to move faster. Judging by the way he held the knife in his mouth and scanned the area for threats, I guessed he was a skilled fighter.

When the trail I normally took home appeared, I moved to the right, but the wolf swiftly moved in front of me and pointed his snout to the left.

Fuck me. My blood cooled as the enormity of the situation settled over me. He was leading me toward Idaho. The territory of a royal-advising alpha whom my alpha couldn't stand.

"Uh...my pack is this way." I tried to lift my arm, but I'd barely shifted it off my chest before my ribs panged as if someone had kicked me. I placed my hand back on my shoulders, covering my bare chest.

The wolves probably thought I was stupid for protecting my modesty. Shifters usually weren't bothered by nudity, but I was, mainly because I'd never shifted.

He shook his head and motioned in the opposite direction.

When I didn't move, he planted himself in my way, making it clear he wouldn't allow me to go the way I wanted.

Normally, I'd be willing to fight him, but not after what I'd gone through. He'd have me down within seconds. Begrudgingly, I turned left and set out again, with him following close behind me.

I didn't know this trail since I'd never ventured to this side of the recreation area. The river ran through it, and it was most definitely too close to the Idaho state line. I had to watch my steps more closely, although my wolf side was strong enough to make me agile.

As we moved farther from my pack lands, cold tendrils of fear unfurled throughout my body. Even though these wolves had saved me from my pack, the closer we came to the state border, the more I'd pay for this misadventure when I finally went home. Charles, Pearl, and the others would surely tell our alpha their version of what had happened.

There was little I could do now, and I continued to force one foot in front of the other, playing Kelly Clarkson's "Stronger (What Doesn't Kill You)" in my head, focusing on the lyrics. I had to believe they were true. I wasn't dead, so I'd survive. I had to.

As soon as we were close enough to hear the rush of the Snake River, the distant pounding of wolf paws hurried toward us. My heart clenched, and I glanced at the wolf beside me, trying to gauge whether he was alarmed. When he didn't tense or glance behind him, I took a slightly deeper breath. "Are those friends of yours?" I didn't know what to call his companions. They all emanated strong power like an alpha, but they were together. I wasn't sure if they had a superstrong pack or if four packs were close enough for all their alphas to be friends. That would be rare.

He nodded, not breaking his leisurely pace.

I couldn't figure out why these four wolves were helping me. Normally, wolves minded their own business, but for whatever reason, they had come to my rescue.

We stepped through the trees and walked down to the rocky embankment. A canoe had been pulled onto the shore, and four sets of clothes were scattered around it, indicating the place where they had stripped to shift.

The chestnut wolf brushed my leg, then dropped my knife at my feet. If they were planning to hurt me, he wouldn't have given me back the weapon. Although, considering how strong they were, I didn't stand a chance against them even with it.

When the other three wolves ran between sage-brush bushes and toward me, the chestnut wolf gently picked up a shirt, jeans, and underwear with his teeth before rushing back into the tree line.

I raised my brows. Shifting in private was definitely not the norm in my pack.

The ebony-furred wolf trotted over to me and sat beside me with his body turned toward the tree line, keeping watch as the other two shifters followed the chestnut wolf, grabbing their clothes and running in the same direction.

With his attention diverted, I examined the ebony wolf. He was larger than any wolf in my pack, including Zeke. Beside my five-foot-ten-inch frame, he came to my waist, and his fur was gorgeous, the color of the night sky.

Twigs snapped, and I glanced back to where the wolves had disappeared. My jaw dropped.

The most handsome man I'd ever seen was marching toward me.

He was tall, even by shifter standards, coming in at perhaps six and a half feet. I knew exactly which wolf he was from the messy chestnut hair that fell over his forehead and his indigo eyes, which appeared lighter against his sun-kissed complexion. My eyes lowered, taking in his scruff, and dropped further to his shirtless body. His lean, muscular form was stunning...not too muscular, but definitely not fat, and I wanted to touch the curves of his muscles. Jeans hugged his body, but I had no doubt the lower half was just as enticing as the top portion was.

"You can go and shift, Miles," he said as he strolled over, his white shirt in hand.

Miles gingerly took his clothes and ran off to join the others. My focus, though, stayed on the sexy man standing in front of me.

His forehead lined as he scanned me. "How much pain are you in?" The concern was foreign to me, especially coming from someone as strong as he was.

I glanced down at my injuries. My hands were covered with drying blood, and soon, they'd be sticky. "I've had better days," I replied dryly. "But it would've been worse if you and your friends hadn't helped me, so thank you." I swallowed, my throat suddenly parched. "I really need to get back to my pack. I'm sure Charles and the others are already telling my alpha everything, and, well, he won't be happy with me."

Brows furrowing, he stared into my eyes. "He won't be happy with *you*? What about them?"

This was a conversation I'd never dreamed of having. "Pack hierarchy. I'm the weakest of us all, so..."

His eyes glowed, and his voice turned gravelly. "Wait. This behavior is *normal*? They've done this bullshit to you before and gotten away with it?"

More power radiated from him, and I lifted my chin, not liking the way he was speaking to me.

The blond and brown-haired men joined us.

"Bodey, chill," the blond said. His hair was longer than Bodey's, with waves that fell into his eyes. He had a similar build, just a bit smaller and shorter, but his cobalt eyes were jarring. "She's been through a horrible experience at the hands of her own pack members, so back off, douche canoe, and don't freak her out more." He winked at me. "I'm Jack, by the way. And you are?"

My face warmed. "Callie."

"Flirting with her won't help." The second dark-haired man rolled his eyes and lifted his hands as he approached me like I was a timid animal. He was almost as tall as Bodey but leaner. His dark-brown eyes matched the shade of his goatee, and they were full of concern. He gently touched my arm, my blood-streaked pale skin contrasting with his tanned hand. He sighed. "We need to clean your wounds before they get infected."

I hated the attention and, worse, that they were treating me like a delicate flower. I didn't know how to react, especially when my own pack treated me with malice. "I'm fine. I should head back home. I need to tell the alpha my version of tonight before he won't listen."

"Just link with them." Jack tapped his head. "Tell him you're with the royal advisers from the other four territories. We'll back your story."

Shit. Now it made perfect sense. These four were none other than Bodey Valor, royal adviser of Idaho, Jack Landry, royal adviser of Washington, and Miles Harper, royal adviser of Wyoming, who had just gone to change, and that meant the man trying to take care of my wounds was Lucas Barret of Montana. They were each the strongest alpha in the state they represented. I hadn't thought all four of them could be from the same pack, but I hadn't expected *this*. They were supposed to be self-absorbed troublemakers, per Zeke, but they were the only ones who'd ever helped me in my entire life.

Zeke was the fifth royal adviser, based out of Oregon, but considering how close-knit these four were, he was the outsider.

I wrapped my arms tighter around myself. "I can't link with them." Now the four of them would decide I wasn't worth the effort. They'd realize how weak I was and finish what Charles had started.

Bodey tilted his head. "What do you mean, you can't pack link? The alpha shut down his connection with you, and you can't communicate with him?"

I wished that was the problem. I shook my head. "I've never been able to pack link, at least from what I can remember. I don't remember much from before my pack took me in when I was a young girl."

Lucas mashed his lips together. "Well, you have to submit and acknowledge the alpha as yours."

"Dumbass." Jack snorted, but it lacked humor. "I'm sure they made her."

"They did, fairly soon after I came here. When I couldn't pack link with them immediately, they thought I needed time to adjust, but it never happened. Then with my not shifting..." I trailed off and shrugged.

Bodey's eyes widened. "That's why you didn't shift when they attacked you. We were wondering."

My face flamed, and I averted my eyes to the ground in embarrassment.

Silence descended until the fourth guy—Miles—joined us. The moon shone down on him, emphasizing his gorgeous bronze complexion. He was two inches taller than me and thicker than the others. He ran a hand through his short ebony hair, and his dark-green eyes were full of kindness.

But I wasn't foolish. These four men *seemed* kind, but they could take me down and anyone else who stood in their way. My wolf could feel it.

Nerves buzzed hard under my skin. The breeze picked up, and I shivered.

Bodey held out his shirt. "Here, do you want to go somewhere and put this on? Your shirt is ruined."

"Thank you." I had no clue why Zeke hated him so much. He was kind and helped me, even though he didn't have to. "But I need to get back before it gets worse. They're gonna want to know where I am."

My cell phone dinged. Grimacing, I removed it from my back pocket and glanced at the message.

Theo: Where are you? I'm at your house, and you aren't here. Charles is telling Dad what happened. He's livid that you were in the canyons and attacked them. Get home now, and I'll protect you as much as I can.

I lowered my phone and turned to the trees. "Thank you for everything, but I have to go."

I'd taken only a few steps when a gigantic, calloused hand gripped my upper arm.

Bodey growled, "You aren't going anywhere."

CHAPTER THREE

BODY RADIATED POWER, so much so that I could feel his command sink straight into my bones. Despite being weak, my inner wolf never considered cowering, not even when my brain told me to. Even when Zeke used his alpha will, I wanted to fight back and usually had to resort to biting my cheek until it bled so that I wouldn't run my mouth.

For the first time ever, my wolf damn near submitted but then decided not to. I straightened my back and faced him. My ribs burned, and I almost whimpered, but I gritted my teeth to hold back the noise and stood my ground. "I have to go. My alpha is looking for me."

Bodey snatched the phone from my hands and stared at the message on the screen.

"Hey," I snapped and took it back, returning it to my pocket. "That's rude. You don't read other people's messages without their permission." I waited for him to put me in my place. I always did this and got myself into more trouble.

"It's going to get worse." His eyes darkened to midnight black. "It seems like your alpha has already decided you're guilty. How is that even possible? He hasn't heard your side!"

"Dude," Jack said as he smacked Bodey on the back. "I'm sure she's well aware of that. Next thing you'll tell us is that the sky is blue and Nirvana isn't the best band ever."

Bodey snarled.

Lucas shook his head. "Not the time, Jack."

Apparently, Jack liked the sound of his own voice, but I needed Bodey to see reason. "It's their word against mine, and the longer I stay away, the guiltier I'll appear." He couldn't argue with that.

"She's right." Lucas sighed. "We should let her go. This is Oregon pack business. Besides, she needs to rest and take care of herself. He can't deny they attacked her—just look at her."

My shoulders relaxed. At least one of them was on my side. "Theo will be there to help me handle his father, the alpha."

"Theo?" Jack's head snapped toward me, interest clear on his face. "As in Theo Stark?"

My breath caught, so I nodded. They'd piece together who I was now.

Bursting out in humorless laughter, Jack ran his fingers through his hair. "Zeke Stark is your alpha. Why am I not surprised?"

By the way Lucas's, Bodey's, and Miles's noses wrinkled, it was clear the four of them felt the same way about Zeke as he did about them. But now I understood why Zeke didn't like them. All four of them were more powerful than he was.

There was no point in denying it. "Zeke is my alpha."

Miles crossed his arms and rubbed the scruff on his face. "Bodey, I get this sucks, and I hate having to remind you, but it's the rule. We can head back with her and tell him what we saw."

Growling, Bodey glared at him and said, "You're right." His jaw twitched. "It's just that none of this should've happened. Wolves shouldn't hurt one another, especially not their own pack members."

I sucked in a breath. "You guys don't treat your weak shifters this way?"

"King Richard was a big advocate for mutual respect and caring for one another, even across territory lines." Lucas's lips pressed into a firm line. "Since we haven't had a king in seventeen years, things have gotten far more lax than they should have, but that will change when Prince Samuel takes the throne in a couple of weeks."

We'd heard about the future King Samuel from Zeke. He was turning eighteen in two weeks and would finally be old enough to ascend to the throne. Zeke had informed us that pack tensions would worsen once that happened, but I wondered if that was because he'd once again have to answer to someone. I cherished the fact it would be someone so much younger.

"The reason the adviser roles were created was that the original pack had grown too large for one person to manage across five states," Lucas continued. "Our job is to ensure we function as one pack, the way it originally was, with everyone's best interests at heart."

This was new information to me, but it didn't

matter. I had to get back to Zeke. "Thank you for helping me, but—"

"Here, Callie." Brows furrowed, Bodey held out his shirt. "Go put this on."

I cringed. I'd forgotten I was nearly shirtless, even though it was why I'd been clutching my chest. I didn't want to obey him, but the last thing I wanted to do was stumble back to my pack this torn up and broken. Accepting the shirt was more for me than about him.

Before I could reach out to take it, he'd placed it in my hands gently, so I didn't have to extend my arm and injure myself again.

My vision blurred at his kindness.

He took a hesitant step back. "I know it'll hurt to put that on. I'm willing to help if you want."

"No!" I exclaimed.

Jack snickered and muttered, "Bodey's stealing my lines."

Lucas thumped the back of Jack's head. "Shut up, man. Not helping."

Face flaming, I cleared my throat. I didn't want to come off like a jackass. "I meant I'd rather do it on my own, but thank you for offering."

"Of course." He gestured toward where the four of them had shifted back into human form. "There's a concealed spot over there if that works for you."

"I'll be just a minute." I shuffled in that direction, needing a moment to myself to process everything—the attack, the four alpha advisers, their kindness, and Zeke searching for me. My head spun, and I wasn't sure if it was from confusion, blood loss, pain, or a combination of all three. I didn't know how to stop them from going back with me. It would only piss Zeke off more, but what could I do? If I ran, these four would catch me, and even if I got away, they knew where Zeke lived. They would show up anyway.

With shallow breaths, I ducked behind a gigantic larch and groaned as I lifted my arms to remove my shirt. Fire sliced through me, and nausea churned in my stomach. I dropped my hands to my sides, trying to think of an easier way to get out of the pathetic excuse for a shirt. The best option I had was to rip the rest of it off.

"You know he won't be thrilled when we go back with her," Lucas said, and I realized I could hear them from their spot on the embankment. "He won't like that we interfered."

"We can't let her go alone. From that text, it's clear there's no telling what she'll be walking into," Bodey replied. "Zeke is an ass."

"Hell yeah, he is," Jack added bitterly. "If he were on fire, I'd find some gasoline to finish the bastard off."

Laughter bubbled out of me before I could clamp it down. Most of the pack revered Zeke, especially the wolves he favored. Zeke had a way of luring people in when he wanted to, but he'd never even attempted to use that charm on me. From as far back as I could remember, my mere presence had incited vicious stares and words.

"It sounds like I'm not alone in that sentiment." Jack chuckled. "I like her more already."

My knees weakened, and I almost fell down. I wasn't used to anyone being nice to me, but he'd actually complimented me.

Me.

The weakest wolf most shifters had ever seen.

I released the shredded fabric of my shirt, watching the pieces float down and settle on the leaf-covered ground. I didn't have many things I valued, and that shirt had been one. Just another thing my pack had taken away from me.

I unfolded the white shirt, and delicious scents of cinnamon and sandalwood swirled around me, smelling just like Bodey. It was one of the best things I'd ever smelled, and the scent seemed vaguely familiar. I lifted the shirt to my nose and took a deep whiff as if I were some sort of perv. Lovely.

"Jack, for the love of gods, keep your mouth shut," Bodey grumbled, and someone's shoes scuffed against the rocks.

Ribs screaming, I tried not to groan as I lifted my arms to put the shirt over my head. A whimper escaped.

Miles exhaled. "We need to take her back."

"Yeah, she needs to clean those wounds and rest," Lucas repeated as if no one had heard him before. "I'm surprised she wasn't harmed worse."

Shirt on, I stumbled from behind the tree. The garment's hem hit my knees, and it looked as if I were wearing a large dress. "*She's* right here and heard everything."

"Sorry if we were rude." Miles cringed. "That wasn't our intention."

"Look, I appreciate everything you four have done and are trying to do. *Really*. But I can go back on my own." I didn't want to cause more problems between Zeke and the other four royal alpha advisers, especially with the pending coronation. They were about to spend a lot of time together.

Bodey karate-chopped the air. "Absolutely not.

We're going with you. We need to tell our side of the story."

I hadn't considered that point. Charles wouldn't have only made me out to be the bad guy; he'd have vilified them as well, probably not realizing who they were. I sighed in defeat.

Jack cackled. "Do you know how many women would love to have just one of us escort them *anywhere* for *any reason*? You're getting all *four* of us. It's like a buy-one-get-one-free deal times two!"

I arched a brow. All four of them were hot, especially Bodey, but the last thing I needed was a distraction. I had one goal, get my own place away from the pack. "You aren't lacking confidence."

"I *am* a superstrong alpha." Jack patted his chest.

"Man, stop talking," Bodey rasped, smacking Jack in the back of the head.

That had happened twice in the past ten minutes. I had no doubt it wasn't an anomaly.

Lucas rubbed a hand down his face. "Let's just go."

Now *that* I could get behind. Instead of waiting for one of them to take the lead, I headed back in the direction we'd come from. My misery had eased slightly, indicating my shifter healing was kicking in. I needed to get home and clean the wounds just to be sanitary. Shifters rarely got infections, but given how weak my supernatural side was, I wouldn't risk it.

The four of them trailed behind me, having no problem with me taking the lead. Zeke—and even Theo—wouldn't have tolerated it, proving how different these four were from my pack.

My phone dinged again, and I winced as I pulled it out.

Theo: Callie? Are you okay? I'm getting worried. Charles said something about rogue wolves attacking them and you running off?

Me: Sorry. I'm okay. I'm heading home now.

After I hit send, I kept my phone in my hand. It put too much strain on my injuries to reach back and put the phone into my pocket again.

Guilt weighed on me. I should've warned Theo that Bodey, Jack, Lucas, and Miles were heading home with me, but I didn't want to give Zeke time to prepare. For once, I would have the upper hand against him.

Bodey caught up to me, his irises back to the gorgeous color I seemed to get caught up in. "Hey, everything will be fine." He smiled reassuringly. "We'll make sure of it. The five wolves who attacked you will get into trouble."

I smiled sadly and kissed my fingertips before holding them up to the moon. "You can't say that. It's a promise on behalf of someone else."

His breath caught, and something shimmered in his eyes. "Why did you do that?"

"Tell you not to make a promise you can't keep? Because Zeke isn't like you and your friends."

He clutched my elbow, stopping us. "No—you kissed your fingers and held them up to the moon. Why?"

"Oh." I shrugged. I'd done it on instinct. "It's something I occasionally do when someone has misguided good intentions. I'm asking the moon to bless them for trying." I wrinkled my nose and hung my head, not wanting to see his reaction. It sounded silly, but it was something I'd always done, though no one had noticed before.

"I once knew someone who did that for the same reason." His eyes narrowed. He scanned my face as if searching for some sort of answer.

I fidgeted under the intense perusal.

"Is something wrong?" Lucas asked, his voice tense. "Is there a threat?"

Bodey blinked, and whatever had come over him vanished. "Nope. I just got distracted."

"By Callie's face?" Jack asked with approval. "I could easily be, too. It's by far the prettiest I've ever seen."

I lowered my head, using my blonde hair as a barrier between Bodey and me. A shiver ran through me—not because Jack was acting like a creeper but because I wasn't used to compliments.

A low growl sounded from Bodey. "She's off-limits, Jack."

My heart skipped a beat, which was foolish. It wasn't as if Bodey was interested in me. He was clearly a nice guy...a good alpha.

I picked up my pace, despite my ribs protesting. I needed to get the confrontation with Zeke over with so I could go to bed and rest. And get some space.

Bodey caught up with me again, but he didn't speak. He occasionally glanced at me, his face strained like he couldn't figure me out.

Five miles later, we broke through the last of the woods that made up Hells Canyon and stepped onto the private land of our pack. Zeke's main pack consisted of two hundred shifters, but he oversaw all the packs in the entire state, so over five thousand shifters in total.

The back of the one-story brick house I called home came into view, and I hurried. All the lights were on, despite it being close to two in the morning, but that wasn't what gave me heartburn. *That* was due to the man waiting in my backyard with Theo.

My parents weren't outside, which wasn't surprising. The alpha would want to speak to me alone.

Even though I'd known this would happen, seeing Zeke there was a whole different experience. His emerald eyes tightened, and his face scrunched in disgust. He had his arms crossed over his black shirt, his short salt-and-pepper hair messy. His face was flushed, darkening his normal olive complexion.

Theo frowned, his caramel hair falling over his forehead and his topaz eyes fixed on me. He was shirtless from his run, and it was noticeable how much more muscular he was than his father. I saw his shoulders dip as he sighed.

I knew the moment Bodey came into view. Zeke's eyes widened, and Theo's jaw went slack. When the other three stepped up behind us, Zeke clenched his hands into fists.

When we reached him, Zeke growled, "What the hell are you doing here? This is *my* territory."

Bodey lifted his chin and stepped closer to me. "Those are your first words? No concern for your pack member?" He gestured at where blood had seeped through his white shirt.

"Gods, Callie, are you okay?" Theo asked, but his attention remained on Bodey.

"Shut up, Theo," Zeke snapped and marched over to me, getting in my face. "She caused problems in our pack, so she got what she deserved. You aren't supposed to go to Hells Canyon." His eyes glowed.

Theo flinched but remained quiet. Any time he pushed to protect me, Zeke punished me harder.

"I know, and I'm sorry." I didn't lower my gaze, but at least I hadn't said anything to make the situation worse. "But Charles, Pearl, and their friends were also there, and *they* attacked *me*," I added, my lips moving of their own accord. Well, there went my attempt at complacency.

He sneered. "I saw Josh's stab wound. That's bullshit. *You* threatened *them* and somehow got rogue wolves and four alpha advisers involved."

"Those *rogues* were us." Bodey gestured at himself and his friends. "And we can vouch for her version. We heard the howls and growls, then a human scream, so we rushed over to check it out. All *five* of them were attacking her at once, and she nicked one when she had no choice but to protect herself."

I expected Zeke to call him a liar, but he remained silent, his eyes still hard...still cruel. He arched a brow. "Is that so?"

"Nope, we're just here for shits and giggles." Jack scoffed. "Oh, wait, there aren't any giggles, but I sure smell a pile of steaming shit somewhere in front of me."

Laughter bubbled in my chest, and as I covered it with a cough, I felt as if I'd been punched in the ribs again.

Zeke's head jerked toward Jack. "What did you say?"

Jack threw up his hands. "And now he has selective hearing."

"Man, quit it," Miles scolded and moved in front of Jack. "What Jack is trying to say is, of course it's true. Why else would we be here?"

"She's bad off," Lucas added. "And needs rest. We should let her take care of herself now."

Bodey scanned me again. "I want to know what you plan to do about your pack members."

"I'll get them under control, but you four need to go. You shouldn't be here." Zeke rolled his neck.

All four tensed as Lucas rasped, "We have *every* right to be here. Just because we oversee other territories doesn't mean we're restricted from neighboring areas under the Northwest jurisdiction."

Zeke's neck corded. "You're right. It's been a long night. Thank you for coming and making sure I heard what you saw."

"You won't punish Callie for defending herself, correct?" Bodey asked and leaned back on his heels, watching Zeke.

"This is my pack business, but since you made the effort to bring her home, I'll oblige you with an answer." Zeke's expression smoothed. "She will not be punished for that. You have my word."

Wow. I hadn't expected to get off that easily. Maybe it had been smart for the four of them to come with me after all.

"Okay." Bodey scratched the back of his neck. "Well, Callie, it was nice meeting you. I just wish it had been under better circumstances."

The other three agreed and said their goodbyes before walking off.

Theo, Zeke, and I stood there, watching the four of them leave. For some reason, it hurt to see them go. I'd only just met them, but there was something comforting about being with them, like I'd known them my whole life.

As soon as they disappeared into the thickening trees and the gorgeous mountains, Zeke murmured low enough so they couldn't hear him, with the usual edge of hatred in his tone, "Now it's time to truly talk."

My heart dropped, and my blood ran cold. I would still be punished, after all.

CHAPTER FOUR

A SOUR TASTE filled my mouth. I'd been foolish to even consider that I might come out of this unscathed. I should've known Zeke had chosen his words carefully.

"Let's go inside where we can talk in case those four don't wander off as they should," he growled as he gripped my arm. "And you'd better not make a noise."

Zeke's and Theo's eyes glowed as they spoke through their pack link.

A moment later, Theo said loudly, "You should go inside and get some rest. I'll come by and check on you in the morning."

I gritted my teeth. Zeke must have told Theo what to say to keep up the illusion.

When Theo opened the door, Zeke shoved me through and into the maple rectangular kitchen table. My right hip hit the edge, and my body jerked. A deep ache ripped through me. I whimpered.

Zeke chuckled, and I hated that I'd made the damn sound. I glanced around the space with its familiar beige-painted cabinets, unsurprised to see I was alone with these two. Zeke had likely commanded the rest of my family to stay in their rooms.

"Dad, was that necessary?" Theo asked as he passed his father and pulled out the chair in front of me on the side of the table closest to the door. "She's already injured."

"She has to learn *her place*," Zeke spat from behind me.

Having him at my back was a good thing because I couldn't prevent my eye roll. He was a pompous prick and, unfortunately, one I had to endure.

Theo lifted his brows in warning.

All that did was make me more frustrated. I gritted my teeth and lowered myself into the seat. Whether I liked to admit it or not, my injuries had zapped me, and my eyelids were growing heavy. As I sat down, my bones felt as if they were separating, and my teeth cracked from how tightly I was clenching my jaw.

"What's hurting you?" Theo asked.

Zeke's feet scuffed the beige tile as he marched to the spot in front of me and leaned against the island.

"My ribs mainly, though my arms, back, and shoulders don't feel great." I didn't want to elaborate because Zeke didn't care.

"Now that we're alone, tell me exactly what happened," Zeke demanded.

This was it, the beginning of my certain conviction. When it came to me, there was no innocent until proven guilty. It was guilty until Zeke pretended to consider my story and still blamed everything on me. I licked my lips, taking a moment to gather my thoughts as the harsh edge of the pain waned. "They told you what happened. Why do you need to hear it again from me?" Anything I added would give him ammunition to hurt me.

"No, they told me what *they* saw, which had started before the four of them arrived." Zeke crossed his ankles, leaning back more. "Charles, Fred, Bryson, Josh, and, most importantly, *your sister* said they caught your scent and followed you when they realized you were heading to Hells Canyon."

"Of course they did," I deadpanned, my mouth running away from me again. Now I had to reevaluate whether I did have a death wish.

Zeke straightened, placing his palms on the dark-beige granite countertop. "Which direction did they come from?"

I knew what he meant, but I couldn't help but be a little contrary. "Technically, there was a lot going on that messed with my bearings."

His lips flattened. "Of course. You're so *weak* that you can't even keep your bearings like a normal wolf. Let me try again. Did they come from behind you?"

Yup. He knew the answer and what he could say to make me tell him what he wanted to hear. I'd been so stupid, thinking the alpha advisers vouching for me would get me out of trouble. I was now certain it was just going to make everything worse.

Defeat crushed me, but I refused to crumble. "From behind, but they were out there before they smelled me."

Theo flinched. "How do you know that?"

My head jerked back as my blood heated, but I didn't take my attention from Zeke. "They were howling, barking, and running around before they grew silent. That was when I knew they'd caught my scent. They weren't out there because of me."

"What would you know about shifting, girl?" Zeke spat, and his face turned its usual shade of pink that manifested whenever he was around me. "You've never shifted. You don't know what wolves sound like when playing or hunting. You don't know *anything*. That's how I know your sister and the others are telling the truth."

I leaned back in my seat, my body protesting. This was pointless. I was guilty. There were five against one, and that one was me. I had no clue why this man hated me so much or why he'd taken me in. "Let's pretend they're telling the truth...you know, for *shits and giggles*," I said, repeating the phrase Jack used to insult him.

"Callie," Theo warned.

"Five of them attacked *me*. I can't even shift to access my magic and strength to protect myself. How is that fair?" I hated being treated like this...viewed like this. "That *is* something the four alpha advisers know. They pulled them off me."

Zeke clutched the countertop even harder, his knuckles blanching. "That might be the case, but I've dealt with you every day for the past seventeen years. There's no doubt they had to do what they did to make you listen. I'm not a fool. I know what happened."

"But—" I started.

"Let me finish!" he barked, cutting me off. "Not only have you made the four other royal advisers aware that one of the weakest wolf shifters to ever exist is in my pack, but they'll think I don't have my pack under control. Do you know how bad this is? Those four always work against me."

I bit my tongue. The more I pushed, the worse the punishment would be.

"It's hard enough to make sure they don't try to take my territory, but then you had to go do something like *this*. It's unacceptable, and you'll be punished."

That had been his plan all along. He wouldn't punish me for the attack but rather for being out there and getting the alpha advisers involved.

Like usual, I bit the inside of my cheek, and blood filled my mouth. This little tic had become somewhat comforting.

"Here's what's going to happen." Zeke pushed off the countertop and slammed his hand on the table, and the loud *thump* echoed off the kitchen's cream walls. The table cracked but didn't splinter. This was an intimidation tactic he used frequently with me, and I *hated* it—not because it worked but because it made me want to fight back harder. I tried to school my expression despite the anger churning through me.

Whatever look crossed my face, Zeke must have approved because he smirked, thinking it was fear instead of barely bridled rage. "You're going to work for Charles in the morning. You'll do whatever he requests. Then you're going to cycle through the other four, your sister being last. Whatever they want, for however long they want." He nodded and locked eyes with me.

My cheek was throbbing, so to stop myself from telling him exactly where he could go, I switched to biting my tongue.

"Do you understand?" Zeke demanded.

"I do." Of course he wouldn't give me a few days to

heal. "But I need to leave by five to get to work on time. I already missed my shift tonight when you had me clean your bathrooms." Which hadn't needed to be done, but I couldn't refuse my alpha.

He shook his head. "You will stay as late as required to finish whatever they ask of you. If it's after five, you'll have to miss work again. Besides, you don't need a job outside of the pack. We provide you with a home, food, and everything you need."

That was the kicker. For whatever reason, he made it difficult for me to work outside of the pack. Even my parents worked for an outside company, although their jobs were remote and they worked from home. Still, there were plenty of pack members who owned businesses and held jobs in Halfway, a town thirty minutes away. "By accepting the job, I made a commitment. I can't keep missing shifts."

Zeke leaned across the table, his face inches from mine. His foul garlic breath hit my face, and I damn near gagged. "You're not *listening*," he breathed. "You'll do what I say, and if you lose your job, so be it. That's not my problem."

My hands fisted, and the urge to punch the prick surged within. I bit my other cheek, giving my tongue a reprieve. Remaining quiet, I didn't falter, keeping my gaze steady as I stared right back at him.

His nose wrinkled. "You're lucky you've survived this long. You'd better watch it. Not only is the entire pack tired of your attitude, but you can't shift. You're lucky we haven't kicked you out. You're worthless, and we tolerate you because we took you in, but even that goodwill is fraying. Learn your place, or I'll be forced to teach it to you, no matter the cost."

A chill ran down my spine. If that wasn't a threat, I didn't know what was. There was no doubt he was insinuating death. Maybe I should cut my losses and run away.

"Dad," Theo said, "I think she got the point."

"She better have. My tolerance is over, and if you leave, your family will pay the price for that, too." He stood again and pointed at me as he continued. "You will be at Charles's house by eight in the morning. Got it?"

I glanced at the clock on the black stove across the room. It read two a.m.

By the time I cleaned up and got myself in bed, I'd have less than five and a half hours of sleep. That wasn't enough time for my injuries to even halfway heal, but that was the point. Gods, I hated this asshole. "Got it," I said bitterly.

"Good." Zeke grinned and crossed his arms. "I'll be there to see you arrive. And if those alpha advisers try to contact you, you'll say nothing of this. Otherwise, life will get worse for you and your entire family."

Every time I thought I couldn't dislike him more, he proved me wrong. I'd better stop tempting Fate. I had to get the hell out of here without causing too many more problems.

Zeke turned on his heel and left via the front door.

When it closed, Theo hung his head. "What did you get yourself into?"

"Clearly, not a good time." These were the moments when he irritated me and reminded me of his father.

"Cal," he said tenderly, his expression softening.

"You know better than to go out there. I've told you to stop."

I unclenched my teeth, and the taste of copper had my stomach gurgling. "I needed to be outside and alone. With the full moon, I knew most of our pack would be running around here, and I didn't want to deal with any judgment because I can't shift. I wasn't trying to disobey. I just needed some peace and silence. That's it."

"We need to find you a better place to go." He pushed up the sleeve of Bodey's shirt high enough to see the first set of claw marks. "They got you good."

"I'm well aware." I tried not to wince. Having him see me like this made me feel too vulnerable, which pissed me off. "Theo, I'm telling you, those five weren't out there hunting me. They were playing, wanting to get away until they caught my scent and decided to have some fun."

"Maybe, but it doesn't matter." Theo's face hardened, his expression slightly cold again. "All of them, including your sister, are stronger wolves than you. You can't keep stumbling into these confrontational situations and disrespecting them."

"Now you sound just like your dad." Even though he was my best friend, one of the few I could count on, he still tended to anger me.

He tilted his head and smiled sadly. "You know I care about you, but I'm not alpha. There's only so much I can do. I need you to follow the rules until Dad hands the pack over to me."

I huffed, and my throat constricted. I didn't believe his father would ever hand over the pack. Bodey, Lucas, Jack, and Miles were their packs' leaders, and they weren't much older than Theo. Their parents were in their eighties, just like Zeke. Wolves in their eighties were middle-aged for our species, but the responsibilities of an alpha were draining, and a shifter's power began to weaken around that age. Usually, if an alpha felt their heir was ready, they passed the responsibility on to them and served in a supporting role.

"Go get some rest. You have a big day tomorrow." Theo stood and helped me to my feet. "If I stay too long, he'll get mad at me, too."

"Yeah, I need to shower and sleep." I yawned, unable to stop myself. Thankfully, my mouth was already healing. I just wished my body would heal faster. "I'll see you out."

I locked the back door, and the two of us walked through the living room, past the tan cloth couch that sat across from the wide-screen television and a family portrait. At the door, he turned to me, his gaze landing on my lips.

I took a step back. I didn't like the way he was looking at me. He'd been doing it a lot this past month, and I should have been thrilled, encouraging his interest. It would help get the other pack members to back off, but I didn't see him in that light. So I winced, playing up my injuries.

The warmth in his eyes vanished, and he frowned. "All right. I'll come by and check on you tomorrow."

I forced a smile. "Thanks."

When he left, I locked the front door and went back through the living room, taking a moment to glance at the family picture from just two years ago. My younger sister stood between me and Pearl, with Mom and Dad behind us. They'd wanted the kids positioned in order of age, which would've been Pearl, me, then Stevie, but Pearl had refused to stand next to me. She'd even tried to exclude me from the picture completely, which hadn't surprised me. She'd hated me ever since I arrived.

The way she treated me always stung, but it wouldn't change. There was no point in dwelling on it.

I turned right and entered the small hallway that led to a bathroom and two bedrooms on the left and right.

Stevie and I shared the bedroom on the right, so I tiptoed inside, only to find her dark-brown eyes glistening as she watched the door. As soon as I walked in, she sat up, her forehead creased as she scanned me. "Are you okay?" Her dirty-blonde hair was braided, and her tanned skin reflected the light from the hall.

"I'll be fine."

She gestured to the white nightstand that divided her navy-decorated full bed from my fuchsia one. "I snatched some Advil and water. I thought you might need it."

I smiled, my chest expanding. "Thank you." I walked over and took the medicine, then set the water back down. "I'm going to take a shower. Get some rest. I'll be crawling into bed soon."

"Good night. If you need anything..." Stevie bit her bottom lip.

"I'll ask you." I placed a hand over my heart. "Promise."

I grabbed a shorts-and-shirt set of fuchsia pajamas and headed into the bathroom. I turned the water on lukewarm, not wanting to unclot my wounds, and climbed in. Getting clean hurt like a bitch, but when it was over and done, I felt better.

I set my alarm for seven thirty and put it on vibrate, then climbed into bed and put the phone beside my pillow since I didn't want to wake Stevie if possible. My eyes closed, and I was out within seconds.

SOMETHING BUZZED, and my eyes cracked open. I reached over with a twinge of pain and turned off the alarm. I wanted to roll over and go back to sleep, but Zeke's words echoed in my head. *You will be at Charles's house by eight in the morning. Got it?*

If I didn't get my act together, he'd ensure that I learned my lesson and that my family was involved. After everything they'd done for me, I couldn't make them a target for his anger. I had to get moving.

I inhaled, realizing I could breathe normally again without discomfort; I'd just need to be careful not to take any deep breaths. I climbed out of bed, trying to minimize my movements while remaining quiet, then grabbed my phone and earbuds and sneaked out of our bedroom to the kitchen. The smell of bacon, biscuits, and eggs greeted me, and my stomach grumbled.

Mom stood by the stove, her shoulder-length ash-blonde hair pulled into a ponytail. She glanced over her shoulder, her aqua eyes filled with concern. "Callie. Thank gods. I was worried you might not be able to fulfill the alpha's punishment."

That validated what I'd already assumed. He'd decided on my punishment before I returned. "Don't worry. I'm up."

A few feet away from Mom, Dad opened the fridge and grabbed the orange juice. "Will you be okay doing the work? I can ask Zeke to give you another day…"

"I'm fine." I wasn't, but Dad talking to Zeke would only make the situation worse.

Mom opened the upper cabinet between the stove and refrigerator and grabbed three plates, then filled each one with food. "If that changes, let us know. You don't need to hurt yourself worse."

They were such good people. Though I was blessed with a crappy pack and a shitty alpha, at least the family who'd wanted me was kind. "Okay."

She brought the plates to the table while Dad poured the orange juice. I sat down, starving, and devoured my food in minutes. Now I needed to get to Charles's place. If I showed up right at eight, Zeke would be annoyed.

Once I took my last bite, Mom said, "I'm sorry you're going through this, but you really shouldn't have been out there, even if it wasn't your fault."

I nodded. I didn't have much choice, but at least she'd acknowledged I wasn't entirely at fault.

"Since Pearl was involved, we're gonna punish her." Dad reached across the table and patted my hand.

I hung my head. *Great.* That would make things worse. But they were trying to do what was right for me.

"You don't have to, seriously. It might get back to Zeke." I squeezed his hand and stood, trying to keep from grimacing. "I gotta go, but I'll be back for lunch." I walked around the table and hugged Mom, then kissed Dad on the cheek.

"Be careful," Mom called as I headed out the door.

Our home was at the very back of the pack neighborhood. At the end of our road, I turned left and passed three houses to get to Charles's. Of course, he and Zeke were already in the front yard, waiting for me.

Every house looked similar here, a sign that this was a shifter neighborhood, and I tensed when I noted three cases of pink peonies and three cases of candytuft with numerous large rocks sitting on the sidewalk near the front of the house by several bags of soil.

As I strolled over to them, Charles grinned. He held a shovel and a pair of gloves, and as soon as I got close to him, he handed them to me. "My parents and I hate landscaping, so it's the perfect time for you to help," he said and beamed, likely because he knew gardening would be excruciating for me with my injuries.

"This won't be a problem, right?" Zeke crossed his arms and lifted his chin.

Hot rage swirled through me, but instead of answering him verbally, I moved to the dead plant beds and began digging them out.

Zeke chuckled and walked toward the road. "That's what I thought. Charles, let me know if she gives you any grief or stops working."

"Oh, I will." Charles laughed and walked into his house.

When the door shut, I paused to pull up my playlist. I put in my earbuds and blared Destiny Child's "I'm a Survivor." Then I went back to work.

My ribs had begun to heal overnight, but they weren't getting better anymore. Not with the way I was digging holes and planting flowers. My only salvation was my playlist of survival songs. That and the fact the peonies and candytufts were pretty.

Pain raged through me, making every movement and shallow breath torment. I tried to focus on the lyrics and the music—anything to distract myself.

They didn't want me to finish. They wanted to break me. I wouldn't give them the satisfaction, even if it killed me.

As I turned to drop a shovelful of dirt on the ground, someone jerked the shovel from my hands.

My stomach tensed, and the hair on the nape of my neck stood on end.

I spun around and immediately hunched over from the sharp pain. But when I saw who stood in front of me, the world stopped.

CHAPTER FIVE

THIS HAD TO BE AN ILLUSION. Why would he be here? But no matter how many times I blinked, I was still staring at a muscled chest, and when I tilted my head up, gorgeous indigo eyes locked with mine.

It seemed like a dream, but the intense way my ribs protested confirmed I was still grounded in reality. This was worse than any pinch could be.

My heart fell into the depths of my stomach.

His expression was strained, his jaw clenched so tightly that I worried it would break. As he scanned me, his eyes darkened.

The anger and power radiating off him had me taking a step back, and I damn near tripped over the peonies I'd been about to plant.

"What the *fuck* do you think you're doing?" Bodey growled, his words barely audible.

And in that moment, I learned there was such a thing as a stupid question.

I glared as anger pulsed through me. "Sunbathing and drinking margaritas." I wished breathing didn't hurt so I could amp up my sarcasm, but alas, here I was. "What does it look like?"

His nostrils flared. "You're injured."

"Oh, wait, is that why breathing hurts?" I needed to shut my mouth. He could do so much worse to me than what Zeke could do, but my mouth had a mind of its own.

He didn't flinch, probably because he was used to Jack. Instead, he ignored my words and asked, "Why are you doing yard work? This isn't even your house."

All my smart-assness vanished. I'd hoped to fluster him and drive him away, but he was standing his ground. *Figures.* Damn alphas.

Now I was in a pickle. If I didn't get him to leave, pronto, Zeke would be alerted that he was here...if he hadn't been already.

I looked around. The front yards were empty. No one else was doing yard work in February—at least, not on a Monday. Mostly because they actually had paying jobs.

I had to answer him, but not in a way that would encourage him to stay. The problem was that I had *no clue* how to do that. Anything I said would only irritate him further.

I removed an earbud, which was blaring Rachel Platten's "Fight Song," and peered over Bodey's shoulder. A new black Jeep Grand Cherokee sat crookedly in the middle of the road with the driver's door open. When I didn't see the other three with him, relief and confusion battled one another.

"I'm still waiting for an answer," Bodey pressed, his jaw twitching.

"Well, I..." I stuttered, trying to come up with a plausible explanation for *this*. If I lied, he'd know. "I..."

He stepped closer, holding the shovel to his side while his scent swirled around me more. "You...?" he prompted and arched a brow.

This was bad. The enormity of the situation had my legs weakening, and if it hadn't been for my ribs, I'd have likely crumpled into a mess on the ground. He was demanding an answer, and I was screwed whether I responded or not. If I didn't, he'd stay. If I did, he would refuse to leave. There was no way out, and Zeke would accuse me of calling him.

"Callie," he said tenderly, placing both hands on my shoulders. "Please tell me what's going on. I'm fairly certain I already know, but I need to hear you say it before I confront Zeke."

Yup, I was screwed. I might as well bend over and take it like a man—er, woman—er, person. Whatever. Any type of person who enjoyed that sort of thing.

I'd opened my mouth to answer when the front door opened, and Charles barreled outside in his flannel pajama bottoms and a black shirt. He rushed onto the sidewalk and stopped in front of us. "What the hell is going on out here?" He gestured to the plants, stones, and mulch. "You're interrupting her work." He sneered.

The tenderness vanished from Bodey's demeanor, and he grimaced again as his anger returned. When he inhaled, my lungs seized. I suspected he'd figured out who Charles was.

"You're one of the jackasses who attacked her last night," Bodey stated, his hands dropping from my shoulders.

Forehead creasing, Charles crossed his arms. "This is *none* of your business, so you need to leave before my alpha gets here."

His threat fell flat as Bodey's hands clenched into fists. "Actually, it *is* my business since I was one of the four who pulled you and your cowardly friends off a single girl in human form." He puffed out his chest as his neck corded, the strength of his alpha wolf emanating from him more strongly than before. He moved in front of me as he continued, "So, please make sure Zeke gets here. In fact, tell him I'm waiting."

Charles's jaw went slack, and he lowered his head. "I've notified him, *sir*." His demeanor had changed, becoming more submissive, though his body tensed, betraying he wasn't happy about it.

The dumbass was too wrapped up in himself and determined to make sure I suffered to realize who he was confronting. I hoped Bodey would put him in his place, though that was a double-edged sword. Charles would take it out on me after Bodey left.

I needed to intervene. I didn't want my family to suffer because of this.

"Bodey, please calm down." The words chafed my throat as if part of me were trying to hold them back...as if part of me were disgusted. I hated when it felt as if someone completely separate was living within me. "It's fine. I promise."

I took a step toward him, wanting him to see my face and realize I was being sincere, but my vision blurred, and I groaned.

The work had taken more of a toll on me than I'd realized.

Bodey spun around, his forehead creased with

concern, causing my breath to catch and another pang to shoot through me. He placed his hands back on my shoulders to steady me. "You need medicine and to lie down and rest."

Something squeezed in my chest. It was odd—uncomfortable but pleasant—and I couldn't help but notice the strong cut of his jaw and the shape of his full lips.

I shook my head, trying to get these random thoughts and feelings out of my head.

"What's wrong?" His frown deepened as he bent so we were eye to eye. "Is your head hurting or something? Maybe we should take you to a healer."

His effort to help me would make things worse, but I couldn't get upset with him for his genuine desire to help. He and the other three royal advisers held a kindness that Zeke lacked.

Every cell in my body buzzed. Why couldn't his pack have been the one to find me all those years ago? If they had, my life would've been so different...better.

Focus, Callie. I bit the inside of my cheek, my teeth digging into the sore spots from last night, and the throbbing, comforting pain embraced me. I'd learned that *what-if*s didn't solve the problem. In fact, they often left me spiraling and expending energy I didn't have to spare. As a child, I'd learned to push them from my mind, but for some reason, this time, they were harder to push away. And there was no doubt why. It was because of the man standing in front of me. He represented the most powerful emotion of all.

Hope.

Hope that somewhere out there, things could be different for me.

But that wasn't the case. Zeke wouldn't let me walk away. He'd use my family against me.

"Callie, talk to me," Bodey begged, pulling me back to the present. "What's hurting you?"

If it weren't for my ribs, I would've laughed. The easier question would've been what *wasn't* hurting. "I'm fine. I need to get back to work."

"See?" Charles said as he moved next to Bodey. "She's fine. You can leave."

He might as well not have said anything because Bodey gritted, "You are *not* fine. You're worse off than when we left you last night. Zeke promised he wouldn't punish you."

Needing a distraction from Bodey's face, I glanced at the flowers to my right. "He promised I wouldn't be punished for the attack. That's not why I'm out here."

His whole body tightened, including the hands on my shoulders, bringing my focus back to him. With his strong, masculine face and muscular body, he could easily pass as one of those statues of gods from back in Roman times.

"Son of a bitch," he growled. "I shouldn't have left. I *knew* better. But this is his pack, and I'd already interfered enough. I wanted to give him the benefit of the doubt."

Two sets of footsteps echoed in my earbudless ear. The lighter set was Theo's. Zeke always clomped as if the harder he walked, the stronger he seemed.

Idiot.

Bodey turned in their direction and dropped his hands from my shoulders as he straightened.

He was getting ready to argue, and this would be a battle of wills in which I—and possibly my family—

would lose. I had to try to salvage this one more time. "Bodey, please. I've got to do this. Just let it go." I placed a hand on my side to support my ribs so I could move a little more easily, but I gasped instead.

"Hell no. I'm not *letting this go*. This is unacceptable." He turned to me again, his face softening. "He can't expect you to do this. Callie, this isn't healthy in more ways than one."

I opened my mouth, but Zeke interrupted, "Did *she* call you?"

I scoffed and turned my attention to Zeke, confirming my worst fear. His face was flushed, and spittle pooled in the corner of his mouth. His hands were shaking.

He was livid and barely holding it together.

"What sort of question is *that*?" Bodey asked as he marched the last five feet to meet Zeke. "Did you tell her not to?"

Theo moved to my other side and scowled. His face contorted as he removed my other earbud and whispered into my ear, "Do you realize what happened?"

I clenched my hands, my nails digging into my palms. For once, I was glad he couldn't link with me. There was no telling what else he'd be saying if he could.

Zeke threw a sneer my way and said, "I'm just asking—did she call you?"

He didn't want to answer the question, and I suspected Bodey knew why. Shifters could smell when someone lied, just like we could smell when someone was scared, aroused, or happy. Any heavy emotion released different chemicals in a person's body, slightly altering their smell. A lie was the easiest to detect because of its foul odor.

"No, she didn't. I wanted to check on her because of how bad off she was last night, and I drove up to find her in one of her attackers' yards, shoveling dirt despite her injured ribs and the claw marks all down her arms and back." Bodey rocked on his heels. "Now that I've answered your question, I want an answer to mine. Did you tell her not to call me or any of the royal advisers?"

My chest swelled. That right there proved what I'd already guessed. Bodey was smart and understood how people thought. He'd worded his question carefully to make sure Zeke would struggle to find a way to answer without outright lying.

"It doesn't matter," Zeke answered, leaning toward Bodey. "She's *mine*. I can punish who I want for what I want in whatever way I see fit. You have no say in the matter."

"So she *is* being punished. You promised last night that you wouldn't punish her."

"No, I did not." Zeke snorted. "I said I wouldn't punish her for the *attack*. This is for other things."

Bodey tilted his head and rubbed his chin. "Like what?"

"Is this guy serious?" Charles gritted out.

Theo's head snapped toward Charles, and their eyes glowed. Then Charles huffed and went inside.

Crossing his arms, Zeke stood as tall as possible. "You don't get to question me. I'm her alpha *and* the Oregon territory adviser. This is *my* territory, and I'll do what I deem fit."

"Is that so?" Bodey asked before beaming and looking down his nose at Zeke. "According to the

Northwest shifter law, if any *person* feels that an alpha is abusing their position and treating someone unjustly or causing undue harm, any alpha can intervene, even across territory lines." He shrugged as if it weren't a big deal. "I know for a fact that Callie didn't commit any heinous crime that would justify this sort of punishment, so I'm invoking my right to interfere."

Butterflies assaulted my stomach. I'd never heard of any such law. Maybe I could get a reprieve, even for a little while. Anything was better than nothing.

Theo stiffened as his father's face turned scarlet.

Breathing rapidly, Zeke spat, "Clearly, we're not putting her at risk—she's already done over half the job already."

Sighing, Bodey pivoted toward me and grimaced. "I'm sorry," he murmured.

A hollow sensation sifted through me as all that damn hope vanished. I couldn't blame him, and in the long term, it would be best if he left. But I feared I'd never see him again.

It was silly. I hadn't even known him for a day, but he stirred something comforting inside me.

I forced a smile. "It's okay."

When he held out the shovel to me, Zeke grinned victoriously.

I swallowed, mentally preparing myself for the torture I was about to endure. Refusing to appear weak, I schooled my expression and grabbed the handle of the shovel.

He didn't release it, and I dropped my arm back to my side. Tears trickled from my eyes. Nausea roiled through me, and I was certain I was going to puke.

Lifting the shovel, Bodey gestured to me. "She can't

finish this job, yet you're determined to force her. You're risking her health and well-being."

Zeke stared at me feverishly like I'd done something wrong. For once, someone was challenging him.

"I want you to listen carefully." Zeke moved forward, stopping inches from Bodey's face. It was almost comical since Bodey had at least three inches on him and was twice his size, but Zeke wasn't daunted. Instead, he continued, "This is my territory and my pack, and you need to leave now. How I handle things here is my business and mine alone. I don't go into Idaho telling you how to run things."

"If I leave, you'll add on more punishment just because I showed up to check on her," Bodey said as he looked down his nose, emphasizing his size and power over Zeke. "Not happening."

"Theo, take her home. *Now*," Zeke commanded as he grabbed my arm and jerked me away from Bodey.

I stumbled from the jolt that zipped through me at the sudden movement, but thankfully, Theo rushed over and wrapped an arm around my shoulders, righting me.

Bodey snarled, but Zeke bellowed, "King Richard is dead, and you're not taking her. Now get off my land."

"It's true we don't have a king," Bodey agreed with another snarl. "But here's the thing. His laws are binding until another royal changes them. Therefore, I'm invoking the law, and I will be taking her home with me."

Theo stilled, and my mouth dropped. Was that possible?

"You don't have that authority," Zeke spat. "I demand a vote review."

"You're right." Bodey removed his phone from his back pocket. "But I can get a review right now." He nodded at me and said, "Callie, this won't take long. Head home and I'll be there shortly to help you collect your things."

Zeke's irises glowed as he stared at his son, but Theo turned before Bodey could see.

"I'll take her home," Theo said and dropped his arms from around me.

The two of us walked away just as Bodey's phone connected.

"Come on, Callie," Theo murmured in my ear. "We need to get a head start."

In other words, they were determined that I was staying, even if the other three advisers agreed.

CHAPTER SIX

I TRIED to keep up with Theo's pace, but I had to slow down, or I'd vomit here on the street.

When I started to lag behind, Theo slowed a little. He rasped, "I'm sorry, Callie, but we need to move as quickly as you can. You know I can't protect you from Dad."

A sharp pang stole my breath, and acid filled my mouth, burning my throat. I swallowed it, trying to ignore the way it felt like fire going back down. My injury worsened with every movement, and Bodey was right. To get better, I needed to lie down and rest.

I stumbled but forced myself forward.

Theo murmured, "Come on, Callie. Just a little farther, I promise. We need to hurry."

My chest tightened. I had no clue what he and Zeke had planned, but it definitely involved preventing me from leaving with Bodey.

I missed a step in my haste, and a yelp left me before I could lock it down.

"Slow the *fuck down*," Bodey commanded from

Charles's yard, only fifty feet away, watching us. "Her ribs are injured."

Huffing, Theo flinched. He didn't like anyone besides his father telling him what to do.

Someone picked up Bodey's call, and Jack's voice filled the air. "Hey, man. Where are you? Please tell me you're getting breakfast to bring back."

That was interesting. I didn't know why, but I'd expected Miles, Lucas, and Jack to know that Bodey was here. The fact that they didn't unsettled me. Maybe they wouldn't be on the same page as him after all. Dread sat heavy over me.

"Can you pick up the pace?" Theo asked, his eyes filling with concern. At least he was starting to act like my friend again instead of his father's right hand. Granted, he did try to do both, which had to be hard.

I nodded and bit my cheek, forcing my legs to move faster. Though the pain was excruciating, I could use my cooperation as proof that I'd attempted to go along with their plan.

"My gods, Callie," he whispered. "You really are bad off." He cleared his throat as if this was brand-new information. The worry rolling off him softened my anger toward him.

Bodey, Zeke, and the other three alphas were talking behind us. I could hear each voice, but their conversation was muffled because all my focus was on putting one foot in front of the other.

Reaching my house felt like it had taken hours, even though mere minutes had passed. Theo opened the front door, revealing Pearl and Stevie sitting on the couch, watching television.

Still dressed in her pajamas, Pearl lifted a brow and

smirked. "What are you doing here? You're supposed to be at Charles's house, working off your punishment."

Groaning, Stevie leaned her head back on the couch. She was dressed in jeans and a black shirt, which was standard for the coffee shop she worked at in town. "She's hurt, Pearl. Leave her alone. Theo is with her, so she's not trying to hide anything from Zeke."

"*She's* right." Theo gestured at Stevie. "Go pack your sister a bag quickly. Make sure she has enough clothes for a couple of days."

"Of course." Stevie jumped to her feet and scurried to our bedroom.

Pearl took note of my hand in Theo's, and her smirk changed into a deep scowl. She'd always wanted Theo, but Charles was the strongest wolf who gave her any attention.

I shivered and turned to Theo. "What do you mean 'a couple of days'?" Where in the hell were they taking me?

He turned to me, his face softening. "Dad told me to take you away for a few days. Long enough for the alpha advisers to calm down and forget about you."

My limbs shook. I hadn't known these four for even a full day, yet I didn't like the idea of them forgetting about me. "But where are we going? And will I be able to get to my job from there?" Every day, this situation with me and my pack became more dire. I had to find a way out.

"Forget the job, Callie." Theo huffed, causing Pearl to smile.

"Theo, not you, too. *Please*."

"I'm *sorry*, but that's the whole point of disappearing. We're heading to a remote cabin owned by the pack. Only a few people know it exists."

Pearl's mouth dropped. "Wait, you're going to stay there with *her*?"

I was appalled, too, but for a different reason. The way Theo had been acting around me for the past month didn't sit well with me. He looked at me as if I held the answer to something, and though it would have been ideal if I were into him, I wasn't. He was my best friend and the future alpha, and I couldn't risk getting into a relationship with him in case it ended horribly.

"We need to go," Theo said, ignoring my sister. "And don't worry. You can still work off your punishment there. Dad already has ideas of things you can do while you take time to heal as well."

Sure. Zeke didn't give a shit about my injuries, but I didn't have enough energy to run my mouth. Worse, it wasn't like I had a choice. If I fought Zeke's request, my family would suffer the consequences.

Mom and Dad appeared in the hallway that led to their room slash home office, Pearl's room, and the garage. Their brows were furrowed, and Dad's mouth was mashed into a firm line.

Dad stopped in front of the door that led to the garage, blocking it. "Are you sure this is a good idea?" He glanced at me, his forehead creased. "She's hurt, and the Idaho alpha adviser is here."

Of course, Zeke and Theo would've informed my parents using the pack link.

"We have no better option." Theo held out his free hand. "For whatever reason, Bodey is determined to take her away."

If I hadn't gone out for a walk last night, none of

this would be happening. Normally, I tried not to dwell on things, but damn, this was a curse that kept on giving. Not only was I being torn away from my family, but I would also face more of Zeke's wrath.

Dad tossed Theo a set of keys as Mom headed over and touched my shoulder gently.

"We're taking one of your cars?" Now I felt even worse. My parents had two vehicles, and if we took one, it would put more of a strain on the family. Though my parents worked from home, Stevie and Pearl each drove a car to reach their own jobs in Halfway.

"They can use mine while we're away," Theo replied, squeezing my hand comfortingly. "I'll let Dad know I gave them permission."

Stevie's footsteps had Theo springing into action. Dad opened the door to the double garage.

I walked much more slowly behind him.

Twirling the keys around the finger of his free hand, Theo huffed and fidgeted. I realized he was getting impatient with me.

Stepping down from the hardwood floor to the cool concrete of the garage, I groaned faintly.

"Please power through a little bit longer. You'll get to rest soon." Theo's voice was tender with concern. "Dad won't come around until later to bring my clothes and some food, so you'll have time to heal."

He was nice...whenever his dad wasn't around, and though I wasn't thrilled at the prospect of being alone with him for that long, at least he'd treat me kindly. We'd been friends for as long as I'd been part of the pack.

Wanting to honor his request, I bit my tongue and stumbled to the car closest to the house door, an older black Buick Lucerne. The other car, an older gray Honda Odyssey, was parked close enough that Theo had to be careful when he opened the passenger door.

He helped me into my seat, but even then, my vision blurred with unshed tears. Somehow, I got into the car without passing out.

Stevie opened the back seat and tossed my fuchsia duffel bag inside.

"I also got your charger since you can't..." Stevie paused, her face scrunching.

She didn't have to finish her sentence. I already knew—*since you can't pack link.*

"So you can communicate with us once you arrive," Mom interjected, trying to remove the awkwardness.

"Thank you," I murmured.

"Sorry, guys, but we gotta go," Theo said and pressed the garage door opener.

That had to mean Bodey's conversation with Zeke was ending.

"You two be careful," Mom said as she and Stevie shut the passenger door.

As the garage door opened, Theo put the car into drive, ready to move as soon as it had risen high enough. Suddenly, a Jeep pulled in front of the driveway, blocking us from leaving.

Bodey.

"Dammit." Theo slammed his hand against the steering wheel, blowing the horn.

By the time the door had fully risen, Bodey was standing in front of us with his arms crossed and Zeke next to him.

I was surprised Theo didn't try to run him over.

The skin around Bodey's eyes tightened, and a vein bulged between his eyebrows. He stared at me.

"Why are your son and Callie in a car, getting ready to leave?" Bodey growled. "Are you trying to sneak her away even after the other three royal advisers voted in my favor?"

My heart pounded. For him to move that quickly, he must have suspected Zeke would try to pull something like this.

Zeke clenched his hands as his neck corded. "This is *my* pack. My territory. You four don't have any rights here."

Spinning toward Zeke, Bodey growled. "The five states we represent are all *one* territory. What happens here is everyone's business. Unless you're going against what every ruler over this area has ever believed?"

"This is bullshit, and you will pay for it if you take her," Zeke vowed, baring his teeth.

"I have the *right* and the *obligation* to take her. If you don't like it, you can talk to Samuel in two weeks once he becomes king," Bodey replied as he marched past Zeke and opened my door. His face softened as he held out his hand. "We need to get you somewhere safe so you can rest and heal."

Theo snarled. "Be careful how you touch and look at her. I plan on making her my mate." His eyes were hard, and his face tightened as he stared the alpha adviser down.

I flinched. That wasn't true, and even if it were, he hadn't talked to *me* about it. His statement was way too forward and assuming.

Bodey didn't miss a beat. He lifted his chin. "I'm showing her kindness, not interest, but you wouldn't know what that looks like by the way you and the others here treat her. How strange that the very man who proclaims he wants to mate her didn't fight his father regarding her situation." He continued to hold out his hand, his gaze landing back on me. "We should go."

Needles prickled the back of my throat. His show of kindness was more than most had ever done for me. I felt safer when he was around.

Taking his hand was all too easy, and when our skin touched, a tingle jolted through my arm. It didn't hurt, thank goodness. His hand closed around mine, revealing it was twice the size of mine, and his callouses rubbed my skin, creating an even more pleasant sensation.

As I moved slowly out of the vehicle, his eyes remained trained on my face to determine how much pain I was in. I swallowed hard as I focused on his touch instead of my suffering. I didn't want him to worry further. He'd already risked enough by coming here.

When we reached the front of the garage, I remembered something. "I have a bag in the back seat."

"Oh, here," Stevie said from behind us. The car door opened as she got the duffel for us.

"I'll be right back." Bodey released my hand and met my sister halfway.

Zeke used the opportunity to step beside me and whisper in my ear, "I hope you enjoy your time with him while your family suffers. You know...the people who took you in."

I couldn't breathe. I didn't know what to do. I hadn't asked to leave.

Bodey appeared beside me with my bag. He asked,

"What did you say to her?" The power radiating off him was stronger than before as his expression turned to stone.

"It's none of your business." Zeke straightened, but sweat pooled above his lip.

"That's fine." Bodey laughed humorlessly. "I can guess what someone like *you* would use against her." He smirked, taking a threatening step toward Zeke. "If you do anything to her family, there will be repercussions. Samuel tends to think very much like his parents did. With the Southwest desperate to gain more ground, maybe, just maybe, we could hand your state over to them and deal with your punishment."

Zeke flinched. The Southwest had fewer wolves than any other area, and being part of their territory wasn't nearly as prestigious as ours. It was all about perception.

They were pushing into our lands, taking advantage of us not having a crowned king. That was one reason the coronation in two weeks was such a big deal—it would help restore stability so that the Southwest, and mainly Queen Kel, would rethink their lofty goals of Western domination.

"Do you understand?" Bodey arched a brow.

"Understood," Zeke growled, glaring at me with such hatred my insides turned cold.

Bodey led me toward his Jeep, and Zeke, Theo, my parents, and Stevie watched us go. As we passed the front of the house, I caught the fluttering of blinds from the corner of my eye. Pearl had been watching from inside.

When we got to his Jeep, Bodey bent down and

lifted me slowly and easily into the passenger seat without jarring me. I tensed, taken off guard.

"Sorry," Bodey said softly. "I should've warned you. I just thought that might be easier than making you step up so high."

Though my ribs had protested, the ache wasn't half as bad as when I'd moved to sit and stand from the other car. "It was a good idea. Thank you."

"No problem," he answered as he gently put me in the seat and buckled me in.

For a moment, I felt like a child. My hands clenched. I hated being this weak.

Bodey shut the door and hurried to his side, throwing my bag in the back seat on the way. I glanced out my window to see everyone still watching us leave. Theo looked tense, and Zeke's expression was stony. Worse, I saw the panicked looks on my family's faces, and I could only hope that Bodey had scared Zeke enough that he would leave them alone.

Within seconds, we were off, and when my garage faded from view, I leaned my head back on the headrest and took in the dark leather interior of Bodey's Jeep. It was hands down the nicest car I'd ever been in. His scent, mixed with leather, had my eyelids drooping.

I was safe...for now.

"I'm sorry about all this," he said, messing with the buttons on his dashboard. "They shouldn't treat you that way. We're about three hours away, so get some rest."

My mind raced as I tried to figure out how to respond. Every time I thought of something, the words got lodged in my throat like a dry pill, so I said the only thing I could, "Thank you."

He didn't say anything else. The two of us fell into a comfortable silence, and before I knew it, my eyes had closed, and everything faded around me.

―――――

A DOOR SHUT GENTLY but loudly enough to stir my consciousness.

"What the *hell*, man?" Jack asked excitedly. "Do you have any idea what shit you've just stirred?"

My heart thudded against my ribs. We must be at Bodey's place. I opened my eyes but remained still. I wanted to hear what they were going to say, and if they knew I was awake, the conversation would end before it began.

CHAPTER SEVEN

"BE QUIET," Bodey demanded. "She's resting."

The voices were coming from behind the vehicle, and that lessened my tension. My eyes fluttered open to find a white wall in front of me. I glanced around and realized there was a door to the left—we had to be in Bodey's garage. A sleek black Mercedes-Benz SUV was parked in the space beside me.

My throat constricted. I hadn't considered that Bodey might be with someone. He wasn't mated—I could tell by his scent—but that didn't mean he wasn't committed.

"Yes, because, clearly, everything is about this *girl*," Jack grumbled but a whole lot more quietly.

I glanced in the rearview mirror and saw the three other royal advisers, along with a man who looked like an older Bodey.

"Son," the man said, placing a hand on Bodey's arm. "Jack has a point, though he could have been less confrontational about it. Do you think bringing her here was wise?"

I rolled my head to the left so I could watch them in the mirror as I listened. I kind of wished I had slept through this conversation. No one but Bodey seemed to want me here. A knot curled inside me.

"Guys, I had to." Bodey rubbed a hand down his face. "I couldn't sleep last night after we left her there, so I drove through the neighborhood this morning to make sure nothing was off."

From his spot between Jack and Miles, Lucas lifted a hand. "Whoa. What do you mean you went and checked on her this morning? Zeke promised he wouldn't harm her. I don't understand why you even went there."

Miles groaned, his face contorting. "We all know how Zeke is. That's why he went."

"Exactly." Bodey's shoulders straightened. "And you wouldn't believe what I saw." His voice hardened. "He had her working in the yard of one of the guys who attacked her last night. She'd already dug up and planted at least seven flower beds in front of the house, and they had mulch and stones out there for her to take care of next."

The older man hung his head. "I knew he was bad news. I advised King Richard that Zeke shouldn't be considered for the open Oregon royal adviser role, but the king insisted he had to meet with him for appearance's sake since he was one of the strongest alphas in Oregon and should be considered for the role. It was supposed to be a formality."

Jack snorted. "But Fate fucked us when Richard found his chosen mate while he was there."

"Now, Jack. Mila was a good woman," the older man countered. "She was just close to Zeke, and that friendship influenced the king to put Zeke in charge, and so here we are...yet again."

My heart squeezed. I'd heard stories about Queen Mila. Apparently, she'd been close friends with Zeke, sort of like I was with Theo, but she'd also been one of the strongest wolves in the pack. Zeke had taken her loss hard, and on the night of her death, he'd come back to the pack with me. I wondered if that was why he hated me—he associated me with her death—but I'd never been brave enough to ask anyone...not even Theo.

"The past doesn't matter. Samuel needs to check into it once he's king." Bodey shook his head. "I wish I'd dragged your asses there with me. If you would've seen..." He trailed off. "I don't even know how she was still standing. If I hadn't seen her stuck in human form and unable to pack link, I would've never believed she was a weak wolf. She shouldn't have been able to do even part of that job, and when I stopped her, I could *see* the agony on her face and by the way she held her body. I don't think I could have done the work with her injuries."

The older man scowled. "He's always been a jackass." Then his shoulders sagged. "You're gonna have to take her to a healer in the coven. We need to take her back to Zeke sooner rather than later. He'll view our taking her as a betrayal and a threat to his power. We have to tread carefully until Samuel is crowned."

Tensing, I reminded myself to breathe. Though our pack protected a coven nearby, we weren't allies with the witches. They helped us only when absolutely necessary, and even then, it was begrudgingly.

"Dad, what would you have me do?" Bodey lifted his hands in surrender. "The four of us witnessed the attack and the complete disregard Zeke had for her. You taught me better than to turn my back on people in need. I couldn't *not* check on her and let Zeke do whatever the hell he pleased. That's not right."

Chuckling, Jack patted his chest. "You know what? I'm here for it. She's hot and nice, and Zeke is a douche. I say fuck him."

"Shut up, man," Lucas growled and smacked Jack on the back of his head. "What Mr. Valor is trying to say is that even though there's a law, now wasn't the time to invoke it, not with the coronation in two weeks. The Southwest is already trying to infiltrate our territory—we don't need to be fighting one another."

I'd been so wrong to come here...not that it had been entirely willingly. But I could've put up more of a fight. By not doing so, I'd caused more problems.

I tried to rise, but my ribs screamed and forced me to lean back against the seat. I didn't know if I'd bruised them or if one might be broken, but one thing was certain, I wasn't going anywhere right now.

"What's done is done." Mr. Valor's shoulders sagged. "She's here, so there's no reason to dwell on it. You should get her inside and let her rest if she's that bad off. We can get the priestess to visit her here."

Bodey's jaw tensed. "That's the problem. Priestess Dina and her coven left to visit family across the state and prepare for the coronation. Some of the preparations need to be done on the sacred ground there."

"Right." Mr. Valor rolled his shoulders. "I forgot about that. It's been so long since we've crowned anyone. Well, then, rest is all we can do for her right now."

"Dude, it's like everything is a surprise for everyone

as we navigate the ceremonies." Jack crossed his arms and smirked. "You'd think with all the shit you guys gave us about taking notes and documenting traditions, you would've taken your own advice."

Arching a brow, Mr. Valor chuckled. "There *is* a book, and it includes descriptions of all the ceremonial rites. Why am I not surprised you aren't aware of that?"

"What?" His mouth dropped. "But you just said—"

"I don't have the book," Mr. Valor interjected. "Miles does."

"So that's how he knows everything." Jack glared. "And here I thought it was because he was silent and had keen observational skills."

Miles rubbed his hands together. "I do. How do you think I knew about the book in the first place?"

"He's got you there." Lucas snorted as he patted Jack on the shoulder.

"You three go be smart-asses somewhere else." Bodey waved them away. "I'll take care of Callie. She fell asleep on the way here, and I don't want her to get sore from sleeping in the car. She's gone through enough."

Butterflies took flight inside me as I watched him walk around his dad toward me. When I noticed the way his dad and friends glanced at one another behind his back, though, those flutters died. They were concerned...and I was certain it wasn't about me.

"After you get her situated, you want to meet us and Samuel at the bachelor pad?" Jack quipped, waggling his brows despite Bodey not facing him.

"It's *not* a bachelor pad," Miles growled. "Stella will be staying with us this weekend, if not sooner."

Lucas shook his head. "You know he said that to rile

you up. It's not like he's planning on strippers..." He trailed off. "Wait. Jack, you don't have strippers coming, do you?"

"I didn't...but maybe I will now." Jack's eyes twinkled. "I could use a little loving, and Bodey made it clear that the pack women here are off-limits."

Miles's eyes glowed.

"You know Jack won't risk Stella's wrath by doing that. She would destroy him." Mr. Valor laughed and led the boys away from the garage. "And Jack, stop being an instigator."

"Thank gods," Bodey grumbled as he moved toward me again. "I needed Jack gone."

The corners of my lips warred with me, trying to tip upward, but I didn't want him to know I'd been eavesdropping. I bit the inside of my cheek, focusing on the sting, and closed my eyes a moment before he opened my door.

He touched my arm gently and whispered, "Hey, we're here. We need to get you inside."

The flutters returned at his touch, and I opened my eyes slowly. My breath caught as I stared into his eyes.

"Here, let me help you out," he said as he carefully reached around me and unbuckled the seat belt, then took my hands, helping me out of the Jeep and onto my feet.

Pain ricocheted throughout my body, but it was a tad better than when I'd left home. "Thank you," I gritted out.

He smiled. "No worries."

My heart picked up its pace. I had to get whatever was going on with me under control. He was nice and kind, but I was a weak wolf, and he was an alpha. For all I knew, he had a fated mate, and they hadn't yet bonded for whatever reason. Nothing would ever happen between the two of us, and I had enough on my plate without pining for someone who would never glance my way.

Seeming unaffected, he opened the back passenger door and grabbed my bag, then led me to the door on our left. He closed the garage and opened the inner door, revealing a sizable white mudroom.

Taking a quick breath, I stepped into the house. At this point, I didn't even feel the claw marks anymore. The torment was all internal.

To my left was a small alcove where a white wooden bench seat was built into the wall. Bodey removed his shoes before helping me with mine and placing them under the bench.

The dark-mahogany wood floor was cool, despite the socks on my feet, and his house smelled very much like him, mixed with a lemony cleaning scent.

"Are you hungry?" he asked as he guided me into the kitchen.

I paused, taking in my temporary living quarters. The kitchen was spotless, with a black stove and matching microwave on the left wall that connected to the mudroom. Right next to me was a black refrigerator surrounded by gray cabinets, and a matching island sat about eight feet away from the stove.

Bodey walked to the sink in the center of the island and washed his hands. Snatching a paper towel from the stand to the right on top of the dark granite counter-top, he turned to me. "Are you not going to answer me?"

"Oh." I shook my head to clear it. "I'm fine. I don't want to be a bother."

"I'm starving, so I'm going to make myself something." He strolled to the refrigerator and opened the door. "It wouldn't be hard to make you something, too."

If I wanted to heal, I needed calories and to take care of myself. "If you don't mind."

He winked. "If I did, I wouldn't have offered. You'll learn that about me soon enough." He gestured to the den behind the island. "Why don't you go sit on the couch and rest while I make us some grilled cheese?"

My stomach gurgled. "Okay." My face heated as I went into the den, not wanting to see his reaction to my noisy stomach. At least I'd told him okay instead of no, so he already knew I was hungry.

I made my way to the tan leather L-shaped couch and gingerly sat on the most comfortable couch I'd ever been on.

"Do you want me to get you the remote?" Bodey asked and gestured at the large flat screen that hung over the beige-tiled fireplace.

"No, I'm good." I didn't even want to listen to music. I just wanted silence. My nerves were coiled tightly, and the thought of not being able to hear the sounds of my new environment put me on edge.

I laid my head back, enjoying the warmth of the room. The den connected to a gigantic covered patio with a rectangular table and six chairs around it, and to my right was a large dining area with a square, light-mahogany table and sixteen matching chairs. This place was nicer than any of the houses in our neighborhood, but what made it perfect was the peace of the moment. There were no vicious stares or impending threats. For the first time since I could remember, my body relaxed, and stress floated off me.

"So, what's your pack like?" Bodey asked as something crinkled behind me.

And the stress returned with a vengeance, my body stiffening once again. This was a trick question, and I was disappointed by his obvious manipulation. "If there's something specific you want to know, why not ask?" My mouth was running away from me again, but I hated people treating me like I was stupid. "You already know Zeke, so you have a pretty good idea."

There was a beat of silence, and I prepared myself for him to tell me to get the hell out of there. Zeke hated it when I got *ornery*, and I was sure all alphas were the same.

"You're right. I should be direct." He cleared his throat. "Do others in your pack get treated as poorly as you do?"

I closed my eyes tightly. Now I wished I'd played along and told him pointless information. I guessed he deserved answers. He was putting his reputation on the line with Zeke and his father and the other alpha advisers. "Not anything like me. I get the brunt of the mistreatment since I can't shift or pack link. But Zeke isn't the nicest to anyone, including my family."

Drool pooled in my mouth at the sizzle of the bread and the smell of melting cheese. I licked my lips.

After another pause, he said, "I'm assuming he sent you to your pack's witch allies to be evaluated. How do they explain your latent wolf?"

"Our pack isn't on friendly terms with the witches who live close by, so we haven't gotten them involved." I rubbed my hands together, knowing I was giving him too much information. I forced a yawn, hoping he'd ease up on me.

Bodey's breath caught, and I heard him move and open some cabinets. "That's unfortunate and something we will need to address. Witches and wolves are allies for a reason."

Now I was intrigued. Most of the packs Zeke was responsible for had witches living nearby, but I'd never known why. Zeke didn't inform us of such matters. "Why is that? He never told us."

"It goes back generations. When witches were persecuted and hunted long ago, our ancestors helped hide them, and we still do today. We protect them and keep them safe, and in return, they help us with things like healing and ceremonies. It's a mutually beneficial relationship built on respect. We're not only allies but friends and part of each other's communities."

That sounded nice. Maybe if we'd had that, I could've gotten answers and wouldn't be in the situation I was in now.

He walked over with two plates. One held two grilled cheese sandwiches, while the other had four. He handed me the one with two and set the other plate on the dark-brown wooden coffee table that was a few feet in front of the couch. "Would you like some water?"

"Please." Unable to wait, I grabbed one of the sandwiches and took a huge bite. I couldn't remember the last time I'd eaten something without meat, but I almost moaned. It was *so* good.

When Bodey came back with two glasses of water, he stared at me with a huge smile.

My mouth went dry. "What? Do I have something on my face?"

"No, you just remind me of someone I used to know." He sat down beside me, opened one of the bottles, and handed it to me. "You resemble her and even have the same reaction to grilled cheese. I have no idea why I made them. I haven't had one since..." He trailed off, pain etched on his face.

He had his own trauma, and of course, it was over a girl.

"Sorry." I put my sandwich down. "I don't have to eat them."

"Don't be silly." He snatched a sandwich from his plate and took a big bite. "I made these for a reason." However, his irises had darkened. Whatever memory I'd triggered still haunted him.

We ate in silence, but the entire time, he glanced my way, watching me. I wasn't sure if it was because of the girl he was remembering or because he wanted answers. Either way, not talking was the best solution for both of us.

He somehow ate his four sandwiches faster than I did my two, and when I took my last bite, he stood. "Let's get you upstairs so you can get some good rest. You can have a room all to yourself."

Now that I had a full belly and was hydrated, my eyes wanted to shut again. "That sounds great."

He jogged through the kitchen to where he'd set my bag in the mudroom and returned. "Want me to carry you? We're going upstairs."

A part of me wanted to say yes, but a larger part of me hated that I'd even considered accepting. "No, I'll be fine. I'll take it slowly."

"If you change your mind, just say the word." He nodded toward the hallway on the right. "It's down the hall there, past the patio and to the left."

Great, he was going to follow me.

I took my time climbing to my feet. Each movement felt like something was stabbing me, but I managed to get up. My vision blurred, but I blinked it clear and slowly moved toward the stairs.

As he'd described, we passed another covered patio area, this one with a round table and two seats, and then a large mahogany staircase appeared on the left, just before a massive living room. I wanted to check out the space, but I needed sleep, so I limped up the stairs.

Like the rest of the house, the walls were painted a light beige, and when I reached the landing, Bodey instructed me to turn right. I walked past a covered deck with three Adirondack chairs, and he guided me to a bedroom on the right.

When he placed a hand on the small of my back, tingles sprouted up my spine. I stepped into the room and surveyed my surroundings, noting the dark-mahogany king-size bed with a matching dresser and two nightstands. One of the nightstands held a trendy black metal lamp, while the other had a clock. To my left was a huge closet, and two doorways on opposite sides led to different decks. The huge one next to the closet had a swing and two rocking chairs.

"If you head down to the hallway across from the stairs, the bathroom is the first door on your left." He set my bag on the gray comforter and gestured at the closet across from us. "When you're feeling better, you can hang your stuff in there. This is your room while you're here." He walked over and shut the blinds on the doors that led to the decks, blocking out most of the sunlight.

I'd never met anyone as kind as him, and the way my chest expanded almost hurt. "Thank you." I couldn't risk saying more. I might fall apart.

"Get some rest." He removed his phone from his back pocket. "What's your number? I'll send you a text so you can reach me. I have to attend a meeting."

Without hesitation, I spouted off the number, and within a second, my phone dinged.

"There." He headed to the door. "Text me if you need anything. I'll be back later, but hopefully, you'll sleep while I'm gone."

When he shut my door, I could barely keep my eyes open. Luckily, he'd put my bag on the bed. I changed into some shorts and a comfy shirt and crawled on top of the comforter, not wanting to get under the covers. As soon as my head hit the pillow, I was out cold.

SOMETHING RATTLED, stirring me from my sleep. Then a scratching noise came from right outside the smaller deck to my left.

My heart quickened as everything filtered back into my mind.

The scratching noise was at my door—as if someone wanted inside.

CHAPTER EIGHT

HEART RACING, I tensed and focused on listening.

Another loud dragging noise came from outside.

I couldn't just stay in bed and allow someone to attack me. I needed to be on my feet before they tried to take or harm me. At least I'd go down fighting.

Adrenaline roared through my blood, and my survival skills kicked in. I sat up, my ribs panging, but the ache ebbed quickly enough.

Still, I moved slower than I would have liked, compensating for my injuries. I gritted my teeth and shifted my legs over the edge of the bed. A quicker movement would've had me crumbling, but I didn't want to be caught with my pants down...metaphorically speaking.

As my feet touched the cool wood floor, I grabbed my phone. The dragging noise of the chair had me quickly standing, and I tiptoed toward the door.

A deep groan came from outside, and the voice was definitely not Bodey's.

Breath quickening, I peeked through one of the

blinds to see a tall man grab the back of a chair and drag it toward me.

He was going to use it to break in.

I fired a text off to Bodey using one simple word: *Help!*

I tossed the phone on the bed and listened. I might be injured, but I'd do everything possible to get the upper hand.

Another scrape of the chair on the wooden deck hit my ears. He'd make his move any second now, and I needed to catch him off guard.

I glanced around the room for a weapon. My gaze landed on the lamp. The metal looked flimsy, but it was better than nothing. I hurried over and yanked the plug from the wall. As I lifted the lamp, agony coursed through my body, but I bit the inside of my cheek to reallocate the pain.

Taking a deep breath, I unlocked the door and charged outside, the lamp raised over my head. Fortunately, I focused my fear and anger on the intruder.

The man spun around, his eyes widening as I swung the lamp at him. A *yelp* left me as the strength I put behind the movement sent an intense ache breaking through my adrenaline. I almost fell to my knees.

"Whoa!" The guy caught the longer part of the lamp, stopping my forward motion. "What the *hell*?"

My breath caught, but I wouldn't stand here and do nothing. "I should be asking you that." I tried to keep as much malice in my tone as I could bear. "You're the one about to attack me!"

He blinked, then released the lamp. "Attack you?"

"Is this a tactic to throw your victim off?" I narrowed my eyes, ignoring the fact his face seemed familiar. He definitely wasn't from Zeke's pack, so where would I have seen him? "You repeat everything they say to...gain trust or something?"

"Victim?" His baby-blue irises darkened, and he ran a hand through his messy dark-brown hair.

I gestured at him. "See? There you go again!"

Footsteps pounded down the hallway, and my heart started to beat again. That had to be Bodey. He'd be here in seconds.

"Look, this is a big misunderstanding." The guy's mouth opened and closed as if he were debating what to say when the doors behind us from the hallway swung open.

Bodey barreled onto the deck, dressed in flannel pajama bottoms and shirtless. He didn't even glance at the man standing beside me as he rushed to my side. "What's wrong? Are you hurt?" he asked as he stepped between the stranger and me. One of his hands touched my shoulder while the other cupped my cheek. "I saw your text and heard you yelp." His forehead creased as his eyes searched mine for answers. He emanated tenderness and concern.

My legs grew unsteady, and I glanced away from his face only to focus on his naked torso. My knees almost gave out as the delicious curves of his muscles greeted me.

"Callie," he said as he placed both hands on my shoulders. "Are you okay? You're about to fall over."

Yeah, I was definitely not okay. He needed to put on a shirt.

"I should've been the one calling for help, not her." The younger man came up next to Bodey and pointed at the lamp. "She swung that thing at me when I was just rearranging the chairs to get comfortable."

I tore my gaze from Bodey and glanced over his shoulder.

Two chairs were now facing each other like he'd moved them so he could use one to rest his feet. That was why there'd been so much noise.

My face flamed, and I wanted to avert my gaze, but something stronger inside me refused to let me cower. I'd been scared and protected myself. I had nothing to be ashamed of.

Bodey's expression changed as he took the lamp from me. The concern washed away as his expression soured. He dropped his hands and turned to the guy. "I told you someone was resting in the bedroom, and you were out here doing *this*?"

The guy, who had an inch or two on Bodey, winced, even though he had an equally strong wolf inside him.

"Honestly...I forgot." The guy grimaced. "I came out here to chill after dinner, which was clearly a mistake."

"No, it's fine. I'm sorry. I was being paranoid." The breeze picked up, and I remembered I was wearing only shorts and a shirt. "I just thought..." I trailed off. I wasn't sure what to say to improve the situation. If Bodey had been concerned about my well-being before, this probably exacerbated the problem.

The guy shook his head. "No. *I'm* sorry. Bodey mentioned you had a bad injury and your alpha hasn't been kind to you. I didn't mean to startle you." He held out his hand and smiled softly. "By the way, I'm Samuel."

Samuel. The almost eighteen-year-old heir to the

throne. The future king of the Northwest territory. His coronation was in two weeks.

And I'd attacked him.

That sounded about right.

When Zeke learned of this, he might actually kill me.

I reached out and shook his hand. "Callie. And sorry for...*that*."

"Hey, a future king needs to be prepared for anything." He chuckled, his irises softening and sparkling in a way that tugged at my heart but in a different way than Bodey's did. "That's what you and your dad always tell me, right, Bodey?"

"Right." Bodey took a step back and smirked. "Though I gotta say...this was unexpected, even for me." He looked at me intently. "You're full of surprises."

"Believe me, I surprise myself sometimes." Way too often for my liking. I glanced off the side of the deck, noting the night sky. The moon was already halfway to its peak. From this angle, I could see the house across from us and a few across the street. They were modern but with a colonial feel to them and in various light, natural colors.

The prickling sensation of being watched ran down my spine.

"Have we met before?" Samuel asked.

That was strange, especially since I'd thought the same thing. I looked at him again, and that eerie feeling washed over me. For the life of me, I couldn't place him. "I don't think so."

He frowned. "Yeah, me neither."

Bodey cleared his throat and strolled past me to the

door that led into my bedroom. He said, "It's cold out here. Why don't we head downstairs? Samuel, Jack, Miles, Lucas, and I ate dinner earlier, but when I checked on you, you were sleeping. I didn't want to wake you, so I put up a plate for you. I'll go warm it up downstairs."

Goose bumps pebbled my skin. "Okay. I want to take a shower. I didn't earlier, and I feel kind of gross. Can I do that before eating?"

"You did a lot of yard work today." He mashed his lips into a line. "Do you remember where the bathroom is?"

I nodded. "I'll be down in fifteen minutes." I went back into my room, relieved to be alone again. All these people unnerved me. Not because of how strong they were but because of the type of people they were and the way they looked at me. It wasn't with judgment, but they saw me as weak.

From my bag on the bed, I pulled out a long fuchsia T-shirt and a pair of black yoga pants. I walked out of the room and down the hall, but I paused in the hallway to the bathroom. The two of them were still outside but weren't saying a word, most likely pack linking.

Finally, Samuel said quietly, "That woman looks like an older version of her, at least from what I've seen in pictures."

"You're not wrong." Bodey sighed. "But we both know it's not her."

Silence descended, and I moved again. Bodey would come inside at any second to head downstairs and warm up my dinner.

As I stepped into the bathroom, the door from the deck to my bedroom opened. I wanted to march back in there to see what was going on, but I just closed the door as silently as possible. I had nothing to hide. Further, I trusted Bodey. Somehow, I knew he wasn't snooping, and this was his house.

Taking note of the cool, dark-gray tile underneath my feet, I turned toward the double sink, choosing to look in the closest mirror.

I froze. I didn't recognize the girl staring back at me.

My long ash-blonde hair was tangled, and my normally bright Caribbean-blue eyes looked dull. Add in the dark circles under them and the paleness of my usually sun-kissed skin, and I looked like an unhealthy version of myself.

My throat constricted. No wonder Bodey was concerned about me. I could pass as death walking—also known as vampires who usually kept to themselves and, despite what books and movies depicted, didn't cause chaos.

I felt bad for the girl I reminded them of, especially if they remembered her like *this*.

A closet behind me caught my eye, and I ran my hand along the granite countertop as I opened the door to find it full of towels. I snatched one up and went through the door that separated the toilet and shower area.

Not wanting to waste any more time, I began the struggle of getting clean with my injuries.

THE SHOWER HADN'T BEEN easy, but it'd been so worth it. Washing off the sweat and slathering my hair in conditioner almost made me feel like a brand-new woman. It had taken longer than I'd hoped, but I was finally clean. Once I managed to get dressed and brush my hair, I gathered my dirty clothes and headed back to the bedroom.

Samuel was still on the deck, meaning I'd be alone with Bodey. I wasn't sure how I felt about that. Spending time with him was making my brain fuzzy.

When I entered my room, my feet stilled. Bodey had set the lamp back on the end table and put new sheets on the bed, including pillowcases. Their fresh, clean smell hung in the air, matching their color—ocean blue. Though it wasn't my favorite, it was still a color I favored.

I dropped my dirty clothes on the other nightstand and headed out. As soon as I reached the top of the stairs, the scent of steak and potatoes filled my nose. Though I hadn't done a damn thing since getting here except sleep and attack the future king, I was famished. Shifters had healthy appetites, but this was extreme even for me. It had to be because I was healing.

Each step down the stairs was like a kick to the gut, but I held in any noises of discomfort as I reached the kitchen.

"Hey." Bodey smiled as he put a big glob of sour cream on top of a loaded baked potato. "You look like you feel much better."

Thankfully, he had a black shirt on now, so it was easier to focus on his words. "Showers and music are two ways to better my world." Usually, I listened to music while I bathed, but I didn't want to force them to listen to it as well.

"Music, huh?" He beamed. "Now that I think about

it, you weren't even aware of my presence this morning until I took your shovel away. You had earbuds in."

I wrinkled my nose. "You've got me there. I'm not usually that unaware, but I was trying to focus on anything other than my..." I trailed off, not wanting to finish that sentence.

We both knew what I was alluding to.

He snatched a bottle of water and grabbed some silverware, nodding toward the den. "Why don't you eat there, and I can play you a song?"

"I'd love that!" I'd never heard anyone play music in person before, and I'd always wanted to experience that. I arched a brow. "You going to sing to me?"

"Nope." He shook his head. "For the first time, let's stick with just the guitar."

He strolled into the living room and placed my food on the coffee table before scooting it closer to where I'd sit, and then he went to the corner of the room, where a black guitar case was propped against the wall.

I must have been out of it when I'd arrived because I'd completely missed that, along with a picture of him, a younger woman who had to be his sister, his dad, and his mother in the space between the deck and the television. He and his dad had similar features, but Mr. Valor's eyes were jade green with crow's-feet lining the corners of his face. Bodey had gotten his eyes from his mother. She had a heart-shaped face, strawberry-blonde hair, and a kindness that wafted from her soul even from there. The younger girl had Mr. Valor's jade eyes and her mom's strawberry-blonde hair and heart-shaped face.

Not wanting my food to get cold, I picked up my plate and sat in the same spot as earlier. As I got settled,

Bodey brought over an acoustic guitar and took a seat on the other end of the couch. He strummed the guitar and tuned it, then slid right into playing "More than Words" by Extreme.

It was one of my favorite songs in the world.

I stopped eating, mesmerized by the song and how his fingers moved over the strings. At first, he didn't seem comfortable, but after several chords, his gaze flicked to mine, and his eyes bored into me as if he'd chosen that song to say something to me that he couldn't say aloud.

It was the first time I could ever remember feeling at peace.

———

I DON'T KNOW how long Bodey and I hung out together, but before I could stop myself, I yawned.

Of course, he noticed immediately and stopped playing. He grinned. "You'd better go lie down again. Your body needs more rest."

He was right, even though I hated it. "Only if you promise to play for me again sometime," I said, not wanting the evening to end.

"That I can do. No one else likes to listen to me play." He winked. "It bodes well for me that I finally found a fan."

My heart did a stupid flutter, and I was at a loss for what to say.

He placed the guitar on the couch beside him and stood. "Here, let me help you up."

When he wrapped an arm around my shoulders, his

scent swirled between us. He smelled amazing, like all man, and my blood warmed.

Stop it, Callie, I chastised. *He's touching you because you're injured. Don't make a fool out of yourself.* But that didn't cool the rush of heat at all.

Focused on these strange feelings, I forgot to be cautious about moving. As I stood, I whimpered.

Releasing his hold, Bodey faced me. His hand cupped my face, his thumb stroking my cheek. He murmured, "Hopefully, the pain will have eased a lot by morning."

I watched his lips move and murmured, "Uh-hmm."

"Okay." He dropped his hand, leaving me feeling bereft. "Let's get you to bed."

That was enough to wake me up and reinforce that my reaction to him was one-sided. Not saying another word, we made our way upstairs.

He paused at my door and smiled tightly. "If you need me, all you have to do is yell."

I snorted. "Hopefully, I won't attack Samuel again."

"Eh, he's already in bed. Besides, it's good for him. I hope you do it again." He leaned against the doorframe.

"I don't." I took a step back, needing distance. When I saw my bed, I added, "And thanks for the new sheets."

He shrugged. "No problem. You slept there before you showered. It was the least I could do."

Oh, but he'd done more for me in a day than almost anyone else ever had.

An awkward silence settled between us as he stared at me.

My phone dinged.

I winced. I'd forgotten to call my parents.

Bodey pushed off the doorframe and backed into the hall. "Okay, see you in the morning. Good night." He shut the door behind him.

Alone, I hurried to my cell phone and saw twenty missed texts.

A few were from Mom, Dad, and Stevie, but the majority were from Theo. The last text from him read, Call me now, or I'm coming to you. Bodey can fuck himself.

He'd sent it at eleven, and it was midnight. Fuck.

I hit call, my hands shaking. *Please don't let him be on his way here.*

CHAPTER NINE

A LUMP FORMED in my throat as the phone rang twice. If he was that anxious to talk to me, I was certain he would've picked up by now—unless he was in his wolf form, racing over here. But then, how would he know if I was trying to call him back?

I sat on the fresh blue sheets, ignoring the sharp ache, and ran my hand along the soft, cool fabric.

The phone rang for a fourth time, and I hung my head. I'd be transferred to voice mail. Before the changeover could happen, the phone was answered.

"Hello?" Theo said gruffly. "Callie, is that you?" The thrumming of an engine filled his side of the line.

He was on his way here. I clenched my jaw. "Who did you expect? Unless I'm not the only one you've sent a ton of texts to," I snapped, then tensed. In fairness, Bodey could have taken my phone and called him back, especially with that last message. "Sorry. I'm just a little out of sorts."

Thankfully, he didn't focus on my smart-assery

"Why the hell did it take you so long to respond?" he bit out.

"I didn't hear my phone." I almost said I didn't have it on me, but that would've led to more questions. Questions I didn't want to answer.

"What do you mean you didn't hear it?"

"I was sleeping." I sighed, wishing he hadn't texted. He'd never been so needy before, but I'd also never left the pack. "That was the whole point of Bodey bringing me here, remember?"

He chuckled darkly. "Oh, I'm aware." His tone softened. "I was worried when I couldn't get a hold of you, especially with how injured you were when you left. I wanted to make sure he was following through on his word by taking *care* of you."

I didn't like how he'd emphasized *care*. "He has. I've slept most of the day, and he even cooked me food." It was sad that an alpha adviser for an entirely different state had helped me when Zeke, my own alpha and the alpha adviser for my state, had been determined to break me.

Worse, Theo hadn't intervened. None of it made sense when I considered that Bodey was twice as strong as Zeke. As the next alpha and royal adviser, Theo wanted to be taken seriously and should've sided with Bodey. That would've been the right thing to do, especially since the other royal advisers had agreed with him.

But it wasn't my place to tell Theo that. It would only lead to an argument and add to the tension between us.

To reinforce that everything was okay, I added, "Bodey's been great."

"*Great,*" Theo growled. "What does that mean? Has he touched you in any way?"

I rolled my eyes. Theo wasn't used to having another man be kind to me, and he sounded extremely jealous. I kept my voice even. "I already told you why he was great. He let me sleep and fed me. He even gave me my own room. That's it. Nothing more happened." Even if Bodey had touched me, it was none of Theo's business. He and I were just *friends*.

"Okay, sorry." He groaned. "I'm losing my mind. I hate you being there." The kindness filtered back into his voice, reminding me of the boy who had befriended me long ago. "I wish I had stood up to Dad instead of *him.*"

"Why didn't you?" I asked. If he was my friend and expected to claim me one day, why wasn't he more invested in how I was treated?

"You know it's complicated, Callie. I can't go against my father. What would the packs think of me? Forcing a takeover would cause mass chaos, and other shifters would think they could do the same thing and challenge me."

Zeke must have told Theo that to prevent his son from challenging him. Zeke wanted to maintain control, even though he was getting older. But he and Theo were acting as if they weren't already pushing the time line for the transfer of leadership.

I eased myself back on the pillows and grunted.

"What's wrong?" Theo's voice thickened with concern.

"My ribs. I'm just lying down. I'm exhausted." I wanted to hang up, but I couldn't rush him. I needed to make sure he didn't come here and make things worse.

After a moment of silence, he eventually asked, "Is there anything you can tell us?"

My eyebrows lifted, and a warning buzzed in my blood. "What do you mean?"

"Well, you're with Bodey in his home." He exhaled. "Have the royal advisers said anything odd? Have you overheard plans they might be keeping from my dad?"

He wanted me to spy on Bodey and the other advisers. My blood pumped harder through my veins. Zeke had put him up to this, but I refused to help them, not after what this group had done for me. "I've been resting in my room like I told you, so I haven't had a chance to learn anything. However, I did meet Samuel briefly." I hoped that would reinforce that I wasn't hiding information from him. "He seems nice. We didn't talk for long, and I haven't seen the other alphas since I arrived." I was thankful he wasn't here in person, or he'd smell my lie.

"Maybe they aren't staying there. I think Jack's main pack lives closer to the Washington border, so he could easily go back and forth. Lucas and Miles are probably staying somewhere nearby since Montana and Wyoming are much farther away."

Wanting to change the subject, I used the opportunity to ask a question of my own. "What punishment has Zeke inflicted on my family?" Dread knotted my stomach. I was certain Zeke had found a workaround for what he'd promised Bodey.

"They're fine. Dad doesn't want to risk causing more problems with the other advisers. And Callie..." His voice deepened. "I'll make sure they're safe. I'll do better where you and your family are concerned. I won't continue to sit idly by."

He'd made vows like that before, but not quite as boldly...more like hints of protection. Maybe—just maybe—he'd follow through this time.

I still couldn't get myself to respond. Anything I said would seem snarky or insincere, especially since it had taken Bodey's involvement to get Theo to this point.

After a few beats of silence, Theo cleared his throat. "So...about what I said earlier."

My lungs quit working. *Please, no.*

He continued, "I've been meaning to talk to you about my intentions and our future."

I was not ready for this conversation in any capacity. "Can we talk about it later? I'm tired, and that's a huge discussion. It's not something we can resolve in a few minutes." In truth, I never wanted to discuss it. Theo and I were just friends. I didn't have romantic feelings for him. I'd never been attracted to him like that, even though he was very good-looking. The feelings of love I'd hoped to develop for him one day had never happened. We didn't quite *click*.

I couldn't see him as my mate.

Further, I'd never seen any indication he loved me like that, except for the stares he'd been giving me lately, but even those seemed contrived.

"Really?" he asked with surprise. "You think it involves a long conversation?"

Of course he'd assumed I would jump to say yes. Typical arrogant man. But I couldn't risk hurting his feelings. I had to reject him in a way that wouldn't put me on his shit list. "Yes, it does. And one you need to reflect on further. The entire pack views me as worthless...a waste of space. I'm a wolf who can't shift or link with anyone else, and you're an alpha and future adviser. You need a strong female wolf next to you to strengthen your standing, not hurt it."

"You're who I *need* beside me," he insisted.

"That's why we don't need to talk about this right now." Pressure built in my head. "Aligning with me isn't best for your future."

He growled in frustration. "I've thought about it, but I'll drop it for tonight. I understand that you want to make sure it's the best move for me."

Some of the weight rolled from my body. As I'd hoped, he hadn't taken it as me refusing him.

I didn't like admitting it, but mating with him would offer me a certain level of protection. Not all-encompassing —the pack would still resent me and harass me—but not in front of Theo like they did with Zeke. But I refused to mate with someone just for protection. I didn't need him—or anyone, for that matter—despite what they all thought.

I yawned, and my eyes grew heavy.

He sighed. "I better let you go. You've had a rough twenty-four hours."

It was hard to believe that only a day had passed. My life had changed entirely. For once, someone was protecting me from my pack. "Yeah, it has been, and I still need to call my parents and Stevie."

"Yeah, you do. They've been worried about you as well."

I didn't doubt that. Stevie loved me—we were truly sisters—but Pearl probably loved having me away. Mom and Dad treated me well and cared, but it was clear I was adopted.

"Just...don't get too comfortable there," he added.

My shoulders tensed. That felt like a warning. Usually, Theo didn't say shit for the hell of it. "Don't worry. I'm not."

"Okay. Good night, Callie. See you soon." The line went dead.

That had been a bizarre conversation. I stared at the white ceiling so hard that my eyes blurred. My life was getting more complicated. Theo wanted to claim me, and I wasn't sure how to get out of it. It wasn't that I was waiting for my fated mate—they weren't rare, but they weren't easy to find, either. Most people settled for a chosen mate, which was what Theo wanted, but I at least wanted love.

Between my injuries and the call with Theo, I wasn't up for calling my parents, but I couldn't *not* communicate with them...not after how I'd left.

Creating a group chat with them and Stevie, I shot off a message.

Me: Sorry I didn't text or call earlier. I've been sleeping all day, and I'm on the mend. I'll give you a call tomorrow. I hope all is well.

Stevie: Thanks for messaging. We were worried. Everything is fine, and Zeke is keeping his promise. Get some rest. We miss you. <3

My eyes burned from her sweet, quick reply. I closed out the text and pulled up my music app, then peacefully drifted off to songs with lyrics that meant so much to me.

A BIRD CHIRPED, overpowering my music, and sunlight hit my face. My eyes fluttered open, and I blinked, taking in an unfamiliar room.

When I shook my head to clear it, the motion made my ribs throb, bringing me firmly into the present.

I glanced toward the smaller deck where the sun broke through the blinds. The scent of cinnamon rolls, sausage, and eggs greeted my nose.

Gingerly, I reached for my phone and muted the music, revealing the faint sound of dishes rattling below. Noises I would've slept through if it hadn't been for whatever bird was loudly serenading me outside the door.

My stomach growled. Lately, I was always hungry.

I took my time standing and sighed with relief. My ribs actually seemed better, but it still hurt to breathe.

Pulling a pair of jeans and a teal sweater from my bag, I got dressed. When I was settled, I texted my place of work, informing them of my injury. I couldn't keep them hanging—if I wasn't already fired. Then I put the phone in my back pocket.

Downstairs, I smelled four distinct scents: Bodey, Samuel's musky rain, and two I wasn't familiar with—a musky vanilla and musky leather.

I'd paused at the bottom of the stairs, considering going back to my room, when Bodey stepped from the dining room into the hallway. He wore jeans and a pale-blue sweater that molded to his chest. His hair hung over his forehead, emphasizing his thick eyelashes and sculpted face.

He smiled, and my heart took off in a gallop.

"Good morning." He nodded toward the kitchen. "Come in and join us. Mom is cooking breakfast while

Dad informs Samuel about everything he needs to know as the future king."

Even if I'd wanted to say no, I couldn't. Not to him. My feet moved before I meant them to, heading straight to him.

"Does she have the lamp with her?" Samuel chuckled from the dining room.

I paused, tempted again to turn around and head back upstairs.

Bodey rolled his eyes and stepped forward, grabbing my hand before I could escape. He leaned forward and tucked a piece of hair behind my ear. "Ignore him. He likes to tease, especially when he's impressed by someone."

The world tilted underneath me at his gesture.

"Which isn't kingly," Mr. Valor scolded.

We stepped into the area between the kitchen and the dining room, and I found Mr. Valor sitting at the end of the table farthest from me, with Samuel sitting on his right. A cup of coffee sat across from Samuel by what must have been Bodey's seat.

In the kitchen, Mrs. Valor was at the stove, flipping pancakes with one hand while scrambling eggs with the other. She glanced at me and grinned. "Good morning, Callie. I'm Janet, Bodey's mom." She was beautiful and wore a stylish olive sweater and ripped jeans.

Her friendliness caught me off guard. "Morning. Is there something I can do to help?"

"Not a thing." She turned her focus back to the food. "Everything is almost done. Please, take a seat before the three other advisers get here."

Bodey gently tugged me to the table. "Come. She doesn't like help in the kitchen. Even when Jasmine is home from college, she shoos her out. You can sit by me and save me from Jack." He pulled out the chair next to his.

"Jasmine?" My heart sank. Maybe he had a girl-friend after all.

"My sister." Bodey gestured to the family picture I'd seen last night.

"Right." I forced a smile, trying to seem unconcerned.

As I came over, I felt Mr. Valor's gaze on me. He crossed his arms, his black button-down shirt wrinkling. My skin crawled. When someone paid attention to me like that, it normally didn't end well for me.

Trusting Bodey, I sat and gritted my teeth, determined not to make a noise.

The entire time, Mr. Valor stared. Once I was settled, he extended his hand. "I'm Michael."

I reached out to shake it, and my ribs twinged.

"Dad," Bodey warned.

Michael cringed. "Sorry, I forgot about your injuries."

"It's fine." I dropped my arm, the relief immediate.

As Bodey took his seat, Michael steepled his fingers, placing his elbows on the table, and said, "It's nice to have you here with us, Callie, though I wish it were under better circumstances."

I mashed my lips together and nodded, unsure how to respond.

Samuel tugged at the collar of his white shirt.

At least I wasn't the only uncomfortable one.

"Were you playing the guitar last night?" Samuel asked me.

I froze, uncertain why he'd asked *me* that. "Uh. No."

"Bodey?" Janet gasped. "You played last night? You haven't done that since..." She trailed off.

My brows furrowed. "Since when?"

The skin around Michael's eyes tightened, and again, he stared at me. "Since he was a teen," he answered.

"I've heard him the past few years, playing on the deck outside his room. He practices late at night when most people are sleeping." Samuel shrugged. "He's gotten a lot better lately."

"You heard me?" Bodey's jaw dropped.

"Man, it's not like you're actually stealthy." Samuel wrinkled his nose.

"So what? I've played off and on through the years. Why do you think I keep the guitar in the den?" Bodey shrugged like it wasn't a big deal and took a sip of his coffee.

Both his parents still seemed tense, and his dad kept staring at me. I needed to do something to distract myself. Coffee would do the trick and help with the headache pulsing faintly between my eyes.

When I shifted to stand, Bodey touched my arm. "What do you need?"

"Just a cup of coffee."

"Stay." Bodey stood again. "I'll get it for you."

Before I could protest, he was in the kitchen, fiddling with the Keurig.

Something inside me stirred, and before I realized what I was doing, I lifted my chin and stared Michael dead in the eye...almost in challenge.

What the hell was wrong with me?

His forehead lined as his brows shot upward.

Thankfully, the front door opened, and three distinct sets of footsteps sounded. The first clambered into the house, and I immediately knew who it was.

"Good morning, my peeps. Your day is now complete since I've arrived," Jack said, more loudly than necessary, as the front door shut.

A more reserved set of footsteps followed, which had to be Lucas, as the last near-silent set reminded me of Miles.

"Dude, you know they can hear you, right?" Lucas grumbled.

"It's my aura. It can't be helped. I'm just noticeable like that," Jack countered.

Jack appeared in front of us, and he stopped and took a big whiff. "I smell heaven, and my stomach is going to be happy very soon."

The three of them made their way to the dining table and grabbed chairs, just like Janet had said they would. They obviously felt at home. Miles took the end spot opposite Michael, while Jack took the vacant seat by me, with Lucas across from him. Miles put a leather-bound book on the table in front of him.

"How are you doing, little ass kicker?" Jack asked as he waggled his brows and leaned toward me.

My jaw dropped, and I huffed. "Bodey?" I couldn't believe he'd told them. I would never live this down.

"Oh, it wasn't him." Lucas snorted and gestured to Samuel. "You can thank that one right there."

"Leave the poor girl alone, or you won't get to eat," Janet scolded as she pulled out some plates and loaded them up. "She was scared and defended herself."

Bodey grabbed my coffee cup and some plates

before carrying them over. He put the coffee and one plate in front of me and sat with the other.

The others got up and grabbed their own plates, and soon everyone, including Janet, was sitting down.

After taking a big bite of food, Miles opened the book and began flipping pages. "We need to go over everything and make sure we have the traditional things in place."

Jack leaned over, staring at the pages. "What's that?"

"It's called a book. It's kinda like an iPad but thicker. Instead of swiping, you flip pages," Bodey said through a mouthful of pancakes.

I pressed my lips together, trying not to laugh, but Lucas and Samuel snorted.

"I meant..." Jack started, then leaned forward so he could wrinkle his nose at Bodey. "Is that what you were all talking about yesterday? Because I thought it was just his notepad."

"It's a bound book of notes." Miles shrugged. "So technically, you aren't wrong."

Samuel leaned toward Janet, his eyes on the book. "What kind of details are in there?"

"The clothing we should wear and the crystals and herbs we need to hunt down. All of it will ease the pain that will occur when the witches use their magic to identify and anoint you as king." Miles flipped a few more pages. "It's quite detailed. The cloth should be made of a material that won't interfere with the spell. Apparently, some man-made materials will repel the magic in the tattoo ink if we aren't careful, and the spell won't work."

The bite of pancake lodged in my throat. "I didn't realize the witches were so involved in the coronation."

All seven pairs of eyes flicked toward me.

"It's how the witches and wolves renew their pledge of allegiance to one another." Michael's jaw twitched. "Both have a huge part in the ceremony. Did Zeke not teach you our traditions?"

I took a sip of coffee to get the pancake to go down before I choked. "Maybe it's just me."

The seven of them glanced at one another.

Bodey said, "All that *is* important, but we also need to send scouts to our borders and make sure Samuel doesn't go anywhere alone. Queen Kel has made it clear that she wants to take over the territory and grow her kingdom."

I could've kissed him—metaphorically speaking, of course—for changing the subject. I wasn't stupid; he'd deliberately taken the focus off me.

The conversation continued, and I concentrated on taking one bite at a time. I didn't want to draw their focus back to me.

When the guys were done eating, they all stood. Bodey took my plate. "We've got to head out and meet Zeke to talk about everything. I'll be back for lunch later."

"Yup!" Jack beamed. "We *all* will." He leveled his gaze on Bodey, and I wasn't sure what I'd missed.

"Text or call me if you need me." Bodey brought our dirty plates and silverware to the kitchen sink.

All the men followed him into the garage, and the door shut, leaving Janet and me alone.

As soon as I opened the dishwasher to help her clean, Janet smacked my hand lightly. "Go to your room and get some more rest." She pointed a finger at me. "I'll take it from here, and then I'm heading next door to my house. I'll lock up when I leave."

The stern look on her face had me obeying, not because of her wolf but because she looked very much like a mom.

Following her instructions, I went to my room and crawled back into bed, but sleep never came.

I was losing my mind. I'd been in bed for three hours, and I was restless. At home, I always had something to do, and I was getting antsy.

As promised, Janet left soon after I'd come upstairs, so I was stuck in a strange house all alone. I got out of bed and straightened my clothes and hair. Bodey should be back soon for lunch, so I headed downstairs.

As I reached the bottom of the stairs, the doorbell rang. I paused but realized I was the only one here to answer.

Slowly, I approached the door.

When I glanced through the peephole, I blinked, not believing who I saw.

CHAPTER TEN

THIS HAD to be some sort of joke, or I was seeing things.

Theo, Charles, and Pearl stood on the other side of the door.

Theo had threatened to come, but why in the *hell* were the other two here?

This wasn't our pack, and I was still injured from what those two had done to me.

Sniffing, Theo knocked on the door again. "Callie, I can smell you. I know you're standing at the door."

I should've stayed in my room, but he probably would've called and demanded I let him in, putting me right back in this predicament. He was the alpha's son and my friend, after all.

Ribs panging and dread pooling in my stomach, I opened the door, blocking them from entering. I remained silent, not bothering to smile. Instead, I arched a brow.

"Hey," Theo said softly, though the warmth didn't

meet his eyes. He took my hand in his, and I had to fight the urge to pull away. I didn't like him touching me.

Before I angered him, I needed to know why he was here.

"Are you feeling any better?" he asked, but his gaze was focused over my shoulder.

Charles glared at me while Pearl wrinkled her nose.

Lovely. This was already going well.

"It's been one day, so not a drastic improvement." My throat clenched from how hard I was trying to hide the disdain that wanted to coat my words. "Are you here to take me...back?" I couldn't say *home*. After being here and feeling safe, I realized Zeke's pack had never felt like home to me.

"Soon." Theo's jaw slackened. "But Dad said I couldn't today. We need to give it a few days since all the advisers, including Mr. Valor, are on board with you staying here. But once you heal enough, you'll definitely be coming home. Don't worry." He squeezed my hand.

The last thing I wanted to do was go back there, so his words did the opposite of what he intended—they discouraged me.

I wanted these three gone.

I glanced up and down the asphalt road, wishing Bodey's Jeep would appear, but all I saw were the houses across the street.

I sighed. Bodey arriving probably wouldn't be for the best.

Pearl touched Theo's arm. "We shouldn't rush her healing."

She didn't want me to come back, either. At least that made two of us.

Theo released my hand, moving his arm so she

couldn't touch him any longer. Pearl flinched and stared down at the white wooden porch.

Theo cupped my cheek, and I twitched. He pretended not to notice, staring deep into my eyes. "Your healing is my priority. I'm glad you're already improving."

I took a step back, forcing him to drop his hand. His touch didn't feel nice or comfort me—not like Bodey's did.

A scowl flitted across his face before his forehead lined again with what was supposed to be worry.

"I should be getting back to bed." I took a step into the house, eager to shut the door in their faces. I wanted them to go, and now. "Thanks for checking on me."

"Wait," Theo said, moving into the frame and blocking the door from closing. "Can we come inside for a minute?"

I tensed, causing my ribs to throb, but I'd rather deal with the pain than the three people standing here. I bit my bottom lip. "This isn't my house, so I—"

Charles snorted. "You forced us to come here, and she's refusing to let you in. Figures."

Neck cording, Theo stared at me expectantly. This time, he didn't ask. "You're staying here. You can invite us in."

I wanted to tell him to bite me, but with the way he was acting, he could very well take it as an invitation. Unsure what else to do, I took a deep breath. He wouldn't back down, and if I pushed back further, it would hurt me in the future. I bit the inside of my cheek again, the copper taste of blood filling my mouth. I had to do something to keep my mouth from running, but even then, the urge didn't diminish.

My chin lifted of its own accord as I stared Theo in the eye and said, "We'll stay in the living room."

Though I didn't truly believe I had a death wish, part of me had to. It was as if obeying and submitting were beyond me.

Theo straightened, his irises glowing as his wolf surged forward. He didn't like that I had put restrictions on him, but he must have realized that was the only way he was getting in because he huffed and rasped, "Fine."

Every cell within me lit on fire, wanting me to stay firmly in place and continue blocking the door, but my self-preservation instinct kicked in and allowed me to step aside. I suspected it was mainly because Theo had agreed to my boundaries.

Theo entered with Pearl on his heels. Around Theo, she was like a wolf in heat, desperate for attention he never gave her. He always sought out my company, which I'd never understood. He and I barely had anything in common.

Charles came in last, and as he passed me, he hit my shoulder with his hard enough to jar me backward. The movement jolted through to my ribs, which had been the point.

He sneered and watched me intently as if he wanted to see how badly he'd hurt me.

I smoothed my expression, not wanting to give him the satisfaction of me reacting to his cheap shot. I'd rather go back to the pack under the guise of being well.

When I didn't react, he scowled and went into the living room, where Theo and Pearl stood in front of the couch, facing me.

Even though I wished I could leave it open, I shut

the front door, not wanting the heat to escape. I would have to face them eventually, so it might as well be on neutral ground.

Charles moved so that he and Pearl flanked Theo. I stood in front of them by the recliner. I hadn't looked around this room fully yet, and I noticed another tiled fireplace like the one in the den. There were wide double windows directly across from the couch, giving us a view of the outside. Instead of a TV, there was a massive picture of people paddling in a blue canoe with a majestic mountain in the background. I remembered the advisers having a canoe when they'd found me, and I wondered if Bodey was the reason. Maybe playing guitar wasn't his only hobby.

My skin began to crawl, and I tore my attention from the gorgeous picture to Theo, whose eyes were locked on me.

"Why are you three here?" I didn't have the energy to play games.

"I did what you asked." Theo beamed as if that explained their presence.

His answer left me only more befuddled. "Meaning?"

"You asked me to think about us, and I have." Theo leaned forward and snatched my hand once more. "I'm even more convinced that you and I make sense, so I'm here to see how you're doing and prove it to you."

I swallowed hard, and Pearl's eyes bulged. Even though she was dating Charles, I knew she had her sights set on Theo. This would cause more problems between us, which was sad since I wanted to remain Theo's friend, not become his mate.

"Her?" Charles gasped. "Out of everyone? Is that

why you forced us to come here?"

Gritting my teeth, I wished I could go back in time and not answer the door. The more people he shared his intentions with, the harder it would be to resolve this amicably.

"You came here to apologize to your pack member, who you attacked while she was in human form and grossly outnumbered." Theo turned his head and glared. "You were the ringleader, and Pearl is her sister."

"*Adopted* sister," Pearl added, disdain dripping from every word.

Whether Theo realized it or not, he was making me more of a target. As soon as they caught me alone, they would gang up on me again.

"We'll be making the official announcement tonight to the entire pack, but I wanted the three of you to hear it first." Theo puffed out his chest. "In two weeks, I'll be the pack's alpha and step into the adviser role, taking over the Oregon territory."

My breath caught.

I hadn't expected that. Zeke loved power. None of this made sense, but if he'd agreed to notify the pack tonight, it must be true. He'd never given Theo a time line before. "Two weeks?" I tilted my head.

He nodded. "After the coronation. That's why Dad hasn't transitioned the royal adviser role to me yet—he wants to be involved in crowning the king since the queen was his best friend and Samuel is her son."

That was hard to believe. From what I'd learned, the queen was an amazing person. For Zeke to be her best friend...that seemed unlikely to me.

"That's great," Pearl said as Charles patted Theo on

the back. Even though Theo had forced them to come here, every pack member always kissed his ass, and with him officially taking over as pack leader, their groveling would only get worse.

I smiled, this time sincerely. "Congratulations." Zeke relinquishing control was comforting, and even though he'd still serve in an advisory role to his son, Theo would be making the final decisions.

"Which brings me back to my reason for coming here." Theo cupped my cheek. "It's time for me to think about my future, and I want to ensure you're part of it. To prove my intentions, Charles and Pearl are here to apologize to you."

Thankfully, shock prevented anything snarky from spilling out of my mouth. My words had lodged in my throat. Finally, I managed to say, "They don't have to." What was the point if they didn't mean it? It would only fuel their resentment.

Theo brushed his thumb across my cheek, the gesture calculated. He nodded. "They do. I already told them they have to."

He turned and nudged Charles's shoulder.

Flinching, Charles cleared his throat and growled, "I'm sorry that you're weak."

I snorted, unable to keep it in, even with my ribs aching. "And that I require oxygen?"

Charles smiled sweetly. "That too."

I appreciated his honesty. There was no point in lying; we'd all know, anyway.

"Not good enough," Theo snarled, his eyes glowing.

A sour taste filled my mouth. This wasn't about them making amends. Not really. This was about Theo acting as an alpha, proving to them that they would have to obey him and proving to me that he would be a good mate. This would get back to Bodey and the others through the pack members next door who were home, and I suspected that was also part of Theo's motive.

"Fine." Charles crossed his arms. "We shouldn't have *all* attacked you."

Still not an apology, but Theo seemed satisfied. Theo nodded to Pearl.

Pearl blew out of breath. "I'm sorry I didn't do more. After all, you're my *sister*." The last word dripped with condemnation.

Yeah, I was sure she was sorry she hadn't done *more*.

Then Theo actually nodded at me as if I were supposed to say something.

I remained silent. I refused to say it was fine or that I forgave them. I wasn't stupid; they hadn't truly apologized, just said enough words that Theo wanted to hear.

He waved a hand at me and asked, "What do you have to say?"

Don't say anything, I told myself. *Keep your mouth shut.* Anything I said would anger Theo because it wouldn't be what he wanted to hear, and I refused to be part of the game Charles and Pearl were playing. "That it's time for you three to go?"

Yup, I definitely had a death wish.

Theo's jaw clenched, and Charles and Pearl smirked. They wanted him to be mad at me.

The garage door opened, and my limbs weakened. Bodey was back, and if Theo didn't leave, things would escalate.

Theo planted his feet shoulder-width apart, refusing to leave.

"Do you think it's wise for you to be here?" I asked, and his eyes narrowed.

I kept saying all the wrong things. The story of my life.

The door to the mudroom opened, followed by heavy, rushed footsteps. There was no doubt it was Bodey.

They marched down the hallway toward us, three sets of footsteps following more leisurely.

Bodey breezed into the living room, his jaw clenched and his face stony. This was the second time I'd seen this version of him. It unnerved me because it lacked the kindness and warmth he normally exuded. This wasn't the lighthearted man who'd teased me at breakfast and played the guitar for me the night before. His alpha power radiated off him in waves.

Theo jerked his gaze up, despite his bottom lip quivering.

Taking a protective stance beside me, Bodey placed a hand on my lower back. The warmth of his touch sent flutters through my stomach. I should've stepped away, especially when Theo's face twisted with anger, but I didn't want to, and my legs stayed firmly in place.

"What the *fuck* is going on here?" Bodey spat.

Sweat beaded Theo's forehead. "Charles and Pearl had something they wanted to say to Callie, and I wanted to check on her."

The three other advisers breezed into the room and came to a stop behind us. I wasn't surprised when Jack snorted and said, "Oh...what did they want to say to her?"

Before Theo could bend the truth, I answered, "That he's sorry I'm weak and require oxygen. Then when Theo pushed him, he said he was sorry they *all* attacked me, while my sister said she was sorry she hadn't done *more*."

Lucas scoffed. "Man, that's fucked up."

Theo's face flushed. "They came here to apologize."

"Then they both failed." Bodey's nostrils flared. "They didn't apologize for *shit*."

Strolling to my other side, Jack looked down his nose at Theo and said, "I thought it was strange that Zeke didn't hand over the alpha adviser role to you at the same time our parents did with us. But now I can see why. You're an idiot."

I coughed, needing to hide my laughter. My chest felt lighter, and I felt myself warming toward Jack. He said exactly what was on his mind fearlessly, which I admired.

Miles warned, "Jack."

"He has a point." Lucas shrugged. "Theo shouldn't be here, but the fact he brought these two has me dumbfounded."

"The four of you got involved in our pack business." Theo gestured to the group. "You came into our territory, into our neighborhood, then took one of our pack members. It's only fair that we get to check on her."

Edging in front of me, Bodey pressed his back gently to my chest, blocking part of me from view. "We took your pack member because you were mistreating her. And you insinuated that you have feelings for her, so I'd think you'd be thanking me for protecting her when you refused to." I could feel him seething.

Theo's right shoulder tensed, and I knew what he was about to do.

Throw a punch.

CHAPTER ELEVEN

MY BREATH CAUGHT as Theo's arm lifted.

"Hey—" I said and stepped forward. My ribs screamed, but Theo threw his punch.

Bodey ducked, causing Theo to hit only air, and then he punched Theo in the gut. The sound was solid, and Theo grunted as he stumbled back into the wall five feet behind him.

Eyes widening, Charles and Pearl watched their alpha heir take a huge hit. Neither of them moved to help him.

Jack cackled behind me.

I wanted to glance over my shoulder to see what was so funny, but the risk was in front of me, and something inside me refused to lose focus.

Theo straightened, nostrils flaring, and his eyes glowed as his wolf surged forward.

If someone didn't stop this pissing match between him and Bodey, things would escalate. I glanced at Charles, hoping he'd do something to intervene, but he just stood there.

The glow brightened. He was going to attack again.

"Theo—" I started, but I might as well have stayed silent.

Lowering his head, Theo charged Bodey, who easily sidestepped the attack. As Theo ran past him, Bodey planted his feet and snaked an arm around Theo's waist, offsetting his forward momentum.

Body jerking, Theo fell, and Bodey growled as he pushed Theo backward. Theo lost his footing and sailed into Charles, who yelped as his legs were knocked out from under him. He landed on top of Theo, his head hitting Theo's thighs, barely missing his crotch.

The room fell silent. Then Jack and Lucas laughed. Bodey's face remained stony, his shoulders tense. He stepped toward Charles and Theo, and I grabbed his arm, ignoring the sharp ache that shot across my chest.

"Please don't, it's over." I understood what Bodey was attempting to do—protect me—but he and Theo were making the situation worse. Theo was making it worse between me and the other pack members, while Bodey was exacerbating the tension between Zeke, Theo, and me. Zeke was already having a shit fit over everything that had led to Bodey taking me. Now Theo was determined to prove he could protect me best. What a mess.

At least this debacle had helped me solidify one thing: I would never go to Hells Canyon again.

Bodey's neck corded, and his body shook as if his wolf and my request were battling. I needed to try again. I murmured, "For me."

His body stilled, but his breathing quickened. Everyone was silent for a moment while Charles rolled off Theo and onto the floor, and the two of them stood. Pearl didn't move an inch to help, her attention flicking among Bodey, Theo, and me.

"We *all* need to calm down." Lucas moved between Theo and Bodey. "This shit isn't helping anything."

"Oh, I don't know." Jack snorted. "After a boring-ass morning, this was exactly what I needed. A little-dicked prick getting his ass beat."

Bodey tensed again, and I squeezed his arm comfortingly, reminding him I was there. He took a step back toward me.

A gigantic form stepped up beside me, and I wasn't surprised it was Miles. He was the quiet one, and I hadn't heard him move. His attention was on me, a slight lift to his eyebrows.

"Little-dicked prick?" Theo rasped, his attention on Jack. "I'll show you—" He lunged, but Bodey shoved him back.

"Oh, please do," Jack taunted. "All of us would love to see the size of your balls."

"Speak for yourself." Lucas winced. "His balls are definitely not on any list of things I want to see."

"You two idiots shut up," Bodey snarled. "Now isn't the time for this shit."

Jack was ratcheting up the tension, which might have been the point. I tried to step around Bodey to get closer to Theo, but Bodey countered my move, keeping me slightly behind him.

Theo noticed. "If Callie wants to come to me, she can. There's no need to prevent her from reaching me."

"Fuck yeah, there is," Bodey growled, his body quivering. "You're irrational and volatile. If you don't like something she says, you could attack her, just like you attacked *me*."

Pearl frowned. Charles remained still as a statue, determined not to get involved.

"You don't get to block me from my own pack members," Theo said, "And you don't get to act like you're better than me. In two weeks, I'll have the same rank as you four."

"Please. You may have the title, but you won't be anything like us." Bodey wrinkled his nose. "You're too obsessed with your pack and your property instead of advocating for your people. You and your dad are pathetic."

Miles flinched. "Bodey..."

Eyes glowing again, Theo bared his teeth. "We aren't pathetic, and we're all equals, so you better watch your mouth."

"Man, you let your pack members and your alpha bully a girl you supposedly have feelings for. Then, when you finally decide you want to be a leader, you force them to come here to apologize when they don't want to, putting a bigger target on her back. So either you're clueless, or you're vindictive. Either way, you're an ass." Jack shook his head. "Frankly, you need what my grandmother calls an ass whoopin'."

Miles pinched the bridge of his nose but remained silent.

This confrontation was imploding, and it was all happening because I was here. I tried not to dwell on what-ifs, but it was damn hard in this instance.

Theo held out a finger, his hand shaking. "Me? *I* made it worse? Do I appreciate you interfering and helping Callie? Yes. But you took it to a whole different level when you came to check on her the next morning. We were handling it."

"Look, guys, *please*." This time, I did step around Bodey, and I released him. "We're repeating the same conversation. If you two would stop trying to piss each other off, my time here would go by much more quickly. The more I rest, the more my body can heal, and dealing with you is *not* resting." I turned to Theo and raised my hands. "I get it. You and Zeke don't like that I'm here, but it's done. Zeke was outvoted, so please let it go. I appreciate your attempt to get Charles and Pearl to apologize to me, but they don't mean it. So just stop. You may be their future alpha, but that doesn't mean you get to tell them how they should feel."

Charles snorted, and Bodey glared at him.

"In two weeks—" Theo started.

"You'll be the alpha," Jack deadpanned. "Believe me. We *know*. You've told us multiple times since I've been standing here." He glanced at me and asked, "Does he always repeat himself this way? Or is your pack so stupid that he has to constantly validate how strong he is?"

I often wondered the same thing. I was sick and tired of hearing about it, but I wondered if it was just me.

"You do realize you'll have to show him respect in two weeks." Pearl kept her gaze on the floor, despite lifting her chin. "When he is your equal."

Leave it to her to side with Theo. She wanted to prove she was worthier than me, and for once, I hoped she did. Maybe she could take some of the attention away from me.

Bodey sneered. "Respect is earned, not given. Just

because he'll have the same title doesn't mean we'll have to treat him differently. But none of that matters, seeing as I was the one who *helped* your sister. Out of anyone, you should be glad she's here."

"*Adopted* sister." She didn't say anything more.

An awkward silence descended, and I wanted to run out of the room. Maybe if the source of the problem wasn't here, everyone would calm the hell down.

Wanting to appease Theo, I walked to him and touched his shoulder. Hopefully, this time, Jack would remain quiet and not ruin my attempt to defuse the tension.

Theo's gaze turned to me and softened, reminding me of the little boy who used to hide with me in the woods. There was my friend. The one I trusted. The older we got, the less often I saw him.

"This is a crappy situation for all of us, and I'm sorry." I forced a smile, and it was the hardest thing I'd ever done. "I'll be home soon."

That seemed to appease him, and none of the advisers added anything. Thank gods.

"You're right. This can't be easy for you, either." Theo frowned. "I hadn't thought of it that way. You're the one they're forcing to stay here."

I didn't have to turn to feel the displeasure wafting from the advisers. Theo was determined to insult them at any opportunity.

I couldn't stand here and let the advisers think I was ungrateful...especially Bodey.

"They've been kind, but I miss my friends and family." Namely, Stevie, but I left that out. She was the closest thing I had to family, but Mom and Dad weren't far behind. They did care about me and tried to treat me the same as my siblings, but it was clear I wasn't blood.

"I'd better let you rest so you can come back home sooner." Theo bit his bottom lip, not happy, but there was nothing he could do. "Let's go," he said to Pearl and Charles.

I dropped my hand from Theo's arm. I'd suspected my touch would calm him, sensing he wanted my approval, but I was surprised that it had also affected Bodey. Maybe he was afraid of brushing me off and hurting my ribs.

"That's an excellent idea," Bodey said as he moved beside me again, placing a hand on my lower back. "But let me be clear—if you come here again without talking to me first and ambush Callie, I'll do more than kick your ass."

Theo swallowed and nodded, though his attention kept homing in on where Bodey was touching me. He strolled over to me and tugged me away from Bodey and into his arms.

I groaned, the pain radiating through my midsection.

Bodey growled, "You're hurting her."

"Oh, shit." Theo released me and stepped back. "I'm *so* sorry. I didn't think about it." He caressed my cheek, and I had to grit my teeth. Just when I thought it couldn't get worse, he bent down and kissed the same cheek. I winced, unable to keep my emotions in check.

His lips were warm and rough, which I now knew was a horrible combination. Not only that, but it was sloppy. As soon as he pulled away, the air hit, making the wet spot cold. The urge to gag was overwhelming, so I reached up and wiped the saliva off with my sleeve.

Jack snorted behind me but thankfully didn't say anything. The laughter only had Theo's neck cording as his gaze remained on me. "I'll call you tonight."

"Okay." I smiled. The thing was that he and I needed to talk more about this whole mate thing he was still determined to pursue. I didn't want to remain with my pack, even when he took over the alpha role. Too much had happened. And the way they'd all disrespected me for the past seventeen years wouldn't change.

"Let's go." Theo frowned and gestured to Charles and Pearl. He walked out first with Pearl on his heels, only nodding at me. Charles didn't even acknowledge me.

As soon as the three of them left, Bodey slammed the door. He turned around, his gaze on me.

My stomach fluttered, and I tucked a piece of hair behind my ear.

Jack snickered. "That was *fun*. I kind of wish he'd run his mouth more so I could have gotten involved."

"Man, this is fucked up. Theo's more erratic than Zeke." Lucas cracked his knuckles. "How are we going to handle what happened? You know Zeke was probably aware he was coming here."

"From what the book indicates about the last coronation, Theo acted just like Zeke once did: desperate to prove his strength and dominance." Miles blew out a breath. "It's best if we don't feed into it."

Rubbing his hands together, Bodey frowned. "I agree. We don't need to feed into it. I need you three to go to my parents' house to inform them of what happened. Mom needs to keep an eye out in case Theo comes back."

My blood heated, and my back straightened. My ribs screamed at me, but I didn't care. Bodey was acting as if I couldn't take care of myself. "I don't need a babysitter."

The corners of Bodey's mouth tipped upward, trying not to smile. "I'm not saying she'll stay here with you. She'll just keep an eye out since you answered the door without telling me."

Did he think that explanation made things better?

"Man, just pack link with your parents the same way we're doing with ours." Jack tapped his head. "You can tell them yourself."

"You better watch it." I lifted my chin, narrowing my eyes at Bodey. "If you say or do something Bodey doesn't like, he might get Janet involved, like he's doing with me."

Lucas laughed, then cleared his throat.

Bodey glared at him, then glanced at me. "I need a moment with Callie."

"Let's go talk to Janet." Miles strolled past me and patted Jack and Lucas on the back. "She's probably made an amazing lunch for Sam and Michael, anyway."

"You had me at lunch." Lucas rubbed his stomach. "I'm starving." He grabbed Jack's arm and dragged him out the door.

"Will you two be joining us?" Miles asked.

"No. Callie needs to stop moving around, so we'll stay here. I'll make something for us," Bodey answered, keeping his eyes on me.

"Okay. We'll be by in thirty so we can head back to Grangeville in time." Miles strolled out the door, leaving the two of us alone.

Neither of us said anything, and my pulse thudded

in my ears. I was still pissed that he wanted his mom to watch over me. I felt like a child, not a twenty-two-year-old woman.

Huffing, he took my hand in his. His indigo eyes were warm as he scanned me. "Are you okay?"

"I'm *fine*." For some reason, I couldn't get myself to remove my hand from his. Unlike Theo's touch, I enjoyed Bodey's, and the warmth eased something inside me.

"I'm having a hard time believing that." He grinned. "Are you upset over your visitors or what I said about my mom?"

My throat constricted. "I can handle Theo, but seriously, your mom?"

He arched an eyebrow and took a step closer, his scent washing over me. "You could've texted me that he was here, and you didn't seem to like the way he was touching you and kissing you. I'm just trying to protect you."

He had me there. "I didn't, but I need to talk to him and tell him that he and I aren't going to be together. I didn't want to do that with Pearl and Charles here." If I rejected Theo in front of people, it would make him look bad. I didn't want that.

"I'm pretty certain he's not smart, so I could see him coming back. What if he brings other pack members and tries to do those things to you again? He obviously knows you won't reject him in front of others." He arched a brow.

I looked up at him, my anger vanishing. He wasn't trying to be a jerk; he was truly concerned. "You do realize that when I go back, you won't be there to protect me, right? So...you might as well let me figure out how to handle this Theo situation while I'm here. I need to get through to him. He's just trying to protect me in his own misguided way."

"Do *you* realize that when you go back there, you aren't getting rid of me?" He cupped my cheek, staring into my soul. "I will still be there for you. You're too special and too kind for someone to take advantage of you. I won't allow it."

His oath had my heart galloping and warmth spreading throughout my entire body, but not like before. This reaction wasn't anger.

I didn't know what was going on, but my feelings for him were intensifying, and we hadn't been around each other for that long.

He lowered his forehead to mine and promised, "I'll always be here to protect you. If anything ever happens, all you have to do is call me. I'll drop everything to get to you."

My eyes burned, and my breathing turned ragged, despite the agony swirling through me. I didn't want him to stop touching me.

I stared into his eyes as they flicked down to my lips. My tongue darted out, licking my bottom lip before I realized what I was doing.

"You're beautiful inside and out," he murmured.

Part of me screamed for him to kiss me, but I was also terrified that he might.

CHAPTER TWELVE

EACH SECOND THAT Bodey's lips hovered over mine, my stomach clenched tighter as dread and anticipation fluttered inside me, fighting each other.

I was frozen, so tempted to close the distance between us, but not brave enough.

Bodey blew out a frustrated breath and leaned back. "Come on. Let's have something to eat and get you back into bed." He took my hand gently and led me to the kitchen.

My body sagged. Even though I was relieved he hadn't kissed me, a bigger part of me was disappointed.

I'd never truly been kissed. No one in my pack ever noticed me, and Theo and I had been just friends until recently when he'd decided to pursue me. Between that and my family homeschooling me, I didn't have a life outside the pack. My world was small.

I wanted my first kiss to be with someone I was interested in and who treated me well, and no one had ever done that until Bodey.

However, I couldn't ignore the fear curling within

me. If we got physical, returning to my pack would be even harder, and I was already petrified that leaving him would be more difficult than I realized. Though he'd vowed to always be there for me, it wouldn't be the same. I already feared the limited coming days.

Whether I wanted to admit it or not, there was something special about him. I couldn't describe how or why, but it was like I'd known him all my life. He was so familiar, so comforting, and he made me feel safe in a way I'd never felt before.

With no other options, I followed along and kept my hand in his, enjoying the rough callouses and warm grip. My hand tingled from his touch, and I tried to memorize how this felt and how he smelled because Theo and Zeke were determined to take me away from here. There was no telling how much time I had left.

Bodey led me to a barstool and helped me up. I sat there as he made sandwiches, and we spent our time in amicable silence.

OVER THE NEXT THREE DAYS, we followed a similar routine. Janet and Michael came over to make breakfast, and the advisers and their parents joined us.

It was strange seeing all these strong men getting along without anyone feeling threatened, but that was exactly what these four families had accomplished. They weren't just allies but friends.

Each morning, when Bodey left, he made me promise I would text him if something happened. He didn't have to specify what because we both knew.

Each day, I agreed, knowing Bodey was worried about me vanishing.

Theo would call shortly after they left—as if he'd waited until his dad had left to meet with the other advisers, knowing I would be alone. I tried talking with him about our future together, that there wasn't one, but each time, he brushed me off, saying that once I returned home, I'd need to give him a chance to prove how things could be.

But the thing was that I *knew* I would never have those feelings for Theo, not with how I felt about Bodey. With each passing day, I grew more enamored with him. Not only with the way he took care of me but with the way he treated his friends and family. The thought of leaving was worse than the pain I'd suffered when my ribs were cracked.

My ribs were healing, but they still ached. In a few days, I would be pretty much back to normal, which meant my time here was coming to an end. I'd probably be back with my pack by Monday.

Growing restless, I paced around the house. I'd been resting and mending, but walking the stairs and sitting on the deck weren't cutting it any longer.

I needed to get outside and breathe fresh air.

Not wanting to worry Bodey, I texted him, informing him of my intent. He responded immediately, asking me to be careful and notify him if I felt the slightest bit uncomfortable.

My cheeks ached, and I realized I was smiling. Yeah, this wasn't good, but I feared the damage was already done where he was concerned.

I wouldn't leave the front door unlocked in case Theo paid a visit, so I headed out the back door, which opened to a deck. If someone tried to come in this way, there was a better chance of Bodey's pack noticing.

I cut through his backyard, the Kentucky bluegrass lush under my feet despite the cooler weather. As I walked between Bodey's house and his parents', Samuel strolled out their front door.

"Hey, you." He smiled. "Fancy meeting you out here."

Unable to help myself, I chuckled and took in his jeans and casual olive sweatshirt. I arched my brow. "I suspect Bodey told you I was taking a stroll?"

"Me and the entire pack." He chuckled, then yawned. "I was hoping you wouldn't mind some company. I just finished my schoolwork for the day and need to move as well."

"Sure." I'd spent a lot of time alone while Bodey was gone, preparing for the coronation. Though Samuel stayed home in the evenings with us, he was usually on the deck with a book in his hands.

The two of us walked to the neighborhood road, and I glanced back, taking in Bodey's modern white colonial house, the place that increasingly felt like home.

As the cool late February breeze kissed my skin, I tilted my face toward the sky. Large, puffy white clouds dotted the gorgeous blue, and the sun was halfway descended. Bodey would be home in an hour or two.

"Why aren't you helping to plan your coronation?" With his future role as king, I'd expected him to be heavily involved.

"Well, I haven't graduated yet." His cheeks flushed. "And there's speculation that the Southwest queen is scouting the area, trying to locate me, so it's best if I stay home and focus on finishing school before I'm crowned."

I glanced forward, watching the road. "That sucks that you're having to homeschool." I'd been home-schooled my entire life, but neither of my siblings nor anyone else in our pack had. Though I would've fit in better with humans since I couldn't connect with my wolf, Zeke had forbidden me from attending public school. I was certain it was because he didn't want the other packs under his leadership to learn his own pack had such a weak wolf.

"Nah, it's no different." He tapped his head. "And they're keeping me informed. When I become king next week, I'll be heavily involved in leading our territory, and things will settle down after seventeen years of unrest."

"That must be nerve-racking." I couldn't imagine suddenly having so much power. He could do pretty much anything he wanted, while I couldn't hold down a job at a coffee shop.

He frowned. "Yeah, that's a good way of putting it."

That wasn't the response I'd been expecting.

We walked in silence deeper into the neighbor-hood. The houses were built along one long road that went on for a few miles until it dead-ended. There was only one entrance and exit, making it unlikely that humans would come here undetected, and all the houses backed up against the woods. They also had a similar modern feel, which told me they must have been built within the last ten to fifteen years. The difference between this area and my family pack's neighborhood was that the houses here varied a little—they weren't all one standard design. Perhaps the wolves here had wanted to blend in more with human neighborhoods.

As we walked, I realized I had many questions. "How does your relationship work with Bodey? Since you're going to be king, are you the alpha of the pack?" That didn't seem right because Bodey acted as alpha here.

"For the moment, he is my alpha." Samuel shrugged and placed his hands in his jeans pockets. "But when the witches' magic marks me as king, my wolf will become alpha over the five advisers, making me essentially part of each pack. I'll be able to communicate with anyone I want underneath them, though it won't be the same as it is for an alpha of a smaller pack. The five advisers will be like my main pack, then the rest will flow downward."

That sounded complicated. "So you and I could pack link—if I'm ever able to do that?" At this point, I had doubts.

"Yes, if I were to connect with you." He sighed. "I don't really get it, but with the subdivision of packs, you all can't necessarily link with me, but I can feel all of your emotions and link with you if needed."

That made sense, and magic worked in certain ways for a reason. If everyone could link with him at will, there was no telling what all the wolves would drag him into. "But the five advisers could link with you any time they wanted?"

He nodded. "Yeah, just like you could theoretically link with Zeke if you want to."

"I still don't understand why you're not the alpha over Bodey's pack." If he was stronger than Bodey, he would be. That was how the shifter world worked.

He rubbed his chin. "When I joined the pack, I was one year old. I couldn't be alpha, and because I was such a young pup, I naturally submitted to them, though I didn't understand what I was doing. I couldn't even shift until I was six."

"But you were able to shift four years ago when Bodey took over the alpha position here. Why didn't that transfer to you instead?"

Samuel chuckled. "Because I didn't want it. I knew my future was to be king, so there was no point in taking over the alpha position here, especially since Bodey would eventually wind up in the alpha position, anyway. Besides, I was fourteen when that happened, and Bodey is an amazing leader."

Fourteen would be young to take on an entire pack. He had a good head on his shoulders, not wanting to take the role from Bodey, even if temporarily, though I sensed something swirling off Samuel even with the smile planted on his face.

Planted.

It reminded me of when I forced a smile to comply with people's expectations. "Do you...not want to be king?"

"No," Samuel answered. Then his eyes bulged. "I mean, of course I do."

I lifted a brow. "Which one is it?" I crossed my heart. "I promise I won't tell anyone."

He examined me and huffed. "I don't. Not really."

My head tilted back. "Really? Everyone seems so excited about your future. I just figured—"

"They've raised me and protected me, which is why I was never allowed to attend school. They wanted to make sure no one took advantage of me as the sole heir and a child, especially with the Southwest rallying for territory these past several years." He slowed his pace and talked more softly. "And I've been blessed. This pack took me in when they didn't have to, especially Janet, Michael, and Bodey. But...I've never had a choice. Ever since I was a child, becoming king was expected of me, and the last thing I want to do is disappoint anyone."

The irony of the situation settled over me. In a way, Samuel and I were one and the same, though on opposite spectrums.

We were both trapped by what our packs wanted from us.

"The truth is, I'd rather *not* lead, but I will because somebody needs to."

"You know, it's funny. I've had the same sort of life as you but for different reasons. I wasn't allowed to attend school like the others in my pack because Zeke wanted me kept home. He prevents me from leaving the neighborhood, making it impossible to get a job outside the pack."

Samuel pursed his lips. "Really? Why?"

I wrung my hands. "I'm assuming they're embarrassed by me because I'm so weak. I can't shift or pack link."

"Well, they're idiots," Samuel said as he touched my arm. "Even though you can't do those things, I know you aren't weak. Hell, you attacked me with a lamp when your ribs were broken. Not even many strong wolves would do that."

Chuckling, I shook my head. "Or it's my damn determination."

He grinned. "Still means you're strong."

My heart skipped. I *really* liked the sound of that, and he, the future *king*, was the first person ever to call me strong. "You'll make a good king, but I can understand not wanting that responsibility. But think about it —you'll be in a position to help others. To make a difference. And you know that Bodey, Janet, Michael, and the other advisers will be there to support you. Even though I would hate the pressure, if I could help someone, I'd do it in a heartbeat. Having that sort of power would be vexing, but at least you could put people in charge who deserved to be there and remove those who didn't treat others with respect."

"Yeah, they're great." He kicked at a pebble on the road. "And Bodey, well, he was born to be the alpha. I wasn't. I was born to be the spare, so none of this should be happening to me."

"The spare?" I clenched a hand. I hated how little I knew about our leaders, and after spending time here, I was certain Zeke had kept me and the wider pack ignorant on purpose. If we'd learned what the advisers and king believed, not all of us would agree with his leadership.

"I had a sister." His lips pressed together, and we descended into silence.

Giving him a moment to collect his thoughts, I turned my focus to the surrounding neighborhood. A few people were out in their yards, and they smiled and waved as we passed by. There were no kids around, but they'd be arriving home from school soon. I noted an older man tending to his garden and a mom outside with her toddler playing chase, a game wolf shifter children especially enjoyed.

"I don't really remember my family," he said after

several minutes of silence. "I've seen only a handful of pictures because most were destroyed in the fire that claimed their lives."

Once again, we were similar. I didn't remember my family, either, just flashes of things I couldn't put into focus. Everyone believed I couldn't remember because I was blocking out trauma. "Were you somewhere else?"

"No, I was in my room. It was late at night, and my father asked Michael to return to the mansion." He wrapped his arms around his body as if the memory were horrible. "When Michael arrived, the house was in flames."

My stomach revolted and my mind conjured the image of flames. "Wouldn't they have informed someone of a fire?"

"It was a gas leak that exploded from the fireplace in my father's study. My mother and my sister were apparently in there because when Michael raced to the wing that my sister and I lived in, she wasn't in her room, but I was in my crib. Michael grabbed me and linked with his pack to call the fire department. There were no other survivors."

My heart ached for him worse than my ribs were protesting from how long we'd been walking. "Wait. Sister? That still would have made you king since she was female, so you weren't really the spare." Shifter society was archaic that way. Zeke had made it clear that no one would follow a female.

"Not true. Michael told me she was already being groomed to lead. Dad and Mom had every intention of naming her the next ruler, and from what Michael said, her wolf was one of the strongest he'd ever encountered." Samuel's face was lined with pain. "Even better, she had a heart of gold. Everyone knew she'd be the type of leader needed to bring peace back to the scattered territories."

I swallowed hard. I hated that he'd been left alone and that this young girl with a bright future had died along with the king and queen. But Fate had a way of making things work out, so Samuel was meant to be king. "What do you mean 'unite the territories'? Aren't we all separate? Or is it just Zeke's?"

"From what I've heard, Zeke was close to my parents back then. He wasn't as ornery as he is now, but that wasn't what I meant." He spread his arms. "The other four territories are scattered through the United States—Southwest, Midwest, Alaska, and the small pack out in North Carolina. Between humans expanding and the packs battling over limited turf, we all retreated within ourselves and haven't been helping one another."

Wow. I almost felt sorry for the little girl. To know at such a young age that her parents and the alphas had been counting on her to unite all the wolf shifters would have been harder to live up to than just trying to take care of your own area. Now Samuel faced this daunting task—and without his family. I shivered.

"Hey, let's turn around and head back," he said gently, his eyes on me. "We probably went too far."

The end of the neighborhood was ahead of us. This was my first time walking so far since I'd been injured, and my ribs were throbbing. I'd gotten lost in our conversation and pushed myself too hard. I nodded, and we turned around, heading back to the house.

"If it's any consolation, I think you'll be an amazing

king." I patted his arm. "Usually, the people who don't want it are the exact people who should be in power."

He chuckled. "Maybe. I still think Bodey is a great leader. He's stringent about the rules and has true convictions about what's right and wrong. It's sort of intimidating, especially when he became alpha and he and I moved into the house next door. I thought he'd relax more once he wasn't under the constant eye of his parents, but if anything, he's even more put together."

"Why did you move in with him instead of staying at Janet and Michael's? Not that you aren't over there all the time, anyway," I teased.

He shrugged. "They gave me a choice, but Bodey and I were close, and he was the alpha. It seemed right that I stayed with him and helped strengthen his role—though he didn't need the extra help. Everyone loves him. The ones who don't fear him. If you become his enemy, he's nothing like the person we know. He's cold and ruthless."

I'd already seen that each time he'd talked with Zeke and Theo, but as soon as he looked at me, his softer side bled through.

"Enough about me." Samuel karate-chopped the air. "Let's talk about you."

And we did, the entire way back. I told him the short version of my life story, including how my pack saw me, how Theo and Stevie were my only salvation, and how I was desperate to get the hell out, but Zeke kept holding me back. I'd never been so honest with someone before, but it felt right with him—not because I expected him to take care of my problems but because I felt an almost familial connection with him. Maybe because, in a way, we'd been raised with similar struggles.

When we reached the house, Bodey was already in the kitchen, along with the three other advisers and what must be their parents.

They looked at us with hard expressions.

CHAPTER THIRTEEN

SOMETHING WAS WRONG. My pulse pounded in my ears. I glanced at Samuel, a little annoyed he hadn't warned me that something was amiss, but I found his brows furrowed and realized no one had linked with him.

"What's going on?" Samuel asked as he scanned the group standing around the island. "What are all of you doing here?"

Bodey looked at me and then at Samuel. "I'm glad the two of you were almost back. I was about to get the Jeep and pick you up." He introduced me to everyone, and it was easy to see who was related.

But this wasn't the time for pleasantries. "It's nice to meet all of you." I turned to Bodey. "But why were you going to pick us up?" I examined his face. His expression seemed stretched tight. Looking around, I found every person wearing a similar expression.

"Scouts from Queen Kel's territory were seen outside of Reggie's neighborhood." Michael was sitting at the bar on the edge farthest from me, rubbing the scruff on his face.

All that told me was that the Southwest queen had people scouting where they shouldn't be. "And Reggie is?"

"Bodey's uncle," Janet answered, placing her hand on Michael's shoulders. "Michael's brother."

"His pack is only an hour away from here," Bodey added, touching my lower back and leading me to the center of the island, opposite the others.

Coming to stand next to me, Samuel pressed his palms to the countertop. "What does that mean? Why would she do that?"

Jack's father, Carl, stood next to him at the other end of the island, his arms around his mate's waist. His hair was a shade darker than his son's, with some gray blended in with the darker color. He said, "It means they're getting braver and moving deeper into our territory. They want us to know they're aware that Samuel is staying with Bodey. They'll probably move farther in, maybe even around here, the closer we get to the coronation. They want to unsettle us, so we'll lose focus or push the coronation back."

Jack grimaced. "That's fucked up."

"Language," his mother—Destiny—said, glaring at him with eyes the same shade of cobalt blue. That was the only thing the two of them had in common. She had long, light-brown hair and a heart-shaped face that many a woman would covet.

Straightening his shoulders, Jack scoffed, "Please. I'm your alpha. I can say what I want."

She smacked him on the back of his head. "You may

be, but I'm still your mother and not afraid to take you down a notch or three."

I snickered before I could stop myself.

No wonder Lucas smacked him often and Jack never got angry. Lucas must have grown up watching Jack's own mother do that to him.

"Be glad I love you." Jack wrinkled his nose at her, grinning.

She leaned over and kissed his cheek, and my heart ached. I'd never had that type of interaction growing up, not with my adoptive parents.

Miles's father, Phil, cleared his throat and took a few steps back from where he'd been standing beside Jack. "Let's stay on topic." He rolled his shoulders as if he'd been squashed and needed to stretch. The setting sun filtered through the blinds in the dining room, shining on his bronze complexion, which was darker than Miles's. He ran a hand over his shaved head. "She could be testing us to see how much they can get away with before we strike back."

"Then we need to show her she can't get away with shit." Lucas lifted his head from his spot at the edge of the island between his parents, Dan and Taylor. "Let's kick their asses."

"That's what she wants, son." Dan's jaw twitched as he placed his hands on Lucas's shoulders. "She wants us to focus on a potential threat instead of securing our future. If we engage in any way, she wins, so she's going to test our boundaries." Dan's brown hair was spiked as if he'd been running his hands through it, and he had dark circles under his eyes.

"What do we do, babe?" Taylor asked and turned to Dan. "If she gets more ambitious, we'll have to respond." Her long, dark hair was so silky that it had to be as soft as cashmere. Like her son and husband, she had a tan complexion that emphasized her dark, soulful eyes.

"I'd like to hear what our sons have to say," Michael said.

Bodey stiffened and stepped closer to me, his arm brushing mine.

A smile spread across Janet's face, startling me. She seemed happy instead of repulsed or upset over his action.

"We don't attack unless they enter our territories." Bodey straightened his shoulders. "Our individual packs can handle them since she's testing us. As long as the number of scouts is low, the packs can handle running them off and warning us about the issue promptly. If more come and our packs need additional hands to resolve the issue, we'll reevaluate and coordinate a strike similar to how Reggie did earlier. The scouts are gone, and there was no bloodshed."

Steepling his hands, Miles leaned on the countertop. "I agree. We don't allow her to provoke us and wait until we see her bigger plan. Also, she could be hoping we'll use our resources to track them, leaving Samuel more vulnerable to kill or capture."

"Great," Samuel deadpanned. "What does that mean for me?"

Bodey sighed and tensed as if preparing for war. "You need to remain in the house, and if you *must* go out, take several pack members with you. Members I approve of."

"Fantastic." Samuel mashed his lips together hard as if making sure no other expression broke through. It reminded me of how I bit the inside of my cheek or tongue to school my expression and not upset anyone when there was nothing I could do to change the outcome.

In other words, he felt trapped.

Once again, our stories were so similar.

I touched Samuel's arm, wanting him to know I was there...that I understood.

His jaw relaxed at my touch as if he got what I was trying to convey. He could challenge any of them, even Bodey—he was strong enough—but he respected the advisers too much to do that, and I admired him so much more for it.

"That's exactly what I'd advise you to do." Michael nodded, his approval shining in his eyes. "Would anyone disagree?" It was a genuine question and not a challenge.

"No, but when Stella and Mom head this way, we need to make sure a few more wolves travel with them. I don't want to chance anything happening to them." Miles tapped his fingers on the countertop.

Phil sighed. "I won't disagree there. I miss Alicia, and I want our mates well protected."

"Then it's settled." Lucas rubbed his hands together. "We have a plan, and we can pack link with our alphas to spread the word."

"And remember, they can't declare retribution on us since they're crossing into royal territories. They're supposed to get permission before coming here," Bodey said and glanced at each person. "That's the law."

For a moment, we all stood in silence, informing me that everyone was still uneasy.

"As much as I enjoy your company, I think I've had

enough for one day and want to head home," Michael said. "After dealing with Zeke's demand to be the one responsible for protecting the clothing and herbs used in the ceremony, and now this, I'm spent." He stepped back from the island.

Jack grimaced. "I don't even know why *he* is an adviser. I get that he's decently strong, but he's the weakest of this group. The former adviser died with no heirs, but...damn, anyone would've been better than that prick. Tell them, Callie."

I jumped a little.

"Don't put her in the middle of this," Bodey growled as he eased slightly in front of me.

"What's done is done." Dan waved a hand. "The late queen chose him because that was her home pack and the two of them were close. She trusted him."

"Until the new king is recognized, we're stuck with him. Though I suspect Theo will be worse since he'll want to prove himself to his father. We need a royal to replace them," Miles added.

Everyone glanced expectantly at Samuel, and even though I wasn't the one in his position, my pulse quickened from the pressure.

Shoulders back and chest out, Samuel didn't flinch. I had to give him credit.

"All right." Janet clapped her hands. "If everyone is tired, let's retreat and get a good night's rest. All our problems will still be here in the morning, and we can continue the discussion over breakfast."

"I'm *all* for that." Jack lifted a fist. "I need some beer, anyway. Bodey doesn't have any."

Jack's parents shook their heads but smiled as everyone eased out the door.

Even though Samuel smiled and said goodbye to everyone as they left, I could tell he was distracted. He had to be worried about his future. And even more pressing, turning into more of a prisoner here until his coronation.

Once the front door was shut and locked, Bodey moved to the hallway. "I'm going to order some pizzas and take a shower."

With the way his body sagged, I could tell the day had taken a toll on him as well. "Okay. Let me know if I need to do anything."

"Nope, I've got it." He smiled tenderly before disappearing from sight.

When I heard him walking upstairs, I tugged Samuel toward the couch. "Let's watch a violent movie." I wanted to do something to put him in a better frame of mind.

"Fine, but only if I can pick it." He looped his arm through mine, and we settled in on the couch.

I smiled. For the first time in my life, it sorta felt like I had another family.

I WRIGGLED AROUND, unable to get comfortable, and finally flopped onto my back to stare at the white ceiling. Samuel was on the deck, and I was tempted to join him, but he wanted space. I'd seen it tonight, even as we'd watched *The Matrix*. He'd been distant, and I didn't want to push him for information. He needed to open up when he was ready.

Unlike Bodey and the others, my day hadn't been insufferable. I'd been alone, talked to Theo, and walked the neighborhood with Samuel. Now it was ten at night, and I was more restless than ever. I felt as if I might crawl out of my skin, and I didn't know how to squash the feeling.

I had to return home soon.

It was the last thing I wanted.

Frustrated, I threw off the covers and stood. Maybe the moon and the chilly night air would help me. And since Samuel was on the other deck, I could hang out on the one outside my room.

I slid my favorite fuchsia sweatshirt over my head, not bothering to change my shorts or put socks on. I didn't mind getting cold, but I wasn't wearing a bra, so I needed a thicker shirt in case wolves were running in the woods and could see me.

As quietly as possible, I grabbed the doorknob and slowly turned it, not wanting to bother Bodey. He'd either already be asleep or close to it. I slipped outside, keeping my footsteps quiet, then eased the door shut.

A deep chuckle came from behind me.

Gasping, I spun around as my heart lurched into my throat, only to find Bodey sitting outside on the swing with his guitar in his hands. I clutched my chest. "My gods. You scared me."

He had the common decency to cringe. "Sorry. I was going to tell you, but you were so cute that I didn't want to say anything."

My cheeks flamed, but then I realized *cute* was something guys called their sisters, not people they were interested in. "I'm glad you were entertained." I stuck out my tongue and wrapped my arms around myself as the cool breeze brushed past me.

The longer I stared at him, the warmer I got. His

hair was messy, hanging in his face, and his thin white shirt hugged every inch of his body. Add in his gray sweatpants, and my mind ran wild with the outline I couldn't help but notice. I was about to combust.

He patted the seat next to him on the swing. "Come join me."

There were three other seats I could take, but the swing would put me close to him. My legs moved of their own accord, bringing me to sit next to him. I sat down gently so I didn't seem overeager, and I pulled my knees to my chest and wrapped my arms around them, needing something to hold on to. "Are you just imagining playing?"

He laughed, then shrugged. "I didn't want to bother you. Lately, I've had the urge to play again, which is strange. I haven't wanted to play for years."

"That doesn't seem *too* strange." I rolled my head so I could look at his face. "Sometimes, you need to take a break to see if you truly love something. I'd say still being able to play like you do after all that time is a sign you needed to find inspiration within yourself or remove whatever block was hindering you."

"Maybe." He strummed a few chords, the sound easing my restlessness. "Do you mind if I play now since you're awake?"

I smiled. "Please. I love listening to you." *And looking at you*, though I wisely didn't include that last part.

"Any requests?" He quirked a brow.

I shook my head. "Nope, performer's choice."

"Well, all right, then." He adjusted his position and leaned slightly over the guitar.

Within the first few chords, I recognized the song

immediately: "Can't Help Falling in Love," made famous by Elvis Presley.

My body smoldered as I watched his fingers pluck the chords. I was stupidly jealous of an instrument, wishing his hands were on me instead. Not wanting the scent of my arousal to grow stronger and catch his attention, I closed my eyes and leaned my head back on the swing, focusing on the chords of the song and the rough timbre of his voice crooning the lyrics.

The strange tide of desire ebbed inside me, but I didn't open my eyes. I needed to focus on the song, the slight rocking of the chair, and the chill that blanketed me.

Bodey fidgeted, and his leg brushed mine. The simple connection had that warmth spreading through me all over again. I wasn't sure what was happening between us or how I felt about him, but my feelings were definitely not appropriate between friends.

His arm brushed mine as he continued to play, and my eyes involuntarily opened and locked with his.

He'd been watching me, but he didn't miss a note as he continued to play.

After the last chord dissipated in the night, he set his guitar down on the table in front of us. When he leaned back, his hand brushed my leg. My breath caught.

When our eyes connected again, my heart pounded.

He leaned toward me, his warm, rough hand cupping my face. "You feel cold."

"I'm not." With him this close, cold was the last thing I felt.

As he had the other day, he lowered his forehead to mine. His breath warmed my face.

"I love listening to you play," I murmured.

He smirked, one corner of his mouth slightly higher than the other. "I love watching you listen to me."

My heart clenched, and I realized how deep in trouble I was. I'd do anything to feel him touch me like this every day and make him smile like that again.

This time, when his eyes focused on my mouth, his thumb pressed gently into my bottom lip, tugging it down slightly. The world tilted.

A heavy breath escaped me before I could hold it back and appear unaffected. I desperately wanted him to kiss me, more than I had the other day when we'd been close like this.

"You're so beautiful," he whispered and closed the distance between us, his lips touching mine as lightly as a feather. They were soft, warm, and inviting, and I leaned forward, wanting more of him.

I had to take my chance. With the return to my pack hovering over my head, this could be the only chance I'd ever have to kiss him.

He growled faintly and nipped at my mouth, making me moan. His breath caught, and I parted my lips, allowing his tongue entry.

His faint peppermint taste washed into me, and I answered each stroke with vigor. My hands wrapped around his neck and slipped into his hair, and I pulled him closer. I didn't want any distance between us.

He leaned forward, his hands gripping my hips and pulling me on top of him. I straddled his waist as our kisses became more desperate, more urgent.

He hardened underneath me, and I trailed my hands down his chest, reveling in every inch of him. The sweet scent of arousal swirled between us and mixed as he slid his hands under my shirt and over my ribs.

A slight ache coursed through me, catching me off guard, and I stilled.

He pulled back, his face creasing with worry. "Shit. I'm sorry. I hurt you."

"No, it's okay." I didn't want him to stop. I needed to taste and touch him more. "It didn't hurt that much." I moved forward, not wanting to waste time talking.

But he leaned back, cupping my face again. This time, his face twisted into a whole different expression... one I couldn't read.

"I'm seriously okay. I promise." I bit my bottom lip. "It's not hurting anymore. Problem fixed."

He hung his head. "That's not it." He glanced back at me, his eyes darkening. "It's just...this shouldn't have happened. I'm sorry."

My eyes stung, and my throat thickened. "Uh... yeah. Clearly." I sniffed and jumped to my feet, my ribs aching. "You're *you*, and I'm *me*. Like, why would you be interested in me?" My pack thought I was weak and worthless, so this wasn't surprising. "You made me forget that no one like you would—"

"No, stop. Don't finish that thought." He stood and took my hands. "That's *definitely* not the problem. You're amazing, and I'd be so lucky to be with you."

I snorted. I'd heard it in shows and movies, but I'd never thought people used that cliché line in real life. "So it's not me, it's you?"

"Sort of, but not really." He blew out a breath and held my hands more tightly. "I've felt something for you all along, even that first day when you were attacked. I've been fighting my attraction to you because if I allow myself to act on it, you will get hurt."

I blinked viciously, determined not to let the tears fall from my eyes.

CHAPTER FOURTEEN

SILENCE STRETCHED BETWEEN US, and even though we were so close, we might as well have been miles apart.

My heart pounded, wanting—no, *needing* an explanation.

He grimaced as if he were searching for the right words and they were evading him.

"If it's Zeke, it's fine. I can survive that." I hated that I'd broken the silence, but I couldn't remain quiet any longer. I wanted to get this conversation behind us and pick up where we'd left off. My lips still tingled from where he'd touched and kissed me.

His face creased. "I wish that were it. That prick doesn't even factor into this equation." He squeezed my hands. "If Zeke were the reason, there would be no problem. Nothing would keep me from you. Not only because of how deeply I care for you but because that would be the easiest way to get you out of your shitty pack."

Instead of making things clearer, he'd just blurred the lines more. "If you feel even remotely how I feel for you, then what's the problem?"

"I...I don't know how to explain this without sounding foolish." He released my hands and took a step back, averting his gaze to the woods behind his house. "Though I've never met her, I know my fated mate is out there."

My breath caught, and my chest squeezed. "What? How's that possible? I've never heard that before." If he'd met his fated, he wouldn't have been tempted to kiss me. There was one couple in our pack that was fated, and they looked at each other as if they were the only two people in the world. Not even chosen mates, despite their genuine love, gazed at each other quite the same way.

"I know. It doesn't make sense, but Callie, for as long as I can remember, I've *felt* her out there." He pounded his chest. "My heart and wolf belong to someone I haven't met yet, and I promised myself years ago that I would find her...that I would wait for *her*." He dropped his head and turned back to me. "And I've never questioned that decision until *you*."

The world shifted under me, throwing me off balance. I planted my feet to make sure I didn't topple over, though that was exactly what I wanted to do. "What if you don't find her? Will you spend your entire life alone? Because I'm here, standing right in front of you, and *she's* not."

"Believe me, I'm well aware." He gritted his teeth, pulling at his hair. "Part of me wants to say fuck it, but what if we move forward, *then* I find her? That wouldn't be right or fair to *you*."

"But what if you don't? Shouldn't I be part of that decision?" He was focused on what-ifs, whereas I had to push those dangerous thoughts out of my mind just to survive. I didn't like living with hope because that could destroy you. That one powerful emotion could only carry you so far.

He shook his head. "I have to decide for you—for both of us—because when I find her, I don't want to hurt you more than I already have."

My stomach roiled. He believed he had a fated, and it'd be selfish of me to ask him not to find her...to choose me instead. I struggled to wrap my head around it. I'd never heard of someone sensing they had a fated before they met them, but he was convinced she existed. Maybe since he was so strong, he could feel her, or maybe his logic was distorted by a misguided childhood hope he still clung to. Either way, it wasn't my place to question it.

He was telling me no. That he didn't want to be with me. If I didn't listen to him, what type of person would I be? The type of person I couldn't respect.

I took a step back, the pain ripping through my chest almost bringing me to my knees. This was worse than anything my ribs had ever inflicted on me. I refused to analyze what that meant, especially since I'd known him for a mere week.

His shoulders sagged. "I've never told anybody this, even when Jack and the others give me hell for not dating, but if the perfect one for me is out there, that's who I should be with, and I wanted you to understand."

A bitter laugh escaped me. "I still don't, but I can't connect to my wolf, so what do I know? I just know what I feel for you." No matter how he explained it, he was still *rejecting* me.

Scratching the back of his neck, he sighed. "I can't take the chance that I'm wrong. What if I choose you and it destroys my bond with her, and something horrible happens to her? Or I choose you, and she winds up with somebody awful? I can't risk it. Fate knows better than we do, and we have to trust her."

I laughed again, causing my ribs to twinge. "Yeah. Fate's a real peach. That must be why my life has been puppies and rainbows. She's so *just* and caring." Though Fate wasn't a person, shifters thought of her like a celestial being. The fact we called Fate *her* was ironic since males thought females were weak, but clearly, she was the exception.

His face fell. "I didn't mean that. I'm royally fucking this up."

This conversation needed to end. In fact, not only was he hurting me, but he was angering me as well. It was easy to trust Fate when your life was great from the day you were born. But to me, Fate seemed more fickle than trustworthy.

I forced a yawn, needing to get away before I did or said something I'd regret. "I'm really tired and should go to bed." My feet didn't want to move, though; they wanted to remain close to him, and I hated that my lips still tingled from our kiss.

Most of all, I hated how much his rejection stung.

But I'd be fine. I'd endured rejection all my life, and I'd stand strong through this, too.

"Callie, please." Bodey stepped toward me. "Don't leave. I don't want our evening together to end like this."

My back touched the door to my room. "Me neither, but I need to go to bed." If I stayed out here, I'd try to change his mind—beg him to choose me, the girl right in front of him—and that would do me no favors. I was in competition with a girl who didn't even have a face or name.

I shouldn't try to sway him. He'd made up his mind, and I'd learned you couldn't change someone's mind when it was set. Whatever you had to say, they wouldn't listen, and they believed in different things than you did. Every person had their own moral code and belief system. That was what made us all different and special.

"Good night, Bodey." I turned my back to him, the hardest thing I'd ever had to do.

I refused to become the girl who chased after someone who didn't want her. I wanted my mate to embrace me the way I wanted to embrace him. If I ever wound up with someone, I wouldn't have to beg them to choose me—I would be all they ever saw.

Maybe that was a fairy tale. Maybe it would never happen. Maybe I was being stupid, the same way Bodey might possibly be, believing he had a fated mate out there.

I opened the door to my room, knowing what I needed to do, even though it was the last thing I wanted. If I remained here, I'd only fall deeper in love with Bodey, and he'd break me further. He had the power to destroy me the way Zeke had tried to do.

As I turned to close the door, I paused, needing to say one last thing. "Thank you for everything, Bodey. I really hope you find her, and I hope you find that happiness. You deserve it."

He rubbed his arms and narrowed his eyes. "Why does that sound like a goodbye? You still have a couple of days before you're healed."

I nodded since that was true. My ribs still bothered me, and technically, I had about two more days to justify staying here. But after what had happened, my time here needed to end. My heart was already cracked, and I couldn't risk it shattering.

But I wasn't willing to tell him that. Not yet.

This moment was hard enough without adding goodbye to the mix.

"Good night. I hope sleep finally finds you." I forced myself to tear my gaze away from him, though I wanted to memorize how he looked. There was no telling if and when I'd ever see him again.

He took a step toward me but stopped when I shut the door.

I wanted him to come after me, and that was the crux of the problem and the entire reason I had to get away. Staying would only give me hope.

The very sentiment I tried to steer clear of.

Get yourself together, Callie. He'd made his choice, and I had to let him go.

I turned the lock, more for myself than him, and leaned my head against the door. The cool wood grounded me, and I wrapped my arms around myself. The tears I'd been holding back finally fell.

I took several deep breaths, but my head spun as if I couldn't get enough oxygen. Soon, I'd lose complete control.

Using the wall to steady myself, I spun and snatched my phone from the end table. I stumbled into bed as I struggled through bleary eyes to pull up Theo's name.

Me: Can you come get me in the morning? I'm ready to return.

My finger hovered over send, which made my blood boil. This was to protect me, yet I wanted to be a glutton for punishment. In the end, I would head back to Zeke's pack with my tail between my legs...metaphorically speaking, since I damn well couldn't shift.

I pressed send, and a sour taste filled every crevice of my mouth. *This is for the best. I have to leave*, I kept repeating as the tears fell faster.

My phone pinged.

Theo: Of course. I'll be there at eight. I'm ready for you to be home.

Perfect. Bodey and the others would be gone before he arrived, which would make this whole thing easier.

Me: Sounds good. SYT.

A sob racked my body, and I dropped the phone next to me. I hugged myself, wishing it were someone else's arms around me, which only ripped my heart further. Somehow...someway...I cried myself to sleep.

I STARED at the white ceiling, counting down the seconds until everyone woke up. The red lights of the alarm clock beside me had been slowly counting down every minute since four this morning.

Unable to lie still any longer, I got up and packed my things, my eyes dry and hot. At least no more tears were coming. I was all cried out, despite the torture my heart was enduring.

After gathering my limited things, I changed into jeans and a fuchsia sweater and paced around the room, afraid to go outside on either deck.

Luckily, my ribs were significantly better, and I experienced only a twinge of pain whenever I moved suddenly. Tomorrow, I would've gone home, anyway.

At seven, the front door opened, and I heard Janet and Michael murmuring as they entered the house. For whatever reason, Janet still came here to cook breakfast for us, which hadn't been the norm until I'd arrived.

I left the room quietly and headed downstairs to help. I needed to keep myself busy.

When I strolled into the kitchen, Michael was at the Keurig, brewing a cup of coffee, while Janet pulled out eggs, sausage, and biscuits from the refrigerator. She snatched some bowls from the cabinet and smiled. "I didn't expect you to be up yet."

"I was hoping to help." The other advisers and their parents would be here within the next ten minutes, and they'd all eat breakfast before rushing to their meeting in the city.

"Fine." She pointed at me. "But only because you're pretty much healed. Why don't you cook the sausage?"

Michael took a sip of his coffee. "I'll set the table."

She placed the sausage on a cutting board and moved so I could take her place. As I cut the meat into patties, she pulled out a frying pan for me. Moving to the spot beside me, she cracked eggs into a bowl. "We heard Bodey playing last night. It's so nice to hear him play again." She glanced at me.

I froze for a second before regaining my composure and placing the meat in the frying pan. I tried to steady my hands. "Yeah, he's amazing."

"Then why have you been crying?" Janet asked, catching me off guard. "It seemed like a good night."

My face burned at the clear insinuation. No matter how many times I'd gone to the bathroom and put a warm washcloth over my eyes, they were still red and swollen. Of course she'd noticed.

Michael cleared his throat as he grabbed the plates and hurried into the dining room.

"It's complicated." I bit my bottom lip and turned the sausage over with a spatula.

She whisked the eggs. "My son is a complicated man who's been preparing to lead since he was a young boy. He believes that rules are made for a reason, so you need to be patient with him. I'm just glad he's playing again and has someone like you in his life."

I went still. She'd pretty much told me she approved of me, but Bodey didn't want to be with me. I wanted to tell her what the real issue was, but telling her wouldn't change a thing. Besides, if he wanted her to know, he would've told her himself. "Thank you," I barely managed to say, fresh tears filling my eyes. I blinked again, desperate to hold them at bay.

"Give him time." She patted my arm. "He needs to realize things on his own terms since being with you would cause a rift between him and Zeke."

I remained silent. I had nothing to say. A rift with Zeke was definitely not the problem, but it wasn't my place to correct her.

The two of us worked in silence as Michael rejoined us. I was certain he'd ensured he didn't come back too soon.

Brisk footsteps sounded on the stairs, and I immediately knew who they belonged to.

Bodey.

My traitorous heart quickened.

He walked into the room, and the hairs on my arms stood on end. I wanted to rush to him and kiss him, but I already knew how that would end.

"Good morning," he rasped, his voice more gravelly than normal.

Unable to stop myself, I glanced at him. There was stubble on his jaw and faint dark circles under his eyes. When our eyes connected, he grimaced.

"Morning, dear," Janet said cheerfully and moved to kiss Bodey's cheek. "Callie decided to come down and help."

Bodey frowned. "She's still not recovered."

"She has enough." She went back to scrambling the eggs and checking the biscuits in the oven. "She'll be returning to Zeke's pack very soon."

"Dear," Michael warned, no doubt knowing what she was up to.

Getting a large bowl from the cabinet, she shrugged. "What? It's the truth."

Luckily, the front door opened, and the advisers and their parents entered.

Jack snickered, leading the pack. "Man, it's not a big deal. You're blowing this out of proportion."

"There is *nothing* natural about walking in on you pooping," Lucas retorted, and the front door slammed shut.

Breezing into the hallway between the dining room and the kitchen, Jack tapped his nose. "I can't help it if you didn't know. Maybe you should be more worried about your wolf not connecting."

"Six men live in the same house. Everything smells." Lucas scoffed. "If I didn't go places where my nose told me there was something smelly, I'd be staying outside."

I chuckled, unable to help it. I could picture the three of them being messy, but I assumed their fathers weren't so bad, or at least their mates were there to clean up after them. Bodey was definitely not messy, and I was thankful I'd been staying with him.

"You guys lived there for over a week before Destiny and I got there." Taylor placed her hands on her hips. "Forgive us if it's taking a while longer to clean things to your standards. Every night, you six come back and mess it all up again."

Destiny wrapped an arm around Taylor. "Everything she just said. We'll give you each a list of chores, so we don't keep repeating this conversation."

"Wait." Miles leaned back. "How many times have you walked in on him pooping? Dude, that's just weird."

"He was in *my* bathroom." Lucas patted his chest.

Jack's face scrunched, and he stared Lucas down as if he was dumb. "Yeah, I don't want to stink mine up and then have to get ready."

"You two, shut it." Dan hurried over and reached for a piece of sausage. "I have a headache, which should be impossible for shifters."

I smacked his hand away before he snatched one. "You can wait with the rest of them."

His eyes widened, and he glanced at Lucas. "I thought you said she was a weak wolf."

"Yeah, she doesn't act like it." Lucas chuckled.

Jack sidled up next to me, threw an arm around my shoulders, and winked. "That's why I've decided we should keep her."

The ache in my heart ebbed a little. Jack had just claimed me as his friend.

He leaned in close, murmuring loud enough for everyone to hear, "You know, if you and Bodey don't work out, I'm single and available."

Bodey snarled.

Jack threw his head back and cackled.

Samuel entered the kitchen. "Hey, what's going on here?"

"Just telling Callie that I call dibs on her when Bodey fucks up." Jack kissed my cheek.

Bodey went as still as a statue.

"Man." Lucas shook his head. "You shouldn't be doing this shit."

As Jack walked past him, Miles smacked him on the back of his head. "Quit it."

"All right, it's breakfast time," Janet said a little too brightly, but there was mirth in her eyes.

I reached for the plate of sausages, and as I passed Bodey, he followed me and took the spot next to me at the table. Janet sat on my other side, cutting Jack off. Everyone but me tore into their food, talking about everything.

I couldn't focus. I played with the food I'd put on my plate and dreaded these last few minutes of being with them.

My phone dinged, and I removed it from my pocket.

Theo: I'm here. Do you need help with your things?

My stomach dropped. He was thirty minutes early.

Bodey jumped to his feet, his chair smacking the wall. "I'll handle this." He turned and marched down the hallway to the front door.

Shit! He'd read the message. I had to do something before he made it out the front door.

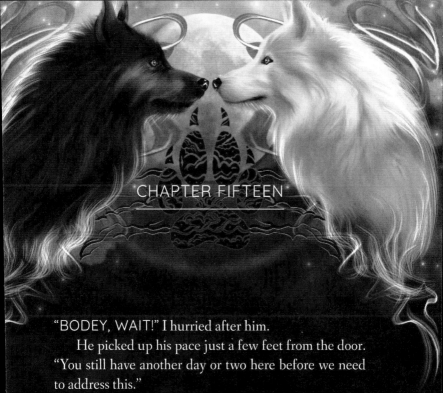

CHAPTER FIFTEEN

"BODEY, WAIT!" I hurried after him.

He picked up his pace just a few feet from the door. "You still have another day or two here before we need to address this."

I wasn't sure what that meant, but it didn't matter. He was at the door. I said, "I asked Theo to come."

Bodey froze. "What do you mean you asked him to come?" His tone was something I'd never heard from him before—deep, angry...and hurt. He kept his back to me, his hand on the doorknob.

My vision burned, and something hard settled in my stomach. "I couldn't—" A sob built in my chest, cutting me off. Being around him would only make me fall for him harder, and I couldn't do that.

I had to get away.

I had to survive.

I'd done that my entire life and I couldn't let someone like him break me. Last night had brought everything I felt for him into clear focus.

Taking a few steps closer to him, I lowered my voice so the others wouldn't hear, but the dining room was silent as they all listened, anyway.

Hands shaking, I murmured. "I've gotta go. I can't stay here."

He slowly turned around, his eyes darkening to onyx, locking on me. "You're not well. You can stay a few more days. This is what the advisers and I agreed upon."

This was harder than I'd expected. With my heart squeezing and my eyes burning, I wanted to crumple into his arms, which was the *entire* problem. "I know, but if I stay here, I'll get hurt worse in a different way." I tucked a piece of hair behind my ear and held his gaze. I couldn't falter. Theo was here because I'd asked him to come. "I don't want to leave, but I have to."

"You don't *ever* have to leave," he rasped, closing the distance between us. "You can stay and become part of our pack."

My heart screamed *yes*, but my brain yelled a louder *no*. Even though his offer tempted me, I'd rather live among people who openly hated me than pine away as he found his fated and fell in love.

At least, with my current pack, I'd have my head on straight and determine a way to leave them behind on my own terms.

Licking my lips, I searched for the right words. I wanted to be honest and not speak out of hurt or anger and regret it later. "I want to. I do. But I can't."

"There's—" he started.

I held up a hand. "Let me finish, please." I needed to get it all out before I couldn't.

He nodded, his jaw ticcing.

"First, staying with your pack would cause more problems with you four, Zeke, and Theo when he takes over."

"Fuck them," he snarled. "I don't give a rat's ass."

Butterflies fluttered in my stomach, but I pushed the sensation away. He wanted to protect me, no matter the cost—and that was both the problem and one reason I was falling for him.

I had to tell him. "Bodey, I can't stay here and watch you find *her*." My voice broke on the last word, and a tear trailed down my cheek. "I wouldn't survive that. I'm sorry."

He hunched his shoulders. "I don't want you to leave for way too many reasons."

Did he want to keep me around in case he never found her? "I need you to let me go." I stared into his eyes, wanting him to see my pain. "I can't stay here. Not after last night."

A knock had Bodey's face hardening. He crossed his arms, blocking me from reaching the door.

If he thought that would prevent me from leaving, he'd soon learn otherwise. I didn't give a damn if he decided to be all alpha-y. Even my own childhood alpha had a hard time controlling me, and I wouldn't cower.

I moved past him to open the door, even if just a crack.

"Callie," he warned.

I couldn't continue this conversation. My resolve would crumble, and I'd wind up staying. I already wanted to give in, so I had to leave...for *me* and *now*.

I opened the door and heard him inhale in frustration.

Welcome to the party. He didn't get to reject me,

then demand I stay close. That wasn't how life worked, even if he was used to it being that way.

I managed to open the door only a crack, thanks to the way Bodey was blocking it, but it was wide enough for me to see Theo's face.

He smiled. "Hey." His smile faltered when I didn't open the door wider.

Snarling, Bodey grabbed the edge of the door and threw it open, stepping between Theo and me so he could hover in the doorframe. He snapped, "She's still not better. It's not time for her to leave."

My hands fisted at my sides, and for the first time, I felt angry at Bodey. I welcomed the sensation. At least it numbed the heartbreak.

Theo lifted his chin. "She asked me to come pick her up today, so I'm here to bring her home. You don't get a say."

Shaking his head, Bodey crossed his arms. "Not happening."

I gritted my teeth. "You aren't the boss of me."

"Somebody concerned with your well-being should be." He glanced over his shoulder at me, his nostrils flaring.

"Bodey," Michael called as his footsteps hurried down the hallway. When he entered the room, he warned, "You're out of line."

Bodey shot his father a death glare but didn't budge. "Not happening."

Alpha will rolled off him in waves so strong I sensed them even from behind him. I could only imagine how Theo felt with it channeling right at him. Bodey wasn't his alpha, so he didn't have to listen, but his wolf would be affected.

I was about to lose my shit. He was acting no better than Zeke, trying to bully others into doing his will.

"Son," Michael added, "if she called him, we can't stand in her way. She's pretty much healed, anyway. There's no reason for her to stay if she asked to go."

"No *reason*?" Bodey's body shook. "Her *pack* injured her!"

"That doesn't change the fact that she wants to return," Michael said, his gaze flicking between his son and Theo.

I wanted to retract my decision, but it was too late. This was why I had to get out of there. "I need to leave. I've made my decision."

"See?" Michael placed a hand on his son's shoulders. "Those are the rules."

Bodey somehow stiffened more, as if he was ready to argue with his dad as well. The comment Samuel had made yesterday about Bodey being a rule follower had hit home.

"I'll go get my bag." I spun and headed up the stairs.

I rushed into my room and grabbed my bag, but my legs froze. I didn't want to leave. This place had been safe but at the cost of my heart.

Soft steps headed toward me, and Janet slipped into the room. "You know he cares about you?" Her face softened. "I don't know what happened between the two of you last night, but it's clear you're both hurting."

I wiped the tears falling from my eyes. "I care about him, too. And that's the real problem because he made it clear last night that we can't be together." I blew out a breath, trying to rekindle the anger I'd had on my way up here.

For a moment, neither of us spoke, and I centered

myself so I could get my ass back downstairs. Turning toward her, I placed a hand on her shoulder and said, "I appreciate everything you've done for me, but it's in Bodey's best interest if I leave. He needs to focus on finding the one he's searching for. And I'm causing more friction when the alphas' focus should be on Samuel's coronation and the queen of the Southwest. I need to return to my family."

I left out the part that staying here would destroy me. Bodey had trusted me with his secret.

Janet smiled sadly. "You're doing what's best for my son. I see that, and all I can do is thank you. I just thought you two had found something special in each other, and maybe you have. But sometimes love isn't enough."

My mouth went dry, and I tried to swallow. If I wasn't careful, I'd start crying all over again, and my eyes were stinging.

She hugged me, and I returned the gesture. I wasn't hugely into physical affection, but I'd grown to care about her and the rest of them.

When she pulled away, she brushed my cheek with the back of her hand. "Remember, you need to take care of yourself. Don't stay in a dangerous situation."

"I won't." That wasn't a lie. I was determined to find a way out of the hell that was my life. I now knew that not all packs mistreated their members, but I had to go back for my family and to find a way to legitimately break free without getting others involved in that battle.

Whatever she saw on my face must have reassured her because she dropped her hands. "If you need anything, all you have to do is call or text one of us." She took my phone from my hand and typed in some numbers. When she handed it back to me, she said, "You have our contact information now. Even though you're not an official pack member, in my heart, you'll always be one of us."

Yeah, she wasn't helping me with my not-crying strategy. I bit my inner cheek to keep from sobbing. "Thank you."

Someone heavier trekked up the stairs, and Samuel joined us in the room. He cleared his throat. "Are you two done? I'd like to talk to Callie for a second before she leaves."

"Of course. I need to go downstairs and check on Bodey and Michael." She hurried over and kissed Samuel's cheek, then left us.

My heart panged. We were both adopted, but my parents didn't show me affection like that. I was happy for him—Samuel deserved it—but sometimes, I wished Fate had been kinder to me.

Enough wallowing.

Samuel rubbed the back of his neck. "I'm really gonna miss you. Out of everyone here, you understood me best."

I mashed my lips into a line to prevent more tears from forming. "That's because we're kinda in the same situation, though our futures look very different." I placed my hands on his shoulders and smiled. "Just know you will be an *amazing* king."

He grabbed my hand and held it tightly. "When I'm king, I'll make things right for you. I promise."

My heart quickened. I wasn't sure what he was vowing to do. "You need to focus on strengthening the territories and settling everything political with the queen. You don't need to focus on helping me. I'll be fine. I'll make sure of it."

Instead of waiting for him to answer, I pulled him into a brief hug, then broke away. I was getting dangerously close to staying.

"Be safe." I placed my phone in his hand. "What's your number? We can stay in touch."

He grinned. "I'd like that."

Once he'd typed in his information, we headed downstairs to find Bodey and Theo standing across the room from each other, glaring. Jack, Lucas, Miles, and Michael stood behind Bodey, all tense as if they might need to reel Bodey in at any second.

When I moved toward the front door, Bodey grabbed my bag and said, "I'll carry it to the car."

Theo shook his head. "I've got it." He grabbed the handle, trying to take it from Bodey.

Bodey didn't budge.

"Man, I don't want her to go, either, but you're going to make it harder on us if you keep doing this shit," Jack chastised.

Lucas huffed. "That's sad when *he's* scolding you, man."

Miles glowered at Theo but remained silent, which I'd learned was his usual demeanor.

Bodey didn't release my bag. His eyes were locked on me, his expression twisted in agony.

He didn't want me to go.

Eliminating the few feet between us, I kissed his cheek. My lips tingled from the memory of last night, and I ignored Theo's low growl of warning.

Leaning toward his ear, I whispered faintly so only he could hear, "I hope you find her." Then I pulled back.

If I thought he'd been sad before, I'd been wrong. His shoulders were hunched, and his Adam's apple bobbed. His eyes remained locked on me as he released his hold on my bag. He looked heartbroken.

Everything within me screamed to stay. "Thank you for everything."

Theo opened the door, and I hurried through before I couldn't.

I'd thought I knew pain.

Suffering.

Anguish.

Nothing had prepared me for this moment. As I walked to Theo's truck, I could feel Bodey's eyes beaming into the back of my head, and I wished he'd run after me, tell me he was wrong. That he didn't need to find her.

But he never did.

So I got in the truck, kept my gaze forward, and left my heart behind as I headed back to my own personal hell.

THE ENTRANCE to the neighborhood appeared in front of us, and a lump formed in my throat. We'd gotten back too quickly, and I wasn't mentally prepared for whatever came next.

I twisted my hands in my lap. I wanted to be back with Bodey, with his arms around me.

"Are you okay?" Theo asked. Rain started to fall, which seemed appropriate in the circumstances, and he turned on the windshield wipers. His expression softened as he examined me, but his eyes were hard. "You seem to be struggling with being back here. You and Bodey looked awfully close."

If I didn't play this smart, he'd grill me for information like he'd done on my first night there. I shrugged. "Not really. It's just that none of them treated me differently there. They were nice and considerate—two things I've never experienced before."

Theo took my hand in his as he turned into the neighborhood.

I wanted to snatch my hand away, but I didn't have the energy to fight. Not when I was struggling to keep the tears at bay.

"You belong with us. You'll see." He nodded sternly. "It's my life's mission to ensure people start treating you differently and that you feel comfortable at home."

"We'll see." I didn't buy it. He was determined to make a difference, but his father had done irreparable damage to me during the past seventeen years.

We drove past the pack houses, heading to my house. I couldn't wait to see Stevie. She was the only highlight of coming home. Being back here felt surreal.

When my house came into view, my stomach clenched. A man was standing underneath the small porch.

Zeke.

Theo pulled into our driveway and put the car into park.

My heart dropped. Oh, gods. What was Zeke doing here? He was supposed to be with the advisers.

There was only one reason I could think of, and Bodey had been right. I never should've come home.

CHAPTER SIXTEEN

ZEKE'S EXPRESSION wasn't his standard scowl, but it wasn't pleasant, either. Tugging down his black polo shirt, he hunkered under the front porch, waiting on the two of us.

"Did you know he would be here?" I asked, probably louder than needed, but with the way my ears were ringing and the sound of rain pelting the car, it was hard to tell. I couldn't believe I'd been so foolish, thinking I'd be safe until Zeke got home from the advisers' meeting that day.

Theo shook his head. "I didn't know. I promise. I have no idea what this is about."

There was no stench of sulfur, so I had no reason not to believe him. He wasn't even trying to be crafty about his answer.

I turned to him just as his irises glowed, indicating he was using his wolf to pack link with his father.

Tearing my gaze from him to Zeke, I noticed evidence of Zeke's wolf surging forward. His brows furrowed, and he pursed his lips.

My body tensed, and my mouth went dry. What-ever Theo was saying would only make this worse, and I needed him to end it now.

Unsure what to do, I squeezed his hand to divert his attention back to me. "Don't. It'll be fine. Let's go see what he wants." I hoped that proactively coming home earlier would be in my favor. This way, he'd know that I'd upset one of his rival advisers.

"Don't worry," Theo murmured, raising my hand to his mouth and kissing it lightly. "I'll be right beside you the entire time."

I flinched, unable to stop myself. His lips on my skin did not feel natural or right. Hell, even his touch wasn't comforting like—no, I had to stop thinking about *him*. There was no other choice. He was searching for his fated mate.

Trying to play off the negative reaction, I kept my hand in his for a beat, even though my skin crawled and I blew out a breath. "Let's get this over with." I pulled my hand away a little too eagerly.

Ready to face the inevitable, I opened the door. I was certain my punishment would come in the form of yard work or cleaning toilets. Anything that involved intense physical labor, horrible weather, or handling literal shit.

Despite the rain and wanting to run away, I forced myself to take casual steps toward Zeke. My heart ached, and the last thing I wanted was to deal with his shenanigans. Maybe for once, I'd actually keep my mouth shut...or I could make the situation worse.

There was no telling which way this would go.

I heard Theo get out, but I didn't wait on him. All I could focus on was meeting Zeke head-on.

Zeke scanned me and said, "You look better." Unlike his normal tone, there was only a touch of malice. For the first time ever, he sounded almost nice, which sent a buzz of warning coursing through me.

I needed to proceed with caution. This was uncharted territory. "I'm feeling better."

Between the anguish coursing through me over leaving Bodey and the uncertainty of what the hell was going on, I wanted to wrap my arms around my stomach, but I refused. I'd only come off as insecure or timid.

"That's one reason I decided to come home." I shrugged, unconcerned. "I'm pretty much healed, so there was no reason to stay there."

He tilted his head, sniffing as if he expected to catch me in a lie.

He'd be greatly disappointed. That was the truth, even if it wasn't my main reason for returning here. He didn't need to know the other part.

I'd take my secret—falling for Bodey—to my grave where it belonged.

The car door shut, and Theo's feet sloshed in the water on the driveway as he joined us.

"You're right." Zeke nodded. "I'm glad *you* decided to come home and didn't let those *four* make the decision for you." He growled in frustration. "But I'm glad to see you back."

My head jerked back. If I hadn't seen his lips move to form the words, I would've thought I'd misunderstood him, but the noises matched the movements.

"Why are you here?" Theo asked, coming up behind me.

The rain fell on us, but I wasn't prepared to get close to Zeke. I didn't trust him. With his nice-guy act, I wouldn't be surprised if he struck me suddenly just to be cruel, especially after Theo had questioned him.

Zeke scratched the back of his neck and looked at me. "I called the advisers when Theo linked, informing me you were heading home, and I told them I'd be a little late due to something important I needed to address."

Ah, yes. There it was. My punishment would be very important to him. However, I remained silent, focusing on the drizzle coating my body instead of the pain from missing Bodey and the dread of what Zeke was about to throw my way.

Theo's chest bumped into my back. I was certain he meant to reassure me, but all I wanted to do was step away. However, he and I had been friends since I'd arrived here, and he was doing his best to follow through on his promise to protect me.

"Don't get your back up." Zeke rolled his eyes. "I wanted to tell Callie I'm sorry."

There was no way I hadn't misunderstood him this time. *Zeke* and *apology* were two words that didn't go in the same sentence together...*ever*.

Theo stiffened as well.

Zeke continued as if this wasn't a strange experience. "This whole situation has made me realize that I haven't been treating Callie fairly."

Theo inhaled quickly as we waited for the punch line, and he coughed from his sudden intake of breath.

Luckily, my emotions were more even-keeled than his, but that's what you got when you learned to school your expression...if only I'd learned how to school my mouth. As if my mouth had to prove it was still in control, I said, "Am I to assume that the possibility of

Bodey and the other advisers coming to check on me has something to do with your change of heart?"

I didn't believe he was being genuine. There had to be a reason that explained why he was standing here, saying all this stuff. There always was with Zeke. His jaw twitched slightly, but he kept his expression smooth, almost indifferent. "I'll be honest. That is what made me reevaluate everything. But I genuinely hope we can start over."

I laughed so hard that my ribs ached. I shouldn't have, but this was either a super messed-up dream, or they were playing a joke on me. I covered my mouth with my hands, ready for things to explode.

He lifted his hands. "Come inside. I have a surprise for you so you can see how serious I am about this."

My legs froze. I didn't want to move. There was no telling what was behind my parents' front door.

He opened it and waved me inside.

My eyes focused immediately on two men I'd rather never see again: Charles and his father, Trevor, who happened to be Zeke's beta and best friend. Both were dressed in suits for their jobs at the realty company Trevor owned. Charles not only expected to inherit the company from his father but also the beta position, which was one reason he acted so cruelly toward me— to gain favor with Zeke and his dad. The two of them could've been twins, except Trevor was clearly older, and his eyes were harder. Even the way they stood was identical, except for the one hand that Trevor was holding behind his back.

Placing a hand in the center of my lower back, Theo tried guiding me inside. His touch wasn't comforting and made me miss Bodey tremendously. I moved forward just to get away from his touch rather than actually meaning to.

As I stepped in, I found Pearl sitting on the love seat close to Charles and my parents on the couch across from them. Pearl scowled. She was dressed in the navy-blue outfit she wore for work at a local family-owned restaurant. Mom and Dad were in their usual jeans-and-shirt attire.

"That man truly took care of you." Mom's eyes softened. "You look like a different person."

My attention flicked back to the two men who weren't bothering to hide the fact they didn't want to be there.

"What's this about?" Theo asked as he sidled up beside me, close enough that his arm touched mine.

Zeke marched over to the two men and placed a hand on Trevor's arm. He answered, "Callie has been wanting a job for quite some time, and we've been holding her back, underutilizing her skills."

"Yes, my amazing toilet cleaning and yard work talents have gone to waste," I deadpanned, unable to keep my trap shut.

Grunting, Charles glared at me. If looks could kill, though, I'd have been dead at five.

"Callie," Dad warned as he pinched the bridge of his nose.

Zeke continued as if I hadn't interjected. "Wanting to make amends, I visited the coffee shop where she's worked a few times, and they informed me she'd been let go."

That was something I was already well aware of. I'd called off on five of the ten nights I was to work, and then I'd informed them I was sick and couldn't come back for a week. There had been no hesitation on their end to fire me, and rightly so.

Smiling, Zeke waved a hand to Charles and Trevor. He said, "Last night, Trevor was telling me they need a part-time receptionist to work during the lunch hour and evenings, which gave me an idea. There's no reason it shouldn't be you."

I stiffened. I didn't want to work for them. There were so many things I'd rather do, like gouge my eyes out, but this would be a way to get myself out of here, especially if Zeke wouldn't impede me from leaving. With human laws, the company would have to pay me. My pride said no, but pride didn't pay the bills. Besides, if I said no, it would backfire on me.

Maybe that was what they were hoping for.

Zeke's eyes brightened faintly, and a moment later, Trevor frowned and cleared his throat. "Yes, Callie. We were wondering if you'd like this job."

My blood warmed, but I fought to remain calm. This was purely a controlling tactic. They wanted to keep an eye on me, but I wasn't sure why.

Well, money was money, and I'd be stupid to let this opportunity pass by. "When do I start?"

Trevor scowled. "How about tomorrow?"

I was certain he'd hoped I would turn down the job. But if Zeke was going to pretend to be lenient with me, even if temporarily, I would take advantage of it while I could. "Sounds great. Anything I need to do ahead of time to prepare?"

He rolled his shoulders and cracked his neck. "I'll have the human girl get the paperwork to you today, so you're ready to go. It'll give you access to our online portal to upload everything you need to get verified and on the payroll. Just jot down your email here." From behind his back, he brought out a binder and a pen.

Pearl fidgeted in her seat and leaned toward Charles, pouting. "Is there another job there that a fellow pack member could fill?"

"Nope," Charles answered, his tone dripping with disdain. "Just one position, and it's for *Callie*."

As I wrote down my email address, the room fell silent. When I handed him back the folder, Trevor bit out, "Seeing as it's almost nine, we've gotten off to a late start, so Charles and I should be going. We already rescheduled a meeting this morning so we could have this conversation with Callie."

Yeah, this was clearly Zeke's doing, but Trevor couldn't resist his alpha. Now I wondered what the hell I'd gotten into. Out of all the people in the pack, *this* was the wolf Zeke wanted me to work for?

He strolled to the door while Charles walked over to kiss Pearl on the cheek. Her body sagged slightly from his attention.

"I'll see you later, right?" Pearl pouted.

"Yeah, I'll pick you up from work." Charles nodded at my parents, then turned around and stalked past me. He paused to pat Theo's arm and say, "Later, man."

I was the one person he hadn't acknowledged. This was going to be *fun*.

Trevor paused at the door. "Oh, Callie. Make sure to dress business casual at a minimum, and please be there at noon tomorrow."

As the two of them opened the door to leave, Pearl glared at me with more hatred than ever before. The door shut, and she jumped to her feet. "See you guys later. I have to get to the restaurant to prepare for the lunch crowd since my future isn't working a desk like *some* people here." She huffed and marched to the garage, leaving my parents, Zeke, Theo, and me in the living room.

I hung my head. "Maybe she should take the position instead of me." I didn't want her to resent me more than she already did.

"Absolutely not." Zeke shook his head. "We already discussed it being you. You're the one without a job." He came over and placed both hands on my shoulders.

I hated feeling Theo behind me and Zeke in front of me. I wanted them to stop touching me immediately, so I bit the inside of my cheek again.

"Rest. Fill out the paperwork. Get better." He dropped his hands and smiled, though it didn't quite reach his eyes. "Let me or Theo know if you need anything. I need to head out since the coronation is soon, but I want you to know you *are* going to feel like a member of this pack now. Theo talked to me about his hopes for your future, and it validated that I need to make this a priority...make things right between the two of us."

Could this day get any worse? Theo must have told his dad that he wanted me to be his mate. I wanted to disappear right then and there. "Thank you," I whispered, unable to speak loudly. Somehow, the words still sounded flat.

As soon as Zeke left, my parents stood and smiled. "We're glad you're home."

Taking a step back, Theo cleared his throat. "I'll let you three have a moment while I bring your stuff in." He bounded out the door after his father, leaving me alone with my parents.

Mom smiled. "I'm so glad that things will be better for you and us. We were worried about what happened, but it's been a wake-up call for Zeke. He even apologized to our family."

Even though no one else in my family was treated with as much malice as I was, they were still stained because I lived in their household.

"Which I'm thankful for." Dad patted my shoulder awkwardly. "We gotta get back to work, but if you need anything, just yell. And if you're feeling better, we'd appreciate it if you could get caught up on the laundry and cleaning the kitchen."

I glanced into the kitchen and bit the inside of my cheek harder. No one had picked up my slack while I'd been gone. I forced out, "Sure."

"Thanks, honey," Mom said, and they headed into their room.

The copper taste of blood filled my mouth. Shit, I'd bitten too hard again. I rubbed my tongue gently across the thrashed skin just as Theo came back in.

He headed to my room without asking. He had a habit of making himself at home. Following him, I watched as he dropped my stuff in the middle of the cluttered room that Stevie had hijacked in my absence.

Gods, I loved that girl, but she was messier than everyone else in this house combined.

"I'm so glad you're back." Theo sighed and took my hands, pulling me into the room.

What I wouldn't give to feel the same, and how I wished I liked it when he touched me. Despite my pleas to myself, neither sentiment was getting better.

"To celebrate, how about we go out to dinner tonight?" He beamed. "Just you and me."

In other words, a date. We'd never eaten dinner out together before.

"Theo, I'm sorry, but I'm tired. Can we do it another night?"

Kissing me on the cheek, he leaned back. "Let me get out of here so you can get some rest, and I'll come to check on you later."

He wasn't going away. Though we were friends, we didn't hang out often, but he was obviously determined to change that. "Okay. Sounds good." I couldn't hurt or upset him. He would be the alpha by this weekend.

"I'll be watching the time until then," he murmured, his eyes flicking to my lips.

Not happening.

Instead, I hugged him and spun out of his hold, plopping onto my bed. "I may take a nap before doing anything."

"Sounds like the perfect idea." He winked and strolled out.

I held my breath, despite my lungs screaming, until I heard the front door open and shut and the sound of his truck pulling out of the driveway.

Once I was alone, I tried to rest, but every time I closed my eyes, Bodey's face appeared. All I saw was the hurt expression in his gorgeous eyes when I walked out the door.

I lay back in my bed, trying to get comfortable, and stared at the ceiling, taking in each kernel of the popcorn texture. This bed didn't feel comfortable...and it no longer felt like home.

The bitter truth hung heavy inside me, weighing me down. Until my stay at Bodey's, I hadn't realized this place had never felt like home.

My eyes burned as more tears filled them. I'd cried more during the last twelve hours than in the last twenty-two years combined. Not only did I want to be with Bodey, to touch and kiss him, but I missed the others as well. Jack's inappropriate jokes and obnoxious laugh, Lucas's amused chastising, Miles's quiet attentiveness, and Samuel's reliable friendship made me feel not quite as alone.

My phone dinged, and I glanced at the screen.

Bodey: Are you okay? Do you need me to come get you? I hate how we ended things.

I wanted to ignore him, but I feared he'd show up here and ruin whatever reprieve I had.

Me: I'll be okay. You have meetings. And Bodey, there's no ending something that never had a chance. Be safe, but I need distance from you to heal. Thank you for everything.

Not wanting to see if and how he responded, I climbed out of bed and left my cell phone behind as I went into the kitchen, needing to busy myself. Needing a way to keep from constantly thinking about him.

Bodey never responded. I wasn't sure if I was hurt or relieved. Maybe a combination of the two. This was what I'd wanted, or that was what I kept telling myself.

When Theo came by last night, I'd already retired to bed. It was pathetic of me, but all day, the only thing I could think about was Bodey. No matter how much I cleaned or tried to listen to music. Every damn lyric came back to him.

I didn't even eat dinner with the family, opting to

take it into my room under the guise of being tired. Stevie got me to watch *The Last Kingdom* with her, but even then, I couldn't stop thinking of *him*.

"What's up with you?" Stevie asked the next day as she turned down the road to Trevor's real estate office, about forty minutes away in Halfway, Oregon. Since Oxbow didn't have a town due to us living in wildlife territory, we had to drive to this area to find jobs if we couldn't work from home.

Trevor had bought a house and converted it into a business office at the edge of town, right up against the woods. If a pack emergency happened, they could shift without causing alarm.

Stevie continued, "You've been acting strange since you got back."

The last thing I wanted to do was discuss Bodey with her. I ran my hands over my black slacks and smoothed out my flowy long-sleeved business shirt, admiring the contrasting colors. "It's been surreal, leaving and then coming back. They were very nice to me there."

"That one guy who demanded you leave with him was quite a looker." She waggled her brows. "I feel like that might have something to do with it."

"He's got a fated mate out there."

Her nose wrinkled. "Oh, damn."

Thankfully, we pulled into the driveway, and I eagerly hopped out of the car. "Thanks for dropping me off." I was ready to end this conversation.

"Yeah, yeah. We still have the ride home tonight, hussy." She stuck out her tongue. "But I'll come by as soon as I get off work."

"See ya." I hurried up the five steps to the door and

entered what must have been the living room and was now the reception area.

To the left was a sizable, vacant wooden desk right across from an identical desk where a brunette human, who looked to be in her thirties, sat. She was on the phone, her nails tapping against the wood. That had to be my desk.

Hurrying over, I set down my black purse and took in the light-blue walls. Someone walked down the hallway and entered the room.

Charles.

"At least you're on time, so that's something." He sneered and grabbed my arm. "Suzy is on desk duty. I have something else planned for you."

His grip was too tight. Even dressed in a gray suit and looking completely in charge, he still had to dominate me.

He led me down the hallway to a kitchen on the right. It was small but modern, with a mustard-yellow backsplash. He didn't pause there but rather led me to the back door.

Once again, it was drizzling, so of course he'd have me do something outside. "What do you want me to do?"

He opened the back door, and we stepped onto a small cement landing that gave way to grass. Charles's family's older pickup truck, which they used for planting, was parked next to the woods.

"Theo's alpha party is this weekend, and we need firewood. We can't risk gathering and chopping wood near the pack lands because he'd be sure to notice, and we want it to be a surprise party and a bonfire."

I glanced down at my black boots. They weren't

stilettos, thank gods, but they weren't hiking boots, either. And this outfit, I suspected, would be ruined.

"I need you to go about a quarter mile into the woods to chop and gather logs where humans can't hear you, then stack the wood in the bed of my truck. I want it full, and then we'll put a tarp over it to prevent it from getting wetter." Charles smirked.

This property had ten acres of land, so finding wood wouldn't be an issue. I just wished Trevor hadn't told me to dress business casual. The only highlight was that, usually, this was something they'd force me to do for our pack without pay. At least this time, I'd get money.

"Fine." I nodded. "I'll handle it."

We walked to the bed of the truck. He unlatched it and handed me an axe. "Great. Make sure you get it done properly. I'd hate for you to have to do it again."

I smiled and batted my eyelashes. "Thank you so much for your concern."

"I can't wait until I can put you in your place," he growled before turning around and stomping back into the house.

Thank gods I wouldn't have to spend the day near him.

Taking a deep breath, I trudged into the woods. My shoes sank into the grass, and rain pelted me. I hadn't brought a jacket because I hadn't expected to spend the day outside, but that was probably part of Charles's plan.

A few squirrels ran past me, a sign that spring was approaching, but other than that, it sounded as if I were alone.

I went to work.

I lost track of time, chopping wood and taking it back to the truck. I'd been out here for around two hours, and my hands were blistering. But I was going to get this truck loaded today because the rain was supposed to be worse tomorrow. I didn't want to be back out here.

The sound of padding paws whispered behind me.

I froze, my heart pounding. Maybe this was why Charles had sent me out here—to teach me a lesson.

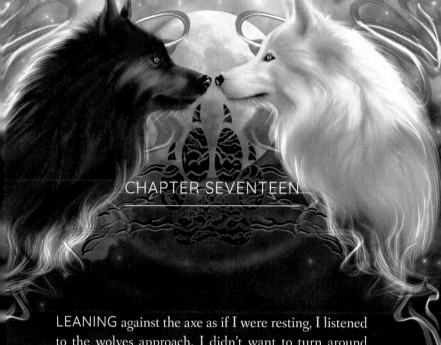

CHAPTER SEVENTEEN

LEANING against the axe as if I were resting, I listened to the wolves approach. I didn't want to turn around and reveal I was aware of them. That would surely cause them to attack. I had no clue how many there were, just that there was more than one.

They stilled. If I didn't continue working, or if I hightailed it back to the office, they'd know something was amiss.

Every cell urged me to scream and run, but I raised my axe and continued to chop the Douglas fir I'd cut down earlier. Instead of focusing on my task, I listened intently.

As soon as I swung the axe, the paw steps came slightly closer, but nothing to indicate an attack was imminent.

I tried to be as quiet as possible, but between fear and exertion, my breathing turned ragged and made listening more challenging.

The hairs on the back of my neck rose.

They were watching me.

My heart leaped. Could it be Bodey? A deep yearning strangled my heart.

My brain took control. Bodey's presence here didn't make sense. The advisers were meeting somewhere south of Grangeville, Idaho, to discuss Samuel's coronation and the security surrounding that, so it couldn't be him.

My pack wouldn't be watching me, either, unless Zeke thought I might be in contact with Bodey. But why wait hours after I'd gotten out here to come watch me? If I were going to reach out to Bodey, I would've done it as soon as I'd freed myself from Charles.

There was no plausible explanation...unless they were scouts from the Southwest territory, here on orders from Queen Kel. But why would they be watching *me*?

A chill ran down my spine, and I continued to work. When they made no move, I took a break. I removed my cell phone from my back pocket and sent Stevie and Theo a text.

Me: I'm being watched in the woods behind Trevor's real estate office.

I sighed, leaning on the axe and wiping the sweat from my brow. I breathed through my mouth, waiting to see if they made a move. I hated having my back toward them, but if I spun around, I was afraid of what might happen. I was alone in the woods, and I thought about calling the real estate office, but all that would do was alert the human, and she wouldn't rush to help me, anyway.

My phone stayed silent. No doubt Stevie was busy at the coffee shop and Theo was handling pack matters in his father's absence. I squatted and picked up an armload of logs, eager to get away. I wouldn't be able to fill the truck today like I'd hoped, but my survival was more important. I'd have to deal with gathering the wood later...hopefully somewhere other than here.

My hands shook, making gathering the logs a challenge. The urge to flee damn near overwhelmed me, but the more scared or out of sorts I seemed, the more they'd see me as prey. They'd be tempted to attack me, even if they hadn't planned on it.

Forcing my lungs to fill and empty slowly, I loaded my arms and grabbed the butt of the axe. This time, I had a better weapon than a knife.

With my grip tight on the axe, I strolled back toward the house. Though a quarter mile would have me back there in minutes, in that particular moment, it felt like a marathon.

My feet sped up without my permission...and the wolves took off after me.

I huffed, annoyed that my fear was taking control as the wolves kept pace behind me. I had to retain control, despite the way my chest constricted.

My arms shook, and a log tumbled and hit my toe, splashing in the muddy path. The benefit of being out here in the cold rain for hours in dress boots was that my feet were icebergs, so I didn't feel much discomfort.

A wolf growled behind me.

I didn't move, not wanting to react to the noise, but they didn't stop moving. In fact, they weren't even trying to be quiet. They were running toward me.

I wasn't close enough to the house.

Holding the remaining logs tightly, I spun around, refusing to have my back toward them now that they were showing aggression.

My eyes scanned the area, but all I saw was rain

and trees. I couldn't see them yet, but I heard them well enough. They'd be on me in seconds. I wished like hell I could tap into my wolf. Even though I had excellent vision, especially by human standards, it paled in comparison to normal shifter vision. I knew because Stevie often talked about the differences in her sight when in human form and wolf form.

As usual, I was at a disadvantage. "I'm not interested in fighting you. I'm merely cutting firewood out here."

Their response came in the signature choking sound that wolves made when they laughed.

This was what Charles did when he was bullying me. "Charles, is that you?"

Three wolves stepped into view. A dark-brown one padded directly in front of me, while a beige wolf appeared between a Douglas fir and a redwood on my left, and a milk-chocolate-brown wolf appeared on the right.

None of them looked familiar, and their musky scents were foreign.

There was no point in feigning bravery, but something inside me still refused to cower. I lifted the axe, hoping I at least appeared menacing. "Don't make me fight you. Just walk away." *Or run.* I wasn't picky at this point.

The three of them lunged at me.

I stumbled back and gritted out, "I guess that's a no."

The two on the sides collided with each other where I'd been standing while the dark-brown one adjusted its attack. I swung the butt of the axe down just as its claws sliced into my left shoulder, but my right hand continued forward, hitting it on the side of the head. The wolf's eyes rolled back, and it collapsed with a loud *thud*. The other two wolves righted themselves and turned to me.

I raised the axe just as they lunged. My heart pounded in my ears, but I couldn't focus on my fear.

Each one targeted a side of my body. Unsure what to do, I moved on instinct. As they jumped, aiming for my neck, I ducked. Luckily, they were already airborne and couldn't change their momentum. They soared over my head, clawing at me, but I was too low. When their bellies were over my head, I jerked up the butt of the axe and hit the beige one. She flipped over and landed with a *thump*.

When I turned to face them, I found the beige wolf on her back, but the light-brown one was already swiping his claws at me. I swiveled my axe in time to block one paw, but the other paw's claws sliced the skin of my right leg.

Pain burned up my leg, unfurling in my stomach, and my left shoulder began to ache, too. Out of the corner of my eye, I watched the beige wolf roll over.

It was back to two against one.

The light-brown wolf swiped at me again, and I stumbled back farther, my left leg screaming when I put weight on it. As he swiped at me, I roundhouse kicked him in the stomach and sent him flying back several feet into a tree stump.

The beige one charged, paw aimed at my already injured shoulder, while its mouth went for my neck.

They were trying to incapacitate me. I bit the inside of my cheek as I moved forward and downward, the will to live springing inside me.

Snapping teeth had my stomach clenching, but the wolf whimpered as it rolled over my back. As she moved, something sharp jerked my head backward, and a clump of hair was pulled free from my head.

Tears burned my eyes as I pivoted toward her, the beige wolf rolling onto her stomach again. I raised my axe and swung, cutting through the back of her neck.

Acid burned my throat. The wolf whimpered as the life drained from her.

I'd never killed anything. I'd never wanted to. But it was literally me or *them*.

The lighter-brown wolf growled as he limped toward me, the injury from hitting the trunk slowing him, but that would only last for a short while. His shifter healing would soon kick in.

I had to do something, and fast.

I didn't want to scream. With how close the house was to human residences, one of them could hear me. If humans got involved, it would put them in danger, make them ask questions, and possibly cause a wolf hunt. Humans were never to know about us, no matter what.

"Just *leave*." My voice cracked.

I raised my axe, the beige wolf's blood dripping from it.

The light-brown wolf remained still, watching me.

Blood coated my entire left side, and it throbbed so much that I was struggling to think clearly...or maybe that was from blood loss.

I couldn't put any weight on my right leg.

Gods, I wished I'd been prepared for battle. I had no clue what to do, so I would have to rely on my wolf to get me through.

With how much I was bleeding, my time upright was limited. I had to end this. I stomped my foot and pretended to charge, stumbling a few steps forward.

The wolf snarled but didn't move toward me.

Dammit. This had to work. I couldn't launch myself at him.

And he knew that.

Taking another step toward him, I raised my axe high, ready to swing. This blow had to count. What if I didn't have the strength to lift it again?

I needed to mess with him, make the wolf irrational.

"It's sad when you're scared of a shifter girl in human form," I sneered, my head woozy. I stumbled another step toward him, unable to keep my balance.

The wolf lost it.

He lowered his head and charged.

At the last second, I jumped to the right, landing on my left leg. I adjusted my hold on the axe and hit the back of his head with the handle.

He dropped forward, and his teeth tore into my left leg.

I dropped to the ground on top of him and rolled onto my back, my arms sprawled out.

My vision hazed just as he jumped on top of me. A sickening wolfy smile stretched across his face, and a hard knot formed in my chest.

This was it. This was my last chance.

With every ounce of strength I had, I swung my right arm upward and forward. I got dizzy, but I felt the axe hit something solid. The brown wolf squealed, and his weight disappeared off me.

I couldn't see. I had to hope the blow had been enough...that I wouldn't die like this.

Blackness engulfed me.

Awareness trickled in as coldness seeped over me. I didn't have the energy to open my eyes. All I could sense was the rain pattering all around me and dripping across my skin.

"Callie," someone whispered.

The wind blew, making the tree branches creak. For all I knew, no one had said my name.

Agony radiated through me as horribly as when my pack had injured my ribs, but instead of it being concentrated in one area, it coursed throughout my body.

The memory of what had happened flooded through me.

I was outside, in the woods, and there was no telling who might find me. The dark-brown wolf could regain consciousness at any second, or the light-brown one might finish what he started.

I hissed through my teeth, grasping for the strength to do something, *anything*. Open my eyes, move a hand, something that would give me a chance to make it out of here. All I got was dizzy.

"Callie," someone called, the voice louder and clearer. It sounded like Stevie.

What was she doing out here? She didn't need to be out here. It wasn't safe.

I needed her to go home. I groaned loudly, my strength thoroughly gone.

"Stop following her scent. It sounds like she's over

here," Stevie commanded, and footsteps hurried my way.

"Dammit, we should follow her scent, just in case. It could be a trap," Charles grumbled.

She scoffed. "Fine. Be *safe*. I'm going to help my sister."

Charles must have been following my scent from when I'd walked into the woods. I'd taken a slightly different path back.

As the people grew closer, my consciousness ebbed. I was so tired, but I needed to stay awake to warn them.

Pack linking would've been super nice right now.

"Oh, my *gods*." Stevie gasped, and her lighter footsteps stomped toward me. "Callie!"

"What's wro—" Charles cut off. Then he asked with disbelief, "Are there *three* dead wolves next to her?"

Some of the dread lifted from my body. The wolves were still out. There was no telling how long I'd lain here.

I'd killed at least one.

My eyes burned, and my heart clenched.

Stevie's small hands touched my arm, and I whimpered.

"She's hurt badly." Her voice sounded broken. "Don't worry, Callie. I'm linking with Zeke and Theo now."

"Of course she's hurt," Charles grumbled. He sounded put out instead of concerned, and I wondered if he'd hired these three. "Wait. One of them is still alive."

So I'd killed two. A lump formed in my throat, and I struggled to breathe.

"Theo's on his way," Stevie informed me, taking my hand. "He didn't hear his phone go off, but I pack linked with him on my way here."

"Dammit." Charles moaned. "We need to get back so I can hide the truck before Theo sees the wood she cut for his surprise party this weekend."

What a shocker that he'd be more worried about keeping the party a secret than my health.

"You had her out here chopping *wood*?" Stevie scoffed. "She's supposed to be an administrative assistant!"

"She was doing something for her future alpha, so you'd better keep your mouth shut," he snapped.

Now I hated Charles more than ever before.

"Whatever. We need to worry about the wolf she knocked out. If he wakes, we might be in danger." Stevie's hand tightened on mine. "We need to get her inside and check out her wounds. Theo won't be happy."

"You're right." Charles huffed. "Can you drag the wolf with us so I can carry her? Callie's bigger than you."

The last thing I wanted was Charles's arms around me, but if that's what it took to get me the hell out of the woods, I'd take it.

"Yeah, I can do that," Stevie said with determination. "We aren't far from the backyard."

Strong arms slipped underneath me, ones that were hard, cold, and unfamiliar. A shiver ran through me, and I wanted to recoil, but I barely had the energy to breathe.

When he lifted me, pain choked me. The world went black again.

A DOOR CREAKED. My shoulder and legs throbbed, but I lay on something soft, not the hard ground. I moved my fingers a little and felt sheets and what had to be a mattress.

Something didn't smell right. This was definitely not Bodey's guest room or home.

Fear seized my lungs, and I opened my eyes to find myself somewhere unfamiliar.

Where the hell was I?

CHAPTER EIGHTEEN

I TRIED TO MOVE, but my body wouldn't listen. Even though agony swirled within, that wasn't the reason I was paralyzed.

It was fear.

I couldn't protect myself, not here. Had I heard Stevie and Charles, or had that been a dream?

Whoa.

In my entire life, I never would've thought *Charles* and *dream* would go in the same sentence.

My mind drifted.

When I turned my head, the room *whooshed*, disorienting me further.

"Callie," Theo said from beside me. Something scuffed against the floor, and he was leaning over me, running a hand over my hair. "Everything's going to be okay."

My eyes burned because his face wasn't the one I craved. "Where—" I cut off, my tongue so thick that I struggled to form words.

222 JEN L. GREY

He sat next to me, taking my hand in his. "You're in the spare bedroom across from my parents' room."

Swallowing hard, I blinked a few times to get the room to come into focus. Soon, the scent confirmed where I was.

Zeke's house.

That was why the smell wasn't unfamiliar, just the room. Even though the blue-gray walls were standard, this room was filled with... "Boxes?" I couldn't get more than one word out at a time.

"Here," he said as he leaned across me, picking up a glass of water from a black nightstand. "Take a sip of this. It might help."

Gently lifting my head, he pressed the glass to my lips. I greedily opened my mouth and took a big sip. The water sliced my throat like a knife. I winced but forced myself to take another gulp. With everything I'd gone through, I needed to rehydrate.

His forehead creased, but he helped me take one more sip before saying, "Not too much at once. Let's give it a minute. We don't need to upset your stomach."

He was right. It wouldn't take much of anything to make me nauseous.

"As for the boxes, Dad cleaned up this room last week, much to Mom's chagrin." Theo chuckled and shook his head. "She thought something was wrong with him, but I suspect he was restless with you away and with the other alpha advisers. He's thought a lot about how he's been treating you."

Thankfully, he didn't expect me to respond—and I physically couldn't—because I had a lot to say. For some reason, Zeke was acting like a nice guy, but the act wouldn't last. I was certain this was solely the result of

Bodey and the other advisers taking notice of me and how he treated his pack. If it saved me from hauling boxes to gods knew where at least some good would come of it.

"Dad's making an effort, and you'll see that Mom is, too. She's the one who tended to your wounds." He brought my hand to his lips and kissed it.

Between learning that Tina had tended to me and Theo's affection, something inside me turned cold; this was not ideal...and I needed to get the hell out of there.

"Your mom?" That was all I got out. I wanted to know exactly what she'd done to me. She was a nurse and worked part-time in a clinic in Halfway.

"She met us at Trevor's office and stitched you up. You were bleeding badly." Theo hung his head. "You were so hurt, and you *texted* me. But I was with Bob, Halfway's alpha, discussing what might happen when Samuel is crowned. I didn't hear my alert go off."

"Wolf?" I hated that I could say only one word at a time, but my foggy head was making it hard to concentrate.

"We have the surviving wolf detained in our basement." Theo's face twisted in agony. "Charles and Trevor buried the other two so no humans would come across them. What were you doing out there, anyway?"

"Charles...needed...wood." I adjusted myself. A stabbing pain flared in my shoulder, and the world spun. My stomach churned.

"He could've cut firewood himself," Theo muttered as he brushed his fingertips against my cheek. "I'll address that later." He chuckled, his eyes warming. "I will say, Charles and Trevor were utterly shocked that you took down three wolves by yourself. They shifted into wolf form to search for additional scents. They were sure someone had helped you."

Of course they were. Asshats. But Charles shouldn't have been surprised. When he, Pearl, and the other wolves attacked me in Hells Canyon, I'd given a good fight. They hadn't taken me down right away, and I'd been more outnumbered.

"They were watching me." The words came more easily, but the room still spun. I took in a ragged breath and focused. They needed to know this, so I had to get this out for their interrogation. "I sensed them, but I pretended I didn't. I pretended to rest and texted you and Stevie." I paused, needing to center myself.

Theo's brows creased. "But they remained even after that? You'd think they'd have realized you were aware of them."

Now that I thought about it, they probably had. Scouts had gotten caught on Bodey's uncle's pack land, so they weren't cautious. Maybe they'd wanted me to know they were there. From what Bodey had said, when the scouts had run away from his uncle's pack, I'd been alone.

"Maybe they did, but I was acting like I didn't, and they kept getting closer." I closed my eyes, but the swirling sensation intensified, so I opened them again. "Maybe they were testing me because they couldn't sense my power and wanted to see how close they could get before I was aware. I don't know."

"Hey, we don't have to talk about this," he replied, squeezing my hand. "You're still very injured."

It was either lie here in silence or talk. I blew out a breath, thankful it wasn't complete torture to breathe.

"It's fine. I want to focus on something other than my injuries."

He bit his bottom lip. "Why do you think they attacked you?"

I paused, trying to clear my mind to answer the question. I'd never understood brain fog until this moment. "I decided to head back because they kept getting closer. I'd hoped they were just curious and would leave, so I grabbed the wood I'd chopped and started to walk but too briskly. Then they knew I was aware of them."

Tensing, Theo scratched the back of his neck with his free hand. "I'm so sorry this happened to you."

That was something he'd said to me hundreds of times growing up.

The bedroom door opened, making it so I could smell Zeke's scent even more.

If that wasn't bad enough, Tina's signature stench of cotton candy and musk followed right after. The combination made me want to gag even when my stomach wasn't upset. I couldn't believe she thought the smell was nice.

"You're awake." Tina strolled past Theo to the other side of the bed. Her carrot-red hair hung loose around her face, which made the look in her onyx eyes more malicious. "We've been so worried. Luckily, I was working at the clinic, so I stitched you up in the nick of time. Any longer, and you would've lost too much blood." Though her words were kind, her eyes held no warmth. In fact, they looked rather dead.

For whatever reason, she was pretending to care, and I'd take fake nice over cruelty.

Zeke stood next to the door with his arms crossed.

"You won't be attacked again. I've already questioned the wolf."

I turned my head toward him, focusing on his face so the world didn't tilt again. "Did you learn anything? Who sent them?" I suspected they were either Queen Kel's scouts or people Charles had hired, but I was smart enough to know not to name them. Zeke would ask more questions if he realized Bodey and the others had talked pack stuff around me.

"Scouts for Queen Kel." Zeke pursed his lips.

Theo gasped. "What? They're now up here?"

His response indicated that Zeke had informed him about the incident involving the pack an hour south of Bodey's home.

"Clearly, they are." Zeke scowled.

"What are we going to do about it?" Tina asked, wrapping her arms around her waist. She still wore her blue nursing scrubs, which had splotches of my blood on the top.

Squinting, Zeke exhaled. "Keep an eye out and make sure everyone takes the threat seriously. No one goes out alone anymore. We need to stay in groups."

They were getting closer to the advisers' homes, almost making a show of it. The advisers had to be right —Queen Kel wanted to distract them from the coronation and focus their energy on her random scout attacks. That way, striking at Samuel before he could be crowned or right afterward would be easier. Attention would be divided.

"What about the wolf downstairs?" I cleared my throat. "Won't he tell the queen his location?" She could send more of her shifters here to free her man.

Zeke *tsk*ed. "You let the men worry about matters

like these. You and Tina don't need to worry your pretty heads."

Lovely. *Asshole.* "I'm sure you and the other advisers will figure things out."

There was only silence, which told me everything. He hadn't told them.

I needed to get out of here. I rose, trying to sit up, and groaned when my shoulder burned as if it were being ripped apart.

"You need to rest," Tina said as she leaned over me. "Especially with the amount of blood you lost. You need to wait until morning to get up."

If they thought I was staying here overnight, they would soon realize how wrong they were. "I need to get home so Stevie and my parents won't worry."

Zeke beamed, the sight giving me chills. "They aren't worried. I've told them what's going on. Besides, this will be your home for the near future."

My mouth dropped open as everything inside me hollowed. "What? No, I need my room."

Jaw twitching, Zeke lifted his chin. "The scouts attacked you, and now Queen Kel knows who you are. The survivor linked back everything. They could attack you and your family. It's better if you stay in the house with Theo next door so we can protect you."

This was my worst nightmare. I was a prisoner in Zeke's house. "I fought off three of them. I'll be fine."

"We can't risk it." Zeke shook his head, and his body tensed. The malice his tone normally held when he talked to me had slipped back into place. "This isn't a request. This is an *order.*"

I wanted to spit and curse, but that wouldn't accomplish anything. It wasn't like I could leave. If I tried, they'd touch me, and I'd crumble. Not only that, but my eyes were burning from fatigue.

"Maybe we should let her rest." Theo released my hand and glanced at his dad.

Zeke rolled his shoulders back. "That's a good idea." His voice had returned to the fake tone he'd been using since my return from Bodey's. "Tina, you should make dinner so she can take some medicine. She's hurting."

My throat constricted. "Advil's fine." I didn't need strong medication that would give me a loose tongue. I'd rather endure the pain.

She moved around the bed to the window. "Sweetie, you need something stronger than that. This isn't a headache."

It was dark outside, making me realize that I'd been out for a while. "I made it through injured ribs." Ribs she hadn't bothered to inspect.

"No one needs to be a hero." She frowned and left the room.

With his attention on where his mate had exited, Zeke said, "Take the medicine. Don't give her grief." He turned to me. "Rest so you can get better. We need you back on your feet."

He shuffled to the door and paused. "Oh, and you don't need to worry about your new job. They know what happened, so they understand." He smiled condescendingly. "The benefits of working for shifters."

Laughter bubbled in my chest, and I covered the sound with a cough. The irony couldn't be denied. Charles was the reason I'd been out there. If I had been doing the desk job Trevor had promised, none of this would have happened.

"Everything will work out. You still have your job, you're safe, and that wolf shifter won't escape," Theo assured me, squeezing my hand once more.

I wasn't worried about any of that. It was being here in this house with Zeke, Tina, and even Theo, at their every whim, that scared me.

Despite the panic sinking its claws into my chest and making my blood run cold, my eyelids grew heavy. Before I realized what was happening, I'd fallen fast asleep.

———

SOMETHING SHOOK ME AWAKE. I tried to open my eyes, but all I could manage was a crack. The room spun like it had that one time I'd downed wolfsbane, and my stomach roiled, ready to empty.

Tina's overly sweet scent had it churning even worse. "Here. Take this pill."

"Mom, she can't take a pill like that on an empty stomach. I can hear it gurgling." Theo sighed. "Let me grab her a protein drink to coat her stomach."

"Chocolate," I said as I heard him scurry out the door. Only the chocolate flavor sounded the least bit appetizing.

A small, rough hand pulled the neckline of my shirt to the side of my injured shoulder.

My pulse stopped, and I managed to open my eyes and glance down. I was wearing a huge shirt...one that definitely wasn't mine. "Who changed my clothes?"

Tina moved the shirt back into place, then threw the tan covers off my legs and began examining them. "I did."

I filled my lungs again.

Footsteps headed back toward us, and Tina replaced the covers over my legs. "Your injuries are already healing, and your skin isn't as pale. You should feel a lot better in the morning."

Thank gods for that. As soon as I could, I'd go home.

Theo returned and sat on the bed next to me. He lifted my head and offered me a few sips of the drink.

It settled hard in my stomach, but I needed protein to heal as quickly as possible.

"Okay, that should be enough to go ahead and give her this." Tina held out the pill again, one that was definitely not Advil.

Biting my inner cheek, I fought against saying something again. They were going to force me to take the medicine, and protesting would only make them suspicious.

I begrudgingly opened my mouth, and Tina placed it on my tongue. She smiled. "There."

Theo held the protein drink to my lips, and I took a sip while I slipped the pill under my tongue and swallowed.

The medicine began to melt and tasted awful. A strong bitterness I'd never experienced before seeped into my taste buds. I forced myself not to react and opened my mouth so they could see that the pill was gone.

"Good girl," Theo crooned, patting my head like I was a dog.

I battled not to let the corners of my mouth tip downward, but it was so damn hard. I wanted him to go away and leave me alone.

Tina sighed. "Now that she's taken care of, let's go eat."

He hesitated. "Do you need me to stay so you can finish this?" He held up the drink.

"Thanks, but I'm good." I forced myself onto my right side and my good arm. "I can finish the rest. Go eat while your food's warm."

Narrowing his eyes, Theo studied me. I tried to keep my expression neutral and my heartbeat steady while sweat pooled in my armpits. Did he know I hadn't swallowed the pill?

"Okay." He handed me the drink. "Just yell if you need me. I'll check on you before I leave."

I'd bet he would.

The two of them left, and I immediately spat the pill into my hand. I took a few more large sips of the protein drink so he'd know I'd drunk more, then dropped the remainder of the pill in there and swirled it around. It should dissolve, and hopefully, they wouldn't pay attention when they poured the liquid out.

Then I lay down and immediately fell right back asleep.

A HAWK SCREECHED, startling me. I blinked against the bright sunlight streaming through the window right on my face.

I jerked to the left and tensed when my shoulder ached, but it wasn't as bad as yesterday.

Bracing myself, I waited for the room to spin, but everything remained in place.

Thank gods, I was feeling a lot better.

One thing ailed me, though, my screaming bladder.

Ready to test the waters, I leaned down and removed the covers with my right arm. I slowly moved my legs, their stiffness causing me some discomfort. I eased my feet onto the floor, taking stock of my wounds. My stitches had already scabbed over, but the area around them still ached. However, nature was calling, and I was at its mercy.

Taking my time, I stood up. Though my legs throbbed, I easily put my weight on them. I'd gotten lucky—my muscles must not have sustained substantial injuries.

With unhurried steps, I made my way to the bathroom just outside my door and to the right and relieved myself. The toilet was between the tub and sink, so I was able to lean on both to lower myself and stand back up.

As I washed my hands, I stared in the mirror. My face was pale, and my eyes were sunken. I resembled death, but I still had a pulse, so that was something.

After wiping the drops of water from the dark-brown granite countertop, I chose not to return to the bed. Instead, I shuffled toward the kitchen, needing something to eat.

As I stepped down the hallway, I noticed Zeke and Tina's bedroom door was cracked open. A box sat on the bed, and a picture had been left out on the foot of the bed. The beat-up box resembled one of the older boxes in the room I was sleeping in, so whatever was in there must have been important enough for him to take it.

I could hear Zeke and Tina in the kitchen, but I

shuffled to the doorframe and narrowed my eyes to make out the figures in the picture.

My heart clenched. It was of an older man and woman and two small children; one appeared to be a baby. Could that be the king, the queen, and the daughter who'd died?

Zeke's heavy footsteps hurried from the kitchen toward me.

Dammit, with the way he was rushing, I suspected this encounter wouldn't go well.

He appeared in the hallway, his expression set in a deep scowl. "What the *fuck* are you doing?"

CHAPTER NINETEEN

I HAD JUST enough time to get my head on straight, and I pushed the door all the way open. "The box on the bed caught my attention. I just wanted to see what I had left to clean up this morning." Even though he wanted me to rest, I was certain "resting" would include cleaning his house.

Zeke moved into the doorway, blocking my view. "You don't need to worry. You're injured, and we already told you to rest," he said and grabbed my left wrist, tugging me toward the living room.

The stitches on my shoulder threatened to rip open. A whimper escaped me before I could force it down.

"Oh, sorry," he deadpanned as he released my arm. There was no trace of remorse on his face. In fact, I could've sworn one corner of his mouth tilted upward.

Yup. He seemed *extremely* regretful.

"What are you doing up?" he asked as he took my other wrist and continued guiding me toward the living room.

As soon as we entered the room, he released my

hand and took a few steps away toward the kitchen, which was connected.

"I needed to freshen up, and I'm hungry. Am I confined to the bedroom?" I arched a brow, scanning the creepy space. I shouldn't be challenging him, but this was my least favorite room in their entire house, which was saying something. The furniture and decor were all pompous and for show. A white couch was placed in the same position as the one in my house, but it had a plastic cover over it. Instead of a television across from it, there was a huge picture of Zeke in a suit. He sat facing the back edge of a wooden chair, staring into the camera. It was over the top and so cringeworthy that it creeped me out every time I came here.

"Of course not." He laughed a little too loudly.

My gaze flicked to the front door. I was so tempted to run for it, but the attempt would be thwarted, and that would make things worse.

He cleared his throat. "Tina was about to bring you breakfast, but if you need to get out of bed for a moment, you can eat with us."

He didn't trust me to return to my room. Lovely. I didn't want to eat in the kitchen with them; being in their house was bad enough.

Besides Zeke's pompous portrait, there were several more normal pictures in the room: Theo and Zeke fishing at the Snake River, a few of Theo playing football on his high school team, and a family picture with Theo between Tina and Zeke.

My skin crawled, and I looked at Zeke to see him standing there, waiting for me to follow.

He lifted his chin. "I thought you said you were hungry."

I shook my head, trying to play it all off. "Yeah. Sorry. I'm out of sorts still."

"Must be lingering effects from the blood loss." He leaned back on his heels. "Do you want food or not?"

He was getting suspicious, so I had to go to the kitchen and bear their company. Luckily, my stomach gurgled. "I think it answered for me."

Ending the standoff, I strolled past him into the kitchen. Tina stood at the sink, looking out the back window, washing a stainless steel frying pan. Greasy water had splashed onto the white granite countertops, turning them several shades darker than the light-gray cabinets around them.

I stood in front of the round glass dining table on the right side of the room. The wood floors were warmer in here, making my feet toasty.

"Good morning," Tina said coldly. She glanced at me and gestured to the end of the counter closest to me, where a plate with a biscuit sat. "I figured that was safest until your stomach settles more."

The smell of bacon still hung in the kitchen, mocking me. Maybe eating grease wasn't smart, but it would have been delicious.

"Thank you." I was half expecting Zeke to grab the biscuit and eat it in front of me. Their kindness didn't make sense. Something was off. There had to be more to the story than Zeke having his eyes opened, but every time I tried to think of an alternative, it came back to the four other alpha advisers.

I took the plate and pinched off some of the flaky biscuit. It wasn't dry, but rather buttery, and I sniffled, hiding the fact I was actually smelling the biscuit before taking a bite to see if they'd poisoned it or something.

Zeke scowled. "Sit down and eat. You're making me nervous, hovering like that."

If it hadn't been for the delicious buttery taste swirling in my mouth, I would've snapped at him—I hated when he talked to me like that. Instead of arguing, I took another bite and snatched the plate, then settled into a light maple chair at the table.

"When you're done with that, you can take another pill," Tina added as she soaped up the pan.

"I'm fine. I don't need it." I took another bite, hunger panging my stomach. I hadn't noticed how hungry I was until now.

"You may feel fine, but you were significantly injured yesterday." Tina scrubbed the inside of the pan with a brush. "You were stiff this morning. A pill will keep you comfortable and allow you to rest well."

In other words, I shouldn't have gotten up. She didn't know I hadn't taken the medicine last night, and despite the pain, I'd slept perfectly fine.

"Okay, thank you." I'd just pretend to take it like last night.

As soon as I agreed, Zeke's face smoothed into a mask of indifference. "Ladies, I must head out." He placed his hands in the pockets of his tan slacks. "I have an hour and a half drive to meet with the other alphas."

Tina rolled her eyes. "I don't know why they can't just come here."

Their entitlement grated on my nerves. Blood heating, I said, "Bodey lives three hours away, and Lucas, Jack, and Miles live even farther. They're meeting in the middle."

Cracking his neck, Zeke leveled his gaze on me. His

body tensed, and I prepared for him to insult or scold me.

"Callie is *right*." The last word dripped with disdain before his tone eased back into the same cadence. "Besides, it won't matter much longer. The coronation is in four days, and we'll all go back to being responsible for our individual states. Unlike the other advisers, I can't venture far. I take my job seriously and have a whole territory to run."

He could spin the truth any way he wanted, but he couldn't fool me. He had to make sure his packs didn't do anything he deemed out of line. He didn't trust anyone but himself. Based on the conversations I'd heard at every breakfast, lunch, and dinner when I'd been with the other alphas, I knew they were keeping in touch with their territories.

Zeke grabbed his keys from the counter and faced me. "You're going to eat, take your medicine, and head back to bed. Right?"

Meaning I was not to go into his room again. Keeping my eyes from rolling physically hurt. "Yes."

"Good." He strolled out of the kitchen, heading toward his room. "Tina, keep an eye on her."

I ground my teeth, causing my jaw to pop.

She didn't say anything, which suggested they were talking through the pack link. But that was fine. I didn't give a damn about what they were saying, anyway.

Some banging came from his room, most likely him dealing with the picture and box, and a few seconds later, the garage door opened and shut. Tina tossed more dishes into the sink, creating a loud crash. How the plates didn't break was beyond me, but she continued to clean with a deep frown. I usually cleaned up after them in the morning.

With the last bite of biscuit, my mouth became dry. I stood and headed to the black refrigerator behind Tina. I removed a bottle of water but paused. I needed something I could dissolve the pill in, so I snatched the orange juice as well.

Tina glanced over her shoulder, watching me like she thought I might stab her in the back.

I hadn't considered that until now, and the thought had merit. But I'd rather not deal with Zeke's wrath and the consequences of that action.

Forcing myself not to tense, I opened the cabinet to her right, grabbed a large glass, and filled it with juice. I put the juice away and took the drink and bottle of water back to the table.

As soon as I was done, she snatched a bottle off the windowsill and brought me another white pill.

I popped it into my mouth like I had last night and pretended to swallow. The combination of the bitterness of the pill and the acid of the juice was harsh, and I nearly gagged. "Thanks. I'm gonna go lie back down unless you need me for anything."

Her face looked strained. "Nope. Just go rest," she replied, way too sweet.

If she thought I'd push more, she'd learn from her mistake.

Taking my juice and water, I hurried back to the bedroom, not bothering to look at the box on their bed. I couldn't risk it; she'd check on me if I didn't go into the right room.

I shut the door and spat out the pill. The bitterness lingered on my tongue, and I gulped half the orange juice to hide the taste. It didn't work, but I couldn't drink more. I needed to leave enough juice to dissolve the pill.

Like last night, I dropped the medicine into the juice and swirled the cup, then set it on the nightstand. That was when I noticed my cell phone on the charger.

Someone had brought it to me.

My heart clenched as I lifted the phone with shaking hands. Part of me hoped I would find a message from Bodey.

But there were only messages from Stevie and Mom.

An intense stabbing sensation hurt my chest, right where my heart was. By now, Zeke would have told the other advisers about the attack. There was no question about that since it involved the Southeast territories attempting to take over our lands. Bodey had been so determined to protect me, and now he wasn't even texting to check on me.

My insignificance to him was too much. For the first time in my life, someone had made me feel important and valued, and for him to treat me like I didn't exist a mere two days later was more than I could stand.

Unable to respond to my family's texts and knowing Zeke and Theo would be keeping them informed, I pulled up my music, looked for the perfect song, and settled on "Stay With Me" by Sam Smith. But when I hit play and tried to get lost in the music, all I could see was Bodey on the back deck, playing his guitar for me. An ache cut through my chest worse than anything before, and I turned the music off and tossed my phone on the bed.

The *one* thing that had always given me solace didn't anymore.

Heaviness pressed on my chest, making it hard to breathe as tears leaked from my eyes like a faucet. The throbbing was so severe that I would have rather had claws slash into my legs again than experience this.

The hollowness I'd lived with my entire life was now an endless void.

I got into the bed, curled up in the fetal position on my good side, and prayed for sleep to take me.

SHATTERING GLASS STIRRED ME AWAKE. I'd fallen asleep after tossing and turning half the night. The past two and a half days had looked exactly the same. I stayed in my room while Tina hovered around the house, cleaning and keeping an eye on me. I'd started streaming TV shows since music was too painful, but my mind kept circling back to Bodey.

"Tina, my gods," Zeke growled. "Clean that up."

"Don't worry about it, Mom," Theo replied. "I'll get it since you're cooking the eggs and sausage."

Not wanting to eat another plain biscuit, I threw off the covers and got out of bed. At this point, I would take being around Zeke and Tina to have a reprieve from thoughts of Bodey.

Stevie had visited me the past two nights and brought some of my clothes. Today, I was able to stand without any discomfort, which meant I was almost healed.

Theo had let me know they'd kept questioning the wolf shifter in the basement, but he wasn't giving up any information other than that Queen Kel had sent him here.

I dressed in jeans and a thin baby-blue sweater and brushed my hair. Then I hurried into the kitchen, not wanting Zeke to come hunting for me. Anytime I left my room, Tina and Zeke materialized out of thin air.

The smell of bacon and eggs met my nose, and my stomach panged. I'd been carb-loading the past few days since carbs were easy to digest, but I needed something more substantial.

When I strolled into the kitchen, Theo was throwing away pieces of a broken plate. He smiled. "Hey, you. It's nice to see you up this morning."

I smiled back without hesitation. He'd been my rock, like usual, over the past few days. Though things had gotten strange between us, ever since the wolf attack, he'd gone back to being the friend I so desperately needed.

He'd sat next to me in my bed and watched war movies with me. We'd shared popcorn until close to midnight, when he'd slip away to his house next door to sleep, never making a move. The strangeness between us was gone now that he wasn't trying to date me.

"You should be in bed." Zeke shook his head. "We need you healed."

"Nothing hurts anymore." I moved my shirt to show him that my wound was scabbed over. "And Tina removed the stitches yesterday."

"She's fine," Tina added as she carried over two plates full of eggs and sausage. The biscuits were already in the center of the table.

"Want some coffee?" Theo asked as he headed to the coffeepot.

That sounded like heaven. "Yes, please."

I tried to be patient and wait for them to get food and sit before I dug in, but I felt famished.

"Grab me a cup, too," Zeke said as he filled his plate.

I forced myself to wait until he was done, then swooped in, snagging two biscuits and filling them both up with eggs and sausage. As I took a large bite, Theo took the seat beside me and placed a cup of coffee in front of me.

He snickered. "Hungry?"

I nodded, grabbing the coffee and sipping. It was perfect. He knew I took a tablespoon of sugar and a splash of half and half.

Tina sat next to me since Zeke was across from me. For a few minutes, we all ate in silence, and then she fidgeted in her seat. "I'm assuming you're well enough to pick up your chores here."

Zeke frowned. "Today? No, she needs at least another day of rest."

Tina's face wrinkled with annoyance before she schooled her features into a blank expression. "I can't take care of the house today. I need to run to the clinic for a shift."

His jaw twitched. "You're supposed to stay home this week."

"I can't." She placed her hands on the table. "We're low on staff, and I'm required to come in. Somebody called out sick, and I can't risk losing this job. You know that."

Theo bit his bottom lip as an uncomfortable silence filled the room. Zeke's and Tina's eyes glowed as they talked telepathically.

"Seriously, I'm not in pain. I can clean the house. It's fine." With them gone, I could search for that box. I had to see what Zeke was so desperate to hide from me.

Neck cording, Zeke flushed. "No. Then you won't be protected."

"If she's better, we don't want to leave her here unprotected." Theo placed a hand on the back of my chair. "I need to run by Lynerd's pack to check in with them. Callie can come with me if she's willing."

My jaw dropped. They'd never wanted me to meet wolves from other packs.

Zeke relaxed marginally, though his face was still flushed. "That's an excellent idea."

This *had* to be a dream or nightmare. I wasn't sure how I would categorize it. "Really?" I was all about leaving this place.

"If you'd like." Theo pursed his lips.

Zeke tensed again. He didn't like that Theo had given me a choice. Figured.

"Sure." I wanted to see how the other packs inter-acted...see if their leaders acted more like Zeke or Bodey.

We finished eating in silence, and soon, Theo and I were loaded into his truck. I was so relieved to be out of that house, which had started to feel like a prison. I couldn't even go to the bathroom without one of them watching me.

Theo pulled out of the pack neighborhood, focused on the road, and after a few minutes, he glanced at me. "You're not going to turn the radio on?"

I usually did that whenever I rode in a vehicle. "Nah. I don't want to listen to anything." I hadn't wanted to since leaving Bodey.

His forehead creased. "Maybe I should take you back. You might not be better."

"No, please." I leaned my head back on the head-rest. "I feel like a prisoner back there, and your dad doesn't want me to be alone in their house for some reason."

"For *some* reason." He scoffed. "You do realize that one of the wolves who attacked you is in the basement. What if he got out?"

I lifted a brow. "And your mom was going to protect me?"

"She can link with the pack to ask for help. You can't. You rely on texts."

I flinched. He hadn't meant to be cruel, but it was yet another reminder that I was different. That I was weak.

"Shit." Theo reached over the center console and took my hand. "I'm sorry. I didn't mean it like that."

"I know. It's just hard to hear sometimes." He'd said what he meant, and I wouldn't pretend to be stupid.

Theo licked his bottom lip. "It came out harsher than I intended. You're the only person who calls me out on things and doesn't let me slide, other than Dad."

That made my anger ebb. "Are you saying you don't like it?"

"It's not my favorite." He winked. "But I like that about you." He squeezed my hand.

Something shifted between us...and I wished I hadn't come after all.

I looked out the window and watched the majestic mountains of the canyons pass by. The urge to head out there was so strong. It was one of my favorite places to hike, and I always found peace there. Maybe

Bodey hadn't taken that from me like he had my music.

"So...Dad informed me this morning that there's a dinner tomorrow night, and he wants me to attend since I'll be alpha soon." Theo concentrated on the road again. "It's being held four hours from here."

"Oh, that's great." Although the thought of being alone with Tina for an entire night didn't sit well with me. Maybe she'd let me go home. "I'm sure you and your dad will enjoy that."

"We're supposed to bring a significant other." His hand tightened on mine. "And...I was hoping you could come."

My head jerked toward him. "Me?" An unpleasant shiver ran down my spine.

"Yeah, we're friends, and you know the advisers." Theo shrugged. "I thought it'd make sense."

"So it'll just be the advisers, Samuel, and us?" That was *way* too small of a gathering. I'd be too close to Bodey.

My heart leaped at the thought of seeing him...until I realized he'd also have a date. What if he'd found *her*?

"Oh, no. There'll be about a hundred people there. All the top-ranking alphas from each state are attending to welcome the new king, and I'd like to have a friend at my side."

A hundred people. I could hide in the crowd, and Theo was asking me to go as his friend, not as a real date, so my talks must have gotten through to him. It'd be awful to tell him no when he was asking for my support. "Sure. I just need to find a dress."

"We're going into Ontario." He grinned. "We can find one while we're out."

That was the biggest city around and should have many shops. "Sounds great."

Part of me yelled at me not to go. That seeing Bodey could destroy me. But if Samuel changed the way pack dynamics worked, I might have to get used to seeing him, anyway. Maybe if I faced losing him now, I'd be able to move on quicker.

Though I doubted it.

I leaned my seat back, not wanting to talk. The dread of tomorrow night sat heavily on me. I pretended to fall asleep, and Theo drove on, letting me rest.

Soon, we were thirty miles south of Ontario, Oregon, pulling into the local pack's neighborhood of massive brick homes. They were all one story but double the size of the houses back home. This pack screamed *money*, which didn't make sense. Zeke was the richest alpha in this state.

As we coasted up to the first house and parked, a large man rushed out of the front door. He grimaced as he hurried toward us.

Theo patted my leg. "Stay here for a minute."

Before Theo could get out, the man yanked his door open. In a deep, growly voice, he demanded, "Why are you here?"

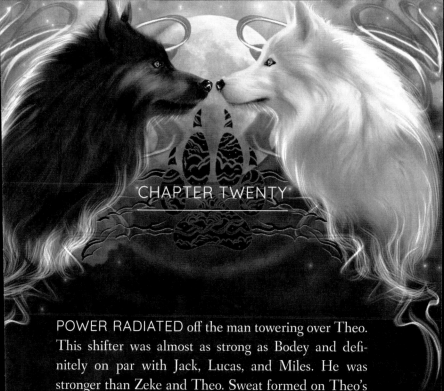

CHAPTER TWENTY

POWER RADIATED off the man towering over Theo. This shifter was almost as strong as Bodey and definitely on par with Jack, Lucas, and Miles. He was stronger than Zeke and Theo. Sweat formed on Theo's forehead.

I wasn't sure why this man wasn't the adviser in Oregon or why he hadn't challenged Zeke for the position. Animosity rolled off him. Wavy dark-blond hair hung in his face, and his cognac eyes took on an alpha glow. His slightly over-six-foot frame tensed as if he were prepared to go to war.

Theo straightened. "I'm here to talk about tomorrow night."

New Guy's nose wrinkled. "You're wondering if I'll behave." He laughed menacingly. "King Richard made Zeke's line the advisers of the state after my uncle died. I may not like or understand it, but he was my king, and I will respect his decree, even if I don't like Zeke—or you, for that matter."

My heart clenched. Zeke was proud that the king

had found him worthy to take the adviser spot, but he hadn't mentioned that story in years. I'd forgotten it until Bodey and the others had discussed it. Apparently, this pack's alpha had been the adviser until twenty-five years ago, when their family line had died out, but clearly, this man had hoped to take the position. Feeling his power, I was confused about why the king hadn't given it to him.

Theo lifted his chin. "You don't have to *like* me; just obey me."

The guy chuckled. "Zeke is bad enough. Let's not get too crazy. I know you're here to do *his* bidding."

No wonder Theo wanted me to stay in the truck. This guy didn't respect him or Zeke at *all*, and Theo didn't want me to see that.

When Theo thrust out his chest, he reminded me of a puffer fish. "I'll be the alpha in three days, so you'll be listening to me soon enough." He moved to get out of the car, but New Guy blocked him.

"I told you I'll behave, so you can leave." He gestured to the road. "You don't need to be here, anyway. You didn't inform us that you were coming."

Nostrils flaring, Theo bit out, "I don't have to. This is *my* territory. I can visit anytime I want."

Now I wished I'd stayed behind. I didn't want to watch two alpha males have their pissing match. Even though I was on the other side of the truck, I could get dragged into this confrontation as an innocent bystander. I didn't know what to do. If they continued, a fight was inevitable. And if they fought, I suspected New Guy would win.

I assumed he was Lynerd, and a fight would have huge implications for him, Theo, and Zeke and could affect Samuel's coronation. I couldn't let that happen. "We're heading into town to get me a dress for tomorrow. We stopped by on our way there."

Lynerd's eyes flicked to me, taking me in. "And you are?"

I smiled and leaned over Theo, sticking out my hand while reining in my emotions. "Callie. I'm part of Zeke and Theo's pack."

His forehead lined. "I'm sorry that's the case. Growing up there couldn't have been too pleasant, especially for a woman." He shook my hand firmly.

I flinched as I removed my hand from his. For him to assume that they treated me harshly meant Zeke must also treat other females poorly across the state. Even though I received the brunt of Zeke's malice, I'd seen how he treated other females in our pack. Not quite as bad, but he disregarded their abilities and opinions.

Theo turned to me, lifting his brows as if telling me not to answer. But that would just confirm everything Lynerd had implied and make the situation more awkward.

"As a whole, it hasn't always been easy." I shrugged, acting as if it were no big deal.

If looks could kill, Theo would've driven a stake through my heart.

"But ever since Queen Kel's scouts attacked me, Zeke and Theo have been kind and attentive to my needs. They've taken care of me and ensured that someone's always watching over me." *Probably to prevent me from digging around in Zeke's room.* "So maybe Zeke's views are changing?" I was certain that wasn't true, so

I'd formed it as a question. I hoped that would be enough to relieve the tension.

Lynerd's attention turned to Theo. Both men stared at each other, and the little bit of tension I'd eased came swirling back between them.

I knew one thing for certain—Theo was determined to get inside, and we weren't leaving until that happened. I wondered if Zeke had told him to do this as a test, but that could just be me thinking the worst of his father.

"You have a beautiful home." I made a point to stare at the impeccable brick house and the neighborhood. Similar to ours, their houses appeared to all have the same layout, but this one was slightly bigger.

"Thank you." Lynerd blew out a breath and blinked, considering something. A conflicted wince shot across his face as his gaze met mine. "You've traveled for a while. I know that's rough on our wolves. Would you like to come inside and stretch for a minute?"

Clearly, he was asking me, not Theo. Regardless, the offer was an olive branch because Theo would come inside with me. I wanted to decline and not push this visit on him, but if I did, a fight could break out.

"Of course we're coming inside." Theo clenched his hands in his lap. "I already *said* that."

A scowl returned to Lynerd's face, and he huffed. I bet he regretted his offer now. Instead of being gracious, Theo reminded me of his father—petulant and entitled.

Not wanting to ruin the progress I'd made, I climbed out of the truck and hurried around the hood. I stretched, emphasizing this was what I needed. Lynerd strolled over as Theo got out of the car and said, "By the way, I'm Lynerd. The alpha of the pack."

Yup, I'd guessed right. "Nice to meet you."

Ignoring Theo, Lynerd gestured for me to come with him. The two of us headed to the front door, with Lynerd walking on the edge of the concrete sidewalk, forcing Theo to either walk in the grass or on my other side.

That was probably for the best, though if they started another argument, I would be the only thing standing between them. Fortunately, no one said a word as we walked the fifteen steps to the front door.

Opening it, Lynerd waved us in.

As soon as I entered the long hallway, I smelled three distinct scents. The first was Lynerd's—a musky pine—but there was also a musky grass and herbal rosemary. I took in every inch of the house and found muted-brown walls and gorgeous crown molding. Thick, dark wooden floors were sturdy under my feet, confirming this place was way nicer than the houses back home. That had to contribute to the contention between this pack and ours.

Lynerd shut the door and led us toward the living room. Two people came into view, sitting on a massive tan couch against the left wall. The musky grass was the scent of the male wolf shifter sitting on the end closer to us. His hair was cut short, and he had a shaggy copper beard. The woman on the other end had to be a witch. I eyed her curiously. I'd never been around one before.

I was beginning to realize our pack was an anomaly. Zeke had warned us to stay away from witches because a witch had killed his best friend, our previous beta. I had no reason to doubt him; I'd heard him tell the story, and he'd never smelled of a lie, but maybe it had been the act of an extremist witch who didn't represent the entire population.

The witch tilted her head, and her long dark-blue hair fell over the bare, dark tan skin of her shoulder. Her gorgeous emerald eyes scanned me. "Hello," she said, her voice reminding me of a classical song.

Her examination sent a shiver coursing down my spine. Theo must have felt something similar because he stiffened.

"Hi." I tucked a piece of hair behind my ear. "Sorry for dropping in." I felt as if we were interrupting something. I took in the pictures of the coast hanging on the walls.

Sighing, Lynerd walked to the center of the room and stood in front of the couch next to the wooden coffee table. "It's fine. We're planning for my absence tomorrow since Sybil and I are leaving to attend the dinner and coronation."

"Do you need some of *my* wolves to help protect your pack while you're gone?" Theo stood tall and lifted his chin. "We just took out three of Queen Kel's scouts."

I wanted to laugh. *I* had taken out the three scouts by myself, but he was making it sound as if he'd had a hand in it. I wanted to correct him, but instead, I focused on what mattered the most. "Were you guys also attacked?" At Bodey's, I'd been kept abreast of the happenings in the territory, but not once since I'd returned to my childhood pack.

"Yes, just yesterday." Lynerd's neck corded as he turned to Theo. "And no, we don't need your pack's help. My beta is well equipped to handle the pack in my absence, and both you *and* Zeke will be gone from yours. You'll need your people there. You know she'll attack while our strongest are all in one place tomorrow night."

My limbs grew heavy. He was right, and I hadn't even thought of that. It would be the perfect time to attack, but if we postponed the coronation and the surrounding festivities, we'd show Queen Kel that her antics were impacting us. Either way, she'd win.

"I suggest you encourage your packs to utilize their witches." Lynerd lifted a brow, a faint grin ghosting over his mouth. He knew our pack's stance on witches. "It'll be the best way to protect the pack until we return."

"Yes, we've already instructed all our packs which have local witches." Theo crossed his arms. "It's too bad you couldn't capture the scouts to get more answers."

"Because your pack has ascertained such *valuable* information." The beta snorted from his spot on the couch.

I wrung my hands as I absorbed the information. "Was anyone harmed?"

Lynerd's eyes softened as he observed me. "None of my people who chased after them were injured."

So far, I was the only person who'd been attacked, likely because they'd seen me as an easy target—alone and female. That was how shifters thought, despite a queen calling the shots. "Good. There's already been too much turmoil."

"Very true." Sybil nodded. "So much has been hidden from us as it is."

Theo rolled his shoulders and cleared his throat. "If you're making plans for your absence, Callie and I shouldn't interrupt. However, if you change your mind about needing more backup, just link."

We'd already imposed on Lynerd enough, and it wouldn't take much to end the civility. Hell, these people hadn't even introduced themselves—a sure sign that they didn't want us here.

"Oh, thank you." The beta chuckled sarcastically. "We appreciate your concern."

"Of course." Theo rubbed his knuckles on his shirt, ignoring the jab. "It's of the utmost importance that the coronation goes off without a hitch."

Lynerd scowled. "You don't have to tell us. We *all* know that."

If Theo's point had been to check in and assert dominance, he'd succeeded, but at what cost? If anything, he'd fueled Lynerd's resentment, and the only reason Lynerd hadn't challenged Zeke for the adviser role was out of respect for the late king. That respect meant he would help to ensure the coronation was a success despite our unwelcome visit.

Before Theo could open his mouth again, I took his hand and smiled. "Thank you all for letting us stretch our legs. Your neighborhood and house are lovely."

"Do you need anything before you head out?" Lynerd's gaze settled on me again. "Like water?"

This pack was considerate, like Bodey's. Zeke would never ask someone that. I was even more clueless about why King Richard had put Zeke in charge. "No, thank you."

"*We're* fine." Theo tensed, interlocking his fingers with mine. "And we're leaving. Let us know if you need assistance."

Sybil cocked her head farther though her gaze remained on me.

The beta mashed his lips together, trying not to laugh, and I couldn't blame him.

However, Lynerd handled the repeated offer well. "Thanks, but we've got it."

"Well, thanks again," I said, tugging Theo away. I was eager to go because Sybil's attention made my skin crawl.

Theo and I strolled to the door with Lynerd on our heels.

Outside, Lynerd touched my shoulder. "Be careful," he murmured, then bit his bottom lip. He appeared concerned, and strangely, that concern was directed at me.

"We can handle ourselves," Theo replied and tugged me toward the truck.

I didn't falter, not wanting Theo to be aware of this somewhat secret moment. "You too. It's not safe out here for any of us."

Soon, Theo and I were back in his truck. As we pulled out, I noticed Sybil and Lynerd standing at the door together, watching us leave. Sybil was telling him something, but her eyes were locked on me.

Even after we turned out of sight, I could feel the caress of her gaze on me, and I shivered.

"Sorry about that." Theo smiled as he turned onto the main road. "I know that encounter unnerved you. It got tense, but I handled it."

Yeah, he'd handled it. Sure. I hadn't helped at all.

I didn't correct him. Let him think I'd been affected by the confrontation instead of the witch and the way she'd studied me.

At least for a moment, she'd gotten Bodey off my mind...sorta.

I STARED at the stranger in the bathroom mirror. A black lace cocktail dress clung to my skin, stopping at my knees, with a deep V-cut neckline that showed off my cleavage. The beading made the dress sparkle when the light hit the fabric just right, and with four-inch heels, I was as tall as Theo. At least the dress had long sleeves, so I felt less exposed.

"Just one more thing," Stevie said as she leaned over. "Since your eyes have a hint of gray, we'll add a pop of color to your lips." She slowly painted my lips red, making sure to accentuate the dip on top.

I'd never had a makeover or dressed up before, and I wasn't sure what to think of myself.

She leaned back. "What do you think?"

"I couldn't have done half as good a job." And I meant that. She'd pulled my light-blonde hair into a French twist and left a few tendrils to frame my face. The makeup she'd chosen made my blue eyes look brighter than I'd ever seen before.

"You look gorgeous." Stevie beamed. "I'm so happy you get to go to this dinner. You deserve a night out."

Not me. I wished I could get out of it. If dates were expected, then Bodey would be there with someone, and I was certain I wouldn't be able to handle it, especially if he'd found *her*. From what I'd heard, when you met your fated, the love was instant. I wouldn't even exist to him anymore—if I still did. He still hadn't messaged me, not even after my attack. Nor had Samuel.

I couldn't lie—it hurt. I thought I'd connected with them, especially Bodey and Samuel, but no one had checked on me. Clearly, I'd felt more connected to them than they had to me, which was ironic since Bodey had forced me to stay with him.

"Callie," Zeke called from the living room. "We need to get going. We're waiting on you." His tone held an edge of warning.

"Coming," I answered. "We just finished."

Stevie rolled her eyes but knew better than to say anything out loud. "It would've taken longer if I didn't have such a flawless canvas."

She looped her arm through mine, and we walked into the living room. Theo's jaw dropped when he saw me, and Zeke scowled.

"You look beautiful," Theo said as he walked over to me. "I mean, you've always been pretty. But *this*..."

"Right." Stevie beamed. "She's gorgeous."

Tina stood next to Zeke. Her champagne dress was high-necked and flowy, complementing Zeke's black suit with a pale tie that matched her dress.

"You're not too bad yourself." I forced a smile, taking in Theo in his black suit. Theo was attractive, but I viewed him like a brother, and I was thankful that my first time going out like this was with my best friend.

"We can continue this on the road." Zeke stomped over to the door and flung it open. "Stevie, you need to go."

"Have fun, sis," Stevie said. She pecked my cheek and gave my face one more look. "Don't do anything I wouldn't do." She winked.

As soon as Stevie left, Zeke slammed the front door, locked it, and led us into his garage. He climbed into his white Mercedes-Benz GLB 250. I slid into the back on the driver's side so Theo would have more legroom behind his mother. The black leather seat was cool, which I needed because my heart was pounding.

We took off, and I cringed, thinking about the four-hour drive ahead. We were heading to a winery in Lewiston, Idaho.

Thankfully, Zeke turned on a classic rock station, which was fine with me. I'd rather be reminded of Bodey and miss him than deal with silence.

I settled into the car and closed my eyes.

LUCKILY, no one wanted to talk. Everyone seemed tense, even Theo, who stared out the window. This was his debut as a future royal adviser, so I left him to his thoughts. If it had been only the two of us, I would've talked to him and reassured him, but there was no way I'd do that with Zeke in the car.

When we finally got to Lewiston, we turned down some back roads that led us away from town. The GPS told us to turn left up ahead and then that we'd arrived at our destination. Zeke turned down the music and glanced in the rearview mirror at Theo and me. "Remember, everyone, be on your best behavior."

"Yes, we *all* should be," I replied, my mouth running away from me again.

He glared at me in the mirror, but he didn't say anything as we drove up the road. The entrance to the winery was beautiful. Rows of vineyards went on for acres if not miles, and Zeke followed the road to a white metal building with large glass cutouts. A patio with hanging twinkle lights had been staged with fifty tables, all covered in white tablecloths and with six chairs each.

This place was gorgeous and seemed fitting for a celebration of a wolf shifter king. It was a mix of outdoors and class.

We pulled up to the front doors, where valets waited. Zeke and Theo helped Tina and me from the car. My eyes wanted to search for *him*, but I forced myself not to.

We headed down the walkway toward the patio. The smells of steak, pork, and lamb made me salivate. There were already a ton of people there, dressed similarly to us, and thankfully, no sign of Bodey.

At our arrival, Lynerd glanced at us, his nose wrinkling as he cupped Sybil's arm and escorted her to the other side of the back patio, away from us, as Zeke hurried off with some alphas, leaving Tina, Theo, and me behind.

Theo leaned toward my ear. "I'll be right back. I'm going to get us a glass of wine."

Before I could protest, he'd disappeared into the building.

"At least we have each other." Tina smiled, though it wasn't very warm.

"That we do." But I'd rather not be here at all.

I wanted to go into the vineyard and get lost among the vines. My chest constricted, and I felt like I couldn't breathe. The world blurred. I needed something to help me get through this.

Theo returned with three glasses of red wine. He

handed one to me, and I downed it in one big gulp. When he turned from handing his mom hers, he eyed my empty glass.

"Uh...do you want another?" He arched a brow, uncertain about getting me more.

"Definitely." I swiped his and drank it in another big gulp.

Then an all-too-familiar chuckle made me freeze.

Gods, no. Don't let it be him.

CHAPTER TWENTY-ONE

LET IT BE MY IMAGINATION, I chanted internally, sending the message to Fate—if she was even listening. I still believed she was a vicious bitch who didn't like me, but maybe she'd feel bad enough about everything else to grant me this one wish. *Or if it is him, don't let him notice me. Please.*

I had to force my lungs to move before I got dizzy, and I wished I had a third glass of wine in my hand. I needed it more than ever.

"Why weren't you this fun when you were hanging with us?" Jack asked from behind me.

There was no doubt he was talking to me.

Fuck. Fate hated me.

If Jack was here, that meant the others would be aware of me soon, if they weren't already.

Tina and I had blended into a corner of the patio, yet one of them had found me within minutes of my

The only response given was Jack tapping me on the shoulder.

"Don't be rude, little ass kicker," Jack said as I turned to him. "You've been missed. Had I known you knew how to party, you could've stayed longer, and we could have loosened up Bodey a little. Gods knows he needs it."

Jack was usually a force of nature, but in a navy suit with a cobalt-blue button-down shirt that made his eyes sparkle, he was a standout in the crowd. His wolf had edged forward on display, and when he smiled his crooked smile, he reminded me of a mischievous little boy. I was certain that was an intentional part of his charm.

I refused to fall for it. "Sorry, I needed to get back and not hang around after I was done healing. Besides, I'm not much into partying." My hands itched for something to hold. Why weren't there any waitresses out here with drinks?

He frowned. "I should've definitely hung out more at Bodey's. I wanted to give you space so you could rest, but now I wish I'd spent more time getting to know you."

Theo cleared his throat, not appreciating Jack's presence.

But Jack didn't budge, and I suspected he was talking to me to get Theo riled up.

"You look nice." Jack beamed, scanning me up and down. "And it's a pleasant surprise that you turned up. I was afraid you wouldn't be in attendance."

I rubbed a hand on my stomach, massaging away my discomfort. "Since I wasn't invited by any of you?"

"Oh, gods, Callie." He tossed an arm around my

shoulder. "You're *always* invited anywhere we go. Did your time with us not teach you anything? You're our little ass kicker."

"Will you stop with that nickname?" I tried to scowl, but dammit, the corners of my mouth tipped upward. I both hated and admired Jack's effect on me. He was endearing and flustering at the same time. It was a special talent.

Taking a large sip of her drink, Tina swallowed and asked, "And you are?" She must have been trying to find liquid courage.

"My reputation fails me." Jack snickered, pulling me closer. "Jack Landry, the royal adviser for Washington."

Tina's eyes bulged. "Oh, and you're *actually* friends with Callie?" Her surprise was evident.

"That happens organically when you hang out for several days back to back. Right?" He winked. "She's kind and funny."

I scoffed. "When did I ever make you laugh? You were too busy running your mouth and hogging all the oxygen in the room."

"See. That right there." He laughed. "Real entertainment. As if she doesn't love hearing me talk. And the way she puts us in our place—it's rare to find someone who does that."

"Callie." Tina's face turned red. "You can't talk to them like that. It's not a woman's place."

"Oh, please." Jack lifted his other hand, which held a nearly full glass of wine. "That's one of her best qualities." He waggled his brows and held the glass out to me. "Do you want the rest?" Mirth danced in his cobalt eyes.

I should have said no, but this situation was growing more awkward by the second, so I swiped the glass and downed it in yet another gulp.

"Maybe you've had enough." Theo frowned and tried to pull me away from Jack.

"We're here to celebrate, so we should all have fun." Jack smirked. "Besides, she'll need all that alcohol before the event's over, I suspect. It's going to be a fun night...at least for me."

Unease trickled down my back. I didn't know what that meant, but I assumed it involved Bodey and me both being here.

As if confirming my suspicions, he asked, "Have you run into anyone else yet?"

I shook my head. "We just got here."

"Oh, *good*." Jack tugged me deeper into the crowd and said, "Let's go see everyone!"

Theo flinched and reached for my hand. He didn't want me to go with Jack, and I was right there with him.

"Thanks, but I should stay here."

"The guys will want to see you, especially Samuel." Jack nodded his head toward his crowd.

My throat tightened. As much as I wanted to see Samuel, he hadn't texted me once. Jack was being nice, but I'd bet he was the only one who wanted me here, and I really didn't want to see Bodey, especially if he was here with someone. "I'm good here, but thank you. Maybe I'll see him before I leave."

"Nope. Come on." Jack took my empty glasses and turned around as a waiter with a tray of appetizers walked past. Jack placed them on the tray, not worried that the tray wasn't meant for dirty dishes.

Sometimes, I wished I could be more like him.

"Sir," the waiter said.

"Oh, yes. Where are my manners?" He beamed. "Thank you." He tugged my hand, and I almost fell over my feet. His strong grip kept me upright until I got my four-inch heels underneath me.

Heavy footsteps pounded behind me, the cadence telling me who they belonged to—Theo. He wouldn't let Jack take me away from him, and my stomach sank further. His presence should've comforted me, but his and Bodey's animosity toward each other could escalate an already uncomfortable situation.

Worse, after seeing how friendly Jack was with me, Theo would interrogate me later. I was certain he didn't realize how much the advisers had hung out at Bodey's and included me in their conversations.

I glanced around the patio. There were so many people here, the men in suits or sports jackets and slacks and the women in cocktail dresses. I was surrounded by the top alphas throughout the Northwest territories. Everyone here was wealthy, and power radiated off them in waves, crashing over me and making me realize how weak I truly was. No wonder Tina had stayed at the edge of the gathering. That was where I needed to be as well.

Out of the corner of my eye, I saw Miles and Samuel. Bodey wasn't with them, thank goodness.

The crowd pressed in on me, and my heart raced. I had to get out of here. I ducked, attempting to free myself from Jack's arm, then pivoted and almost ran right into Theo.

Theo's eyes bulged at my sudden change of direction just as Jack gripped my wrist.

Jack arched an eyebrow. "Where do you think you're going?"

"If she doesn't want to talk to Samuel, she doesn't have to," Theo growled and puffed out his chest.

Lovely. This was one reason I wanted to avoid them. I had to de-escalate this before we ruined the dinner. Besides, Jack *had* to know why I was trying to escape. I refused to humor him. "This is Samuel's day, and he's clearly busy."

"Exactly why you should say hi to him." Jack's usual mirth vanished, replaced by a strained expression. "He's missed you, and he wanted to call and invite you here himself."

My throat constricted. "But he never called."

"Jack, what the hell?" a *way* too familiar voice said.

I couldn't move or breathe. Bodey stepped up beside Jack...and the world tilted.

"Callie," he breathed, sounding just like the best lyrics to a song I'd ever heard.

He looked more handsome than I remembered, which shouldn't be possible. I'd heard the saying, "Absence makes the heart grow fonder," and boy, did those words suddenly make sense.

I'd hoped that time apart would heal my heart some, but the agony of his rejection swirled tightly in my chest again.

His black suit fit his body like a glove. He wore a white button-down and a black bow tie that he somehow made sexy as hell.

We stared at each other, and the rest of the world disappeared around me. I wanted to kiss him, but that wouldn't be welcome. My eyes burned, and despite myself, I took a step toward him. "How are you?"

A sharp ache streaked through my heart, forcing me to suck in a breath. This was worse than I'd imagined.

A possessive hand landed on the center of my back as Theo moved up beside me. Everything inside me wanted to veer away, but that wouldn't be fair to Theo. I had come here with him, and more importantly, Bodey had let me go.

Bodey's head jerked back, and his indigo eyes darkened, but when his gaze landed on me, he smiled sadly. "I've been better." He leaned toward me as he murmured, "You look gorgeous."

"Thank you." I didn't know why, but Theo touching me felt all kinds of wrong. His hand was too warm, and he wasn't the person I desired.

I had to remind myself I wasn't doing anything wrong. Theo knew we were only friends.

But guilt churned in my stomach.

A gorgeous woman close to my height without heels strolled over to Bodey. She was the opposite of me in every way: long, dark, and wavy hair, dark-violet eyes that reminded me of wild iris, and curves I'd kill for, which she was showing off in a tight red dress.

When she touched Bodey's arm, I wanted to slap her. Instead, I took a deep breath. Maybe this was his fated mate. They looked amazing together and would have beautiful babies.

My heart fractured more, and I wondered, once it was confirmed who she was, whether I'd have any pieces left.

"Hey, the others are looking for you two." She gestured to the spot where I'd seen Miles and Samuel earlier. I followed her gaze and found the other royal advisers, their parents, Samuel...and Zeke.

Right next to them was a group of women who radiated a different sort of power.

One of the women glanced at me, her head tilting like Sybil's had at Lynerd's house. I noted she had curly, dark-auburn hair. Her smile vanished as she examined me, and I looked away, which wasn't normal for me. But this wasn't about submission. I sensed she was seeing something within me, and that unnerved me.

"We'll be right there," Jack said, and I glanced back at Bodey.

The woman with him had dropped her hand and was smiling at me.

Ugh, she was nice. Add that to her ever-growing list of wonderful attributes. At least Bodey deserved someone like that.

She extended a hand toward me. "I'm Stella."

Stella. Miles's fated mate. I exhaled.

"Theo." He took her hand instead and shook it. "This is my *date*, Callie."

I stiffened. If that wasn't Theo figuratively peeing on my leg, then I didn't know what else it could be. I moved forward, causing Theo's hand to fall, and shook her hand on my own. I said, "Are you Miles's fated mate?" *Please say yes.*

"Yes." She beamed. "And you must be that special visitor of Bodey's. I've heard *all* about you. Why don't you—" She paused and glanced at Theo. "Join us?"

"Actually, Callie and I need to get back to my mom. We left her alone." Theo took my hand, interlacing his fingers with mine. "But thanks."

"Your mom is an adult." Jack shrugged. "I'm sure she'll be fine. Better yet, you should go back to her, and Callie can come with us."

Theo tensed. He didn't like the idea, and I didn't want to hang around Bodey and his date whenever she did appear. "Thanks, but I'd better stay with Theo."

Bodey mashed his lips together and nodded. "Yeah, that makes sense. I hope you have a good time."

I could've sworn pain flashed in his eyes. But he turned and moved away.

"You're off the hook for now." Jack booped my nose. "But I'll be back." His Terminator impression was horrible.

Stella laughed. "Never do that again." She grabbed his arm and dragged him toward their group.

I watched them leave. Bodey glanced over his shoulder, and our eyes locked one more time.

"I didn't realize you'd gotten so close with them," Theo said. He nudged me back toward the edge of the patio, where Tina still stood.

I shrugged. "They were nice to me. Everyone came to Bodey's house for breakfast and dinner." Hell, even lunch most times. "I was around them a bit."

I wondered still why none of them had messaged me once they'd heard about the attack...particularly Samuel. The only person I'd had a falling-out with was Bodey.

My gaze clung to Bodey. Under his suit, I could see the outline of his muscles, and I remembered what it felt like to touch them.

"Mom's probably freaking out. Let's hurry back."

I forced myself to follow Theo. Bodey had made his choice, and I'd made mine. If I wanted to find happiness, I had to let him go. I had to decide not to be miserable. No one deserved a life of regret.

When Tina came back into view, I regretted that

we'd left her. She was still in the corner of the patio with her arms wrapped around her stomach. Her wine was gone, and I was fairly certain I'd drunk it. She was watching people around her like she didn't belong.

Seeing her like that was strange. She wasn't a weak wolf, not in the least, so to see her cower was unsettling.

When she noticed us, she relaxed and dropped her arms, standing taller. "I was about to go look for you two."

We two, not Zeke.

Another waitress strolled by, this time with a tray of full wineglasses. I snatched two, needing more to drink. Seeing Bodey had been harder than I'd expected, even without his date present.

Theo's forehead wrinkled. "Are you sure you should be drinking that much?"

Great. Of all nights, tonight would be the one he chose to be my keeper. "I won't drink it as fast. I just don't know when they'll come back around again."

His brows lifted. "Okay." But his tone indicated it was, in fact, not okay.

"I'm just uncomfortable here." I hated showing vulnerability, but it was the truth. Maybe he'd be more understanding.

Tina followed my lead, taking two glasses of her own. "I am, too."

"Fine." Theo frowned and grabbed one for himself. I wondered if he hadn't taken two in case I tried to grab one of his.

Then the three of us drank in silence.

As I DRAINED my second glass, Theo placed an arm around my waist, drawing me to his side. I'd made it clear that we were just friends, and this was the second time he'd made a possessive move. I didn't like it.

"Theo..." I started.

"Callie," Samuel said from behind me.

That had to be why Theo was acting territorial. I turned.

Samuel was dressed in a royal-blue suit with a golden paw print over his left breast. Of course, he noticed the two empty glasses of wine in my hands and smiled. "Having a fun night?"

I winced. If only that had been my goal.

He must have noticed because his expression fell.

"I'm Theo, as I'm sure you know, and this is my mother, Tina," Theo interjected, extending a hand.

Samuel paused as if he might not take Theo's hand, but then he shook it and schooled his features. "Hello." He turned to me again and asked, "Can I steal you for a minute?"

"Of course you can talk to us." Theo stood taller.

"Just Callie." Samuel lifted his chin. "I want to talk to her. Alone."

It wasn't like Theo could say no, but I watched his eyes flash as he considered it.

Extending an arm to me, Samuel raised a brow. I moved to slip mine through his, then paused.

He laughed, taking the glass from that hand. "There. Problem solved."

I smiled. Being with him felt nice. I slipped my arm through his, and we walked into the crowd. Unlike with Theo, people parted for us, giving us a walkway.

Once we were a safe distance from Theo, Samuel sighed. "I've been worried about you."

"Really?" I observed him, taking in his tall frame. He was still two inches taller than me in my heels, and his wolf's magic was pouring out of him more than normal. "You never texted."

He winced. "I was going to, but we've been busy planning, and Queen Kel has been sending scouts out *everywhere*. Also, Bodey said you needed space, and I didn't want to disrespect that. I know something happened between the two of you."

"Zeke has been kinder to me since I returned." Though I wasn't certain how long that would last. I changed the subject. "Will your date get upset with you for walking with me like this?"

"Date?" Samuel laughed. "Nope. Don't have one of those. In fact, the only royal advisers who have dates are Miles and Zeke, and Zeke isn't currently with his wife."

I stared at him, probably looking deranged. "I thought everyone was bringing a plus-one."

Samuel rolled his eyes. "I assume that's how Theo got you to come with him?"

My cheeks burned, providing his answer. However, all I could think about was that Bodey was alone.

He hadn't found her.

Not yet.

"We've all been worried about you." Samuel stopped at the edge of the patio that overlooked the vineyards. "Everyone." Then his eyes glowed, and he glanced behind me.

I spun around and saw the auburn-haired woman who'd been watching me before marching directly toward us. Her charcoal eyes were narrowed with distrust or malice. Worse, Bodey was on her heels.

When she reached us, her herbal scent assaulted my nose.

"Dina," Bodey said, grabbing her arm. "She's a friend of ours."

Friend.

I cringed. The word hurt worse than anything.

Her gaze never left mine as she lifted her hands high. "Leave here *now*...or I'll make you."

CHAPTER TWENTY-TWO

I BLINKED, unsure what to do. Part of my brain screamed for me to leave, but a larger portion was stunned. Dina was treating me like a threat.

She lifted her hands, getting ready to carry through on her threat, but Bodey pushed them down and growled, "I said she's a friend. What is your problem?"

The witch forced her gaze from me to Bodey. "Can't you feel it? Sybil mentioned feeling something similar not too long ago. It had to be her."

His brows furrowed, and Samuel cleared his throat, stepping in front of me.

Panic constricted my chest. If she performed magic, he'd be hit.

Samuel lifted his hands. "We don't feel anything, and like Bodey said multiple times, she's our friend. If you harm her, you'll create a divide between us."

Despite the warmth surging through me at their show of loyalty, I didn't want to cause problems. Each time I was around them, they had to deal with a confrontation, whether with Zeke, Theo, or now Dina. Eventually, they'd realize I wasn't worth having around.

"I know wolf shifters can't feel witch magic, but with the amount pouring off her, I don't know how you *can't* feel it." Dina stared at me, her nose wrinkling. "It's not safe to have someone who's influenced like that around us."

I jerked back. There was *witch* magic in me? I glanced at my hands as if they'd have answers. I didn't know what I was expecting—colors to shoot from my fingertips or mist to swirl around me—but there was *nothing*. "I've never had so much as a hint of magical abilities. I have no clue what you're referring to." Granted, I didn't know my birth family, so maybe I'd inherited something, but surely the magic would've manifested by *now*.

"You're not a witch." She shook her head and crossed her arms. "But you're working with someone who is."

The world blurred as if I couldn't get enough oxygen. I didn't like being accused of things, but this was worse than usual because I didn't understand the potential repercussions. With pack business, there was usually some sort of manual labor punishment waiting for me. "I haven't worked with *anyone*."

"Impossible." Her hands clenched. "You're lying."

"She's *not* lying," Samuel said with authority. "We would smell the stench of her lies if she was. Besides, her heart is racing from panic, not because she's deceiving us. She doesn't know what's going on, so why don't you tell us?"

Dina paused and examined me once more, tilting her head as if I were a puzzle.

I'd grown tired of witches looking at me that way. She'd better provide some answers.

She removed her hands from Bodey's, and he growled in warning.

"I won't do anything," she gritted before refocusing on me and sneering. "Blood magic is coating every inch of her."

Blood magic? I didn't know what that was, but I sensed it wasn't good. "I haven't given my blood to anyone."

"Your blood wouldn't be required for something this strong." She arched a brow, studying my reaction.

A chill crept down my spine, and even though I didn't want to know the answer, I asked anyway. "Then what caused it?" If I'd had magic cast over me, I needed to understand how it had happened.

"A spell like this requires the death of the person you love the most at the requester's hands. That blood must be provided to the witch who casts the spell."

My stomach roiled. There were only a handful of people I cared about, and the people I valued the most were Stevie, Bodey, and Theo, with Samuel coming in close to the top of the list, too. I just hadn't spent as much time with him. "I haven't sacrificed *anyone*," I said a little too loudly. A few people nearby stopped their conversation and looked at us.

Bodey slid between Dina and Samuel and stood next to me. He wrapped an arm around my waist, pulling me close to him.

His touch sent my heart soaring. Even through my dress, his hand was warm, and the heat sank into my skin. I wanted to lean into him and forget how things had ended between us.

Her forehead creased. She took in Bodey's stance beside me and Samuel's in front of me. Their body language was clear—they were protecting me. She sighed. "For her to carry a spell that strong, she's *got* to be hiding something."

Tears burned my eyes as my cheeks warmed. If this witch was part of Bodey's community, then I knew they respected one another. I feared what would happen if she convinced him I was a traitor. It was one thing for Bodey and me not to be together, but it would be another thing entirely if we became enemies. "I don't know what you're talking about. I'm not hiding anything. I can't even connect with my wolf. If I were going to use magic for *anything*, it would be to have stronger wolf magic."

Her head tilted back. "You can't connect with your wolf?"

I nodded. "I can't pack link or shift."

"That makes *no* sense," she said and moved to step around Samuel, but he countered her just as Bodey tugged me behind him.

Now they were being overprotective. If I was spelled, I needed to find out why. This might be my only chance to get answers.

"I won't hurt her." Dina straightened her shoulders. "Let me by."

Samuel didn't move.

I placed a hand on his shoulder. "It's fine."

He turned and took in my expression. Then he huffed and moved beside me so he and Bodey flanked me.

Dina rolled her eyes and placed her hands on my shoulders. Bodey tensed, and for a minute, I thought he might remove her hands from me. Instead, he stayed still with his arm taut, ready to strike if needed.

"Your wolf is strong. One of the strongest I've ever encountered." Her gaze leveled with mine. "I can feel it inside you."

My body tingled from her touch. "How is that possible? I can't shift or link. I can't do anything that other shifters can do."

Bodey said, "The spell must have been forced on you to prevent you from accessing your magic." His expression looked strained. "Which makes sense because you sure don't act like an omega."

My lungs quit working. "Why would someone do that? And why would I not remember?"

Dina lifted her hands. "If a witch spelled you like that, they likely also messed with your memories. What's the first memory you have?"

I thought back, but all the images I conjured in my head were blurry. I remembered a beautiful, elegant voice singing, though I couldn't make out the words. All I could hear was the melody, and I felt so loved by the singer. The memory was what had drawn me to music, especially lyrics because I'd always wanted to know what she'd been singing. "I..." I blinked a few times. "I don't remember much before I was carried into Zeke's pack and given to my adoptive parents."

"Zeke?" Dina's face twisted with disgust. "Well, no witch would work with him willingly."

"It must have been cast as part of the reason you were abandoned." Bodey scowled. He pressed so close to me that our entire sides touched.

"How does she unblock it?" Samuel frowned. "That might alleviate her problems with her pack."

If I were stronger, the pack wouldn't treat me like shit. Although I doubted it would change much. After all, I was female.

"I don't know." Dina bit her bottom lip. "I didn't create the spell."

"Can it be broken?" Bodey's body shook, and I wasn't sure if it was from fear or anger.

She nodded. "Magic can't be limitless—there is always a way to end it. I don't know how, though. Only the witch who spelled her can provide that information."

I might be unable to connect with my wolf for my entire life. At least now, I knew there was a reason why, but I wasn't sure if that knowledge had improved my situation. In some ways, knowing I should be able to shift made my inability that much harder. Before, I'd thought I was broken. Now I knew my ability had been stolen from me.

"What's going on over here?" Zeke's voice boomed behind Dina.

I stiffened. I'd been so focused on this revelation that I hadn't noticed his approach. I didn't want him to know that a witch had spelled me. He hated witches, and I could see him casting me from the pack for this. Even though I wanted to leave, I didn't want to be homeless.

"Just chatting," Bodey said easily. "Dina was giving us an update and introducing herself to Callie."

Zeke homed in on Bodey's arm, which was still wrapped around me. He tugged at his collar. "Callie should be getting back to her *date*, not wasting time talking to *witches*."

I'd expected his reaction. A witch had betrayed him

and hurt his best friend. I wanted to stay here with Samuel and Bodey and learn how spells worked, but Zeke would hover until I left, so my best bet was to oblige him and hope I could find Dina later and ask a few more questions.

I began to step forward, but Bodey's hand gripped my waist, holding me in place.

"She's staying with me."

My heart squeezed.

"She's here with Theo. Not *you*." Zeke straightened to his full height. "And she's my pack member. I don't want her talking to witches. She needs to move. *Now*."

Samuel lifted his chin. "Tomorrow, I'll be your *king*, and I say if she wants to stay here and continue this conversation, she can."

Zeke's hands clenched. "This is unacceptable. A king shouldn't get involved in such affairs."

The silence that followed was heavy with tension. Zeke was arguing with Samuel, who would be crowned in less than twelve hours. Almost anyone would know better than that.

"A king will do what he thinks is necessary and fair if an alpha is abusing their power." Samuel placed his hands on his hips, holding his ground, his strong wolf pouring off him.

For not wanting to lead, Samuel was already doing it well. Pride soared through me.

Zeke glared at me, his hatred for me sliding back into place as if it had never gone away. The message was clear—this confrontation was *my fault*.

If I didn't salvage this, who knew what torture lay ahead for me? "It's fine. I'll head back to Theo and Tina."

"See?" Zeke said. "She wants to go. Are you going to tell her she can't?"

Faltering, Samuel turned to me.

I'd undermined him, though that hadn't been my intention. I'd spoken without thinking of the repercussions for him, but instead of anger, his eyes softened. There was no judgment, no malice, no hatred. He understood why I'd done it.

Readying myself to step away from Bodey's comforting embrace, I smiled. "It was nice to meet you, Dina." I prepared for the arm that provided safety and shelter to fall from me as I stepped away.

Bodey stepped with me, keeping his arm firmly in place.

"What are you doing?" I murmured. My heart raced, and my mind struggled to calm it.

"I'm not leaving your side," he growled, then spoke softly, "I know you want space, but you're not getting it anymore."

I'd wanted to hear those words and more from him, so I didn't reply. My throat constricted with all the emotions swirling inside.

The two of us strolled toward Theo, and Bodey took my hand in his free one. He whispered, "I've missed you."

"I missed you, too," I croaked. "But—"

"No buts." Bodey winced. "We need to talk, but not here." He nodded, forcing me to note that Theo and Tina were less than ten feet away.

Theo's attention was already locked on me, and his scowl deepened when he noticed Bodey embracing me. His scrutiny made me realize that during our heartfelt exchange, I'd stepped closer to Bodey's side.

Theo spat, "What are you doing with my *date*?"

Beaming, Bodey leaned his head against the top of mine. "Escorting her back to you. Is there a problem with that?"

"*Thank you.*" Theo took my hand from Bodey's. "She's back now, so you're free to leave."

Bodey didn't release his hold on my waist. His fingers dug into my side, steadying me against him. "That's kind of you, but I'm in no rush."

His scent swirled around me, making me dizzy. I should have encouraged him to leave, but I feared if I did, I'd never feel his touch again.

Clearing her throat, Tina extended her hand. "I'm Tina."

"Bodey," he replied, using the opportunity to bat Theo's hand out of mine while reaching over to shake Tina's hand. His attention landed back on Theo as he asked, "Have any more scouts been around? And have you gotten more information out of your prisoner?"

He'd changed the subject to pack business so Theo couldn't rush him off without appearing as if he were hiding something.

Still, Theo remained silent, his neck cording.

They were having another pissing contest. I needed to intervene. The other advisers had the right to know everything as well. "Another pack outside of Ontario, Oregon, ran across a scout the other day and chased them off, and as far as I know, the surviving wolf of the three that attacked me hasn't divulged any more information."

Bodey turned into a statue as his nostrils flared. "What do you mean, the three that attacked *you*?" Anger pulsed off him.

I swallowed hard.

"No, we haven't gotten any additional information yet," Theo cut in.

"That's not what I'm worried about." Bodey turned to me, his stare pinning me in place. He rasped, "What attack, Callie?"

I'd never seen him mad at me before. We hadn't known each other long, but the hurt and rage pouring off him made the ground so very interesting. "The one in Halfway."

"You were attacked?" His jaw clenched hard.

I inhaled. They hadn't told him that the wolves had targeted me. I glanced at Theo, who had his eyes closed, ready for the explosion.

Bodey pivoted all that anger onto him and spat, "Why didn't Zeke tell us Callie was attacked?" He cupped my face with his rough, strong hands. "Were you hurt?"

His tenderness had all my resolve slipping away. Maybe it wouldn't be so bad to be with him until he found his fated. Maybe I'd have a few years of happiness. "I'm better now."

"You *did* get hurt." His gaze searched me for signs of injury.

Luckily, the pink scratch on my shoulder was hidden, but his hands fisted at his side the moment he saw the marks on my leg.

I was relieved he hadn't known because that was the reason he hadn't called to check on me. I'd thought they'd forgotten about me. They wouldn't have thought to ask if I'd been attacked since the attack had happened in Halfway. They all knew Zeke didn't like me leaving the pack neighborhood.

"Did they hurt you anywhere else?" He sounded broken.

I didn't want to lie to him. He'd know if I did. I also didn't want to tell him.

He snarled, his eyes glowing as his wolf surged forward.

"We informed you about the issue. When it comes to our pack business, you don't get to be privy to all the details. They aren't your concern," Theo bit out, stepping toward me. He took a stronger hold on my arm and tried to tug me away from Bodey. "She came home to us, and we've taken care of her. She's even staying with my parents now."

My legs weakened. Theo was foolish to think *that* would go over well.

Bodey stepped in front of me, removing Theo's hand from my arm, then turned his back on him. He brushed a tendril of hair that framed my face and breathed, "You're fucking living with Zeke?"

I tried to school my expression. If he realized how much I hated living there, this situation could explode. "He wanted to protect me after I was attacked in the woods at Halfway."

As Theo moved beside us so he could be part of the conversation, my head swirled. Bodey's touch and scent had my stomach fluttering, and it was as if only the two of us were here, except for Theo's heavy breathing.

Pretending Theo wasn't there, Bodey asked, "Why were you in Halfway?"

"That is *none* of your business," Theo growled. "Now, step away from my date. You've had your hands on her way too much, and my patience is gone."

Footsteps pounded our way, and I heard a few gasps

as if someone were running into people. I didn't have to turn around to know who was coming—Zeke.

I'd feared that coming tonight was a horrible idea, but it was becoming way worse than I imagined. The more Bodey learned, the angrier he became.

"Callie, why were you in Halfway?" He ignored everyone as he waited for my answer. With each passing second, his face became redder. He was going to explode.

"I work for Charles and Trevor now."

"*Charles?* The asshole who led the attack against you the night we met?" His words were so low I almost didn't hear them. He pulled me to his chest, no space separating us.

I shuddered, not because I was scared, hurt, or angry but from the force of his fury and anguish as it slammed into me.

He held me so flush against him that I struggled to fill my lungs, but I loved it. I'd missed his touch so damn much.

"What the *hell* is going on here?" Zeke demanded.

Bodey spun around, tucking me between himself and the nearby wall. Even though I couldn't see his face, judging from the way his back tightened, I had no doubt his expression was downright scary.

I edged out from behind him to see Zeke.

"You failed to mention that the scouts attacked Callie," he snarled.

"That was irrelevant. I informed you of the incident." Zeke lifted his chin. "Oregon is my territory. Idaho is yours."

Michael hurried over, with Samuel, Jack, Miles,

and Lucas filing in beside him. Each one wore varying expressions of horror.

The buzz of conversation stopped as people turned in our direction.

"Anything that happens to Callie is *my* business." Bodey reached behind him and took my hand.

"She is *not*. She's been part of my pack since I took her in. I *saved* her. I made sure she had what she needed growing up." Zeke's breathing quickened. "You met her a week and a half ago. She's not your responsibility. She's *mine*."

This was getting out of control, and I was the one who had to ride back with Zeke and deal with the consequences. "Bodey, it's fine."

"You heard her," Theo interjected, stepping beside his dad.

"Son, this isn't the time or place," Michael warned, though when he looked at me, his face twisted in concern.

Jack laughed. "Fuck that, Michael. I agree with Bodey, especially after how we met her."

This was worse than I'd ever imagined. The advisers were challenging Zeke in front of the strongest alphas in our territory. He was going to have a shit fit later.

"Get away from him, Callie," Zeke warned, glowering. "He's gone too far."

Placing his hands on my waist, Bodey held me in place and replied, "Oh, I haven't gone far enough."

"Do you want to challenge me?" Zeke removed his jacket and tossed it on a nearby table. "Do you want to lead two states?"

"Son, this isn't the way to handle this," Michael warned again.

Bodey went still. He blew out a breath. "No, I don't want to fight you. But I'm taking Callie back with me."

Spit pooled in the corner of Zeke's mouth as he snarled, "You have no right to her."

"Yes, I do." Bodey lifted his chin and glanced back at me. "She's the woman I love."

My jaw dropped, and my heart began to race. Had he just confessed to everyone what I thought he had? Was this a dream?

No one said a word.

Bodey turned to face me and pressed his forehead to mine. He murmured, "I love you."

I wanted to say it back—it was on the tip of my tongue—but howls sounded from the vineyard not even one hundred yards away. Everyone turned in that direction.

Lucas growled, "The wolves guarding us are under attack, and more than one hundred fifty wolves are heading this way."

My lungs seized. The queen had arrived.

CHAPTER TWENTY-THREE

I WANTED to laugh despite the threat, proving that my reactions were out of sync with my mind. This proved, once again, how much Fate hated my ass.

The bitch.

Since meeting Bodey, my dream had been to hear those exact words come out of his mouth, and when I did, they were immediately followed by wolves attacking.

Bodey snarled as he turned back to them, his body vibrating from the sound as he pressed against my chest. He spat, "We all know who's behind this."

Everyone nodded.

"We need to get Samuel to safety," Miles said, glancing at Stella.

Michael said, "We need to split up. Some of us can get Samuel to the car, and the rest can protect our people here."

I glanced left. We were near the exit, which I doubted our attackers had expected since Samuel was the guest of honor. At least the drama had made one good thing happen.

Bodey tossed Samuel his keys and instructed, "You and Callie go to my Jeep. I can jump in the back in animal form. If I don't, you two need to get the hell out of here. I'll meet you at the house."

"No." I shook my head. Everything screamed at me not to leave his side, especially not after he'd told everyone he loved me. "I'll stay here to help."

"*Theo* and *I* will make sure Samuel makes it to the Jeep, and Callie will be heading home with us where she belongs," Zeke rasped.

Jack clenched his hands. "You're not even going to stay here and help defend our pack mates who will join the battle to protect Samuel?"

"I'm no use to anyone if I'm dead," Zeke snapped as he reached for my arm.

Bodey shoved him back and snarled, "She's going with me."

"Not a chance," he snarled.

They stared each other down.

"Maybe Zeke would be more helpful dead. Then he wouldn't be here fighting over one wolf when we're all under attack." Lucas lifted his chin, annoyance floating off him.

He was right. We were wasting time.

People shifted on the patio as Bodey and Zeke continued to stare at each other in challenge.

With a strangled cry between human and wolf, someone yelled, "They're here."

I glanced across the patio to see a hundred wolves racing toward us.

Snarls sounded as our wolves ran toward them. We had to move.

Samuel stepped between Zeke and Bodey and took my hand. He commanded, "She's coming with *me*, and as your future king, I command you to obey." His eyes glowed, taking in both Zeke and Bodey, his wolf surging forward.

They didn't know what to do, and I was over this stupid fight. Samuel's life and the lives of others were at risk, and they needed to act like advisers and stop grandstanding.

"Go fight the real enemy," I growled. "We're standing around arguing instead of fixing the actual problem." I didn't want to leave Bodey, but I was a distraction. "Move." I snapped my fingers and took off running toward the exit, dragging Samuel with me.

Jack's laughter rang in my ears. "Too bad Bodey claimed her. I think I just fell in love."

"Just shift," Michael snapped as a scream rang from the farthest corner of the patio.

Bones cracked as they shifted.

My heels hit gravel, and I almost toppled over. Samuel caught up to me and clutched my upper arm, helping to stabilize me. "Thanks," I said and sniffed, searching for smells to indicate where the cars were parked since we'd valeted when we arrived.

"They're over there." Samuel pointed to the left, where the gravel continued around thick Douglas firs.

Of course the parking lot would be hidden a ways away. Anything to keep the place beautiful and unblemished.

I took another step, and my ankle almost rolled. Why did women wear heels? I liked the extra height, but damn, trying to escape on them was problematic. Knowing I'd move better without them, I paused. "Go on. I'll be right behind you."

Samuel spun around, his forehead creased. "If you think—"

I bent down and removed my shoes, then rolled my eyes. "I really meant I'd be right behind you." If I did something foolish, I'd distract Bodey. That was why I hadn't tried to fight alongside him.

He flinched. "I see that now."

Instead of dropping the heels, I held one in each hand in case I needed a weapon. I'd lost my knife in the battle with the scouts, so I needed something to make me feel more secure. "Let's go!"

"Callie, wait!" Theo called.

I glanced over my shoulder to see Theo, still human, closing the distance between us.

Why in the hell couldn't Zeke and Theo let this go? At least until after the attack?

Samuel's jaw tensed. "We don't have time for this. I already said—"

Lifting his hands in surrender, Theo shook his head. "I'm not here to argue. I just want to protect her."

Me. Not Samuel. Some of my anger toward him thawed again. He was trying to be a good friend, even after another man had professed his love for me when I'd come here as Theo's date.

"As long as that's it." Samuel waved us on. "Let's get to the Jeep."

As if Fate were toying with us, three wolves appeared on the left side of the building, heading straight for us. If I ever met Queen Kel, I'd totally give her the finger.

More paws pounded to our right. Twenty wolves ran around the patio. Those twenty were a whole lot closer than the first three.

Samuel's steps faltered. "Run."

Not needing to be told twice, I moved as quickly as possible. The gravel bit into my feet, but I ignored the pain. Those wounds would heal—death was permanent.

I wasn't fast enough, thanks to being barefoot. Samuel and Theo slowed, flanking me.

I opened my mouth to tell Samuel to run ahead—after all, *he* was their target—but he said, "I've warned the others."

"And I've informed Dad," Theo added, placing a hand on my arm.

So we'd have backup, but I hated that people would be putting their lives in danger for me. The stronger wolves needed to be saved. They were our future and what made us formidable. Not *me*.

"Here, this will be faster," Theo said as he ran in front of me. He lifted me by my waist and threw me over his shoulder.

My head hung down his backside, giving me a clear view of his ass. He took off, moving much faster and proving how much of a liability I was, even more than I'd realized.

The wolves ran toward us, and each step Theo took jarred my body. Thank gods my ribs had healed, or I'd have passed out, causing more issues. Though I couldn't easily lift my head to see what was happening, I knew without a doubt that the wolves were gaining on us. We were slower in human form.

Paws pounded so close that they sounded like the

drums of war. "Theo!" I exclaimed and gripped my shoes tighter.

Though I couldn't see them, I sensed two wolves coming at me—the air changed when they lunged.

Theo spun around. I smelled blood and heard a whine. After a second, Theo put me down. My legs almost gave out.

The world swirled, but not so much that I couldn't make out the attack. Wolves from the patio had arrived, and my gaze landed on a large, strong, dark wolf I instantly recognized.

Bodey.

He ripped out the throat of the dark-gray wolf. Then his gorgeous eyes locked on me, and he raced toward me.

My eyes flitted back to the other wolves who were defending us—Jack, Lucas, Zeke, and ten others I didn't recognize.

Theo, Samuel, and I weren't at a large disadvantage, and all but five of the attackers were still on their feet, overtaken due to how strong my friends and allies were.

A hand touched my arm, and I spun around, ready to use my heel as a weapon, but I stopped short when I realized it was Samuel. Of course it'd be him or Theo. They were the only two still in human form, other than me.

"Jeep," he rasped, tugging me toward the tree line twenty feet away. In a short time, Theo had gotten us far.

I glanced back. Bodey and the others were taking care of the remaining Southwestern wolves, which meant Samuel needed to get out of there. The thought of leaving Bodey behind was unbearable. I couldn't leave him, but he was safe. I could see that.

Samuel and I took off together. I glanced at him, noticing blood spatter on his navy jacket. I suspected he hadn't shifted so he could still communicate with me. Once again, my weakness was causing problems.

Theo's caramel wolf ran up beside me. He must have shifted while I was distracted by Bodey.

Figured.

As we reached the bend in the road, some stress fell from my shoulders. The wolves behind us had been neutralized; Bodey and the others wouldn't allow them to get near us.

But when the parking lot with over seventy-five cars in it appeared, my stomach roiled. Fifty wolf shifters were spread out across the lot. Bodey's car was close to us, but ten wolves stood between us and the vehicle.

The three of us stopped, taking in our enemy.

I rasped, "They planned this."

All fifty of them raised their hackles as they took us in. They knew we'd hurt their allies, but they'd maintained their positions.

"Stay here until the advisers come," Samuel said and placed a hand on my arm.

I wasn't sure if he meant to comfort me or make sure I didn't run headfirst into battle, but I wouldn't stand by and let them injure anyone I loved.

I stepped forward, and a sharp pain stabbed my feet. A large charcoal wolf in front of the Jeep tilted its head at me.

Yeah, I was wearing a dress, and I was barefoot with my heels in my hands. I didn't look intimidating, but I'd be damned if I didn't at least bruise some of them before I went down.

"Bodey's coming," Samuel informed me just as Theo stepped in front of me.

The two of them wouldn't let me get very far, so I'd bide my time.

The forty wolves not surrounding Bodey's car charged at us.

"Do you have your knife?" I asked, gripping my shoes.

Samuel bent and retrieved it. "Maybe I should shift."

Considering how strong of a wolf he was, that would be hugely beneficial. "You need to. Give me the keys, and I'll get the Jeep in position so everyone can jump in."

"Take this, too," he said, handing me the knife and keys.

I happily dropped one shoe and took them. I kept the knife in hand and tucked the keys into my bra so I wouldn't drop them.

Bodey and more of our wolves ran by as Samuel shifted, his clothes ripping off his body. The forty wolves were almost on us, and he needed a few seconds to shift. They'd want to attack him while he was vulnerable, so I ran after the others, Theo at my side.

Theo snarled, not happy with me, but I didn't give a damn. If anyone was going to survive this attack, it needed to be Samuel. I could take out at least one wolf.

I focused on the ten surrounding the Jeep. The one in front of the driver's side needed to move so I could get in. Then I could run the rest of the assholes over. I didn't need a strong wolf for that.

Theo's caramel wolf remained beside me. When I peeled off from the others, he nudged his head into my side to get me to alter my course.

Bodey's and Zeke's wolves cut in front of me, heading toward the Jeep. There was no doubt that Samuel and Theo had ratted my ass out, though I was grateful. The forty would focus on the twelve allies Bodey and Zeke had left behind, and we could clear the car.

Theo ran ahead, and the three of them went after the wolves by the Jeep. Two of the queen's wolves attacked each of them while the remaining four kept their attention on Samuel and me.

When I was fifteen feet away, two of the four charged at me—one slate-furred and the other ash. I gripped the knife in my hand, the weapon foreign. For some reason, the shoe felt more normal in my hands, heel pointed outward, which meant I definitely needed training.

As they lunged, I didn't allow myself to think; I just reacted.

I hit the slate wolf in the snout with the heel as my other hand sank the knife into the ash one's shoulder. The slate wolf yelped and recoiled as the ash wolf crumpled to the ground. I yanked hard, removing the blade from his shoulder just as the slate wolf got to her feet.

My heart ached as I listened to the snarls and growls of battle around me, and I could only pray that Bodey and the others were all right.

The ash wolf stood, and the enemy wolves moved slowly to circle me. I moved with them, refusing to have them directly at my back.

The ash one moved more slowly as blood ran down his leg. Both of them sized me up, determining how they wanted to attack. The ash wolf lunged first, catching me off guard since he was injured. He ran into my legs and knocked me onto his back.

I wrapped my legs around his middle, my dress hiking up as I anchored myself to him. His tail lifted, the fur of it landing in my face as I tried to bat it away to see what was happening.

Knowing the slate one would attack, I stabbed the ash wolf in the thigh. His back half landed hard on the ground as he yelped, and a shiver ran down my back as I tried to heave myself off.

It was too late.

The slate one landed on my back, her teeth slashing into my shoulder. Anguish ricocheted through me, and I yelped, unable to hold in the noise.

With his injuries, my weight, and the slate wolf, the ash wolf collapsed. I gritted my teeth as the slate wolf's jaw clenched tighter, and her teeth ripped deeper into me. Unable to free my knife, I tightened my other hand on the shoe and slammed the heel over my right shoulder into the slate wolf's face.

Squealing, the wolf released me, and I rolled off the ash wolf and spun around to face my enemy.

The heel of my shoe was stuck in her eye. She batted at it, snarling as drool dripped from her teeth.

I reached over to get the knife out of the ash wolf's leg, but he climbed back to his feet.

Shit. I was injured and didn't have a weapon.

I was going to die.

This was the end.

I never got to tell Bodey I loved him.

CHAPTER TWENTY-FOUR

MY HEART POUNDED as I stood tall. I refused to cower to these two assholes, and I pushed through the agony ripping through my shoulder.

I'd wound up fifteen feet from the Jeep, yet it looked so far away. I had to reach the vehicle first because I was the one with the damn keys stuffed down my bra.

Blood spilled down my shoulder, chest, and back, the warm liquid disconcerting with the strong metallic stench swirling around me. Even breathing pulled at the wound, and I tried to concentrate on my attackers in vain.

That, of course, was when they jumped at me, their strike coordinated and quick.

Something dark brown flashed past me and slammed into the ash wolf while the slate one continued to sail toward my throat. I moved to the side enough that it wasn't a death blow.

As I braced for the pain, the slate wolf dropped barely a foot in front of me. Wind whooshed past me and pounded the wolf to the ground. I gasped, not understanding what the fuck was going on.

The wolf whimpered as it tried to swipe at my legs with its claws, but I pivoted out of range. I reached down and slid my shoe heel from its eye socket. The sickening suction had acid roiling in my stomach. I bit the inside of my cheek, using my common coping mechanism to ground myself.

It was her or me. I stabbed the heel into the wolf's other eye.

She snarled and tried to bite my hand, missing only by millimeters.

I stumbled back just as Dina appeared at my side. Her hair swirled around her as she stared at the wolf, her forehead creased. The wolf stood and sniffed, trying to locate me, but Dina lifted her hands and chanted, "Force the attacker to the ground once again."

The wind picked up with so much force that the wolf's legs bowed under the pressure. I blinked, not believing my eyes. I'd known most witches were connected to an element, and the strongest were capable of healing and mind manipulation.

Dina held her hand out and channeled the wind to keep pummeling it.

"Do you have a weapon?" I asked, desperate to end this.

She shook her head, her focus entirely on the wolf.

Lovely. There was one thing I *could* do, though the thought made my stomach more upset.

I walked over, ready to break the wolf's neck. She snapped at me again. Between that and the wind, there was no way I could end her without getting injured.

To the right, Bodey was fighting the ash wolf. He

was on top, his teeth sinking into its throat. Samuel was finishing off his second attacker.

We needed to leave. If we got Samuel out of here, maybe the fight would end. That was the best way to save more lives.

Zeke, Michael, and Theo were still fighting their opponents but weren't at a disadvantage. They were stronger than the Southwest wolves...but the Southwesterners could have reinforcements coming at any second.

A chill ran down my spine. Gingerly, I removed the keys from my bra and pressed the button to unlock the vehicle. Bodey and Samuel jumped toward the Jeep, and I stepped over the ash wolf, which Bodey had just killed, and opened the back door.

Samuel climbed into the back seat while Bodey stood by the door, waiting for me. He nodded to the driver's seat, indicating I should climb in.

"I have to shut the door," I said, flustered. I understood he wanted to protect me, but something had to give.

"I'll get it," Dina said as she raced around the vehicle, still holding the blinded wolf down. Apparently, she was coming with us. That was more than fine with me.

Snarls caught my attention. A wolf broke away from Theo, Zeke, and Michael and charged toward us.

Shit. Bodey and I jumped into the car, and Dina's wind moved from the slate wolf's body to our doors, slamming them shut. Dina ran toward the passenger side as I started the car.

The three wolves lunged against the Jeep's side. It

rocked hard, and my stomach sank. They were going to push it onto its side if we didn't get out of there.

Dina got in and slammed the door, and I punched the gas. Gravel spewed everywhere, hitting every vehicle and wolf close by and creating a huge dust cloud.

Before the dust obscured everything, I saw the other wolves attacking our people, and my body tensed. Twenty more shifters had left the patio to defend Samuel, so we weren't as grossly outnumbered, but dead wolves littered the ground. There was no doubt lives had been lost on both sides.

Wolves raced to follow our Jeep. My shoulder throbbed, but I kept both hands on the wheel and maintained control. I couldn't drive as fast as I wanted, but the wolves couldn't catch up. As we drove around the trees, twenty more wolves raced toward us. Every few seconds, more joined them.

Pressing the pedal, I increased our speed, aiming straight for the onslaught of wolves. They didn't hesitate, racing straight toward us. They either had a death wish or thought I'd stop.

Dina leaned forward, bracing her hands on the dashboard. "If you need my help, let me know. I need to conserve as much of my magic as possible for Samuel's coronation."

I stayed focused on keeping the Jeep upright. I didn't drive often.

Bodey's big wolfy head appeared between my seat and Dina's, staring out the windshield.

Wanting to prove a point, I pressed the gas harder. The car swerved a little, but I maintained control. I never took my gaze off our aggressors. These assholes wouldn't see me flinch or hesitate. I'd take out every single one if it meant saving the people I loved.

I gritted my teeth, prepared for the inevitable impact. "Everyone, hunker down." There were only fifty feet between us and them, and more were running in front of me.

They weren't going to move.

That's their choice, I chanted to myself as the last bit of distance was erased. The first thumps were the worst. The wolves right behind the first five I'd hit jumped, smacking the windshield. The glass cracked but remained intact, though blood oozed down it. Every few seconds, more thumps hit the car, and sickening whimpers and howls filled the night.

Something wet and warm landed on my chest, but I didn't dare look down. I was struggling to keep the car upright. I hadn't expected this. I thought they'd dodge out of the way, but they kept coming, desperate to halt us.

"Move them," Dina commanded, her voice cracking. Wind rocked the Jeep as the wolves on the hood were pushed off.

The blood remained splattered on the windshield, reminding me of what I'd done.

The road to the interstate came into view, and some of my tension lifted. When we reached the asphalt, I could drive faster to get us away from this hellacious place. I exhaled, and pure agony ripped through my right arm, but I couldn't focus on it.

After a sharp turn onto the road, I didn't slow down. The Jeep tilted onto its right side. *Fuck me.* I groaned, afraid I'd grossly underestimated my speed, but the Jeep fell back onto all four wheels, and I could breathe once more.

"The goddess has to be with us," Dina whispered, clutching her chest. A few tears dripped from the corners of her eyes.

If someone was helping us, the goddess made sense because Fate was a bitch. I believed that then more than ever. "Thanks for helping me, not—" Pressure built in my chest, and I stopped speaking, not wanting to risk releasing the sob.

"I would've done it sooner." Dina hung her head. "I didn't expect them to..." She trailed off.

One thing was certain, this night would haunt us both.

Wincing, I lowered my right hand to my lap to take off the pressure from keeping it on the steering wheel. Fresh, warm blood trickled over the sticky, cooling mess, and I wondered how much I'd lost.

Shuffling sounded from behind me, and I glanced in the rearview mirror as Bodey jumped into the cargo area. Samuel raised his head and watched as bones cracked.

Then Samuel jerked his head forward as Bodey shifted back into human form.

There was a zipping sound and more shuffling as if he were putting on clothes. He called out, "Dina, can you heal her?"

She went still, then turned around.

A low, deep sound I'd never made before vibrated out of my chest. The thought of her seeing him naked bothered me. I glanced in the mirror to find only Bodey's face showing over the back seat and not an inch of his potentially naked body.

"Of course I can. But not while she's driving." Dina gestured to the road. "Healing will require my magic to merge with hers, and with her injuries, she needs all her focus on the road."

I kept glancing in the rearview mirror as he pulled a shirt over his head, then managed to climb over the back seat somewhat gracefully, despite his size. He leaned forward again, gently touching my arm as he examined my wound.

Even his faint touch caused me to flinch.

"They fucked you up," he snarled. "I don't even know how you're conscious."

"She's an incredibly strong wolf," Dina reiterated. "I told you that earlier."

A few vehicles passed us, going in the opposite direction, and tension rolled off me. We were around humans, which meant Queen Kel's wolves would have to be careful not to be seen.

My eyelids grew heavy. "I hate to interrupt, but I'm not sure how much longer I can drive safely."

"The wolf nicked an artery." Dina leaned closer to me, inspecting my wound. "We need to pull over. If you're feeling woozy, you're close to losing too much blood."

"Not yet." I shook my head, forcing my eyes to stay open. "We aren't far enough away."

"I promise we are," Bodey vowed. "An accident won't help anybody."

A gas station appeared up ahead with several cars parked in the lot. I didn't want to stop there with the blood on the windshield and a wolf in the back seat, so I eased over to the side of the road. As soon as I put the

Jeep into park, Dina leaned over the console and said, "Move if you want me to help her."

Moments before she touched my shoulder, I murmured, "You said you need to conserve your magic for the coronation tomorrow." Not only that but I'd been raised not to trust witches. Having her hands so close sent a chill through me so strong it stole my breath.

"If I use enough to help you live, I'll be fine tomorrow. I just can't heal you completely." A tender smile flitted across her face as she touched my wound.

I flinched at the feel of her cool hands. Then something warm and comforting soared through me, and the pain eased.

I'd always thought that a witch's magic would feel invasive, but this felt safe and tingly.

She lowered her hands. The warmth disappeared, but the discomfort didn't return. She murmured, "That's the best I can do. I'm sorry."

I looked down...and my mouth dropped open. She'd healed more than I'd expected. A thick scab covered the wound, and I could tell it would be healed completely in a day or two. I rolled my shoulder and felt only a faint sting. I smiled and breathed, "Thank you."

Something unreadable crossed her face. "It was my honor."

Though I was healed, I'd lost enough blood that I didn't want to risk driving. "Can one of you take my spot?" My voice sounded slurred even to my ears.

Bodey jumped out, and Dina moved into the back seat, taking the spot beside Samuel. I was confused about what was going on until Bodey opened my door, lifted me up, walked me around the car, and put me in the passenger seat. I leaned my face against the cool window, enjoying the chill as Bodey slid into the driver's side.

He put the car into drive, and we took off.

"I'm sorry about the mess." My eyes shut.

"What mess?" Bodey muttered.

I laughed, the sound strangled. "Fair. I ruined your Jeep, and you're sitting in my blood."

The silence made me uncomfortable enough to open one eye. Bodey had gone rigid, his hands clenched on the wheel. His expression was tense, and the muscle in his jaw twitched. Finally, he rasped, "You have *nothing* to apologize for."

My eyes closed of their own accord, and I didn't have the energy to respond.

"She isn't what I expected," Dina said from her spot behind me. "When I felt that magic roll off her, I thought the worst. But to see her protect Samuel... protect all of us tonight...."

Samuel whined from the back seat, and then I heard a flop like he'd given up and lain down.

"Unique." Bodey cleared his throat. "She's unique, loyal, and doesn't let her weakness define her. Something this world desperately needs."

Warmth surged through me. The way he'd described me meant more to me than if he'd called me beautiful. Those qualities were things that would never change, whereas beauty was nice but fleeting.

"The others?" Dina asked. "Did we leave them to die?"

"No. Just like we expected, once Samuel was out of reach, Queen Kel's wolves dispersed."

"She'll try again tomorrow." Dina asked, "What was the loss on our side?"

"Ten alphas. They lost four times as many. And they don't know where the coronation is being held." Bodey exhaled. "So let's be careful and hope everything will be fine."

I wanted to keep listening, but instead, I drifted off to sleep.

THE ENGINE QUIETED, stirring me from my slumber. My eyes popped open, searching for a threat, but I found myself somewhere familiar.

Bodey's garage.

I lifted my head just as Bodey and Dina opened their doors. Samuel jumped out after Dina and stopped at the door that led into the house while I struggled to sit up. Luckily, I wasn't dizzy or extremely fatigued anymore.

As soon as I reached for the handle, my door opened, revealing Bodey. He bent to scoop me up, but I shook my head. "I can do it." For some reason, it was important for me to walk on my own. Maybe because he'd professed his love to me, and I didn't want him to believe I was weak.

My blood coated his side. I winced, but remembering how he'd reacted to my apology earlier, I kept my mouth closed.

Seeming undeterred by my state, he placed a hand on my back, which was sticky with dried blood, and guided me toward the door.

"I'm walking home unless you need me to stay."

Dina stood at the garage entryway.

My head was foggy, but I remembered that the witches lived at the other end of the neighborhood. I tended to forget that Zeke's pack was an exception since having no witches nearby had always been my norm.

"Go." Bodey nodded. "We'll be fine here. We'll just need to leave for the ceremony earlier since we didn't anticipate having to come home."

"I'll be here at nine." She smiled at me before turning and heading away.

After hitting the button to close the garage, Bodey opened the door to the house. Samuel darted in, heading toward his room. As we entered the mudroom, a sense of peace washed over me. This place felt like home, and I hadn't been at ease since I'd left it behind.

The two of us walked through the kitchen and took a right toward the stairs. I was eager to be back in the bedroom I'd slept in, the one right next door to Bodey's. Just being this close to him had me lowering my guard.

I could hear Samuel shifting in his room as Bodey guided me to the bathroom. "I'll get you some clothes. You can warm the water and grab a towel if you'd like."

A shower would be amazing. I needed to wash off the blood that was crusted on me.

Bodey disappeared, and I turned on the water. By the time I placed a towel on the counter, he was back with one of his black shirts and boxers. "Sorry I can't do better than this."

My heart fluttered at the thought of wearing his clothes. "It's fine."

When he turned to leave, I winced and said, "I hate to ask, but can you help me?" I turned so he could see my dress's zipper. "I can't reach it." Not with my injured arm, which was still stiff.

I heard him swallow hard.

His fingertips brushed between my shoulder blades, sending tingles down my spine. As he unzipped my dress, something warm unfurled in my stomach. His soft touch and the slow way he moved had my heart thundering.

I could feel the moment he finished. "Do you need help with your..." He paused. "Bra?" His voice rasped even lower.

Unable to stop myself, I squeezed my legs together tighter, afraid that I might attack him. "Please."

As with the zipper, his fingers moved firmly but slowly. I hoped he felt the effects just like I did.

I clutched the material to my breasts to ensure it didn't fall away.

"Okay, there." He then stumbled out of the room and called, "Let me know if you need anything else." Then he shut the door swiftly.

The loss of his presence hit me hard, but the urge to get clean overwhelmed me. I stepped into the shower and washed my hair, face, and body. I turned the water superhot, wanting to steam the memories of the horrible night away. There was no telling how many people I'd killed, and I didn't want to learn the number. I feared it might change me.

To clear my mind, I rinsed off, got dressed, and shuffled toward my bedroom.

Samuel stepped out of his room, blocking me. He had clothes in his hands as well, but his eyes met mine.

"Are you okay?" he asked, examining me.

"After Dina healed me, I'm a lot better." I placed a hand on his shoulder and asked, "Are *you*?"

"I'm ready for tomorrow." He ran his free hand through his hair. "I need to take my position and calm things down. Queen Kel will keep attacking me until my reign is secure."

My chest expanded. "You're going to be an amazing king."

"And you're going to be at my side," he vowed. "You're not going back to Zeke's pack."

I froze, my heart lurching into my throat. What was it with men thinking I needed to mate with them to protect me? "I *can't* be your mate."

CHAPTER TWENTY-FIVE

I CROSSED MY ARMS, ignoring the jab of discomfort in my shoulder. I was putting my foot down. No way would I mate with someone for protection—I'd find a way to be fine on my own without settling for anything less than love.

Bodey's door opened, and footsteps pounded down the hallway toward us.

Face contorting and eyes bulging, Samuel lifted his hands and dropped his clothes. "No, no..." He shook his head vehemently as Bodey turned the corner, growling. "Just *no*," Samuel insisted, his gaze flicking between Bodey and me. "That's *not* what I meant."

For a moment, I was distracted. Bodey stood there wearing a heather-gray shirt that clung to his damp skin. His hair was dark from being wet, and his black sweatpants didn't leave much to the imagination. Though I shouldn't, I kept admiring the sizable bulge outlined there.

"That's *exactly* what it sounded like," Bodey

crossed his arms and stopped beside me. "I heard you clearly in my room."

Oh, right. Samuel had insinuated he wanted to mate with me. I'd forgotten what the entire conversation was about, and my stomach swirled at Bodey's reaction.

"I meant she could work for me." Samuel scratched his head with both hands. "I mean, obviously not as an adviser—all those roles are filled—but...like...as *something* to me. But not my *mate*. Definitely not that!" He winced. "Not that you aren't an amazing person or pretty. I mean, you are. You're one of the nicest and prettiest women I've seen."

Bodey snarled and edged partially in front of me.

"But totally not my type." Samuel stepped back and hung his head, realizing he was digging himself a grave.

"Oh, really?" I teased and pressed my lips together, trying not to smile. Now that I knew he wasn't asking me to mate with him, I was fine, but tomorrow, he'd be king. I had to give him as much hell as possible until then. "So...what don't you like about me?"

Bodey clenched his hands. "There is absolutely nothing less than fantastic about her."

Samuel pinched the bridge of his nose, huffing. "Look, she's strong, smart, and gorgeous, but I don't feel *those* types of feelings for her." He lifted his head, homing in on me. "I know it's odd, but in the short time we've known each other, you've become a close friend, and that's all I ever want us to be."

"I'm just giving you a hard time." I stepped forward and hugged him. "Though, at first, I did think you were trying to pull the mate-me bullshit."

When I pulled away, Bodey was quivering.

Okay, I had to defuse the situation, so I moved toward Bodey and said, "Theo keeps telling me that, and I don't want to mate with someone for protection." I squeezed Samuel's arm and said, "I'll figure a way out." A lump formed in my throat.

Bodey flinched, his nostrils flaring. "He's still on that shit?"

I nodded. "But I made it clear there's no way that's happening." I hated that I'd added that last part because I sounded desperate. Even though Bodey had professed his love to me, that didn't fix anything. He still believed his fated mate was out there.

If Samuel offered me a job, I would take it. That could be my ticket out of Zeke's pack and the abuse that came along with it. I'd seen how Zeke had looked at me tonight—his hatred was still strong. He'd been nice to me only because of the advisers. Hell, he'd probably forced Theo to ask me to the dinner so the advisers would see he'd been treating me well.

"Nothing about the situation makes sense." Samuel pursed his lips. "That pack has treated you like shit for so long, yet they don't want to give you up."

"It's about ownership." I shrugged. "Zeke craves control and power. He doesn't like threats or losing anything he perceives as his. Even though he hates me, the thought of someone taking a member of his pack away enrages him. He must have guessed that I got a job outside the pack so I could leave." A sour taste filled my mouth at that truth. Worse, it had taken me seventeen years to understand the real issue. "But Theo is a good guy." Lumping him in with his dad didn't feel right. He'd been there for me as much as he could.

Bodey gritted his teeth. "Yes, such a *great* guy. He

stood there and let his father punish you for stuff that wasn't even your fault."

That was both fair and unfair. I straightened my shoulders, upset that Bodey was denigrating one of my few friends from back home. "Zeke is his father and the pack alpha. Though Theo could have made a *little* difference, if he'd stood up for me too much, his life would've been hell, too." I could still remember the time he'd tried to take the punishment for me when I was eight. I'd tripped at a pack dinner and spilled my Pepsi all over Zeke's shirt. Zeke had increased my punishment tenfold for Theo's interference. "The only reason he wants to mate with me is because he believes that's the best way to protect me. Even when Theo becomes pack alpha, Zeke will be an adviser and have some sway over the pack. If I'm the alpha's mate, others will have to tolerate me in public."

"Yes, that's *so* considerate," Bodey hissed.

The malice in his voice had my head turning in his direction. His entire body was rigid again.

"Uh..." Samuel bent and snatched his clothes from the floor. "I think I'm going to take that shower now. I need to get some sleep for tomorrow."

Sleep. That sounded good. Being near Bodey after hearing he felt the same way about me as I did him was making it hard to be around him. Besides, I hadn't slept well since I'd left here. Maybe tonight, I could actually get some rest.

"Dina said she'll be here at nine in the morning." Bodey was so stiff that his words sounded slightly muffled. "We need to be ready to leave by then."

"No problem." Samuel smiled sadly. "I doubt I'll get much sleep, but I'll try."

A tingle ran down my spine, and I didn't have to look to know that Bodey was staring at me. His scent swirled around me, and I needed to get away before my brain short-circuited. "Right. Sleep. I should get on that." I squeezed Samuel's arm and froze. I had no idea how to proceed with Bodey. Did I just...punch him in the arm, or not touch him at all? If I hugged him, I might rub my body against him like a dog in heat.

The sad thing was, this was the closest I'd ever felt to having animalistic tendencies, and of course, the animal would be a *dog*.

Unsure, I forced a smile and nodded. "Night."

Bodey's brows furrowed, but his Botox-stiff expression finally melted away.

Needing to escape, I breezed past Samuel and headed toward my bedroom.

The guys murmured, "Good night," and Bodey's footsteps followed me. The bathroom door clicked. Bodey and I were now alone in the hall.

When I reached the bedroom door, he cleared his throat behind me.

My heart pounded so hard I was sure it would explode from my chest.

"Can we talk?" he rasped.

"We don't have to." I kept my back to him, fearing what I'd see on his face. "We've already had this conversation, and...what you said earlier tonight doesn't change anything."

His breath caught. "Please, Callie."

I placed my fingers to my lips and blew out a breath, then raised my hand toward where I believed the moon to be. I had to remind myself that Bodey had good intentions.

"Fuck anything I said before tonight," he growled. "I need a second chance to have this conversation."

Everything inside me screamed at me to ignore him...to run into my room. But I'd had way too much time to think about our relationship, and I wouldn't be as reactive as last time. Maybe if we talked, I could get the closure I currently lacked.

Forcing myself to turn around, I locked eyes with him and nodded. I wouldn't run or hide, no matter how badly it hurt. I would listen and accept what he said, no matter how my heart shattered.

Hell, maybe my own fated mate was out there.

With that thought, I couldn't imagine wanting to be with anyone other than Bodey. How could any man be better than the strong, caring, protective, sexy man standing before me? I couldn't fathom it.

He swallowed audibly. "Can we go on the deck?" He nodded to the one where we'd shared our kiss, and the memory of how he'd felt and tasted flitted into my mind.

My throat was so thick I couldn't respond, so I opened my door and led the way to the deck. He followed me, and when I stepped outside, I spotted his guitar. It lay against the railing next to the swing.

A candle glowed on the round table in the center of the deck, the slightly cold February breeze making the flame flicker.

I hurried over to sit on the side of the swing where I'd been *that* night. I needed to be able to fidget.

Bodey shut the bedroom door behind him.

I didn't know what I'd expected, but it wasn't him stalking over to me, taking the spot on the other side of the swing, and picking up his guitar.

As if this had been his plan all along, he arched a brow. "Do you mind if I play a song? Sometimes, music helps get my message across better than words."

That I understood all too well.

A smart person would have said no. When he played, something deep inside me yearned for him even more. I was most vulnerable to him when there was no question he understood me in a way no one else did.

I couldn't bring myself to deny him. "Are we going to bother your parents?" I glanced at their house. All their lights were still off. The last time we were out here, his mom had noticed us and made comments.

"No." He positioned the guitar on his lap, getting ready to strum the chords. "They're staying at the motel with the other former alphas to keep tabs on the queen's next move. Everything is handled. They're dealing with the wolves we lost tonight."

"Then why did *we* come back here? Shouldn't we have stayed and helped?" I placed my hands in my lap, looking for somewhere safe to put them. I already wanted to touch him.

He strummed a short chord. "This is the most secure spot for Samuel. Our pack is strong, and most of them are here, along with the coven. Our wolves are patrolling the area, and the witches are placing perimeters spells. If the queen is dead set on attacking Samuel, we can stop her here. Jack, Lucas, Miles, and Stella, along with their alphas who were attending the dinner, will be here within the next hour. They'll spread out in the bachelor pad and at my parents' house. We'll all ride together to the coronation tomorrow to protect Samuel."

He was so honest and forthcoming, with no hidden

agenda. It was one reason I loved him.

I noticed his hands were shaking. He'd never seemed nervous about playing around me before. I opened my mouth to ask why, but then he began playing a song.

After a few chords, I recognized it: "Perfect" by Ed Sheeran. As he played, the lyrics filtered through my head. My stomach fluttered as tears blurred my vision. A tear trailed down my cheek, and I wiped it away. I sucked in a breath as our eyes locked, and he continued to play.

I didn't know why he was playing *this* song for me, but when he reached the second chorus, I touched his arm. I couldn't hear anymore. Ever since I'd left that place, lyrics had become too painful, and to hear him play this song next to me was worse than him telling me we couldn't be together. It was like he wanted me to know he loved me despite us remaining apart.

He frowned and bit his bottom lip. "What's wrong?" he asked tentatively, which wasn't like him.

One thing was certain—I shouldn't have come out here. I'd thought I could handle this, but I'd been *so* wrong. A sharp ache shot through my chest, and I stood. "I'm sorry. The song is beautiful, but I can't do this."

Hurrying toward the bedroom door, I heard him set down the guitar. When I reached the door, his rough hand caught mine. He gently turned me toward him, his forehead creased as he murmured, "Do you not feel the same way about me anymore? I wouldn't blame you if you didn't."

I inhaled and snorted at the same time, making myself cough.

His head tilted back, and he dropped his hand.

Great, now he thought I was covering up laughing at him. How much less smooth could I be? I tucked a piece of hair behind my ear, the seriousness of the situation weighing down my limbs. "Of course I do. I've been miserable the entire time I've been away from you." I hadn't meant to be that honest, but I was over-correcting.

His indigo eyes lightened to cobalt as he moved just shy of our chests touching. He lowered his forehead to mine. "Then why are you leaving?"

My eyes closed, and my heart constricted. "You've made it clear where we stand with each other."

"Exactly." His minty breath fanned my face. "I have. So why are you leaving me out here alone on this deck?" His fingertips brushed my cheek.

His touch was like a drug, but his words were dangerous. Hope flared inside me, and I feared what would be left when it was squashed. I had to shut this down fast, even if I didn't want to. "Your fated mate is out there." I moved back, breaking our contact, my back now pressed fully against the door. The sharp ache became unbearable. I *couldn't* risk falling even more for him, only for his fated to show up. If I thought I was destroyed now, I'd be obliterated if that happened.

His body sagged like the weight of my words had crushed him. He hung his head and said, "I'm so damn sorry."

His apology reinforced that nothing had changed between us. "It's all right. I get it." The scent of my lie swirled around us.

He laughed and wrinkled his nose. "It's not all right. Clearly."

My face burned. I should've known better than to

lie. I turned around, my hand on the doorknob. "Good night, Bodey." I needed to disappear and regretted ever coming out here with him. I'd hoped for closure, but instead, I'd ripped out another piece of my heart and handed it to him.

"Callie, *wait.*"

I paused, keeping my back to him.

"Face me, please," he said as he removed my hand from the doorknob. "I didn't get a chance to finish what I wanted to say."

Spinning around, I lifted my hands. The words were like knives to my throat. "Bodey, I can't do this. I can't hold on to hope that one day you will change your mind, and if you do, you'll be settling for me. You made it clear you're looking for your fated mate, that this is the *person* you want to be with. I can't compete with that. It's not fair for me to even entertain competing with Fate. I want you to be happy, just know I'll be okay. You don't have to worry about me."

"Here's the thing," Bodey said as he stepped closer. "I *did* say all that, and I'm so *fucking* sorry. It took you walking away and seeing you with *him* tonight to realize how badly I messed up."

My lungs seized.

"I realized it as soon as you walked away, and I was a dumbass for not chasing after you and bringing you back." He cupped my face with both hands and growled, "I don't give a fuck if my fated is out there. Whoever it is *can't* be more perfect for me than you."

Eyes burning, I blinked back the tears. I wanted to take in his face and listen to his words. "What are you saying?" I needed to hear him say the words to ensure I didn't misunderstand him.

He lowered his head so we were eye to eye and rasped, "I choose you. Screw Fate. But that's only if you still want me. You could have a fated out there, too."

The world tilted. His hands on my cheeks were the only things keeping me centered. "What if my wolf never gets free? What if I'll always be this weak? You're a royal adviser."

"I don't give a shit that you can't shift." He moved closer, our chests now touching, the heat of him searing me. "You're not weak. You're the strongest person I've ever known—supernatural or human. I don't care if we can't pack link or you can't shift and run in the woods with me. I won't lie, it would be fun if we could, but I don't need that. All I need is you. Dammit, Callie, I *love* you."

The wall I'd placed around my heart crumbled. Here was the man I loved, standing before me, telling me he felt the same way. Despite having a fated out there, he wanted *me*. My chest expanded so much that it hurt in the best possible way. "I love you, too, but I can't risk being with you and you finding her. That would destroy me." I had to keep my head on straight and not run straight into a dumpster fire.

His lips touched mine, the kiss so brief and tender. He pulled his mouth away and peppered kisses down my neck, stopping right where my pulse throbbed. His teeth gently grazed my skin, stirring something wild within me.

"It won't be a problem," he whispered across my skin, his tongue licking where his teeth had grazed. "Because I have every intention of making you my mate."

CHAPTER TWENTY-SIX

MY PULSE THUDDED, and I held my breath, hoping he would bite me. A substantial part of me wanted to be lost in the moment.

But I cared too much about him to truly want that. I didn't want him to make a mistake he'd regret. That wouldn't help either of us.

"Bodey," I whimpered, tilting my head so he had more access to my neck, my brain telling me to stop.

"Yeah," he rasped, his teeth grazing my skin again, scratching it just enough for blood to well and the metallic scent to swirl between us.

The sting shot heat through my body, and something inside me began to churn like never before. "I don't want you to make a rash decision and do something you'll regret. I don't want one moment of pleasure to lead to resenting me." My breathing turned ragged from desire and fear, and my traitorous hands wrapped around his neck, pushing his mouth closer to my neck. Every cell in my body wanted him to claim me.

He chuckled as his tongue licked my blood. I sagged against the door.

"This isn't a rash decision." His hand slid under my shirt, touching my bare skin. I shivered. His touch was intoxicating, and when he pulled back, I groaned in protest. He freed a hand and tipped my head. We locked eyes. "I've been miserable ever since I told you we couldn't be together. Your leaving the next morning left me devastated." His face twisted in agony. "I've barely been able to function. The only reason I carried on was so that Zeke wouldn't see he had control over me through you. But Callie, I'm done pretending. I need you."

"Why didn't you contact me?" Now that his teeth weren't so damn close to my neck, some of my logical thinking reappeared...some, not all. His hands were still on me.

His hands stilled. "Because you asked me not to. I thought I'd lost you, especially when I saw you with *him* tonight. I was terrified I'd missed my chance to make it up to you."

Placing his forehead against mine, he held my gaze. "You don't have to decide now." He winced as if the thought of me not giving him an answer would be agonizing. "After all, you could have your own fated mate out there. It isn't fair for me to decide for us both."

"Bodey, I don't care. I never have." I cupped his face with my hands. "I love *you*. I don't want anyone else, even if Fate has chosen them for me. That's never been a question for me."

He flinched. "I feel the same way. It just took me a minute to get there. My whole life, I've sensed that someone is out there for me. I grew up determined to be with her. I needed time to wrap my head around the fact that even though it's what I've wanted my entire life, you changed me fundamentally."

Guilt weighed on me. "I'm not trying to make you feel bad."

"You aren't. I hate that I was a dumbass." He shook his head. "The first time I saw you, something about you captivated me. A wolf shifter in human form, fighting five wolves. You'd been fighting them for a while before we got there, and you were still standing." He smiled sadly. "No one, not even my strongest pack members, could've done that, but there you were. I see that strength in you every day, yet you're so kind, beautiful, and loving. There's no question you're who I want. I just needed time to realize it, and I'm sorry I hurt us both and that it took me so long."

The sincerity of his words washed over me like a rainstorm on a hot, muggy day. But there was one more thing I had to be certain of. "You don't want to mate with me to protect me, do you? Because I don't need that. I want love and to make a family, not be someone's charity—"

He kissed me, cutting off my words. Then he growled, "That is *not* what this is about, Callie. I swear. I know you don't need protection. I've always known that. Even when I helped you with your injuries, it wasn't because you couldn't handle the torture. It was because people were taking advantage of you." He removed one hand from my shirt and rubbed his thumb over the juncture of my neck and shoulder where he'd broken the skin. "Just tell me when you decide you want me forever, and I'll be here waiting for you." His irises glowed as his wolf surged forward, man and animal making the promise.

All hesitation melted away, and I sank into his chest. In two weeks, I'd completely fallen in love with him because he was that damn amazing.

Unable to resist him anymore, I kissed him. My tongue slipped into his mouth as my hands fisted his shirt.

He moaned, dropping his hands to my waist again. Our tongues collided, and it wasn't enough. I'd been craving him for way too long. I slid my hands over his body, desperate to touch every part of him but also wanting to take my time. The conflict was torture, yet the best feeling in the entire world.

He chuckled and pulled back slightly. "I need to know your answer before we move forward. Was that a yes to being my mate, or are we going to take this slow?"

I couldn't process his question. I was on a high, and he was refusing me my drug of choice—his lips. Then his words replayed in my mind, and I placed my hands on his chest, feeling his rapid heartbeat thumping under my palms. My heart was so full that I wouldn't have been surprised if it had burst. "I feel the same way. There's no reason to take things slow." I wanted him more than I needed oxygen to breathe.

A deep growl ripped through his chest as he pressed my body back into his. His tongue swept into my mouth as he walked backward toward the swing. I stumbled forward, unable to focus on anything but the carnal need clenching deep within me.

My lungs caught when we moved past the swing, and he pressed my back against the door to his room.

His hand gripped the doorknob, and he held my weight against his body as he opened it.

Our mouths remained fused together. He sucked on my tongue, sending shivers down my spine, and I nipped at his lips. My hands were around his neck, my fingers tangled in his hair. In this moment, we were the only two beings in existence.

He moved me backward again, and I didn't put up a fight. I trusted him, and I wasn't surprised when the back of my legs hit the top of a mattress. He gently lowered me, and my scent became stronger and surrounded me. How was that even possible? It was like I was on my own sheets.

I hesitated, my mind foggy. I detangled my hands from him and ran them over the comforter.

He raised himself up. "What's wrong?"

I glanced down and remembered the white comforter from when I'd slept in the other room. It was on his king-size bed, a little too small. "Is this...?"

"Your bedding from when you stayed here?" Bodey scratched the back of his neck and blushed. "Yeah. I told you I missed you."

My cheeks hurt from how widely I was smiling. "You brought my comforter in here?"

"And your pillows." He nodded toward the top of his bed. Sure enough, two pillows covered in white pillowcases lay next to his mustard-colored ones.

"Bodey," I whispered. He'd been in as much torment as me. In fairness, it might've been worse for him because he had memories of me around him.

I glanced around the room, taking everything in, wanting to learn more about him. His decor had similar colors to the rest of the house, but above the bed hung a huge drawing of a guitar. He had black nightstands on either side of his bed and a matching dresser across from the foot. A maroon sports jersey with the name Valor and the number sixteen underneath hung on the wall with no windows.

"Did I freak you out?" he asked quietly.

I blinked, trying to understand why he'd ask that. "Not at all. I think I just fell for you a little more."

He exhaled and leaned over me again. "Good. Now you can focus on me instead of my room. After the coronation, you can redecorate however you want in here."

I opened my mouth to ask him what he meant, but then his lips touched mine again. The need I'd felt moments ago slammed back through me. He rolled to his side next to me, snaking his hand underneath his shirt that I wore. Goose bumps trailed over my skin as he devoured my mouth.

When he peppered kisses down my face, I almost whined, but his lips felt nearly as good there as on my mouth. He drew up my shirt inch by inch, revealing my stomach, which he then nipped and licked. With each movement, he raised my shirt higher until he was gently removing it from my body.

So low that his words were almost indistinguishable, he growled, "You are so fucking beautiful."

He lowered his head so that his mouth hovered over my breast. I moaned as his breath warmed me. Then he licked my nipple ever so softly, and my head fell back.

"Bodey, *please*," I murmured, wanting his body all over me.

Instead, he took my nipple in his mouth and rolled his tongue over it. My fingers tangled in his hair, tugging gently, wanting more of everything.

I slipped a hand under his shirt and traced the curves of his muscles. The room spun, but I never wanted it to stop so long as he was the cause.

He nipped my breast lightly, igniting a spark inside me. "Oh gods," I moaned.

My body was on fire, and there was only one way I'd be satiated. When he lowered his hands to the boxer shorts I wore, my stomach clenched tightly with need.

He paused, his lips moving across my breasts as he asked, "Is this okay?"

"You better not stop," I threatened, pushing his hands lower.

A deep noise vibrated in his chest as he sucked each breast again and slipped one hand under the boxers and between my legs. Carefully, he circled a finger between my folds.

If I'd thought the friction was intense before, nothing had prepared me for this. I panted, on the brink of ecstasy.

"Tell me if I'm doing this wrong," he whispered, rolling his tongue over my nipple again.

"Per—" I tried saying, but I couldn't manage the rest of the word. All my focus was on my southern region.

He must have understood the message because he slipped his fingers inside me and thrust gently.

My insides clenched, and ecstasy exploded through me. I circled my hips, grinding as he kept tempo with my body.

But even when the pleasure eased, it left me with a more urgent need for him. If it felt like that with just his hands, I wanted to experience an orgasm with him inside me.

Dazed, I glanced at him to find he'd been watching me fall apart.

"That was so damn sexy." He smirked and circled his fingers against me again.

Need knotted in my stomach, but I pushed him away. He'd pleasured me and gotten me ready—now it was my turn to touch him. "Lie down," I commanded.

"But..." He pouted until I slid a hand inside his sweatpants and took hold of him.

His eyelids drooped, and he leaned up, capturing my lips with his. Our tongues collided. In sync with my pace as I stroked him. His hips jerked, and his hands cupped my breasts. We caressed each other, lost in the moment. Nothing existed outside of him and me, and I never wanted that to change.

"Stop," he rasped and grabbed my hand. "This isn't how I want to finish." He rolled me onto my back and stood in front of me. He then removed my boxer shorts and scanned me as he undressed.

He'd always been handsome, but to see him like this —bare in front of me—was hotter than anything I'd ever seen before. Every inch of him was hard and perfect.

I scooted back to give him room, and he positioned himself between my legs. He guided himself to my opening, and I was desperate for him to slip in. But he paused.

"Are you sure?" he breathed, his indigo irises glowing. "There's no going back if we do this. I'm barely able to keep myself from claiming you now. If we—"

Instead of responding, I arched against him, and his tip slid inside me. He hissed, his body shuddering, then he drove in a little deeper before pausing again. His eyes widened. "You're a virgin."

I nodded. Wolves usually had a high sex drive, but with how terribly my pack treated me, I'd never met anyone I wanted to sleep with. "I am. I'm sorry if that—"

"No, I'm relieved." He beamed. "I am, too. I've been waiting for you my entire life."

My heart melted even more, which shouldn't have been possible.

He bent down and kissed me. Every few seconds, he slid deeper and paused, allowing my body to adjust to him. But there was no pause in his kisses and sweet touches.

Once he'd filled me completely, I was certain I'd burst. I'd never felt so full before, both physically and emotionally.

"Are you okay?" he gritted out. "I'm trying not to hurt you, but damn, it's so hard to go slow with how good you feel."

"I'm better than okay." I moved against him, showing him I was completely fine.

He moaned, a sound so deep and sexy that I wanted to hear it forever. He moved in solid, slow thrusts at first, and soon, my slight discomfort was replaced by pure pleasure.

My fingers dug into his back as I wrapped my legs around his waist, pulling him deeper. He thrust faster as my mouth captured his. I wanted to taste, touch, and feel him. I wanted to be surrounded by him.

The pleasure built higher, and he tore his mouth from mine, kissing my neck. His body tensed as he moved even faster, both of us nearing ecstasy.

When his mouth reached the bottom of my neck, he raked his teeth across my skin, asking for permission. I tilted my head, giving him clear access. If he didn't bite me soon, I'd make him do it. Something wild surged through my blood, desperate for him to claim me.

Finally, he bit me, and every muscle in my body tensed for release. Something warm and animalistic surged through me, and pleasure that didn't come from my own body poured inside.

I needed *more*. This wasn't enough, so I rolled us over and pushed him onto his back as I climbed on top of him.

His eyes glowed brightly as he slid deeper inside me. I leaned down, not asking for permission. There was no stopping this moment, and when his wolf surged inside him, I felt its desperate need for me to claim him, too.

I rode him as I bit into his neck. Just as I'd felt something pour into me, something poured out of my body into his. An orgasm rocked through us both, our pleasure melding together.

If I'd been worried about his feelings for me, I wasn't any longer. He loved me the same way I loved him. The intensity of his emotions blanketed me as the quivering of my body shattered me.

I love you so damn much.

My pulse surged. I'd heard that in my mind. Were we...?

He kissed me, and the taste of our blood combined and lingered in our mouths, adding to the bond and befuddling my mind. We'd intermingled everything we possibly could—our souls, wolves, love, bodies, and blood.

As our pleasure continued to peak, I didn't break my rhythm, wanting to keep the pleasure rolling between us for as long as possible. *I love you, too.* Had he heard me?

All too soon, the pleasure eased, and I lay across his chest. He wrapped his arms around me, hugging me close despite our sweaty bodies.

We can mate link. He kissed the top of my head.

I nuzzled into his chest, listening to our hearts beating together. I replied, *We sure can.* I didn't know what I'd expected, but this wasn't shocking. At least with Bodey, linking felt like the most natural thing in the world, similar to breathing.

Something deep inside my chest that I'd never noticed before shifted. A coldness I hadn't realized was there, maybe because I'd gotten used to it? Then heat sparked, and I threw myself off the bed and landed in a heap on the floor.

Bodey jumped up, his eyes wide. "Callie, what's wrong?"

I couldn't answer. Heat swirled around the coldness as if to melt it. Then the spark turned into flames, and the cold dissolved.

A loud howl filled my head as something exploded through my body.

CHAPTER TWENTY-SEVEN

I CURLED into the fetal position, something pulsing through my blood as more warm pockets sprouted throughout my chest. The sensation wasn't awful, but cold tendrils of fear wrapped around my heart.

Bodey dropped beside me. "Callie! What's happening?"

More and more warm spots flared in my chest, feeling like pockets of air but not gas. Was this how bubble wrap felt before you popped it? I tried to speak, but the words died in my throat as another loud howl echoed in my head.

I whimpered, clutching my ears, but that didn't help. The sound was inside. *I don't know*, I linked, unable to communicate any other way. Or I thought I communicated with him. With our link being so new and these strange sensations flaring through me, I could've been answering myself.

He rubbed a circle on my back. "Where does it hurt?"

I didn't know how to answer that. My skin tingled, and I tried to scratch my arms, but they wouldn't move. I was frozen in this position. *My skin.*

"Your skin hurts?" He sat upright, examining my body.

Not hurts. I breathed through clenched teeth. *Tingles.*

"Uh, Callie," he said, his surprise filtering into me, adding more discomfort to an already strange situation. "Fur is sprouting over your body. That's why your skin is tingling."

Fur?

What the hell?

I couldn't shift, so that shouldn't be possible.

Then my bones cracked, and my spine felt as if it had broken in half. Pain swirled through my body, and I groaned as my stomach roiled. This was worse than when my ribs were broken, and my head was now resting against my forearms from the way my body had moved.

Something's wrong. My vision blurred with unshed tears, and I tried blinking, but it didn't help. The hurt eased, but I couldn't move anything.

Bodey's own fear added to mine. He said, "You're shifting. The first time is always slow."

Shifting. The word rang in my ears as another howl soared inside my mind, my wolf confirming it.

"Baby, I'm right *here*," he said, the last word breaking. Through our link, I sensed his own battle over watching me go through this. "Just know it."

Despite our link, he was speaking out loud to me. I didn't know why I noticed it, but it calmed me. Hearing his voice was familiar, unlike speaking telepathically, sprouting fur, and having my bones break.

I thought shifting didn't hurt. I groaned, and another crack in my body echoed off the walls as a new wave of misery washed over me.

"It's uncomfortable the first time, but it usually happens while we're young before puberty sets in. You're the only person I've heard of doing it first as an adult."

He kept petting me, but his emotions swirled with mine. We were both helpless...clueless...powerless...and our emotions fed off each other's.

Footsteps pounded down the hallway as my spine broke again. I yelped. What if I could never walk again?

The door swung open, and Samuel rushed in. He paused, then cleared his throat and asked, "What's going on?"

Bodey snarled and moved around me, blocking my bare ass from Samuel.

For a moment, I relished the torture, focusing on that instead of thinking of the view Samuel had of Bodey and me naked and on the floor.

"What are you doing here?" Bodey snarled.

"I felt a new pack member, and then I heard a cry."

Suddenly, the misery eased, and I could stand and lift my head. My body shook, and the swishing of fur shaking sounded all animal. I glanced at my arms—no, *legs* and found light-blonde fur the same color as my hair covering my body.

Bodey, I linked, my vision sharper. *Am I...* I trailed off, not believing what I was seeing.

He laughed as the tension from his emotions eased. "You're a wolf!"

I glanced around, taking in the room in more detail. My vision had always been better than a human's, but a dark room had always looked dimmer. Not now. This room looked as bright as if all the lights were on and the sun was shining in.

"She's *huge*," Samuel said as he walked around me.

His comment made me want to strut around. Was this how men felt when someone complimented the size of their penis? Although I had no control over my size, I still wanted to puff out my chest.

Bodey chuckled, and his humor wafted through our bond, making me happier. "She very much likes your description of her."

Suddenly, the walls seemed to close in on me. I needed to escape. I also wanted to be with Bodey. I pawed at the floor, the two conflicting emotions at war as heat expanded in my body. I sensed that if I ran, it would make whatever was happening inside me easier.

"She needs to run," Bodey said, and he nodded to the door. "Can you open the front door for us? I'll shift and go with her."

Samuel continued to stare at me, not blinking. "Yeah, but how is this possible? Tonight of all nights?"

Needing to be close to Bodey, I brushed against his naked legs.

Samuel sniffed, and his eyes bulged. "Wait. You two completed a mate bond? Is that how this happened?"

"I don't know." Bodey ran his fingers through my fur. "But we can talk about it *later*."

I whined and nudged his naked body toward the door. I didn't want him to go outside naked, but I didn't want to leave him. Damn him for being so sexy.

"Just be safe." Samuel hurried down the hallway. "I'll get the front door."

"Can you give me a second to shift?" Bodey asked as he squatted in front of me. His blue eyes were so warm, I could have stared into them forever…if I didn't want to run.

Hurry. I licked his face, enjoying the saltiness of his skin. *I need to be with you and nature.*

Dark-brown fur sprouted across his skin, and his eyes took on the glow of his wolf. *That sounds perfect to me.*

I watched in awe as his bones cracked and re-formed. Unlike mine, his shift was fast and without agony. Within seconds, he was on four legs. His tongue rolled out as he jumped on my side playfully.

Let's run, he linked, licking my nose.

Run.

My legs scurried, feeling off balance in this form. At first, my paws skidded against the wooden floor until I pressed them down, gaining traction. Then I took off down the hallway, racing toward the front door.

Bodey stayed behind me, letting me lead and get acclimated. His warmth mixed with mine, and my chest grew even hotter. I needed to be out in the cool air to ease the escalating sensations swirling inside me.

As I raced to the front door, Samuel beamed, watching me. *Have fun!* he linked.

His voice in my head made me falter, and I planted my front paws on his chest and then sprang out the door. His deep laughter quieted as I rounded the corner of the house and headed to the woods.

The soft grass brushed my paws with each step, and I wondered why I'd ever worn shoes. Rain was now drizzling, the scent dewy and fresh, the mist cooling my fur and making my muscles move more easily.

Bodey caught up and ran beside me. He turned his head to me, his tongue lolling out of his mouth. *Let's have fun, but we can't go too far. I told our scouts that we're out here, but we can't be reckless. Let's not go farther than a few miles out.*

Okay. As long as we were outside, I'd take what I could get. Unable to stop myself, I pounced on him, our bodies tumbling over each other toward the trees.

He crouched. *You'd better run!*

I took off. The sound of his pursuit urged me to push my legs faster. Unlike when I was in human form, animals didn't scurry as I passed. Raccoons didn't shy away as they scavenged for food, and two foxes kept hunting nearby.

I was a part of nature, no longer an intruder.

Bodey and I weaved through the trees. He'd catch me, and then I'd chase after him. Each time, we tumbled over each other, licking and pawing.

The warmth in my chest eased, or maybe I was acclimating. My wolf, finally part of me. I slowed, listening to the rain patter against the trees and ground. *What does a pack link feel like?* Maybe that was the warmth inside my chest. I hadn't noticed how ice cold and hollow I'd always felt until the sensation had shattered and filled with heat.

Bodey trotted beside me, his head tilting. *You weren't able to feel your pack mates?*

I flinched and shook my head. Shame flowed through me, and I averted my gaze.

Oh, baby. I didn't mean it like that. He nuzzled my neck, and my skin buzzed where he touched me. *Each pack member has a spot in your chest that you can sense. You can get a general idea of how each member feels if they choose to open their link and share that with you. The alpha always feels everyone. That's how we link and communicate.*

My limbs lightened. Those spots had to be pack members, and from what Bodey said, he had over two hundred wolves in his pack. *That's what I'm feeling.*

You're part of my pack now. His tongue lolled out again and hung to one side.

The largest spot closest to my heart pulsed with his emotions. *And since you're my alpha, your spot is the largest?*

And we're mates. Yours is now the biggest for me, too.

That was so romantic. *As it should be*, I teased.

Oh, I agree, he replied, licking my face.

Can I link with Jack, Lucas, and Miles? Bodey could, and we were mates.

He shook his head. *My bond with them is an odd one, and we didn't form it on purpose. It happened after the king and queen passed, and the advisers—our parents at the time—spent a lot of time together, trying to settle the unrest. The four of us hung out constantly. We didn't submit to each other, and our parents were just as perplexed as we were as to how it happened. But it works well for us.*

It's like you four forged your own separate pack. What had it been like growing up with such close friends? Stevie and I were friends and sisters, but we hadn't forged a bond like that. Granted, my wolf had been blocked.

You're right. I hadn't looked at it that way. Just know

that you're *my home, Callie. In this entire fucking world, you're the one who matters most to me.* He rubbed the side of his head along mine.

The sizzle of our connection had my lungs seizing. I'd never experienced anything like this, and I became even more addicted to feeling him.

Gods, I can't stop touching you, even in wolf form. He whined, and it wasn't from pain.

I wanted to do a whole lot of things with him, but not here while members of our pack were nearby. *Why don't we go back to the house?* My need for his body had officially surpassed my need to be in nature.

He huffed. *You're right. It's late, and we have an early start tomorrow. We should head inside and make love one last time before we sleep.*

That sounds better than perfect to me. Though I hated thinking about him leaving me tomorrow for the coronation, that separation would be temporary, and he had to be there. I'd just force him to make it up to me multiple times when he returned home to me.

Home. I needed to call my parents and Stevie in the morning to inform them I was no longer part of the pack. Dread knotted in my stomach, but it didn't lessen my happiness. Bodey was mine forever.

I won't wait long to chase you, he teased.

I took off, and he ran after me. My muscles burned in pleasure from the workout as well as from knowing we'd soon be home and naked again.

We ran out of the woods, and Samuel was on the back patio with the door open. Bodey must have asked him to let us back in.

Glad to have you back, Samuel linked to us. *Now I'm going to bed.*

Good night, Samuel. Thank you! I raced past him toward the stairs. Though I cared about him, there was something way more important to focus on, Bodey naked in our bed.

Inside the bedroom, I paused. I wasn't sure how to shift back into human form. I turned around as Bodey joined me, and my wolf retreated. She inched back from my mind, and magic poured into the area that had always been cold.

I braced for the torment, but only slight discomfort shot through me. My skin tingled as the fur vanished from my arms and my spine reshaped. Soon, I was standing before Bodey, both of us in human form. And naked.

He wrapped an arm around my waist and tugged me to the bed. My skin sizzled everywhere we touched. Then his lips were on mine, and the world fell away.

———

Buzzing sounded, and my consciousness fluttered awake. I found myself warm from the large arms wrapped around me. I'd never woken up being spooned before, and I never wanted to wake up any other way again.

Bodey groaned and leaned over to turn off the alarm. Just when I thought he'd crawl out of bed, he snuggled more deeply into me. His lips touched the base of my neck in the very spot he'd bitten me the night before.

A new type of buzzing rocked through me, need pulsing between my legs. Bodey turned me onto my back. His lips found mine, and he slid between my legs.

I was already desperate for him, his arousal mixing with mine. He pushed himself inside me, filling me whole. He tore his mouth from mine and kissed down my neck, thrusting into me slow, hard, and loving.

Thank gods you made time for this. I moaned as friction built inside me.

Sorry it can't be slower, but damn, I wouldn't make it through the day without feeling you like this. His mouth fused back with mine, and our tongues tangled.

An orgasm rocked through us, the pleasure and buzzing of our skin making the world hazy.

When we came down, he rolled onto his side but continued to kiss me. *We'd better get ready.*

I wanted to persuade him to stay, but that wouldn't be right. Instead, I forced my mouth away from his and cuddled deep into the pillows. That'd have to do while he was gone.

He climbed out of bed and chuckled. "So, you're a push-it-to-the-last-minute type of person. I didn't see that coming."

Turning my head, I stuck out my tongue. "The wicked never rest, and clearly, I'm *not wicked.*"

"True, but even good people can be late to parties." He arched a brow. "If that's your plan, Samuel will kill you. He likes to arrive early."

I lifted my head. "Wait. You want me to go?"

He sat on the bed and took my hand, linking, *Of course I want you to go. You're my mate. Do you not want to be there? I figured you'd want to see Samuel get crowned, and I know he wants you there.*

I hadn't expected to be invited. I'd spent my entire life on the sidelines of the pack, excluded from everything. *I...just didn't think...* I trailed off, my face warming. I should've known he'd want me there. He was nothing like Zeke.

I'm an alpha and a royal adviser, but my most important role now is being your mate. He squeezed my hand and kissed my forehead. *I want you by my side for everything, especially when I travel the state to meet with our packs.*

I sat up, not bothering to keep the sheet over me. After everything we'd done together, I didn't feel embarrassed. *Then I'd better get ready.* I froze. *Wait. I have nothing to wear!*

He winked. *Stella is bringing over some options for you. She's got several dresses with her. I figured she'd be a safer bet than us scavenging Mom's closet. We can go shopping for you soon, though I do prefer you naked.*

I arched a brow. *Maybe I should go to the coronation in my birthday suit.*

If you want me to kill everyone there, fine. He growled. *But I don't think Samuel would appreciate that.*

Gods, I love you. I kissed him and continued, *Nothing turns me on more than you threatening to kill people for looking at me naked.*

His chest shook with quiet laughter. *You will be the death of me.*

My phone rang from the nightstand. My stomach sank. It was probably my parents, Stevie, or Theo calling to check on me. I should've called them last night, but after all the blood loss and massive life changes, I hadn't been myself.

Stevie's name scrolled across the screen, and Bodey

kissed my cheek and stood. He linked, *I'll take a quick shower while you talk to her.*

In other words, he was giving me privacy, something I'd never been offered before.

I answered the phone while watching his naked ass walk to the bathroom. With each step, his muscles flexed, and I wanted to toss the phone down and join him.

"Callie?" Stevie's voice echoed on the line.

Oh, right. "Hey."

"Where are you?" She sounded worried.

"I'm sorry. I should've called you last night." Thankfully, Bodey had shut the bathroom door, cutting off my delectable view, or I still wouldn't have been listening. "Something happened at the dinner, and, uh, I didn't come back with Theo and Zeke."

She paused. "They aren't here, either."

That wasn't surprising. They were probably with the advisers' parents. Zeke wouldn't want to be left out. "Oh, well, I'm sure they'll be back later today."

"They? Not you?" Now Stevie sounded relieved.

"Yeah, uh..." I didn't know how to tell her I was mated. She'd seen how upset I'd been when I came home, and Bodey and I had moved fast.

"Thank gods," she sighed. "I thought they were taking you to the coronation. Are you and Tina heading home?"

"I'm not with them. I'm with Bodey."

"Bodey? The guy who broke your heart?"

I flinched. "Yeah, but we figured everything out."

"Good, but I need you to come home."

My stomach soured. "Yeah, I can come by later." Telling my parents and Stevie about Bodey and me in person would be best. "Bodey and I will drop by after the coronation."

"What? No!" Her voice grew urgent. "I need you here *now*. You can't go to the coronation!"

My head jerked back. I'd never heard her sound like that before. "Stevie, what's wrong?"

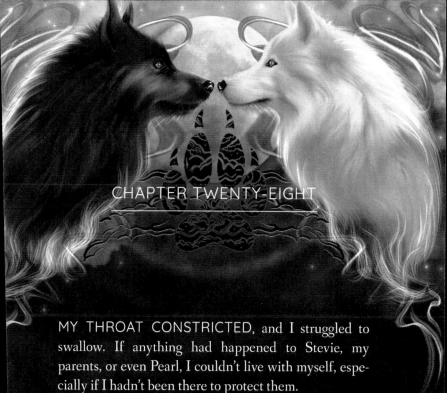

CHAPTER TWENTY-EIGHT

MY THROAT CONSTRICTED, and I struggled to swallow. If anything had happened to Stevie, my parents, or even Pearl, I couldn't live with myself, especially if I hadn't been there to protect them.

"I'm *fine*." Stevie's emphasis on the last word made me tense even more. She was deflecting, which usually meant she was hiding something from me.

"What about Mom, Dad, and Pearl?" Even though Pearl hated me, she was part of my family. The last thing I wanted was for something bad to happen to any of them.

Stevie huffed. "We're all okay."

"Then what's wrong? Why do I need to go there?" The plastic on the phone popped, startling me. My hand had clutched it so tightly that the plastic was about to break. I hadn't even noticed.

"Just...after the attack last night, I need you here." Her words grew louder as if she were holding in a sob.

I loosened my grip, not wanting to snap my phone in the middle of the conversation. Some of my fear ebbed, and the lump in my throat shrank. "Stevie, I swear, I'm okay. I got injured a little, but the priestess from Bodey's coven healed me almost completely. It's just a scab this morning."

She gasped. "You let a *witch* touch you? That's not safe."

A month ago, if she'd told me a witch had helped her, I would've had the same reaction. Our entire pack didn't trust witches because of Zeke. His bias had made us jaded, and maybe the covens that had been part of our pack were different from the rest. I didn't know, but Bodey trusted Dina, and after seeing how protective she was of his pack, I had no reason not to trust her either. "She's nothing like what Zeke painted the others to be."

She paused. "Callie, I'm worried about you. After watching all the shit you were handed with this pack and the way our family is treated, I need you here. It's always been you and me, and now I'm sort of alone. I just—" Her breath hitched. "I need to know you're safe."

Are you okay? Bodey linked, his concern wafting between us.

Yeah, Stevie is begging me to go there. She's afraid I'll get hurt after the attack last night. I wished I could hug her. She'd been my one constant blessing in life and the reason my sanity had survived, even more so than Theo. "I promise I'm safe," I assured her.

His alarm switched to warmth between us. *Tell her the coronation is being held off-site,* Bodey linked. *Only those attending the coronation are aware of the meeting location, and they found out just minutes ago.*

I repeated what he'd told me, wanting to ease her

mind. "Between that and the patrols both there and here, we'll be safe."

She didn't respond, and I hated that I wasn't rushing back to her. The truth was, I wanted to be there for Bodey. When I'd thought he would leave me behind, I'd wanted to pout, even though I understood. Now that I knew he *wanted* me there, there was no way in hell I wasn't going. Not only that, but I cared about Samuel and wanted to be part of his big day.

Bodey and Samuel were part of my pack now, and the horrible truth of the matter was that Stevie and my family were clueless that I'd switched packs. That was how out of sync I'd been with my wolf and that pack. It was hard to fathom, given how connected I was with Bodey and our pack.

"You should be here with us, especially if you were injured. I can't believe Zeke was okay with you going off with those royal advisers *again*."

The water turned off, and I heard Bodey stepping from the shower. Part of me realized he was completely wet and naked in there, but I couldn't rush Stevie off the phone. "He didn't have much choice." Yesterday, that would've frightened me, thinking about what I'd be heading back to. But not anymore. I couldn't be forced to go anywhere with them. "There was a lot going on."

There was an awkward pause, and I didn't have to be there to picture the expression on her face. She'd have her brows furrowed in a deep scowl, but that wouldn't change my mind. In fact, I was certain remaining on the phone with her was only making her more desperate.

"Callie, he broke your heart. It's not smart to stay with him."

I sighed. "Don't tell anyone yet, but I need you to know so you understand. We're mated now." Stevie's words hurt, but they had come from a place of caring. "During our time apart, he realized he wanted me, too... no matter what."

She was only trying to protect me, and I didn't want to lash out unfairly. She was the closest thing to blood I had, including Theo. Theo was a friend, but that was it. Stevie had been my friend, confidant, and supporter.

"So?" She scoffed, undeterred. "It's still not your place. You should stay home, like Tina."

The bathroom door and the front door opened at the same time. Bodey strolled into the bedroom, and I pouted. He was dressed in black slacks and a thin undershirt, which meant I didn't get to ogle his naked body again. Though even with his clothes on, I still wanted to rub my entire body all over him.

"Are you still there?" Stevie asked.

Yup, Bodey had a way of making me lose focus on anything other than him. "Yeah, sorry. Our relationship isn't like Zeke and Tina's. Bodey wants me there, and I need to go."

Bodey snatched the large shirt and boxers from the bed and tossed them at me. He linked, *I hate to ask you to cover yourself, but Stella will be up here soon.*

I'd forgotten about someone entering the house. I was doing amazing.

I tossed the phone on the bed and pulled the shirt over my head.

"But Callie, it's too dangerous." Stevie's voice broke.

Picking up the phone, I ignored the small part of me that said I should do what my sister asked. Making my family happy had always been my default, but Bodey was my mate and priority now. "I'll call you on our way to the house. You'll see me a few hours later."

She blew out of breath. "There's no way I can talk you out of this?"

"Absolutely not," I said firmly, despite the twinge of sadness. "I know you think I'm being foolish because Bodey hurt me not even a week ago, but things are different. You'll see, and I wanted to tell you and Mom and Dad in person."

"If you come home, you can tell them right away."

I smiled. There was my sneaky sister rearing her head. "I'll be there tonight. I promise. I love you." I slipped on the boxer shorts.

"I'd better get going," she said a little too curtly. She wasn't happy with me, and that hurt. She'd been upset with me only a few times.

"Stevie," I started. "Listen—"

"I've heard enough," she said. "Besides, I know how you are once you make your mind up. No one can change it, not even your alpha. It's something I've always admired about you, even if it's frustrating me now. But you're right. We need to go. I'll see you soon."

That was the thing with Stevie. She might not understand me completely, but she accepted me for who I was. "I love you, Stevie," I said again, needing her to know more than ever.

"I love you, too," she whispered before hanging up.

I kept the phone to my ear even without her on the line. My heart ached, but I couldn't do anything about it.

Bodey took the phone from me, then interlaced our fingers and rubbed his thumb against my palm. The sizzle between us sent need clenching in my stomach. "If you need to be with your family—"

I shook my head. "You're my mate...my *family*. I want to be there with *you*."

He smiled tenderly. "Yes, I *am*. And gods, I love the way that sounds."

Not wanting him to get too much of an ego, I wrinkled my nose. "Besides, Samuel is a pack member and my future king. I want to watch him be crowned."

Pack.

That word had so much more meaning now.

I'd always understood what that meant based on the way the others treated one another, but understanding it and experiencing it was completely different. Even though I didn't know most of the two hundred other pack members, I cared about them already. We were connected, literally and figuratively. No wonder Zeke had so much influence over his pack.

The sound of heels stepping up the stairs pulled me from my thoughts.

"He wants you there, too," Bodey answered and kissed my lips.

My skin buzzed, and something inside tugged me closer. I pressed myself to him until there wasn't any space between us, but it still felt like he was miles away. The tingles increased, and I needed more.

Do you feel that, too? I linked, moving my head so I could kiss him deeper. *The buzzing whenever we touch?*

Fuck yeah. He growled in his throat. *It's intoxicating, mixed with how you feel, taste, and smell.*

"I'm here with the dresses," Stella called from the hallway, getting closer.

We stopped kissing, but our bodies were still touching. I couldn't bring myself to step away.

He growled as he took a step back, his irises glowing, and moved to the door. When he opened it, Stella stood there in a strappy burgundy dress that hugged her body, with a deep *V* that cut between her breasts. The gown was floor length, and her hair was pulled back and fell down her back in supertight curls. Her lips were painted a deep red that complemented the dress, and the rest of her makeup was so natural, you'd think she hadn't put any on, except for the hint of dark mascara on her eyelashes and the trace of blush on her cheeks.

"You look amazing." I wouldn't be able to pull off that look even if I had my makeup with me.

She winked. "Girl, you will, too. Believe me, I brought enough shoes, dresses, and makeup to make sure you're done up right."

I nuzzled into Bodey's arms, needing his comfort. I was putting all these people out so much. "You don't—"

"Please." She rolled her eyes. "Don't say what I think you're about to say. We are all thrilled that Bodey finally settled down. Out of all the guys, I was most worried about him. So, it's an honor to have another female in the"—she raised her fingers in air quotes—"'bachelor's club.'" She lowered them. "Jack swore that when there was one more of us mates, he'd stop calling it that."

I laughed, the noise catching me off guard. "I doubt he'll keep his promise." I believed he said things for the sake of saying them at times.

"We're holding him to it." She turned her gaze to Bodey. "And you're going to have to pry your body off hers. I've set up shop in the room next door, per Samuel's instructions."

Samuel.

I cringed. I hoped he hadn't heard us having sex this morning. Lost in all things Bodey, I'd forgotten he was here.

Leaning down, Bodey kissed me. I was pretty sure he'd meant to be quick, but then he growled and slipped his tongue into my mouth. The buzzing intensified, and magic pulsed through me, stronger than last night. My wolf surged into my head, enjoying his touches as much as I was.

Stella cleared her throat. "Guys, I get it. I've been newly mated. But we're going to be late, and Miles is getting stressed."

Sighing, Bodey stepped away. "Only because it's the coronation." He circled me, his hand brushing my ass before he linked. *We'll have to make up for all the time our hands are off each other tonight.*

The promise had desire pooling inside me.

He strolled back into the bathroom and shut the door loudly.

Stella looped her arm through mine. "Come on."

I found three dresses on the bed. One was black and strapless, with a sweetheart neckline. Sequins were sewn from under the breast to the waist like a belt, and a fuchsia skirt flowed to the floor. The second dress was dark purple and shoulderless. The top was full of sequins, and the skirt was a little fuller, with sequins fading toward the bottom. The last dress was navy blue, also with a sweetheart bodice and a sheer top portion that went all the way to the collarbone. It beaded at the waist before falling to the floor.

When Bodey said she was bringing me something to wear, I hadn't expected options. "These are gorgeous."

She shrugged. "I wasn't sure about your style, so I brought them all."

"Are you sure you don't mind me wearing one?" All three looked expensive, and I didn't want to mess them up. "I don't have a good track record with clothes lately."

She waved a hand. "If the dress gets ruined, it's not the end of the world. I promise. Besides, I have a knack for getting stains out. Otherwise, Miles would be running around with ketchup stains on his shirts all the time."

I laughed. "He does put ketchup on his eggs."

"It's gross, right?" She wrinkled her nose. "But anyway, take your pick."

I bit my bottom lip and decided to go with the one that drew me in the most, the black strapless dress with the fuchsia skirt. I lifted it, touching the material. It was smooth like silk.

"I would've picked the same one." She nodded. "It's going to make your eyes pop."

Her validation made me even more certain.

"Let's get you dressed and do your makeup."

IN LESS TIME than I'd expected, I was staring at my reflection in the mirror of the dresser across the room. We'd left my hair straight, and it cascaded down my shoulders and back. Stella had blended various beige, bronze, and chocolate colors across my lids, giving them a smoky tone that made my blue eyes shine brighter, and she'd finished the look with a faint pink gloss that gave my lips a natural appearance.

I didn't recognize myself. Stella was a wizard with a brush. Stevie had done my makeup well, but Stella had taken it to new heights.

I hate to rush you, but will you two be done soon? Bodey linked, our connection warming in my chest.

Her eyes glowed as well, probably from Miles following up with her.

Coming now, I replied and slipped on my tennis shoes.

Stella arched a brow. "I brought heels." She gestured to a sparkly pair that would've gone with any of the dresses.

"With how long the skirt is, I can wear these, and no one will notice. I'll be more comfortable." After running in heels last night while under attack, the last thing I wanted was to put on another pair so soon.

I expected her to argue, but she shrugged and headed to the door, saying, "Just be careful when you sit so they don't stick out from under your dress."

Usually, people challenged me when I didn't listen, but here she was, giving me sound advice. I contemplated changing into the heels just because she wasn't pressuring me, but then the clear disadvantage I'd been in last night had me marching after her.

We headed down the stairwell, Miles and Bodey waiting at the bottom.

Bodey's mouth dropped open when he saw me, and the scent of arousal shrouded him. With the approval in his stare, his scent, and how mouthwatering he looked, my legs propelled me toward him faster, and I didn't care if I fell. His black suit clung to him, every curve of muscle visible through the thick jacket. He wore a light-blue shirt that made his eyes seem lighter.

When I reached him, his hands slid around my waist, the jolt between us springing to life and stealing my breath away. *You're always beautiful, but this...* His breath caught, and his hand cupped the back of my head. *I don't even know how to describe you.* He moved to kiss me, but Stella clutched my arm, pulling me away.

"Do *not* mess up her lipstick," she snarled. "You can wait until after the coronation to kiss her."

Bodey pouted and shook his head. "I'm certain I can't." When he bent to kiss me again, I turned my head so his lips brushed my cheek. Though I wanted his lips desperately, I didn't want to upset Stella.

Jack's laughter forced my eyes away from Bodey and toward the living room. Jack, Lucas, Samuel, and Dina stood waiting by the front door.

You look beautiful, Samuel linked. He wore a suit similar to the one from last night, giving him a very kingly look, which, no doubt, was the point.

Lucas, Jack, and Miles wore black suits as well, while Dina wore a white dress that made her look like a goddess. It was low cut, and the flowy skirt had a slit up the front, revealing her thigh when she walked. She wore no shoes, and there were two ropes intricately tied around her waist.

She tilted her head, staring at me. "Her magic. It's unleashing. The mate bond must have broken the spell, but not all of it is free yet."

"It's not?" Lucas's brows lifted. "She's already almost as strong as Theo."

I stiffened. I must have misunderstood him. Though I could connect with my wolf, I didn't feel stronger than the people around me.

Dina licked her lips. "The spell isn't completely gone."

"You can check her out more later," Miles said, taking Stella's hand. "We've got to get to the coronation."

"Yeah, yeah." Jack scoffed and pulled out a pair of keys. "You've been saying that for the past thirty minutes. We got it. We have a long-ass drive, and I swear, if you don't shut up about it, your ass will be walking. My Navigator is a whine-free zone, and anyone who can't comply will be working the corner."

Lucas arched a brow. "You mean hitchhiking."

"Ha!" Jack snorted. "You think anyone would pick up his grumpy ass? He'd have to work the corner to get some money to get an Uber to drive him the rest of the way."

Stella growled. "Or we could just use a credit card."

"Yeah, if you want to be boring." Jack shrugged. "Depends on—"

Stella's snarl was so loud that it cut Jack off. He grinned wickedly.

I would've reacted the same way to someone talking about Bodey pimping out his body. "Okay, let's go." I clapped my hands. "We don't want Dina and Samuel to be late to the very thing you've been planning for months."

I grabbed Jack's arm, pulling him toward the garage. He beamed at Bodey as we walked by and said, "Your mate, unfortunately, woke up one night too soon to realize she picked the wrong guy."

Now it was Bodey's turn to snarl.

"Can you behave for a minute?" I held back my smile. *And I don't want Jack. I'm only trying to hurry us along.*

Oh, I know. That's the only reason he's not dead, Bodey replied. He was right on our heels, breathing down Jack's neck.

Somehow, someway, we all got into the vehicles without Jack saying another word. Jack, Lucas, Stella, and Miles rode in Jack's white Navigator while Bodey, Dina, Samuel, and I rode in Bodey's Mercedes-Benz SUV. The inside was tan leather with a dark interior. It was nicer than the Jeep. *Why don't you take this more often?*

Don't know. He shrugged, pulling out of the driveway. *Sort of a Jeep guy.*

I'm glad. Though the vehicle was nice, the Jeep fit him better.

Soon, I was watching the trees fly past, and Bodey linked, *Any updates?*

For a second, I was confused until Michael replied, *We should be asking you two that question.*

Three warm spots in my chest expanded as if something had activated them. I froze. One was Bodey, the other Michael, but the third, I wasn't sure.

Oh, leave them alone, Janet interjected. She was the third. *Congratulations. I can't wait to celebrate your mateship with the entire pack later!*

My chest became uncomfortably full.

Me too, Bodey replied as he took my hand. *I can't wait for everyone to know she's mine.*

My cheeks hurt, and I realized I was smiling. The

fact he was proud of me...of us...made me happier than I'd ever thought possible.

This brings me back to my original question because both Callie and Samuel need to be protected. Bodey watched the road and the area around us as if searching for a threat.

All is calm, and Hells Canyon is prepared, Michael answered. *No one unknown has been in the area.*

Hells Canyon? Why did everything lead back there? I'd always been drawn to the canyon, and I'd met Bodey and the advisers there. Now it was the site of the coronation.

If you see or sense anything, let us know, Bodey linked and squeezed my hand.

Michael chuckled. *We will, son. Now focus on getting our daughter and Samuel to us so we can hug them both.*

Heart near bursting, I leaned forward and turned on the music, craving it after not being able to stand listening to anything for weeks.

As soon as Alanis Morissette's "Ironic" came on, I leaned my head back and kept a tight hold of Bodey's hand.

I, for one, held my head up high as Bodey and I followed Dina toward the sacred ceremony grounds. Dina led us to the Snake River, where ten witches were getting the materials needed for the ceremony ready. The guys' parents stood twenty feet back from the witches, with Theo and Zeke a few feet away from them. Trees were sparse this close to the riverbank.

The area was gorgeous, a perfect place for a coronation, with the canyons arching on both sides of the river and the greens of the grasses and tree line adding to the beauty. The sun was high, and the scattered clouds held no threat of rain.

How were the witches chosen for the ceremony? I linked with Bodey, wanting to know the details of everything he'd had a hand in planning.

They're the witches of the royal coven—they used to protect King Richard and Queen Mila. When the king and queen died and Samuel came to live with our pack, the royal witches joined our coven. When Samuel gets inked, if he decides to leave, the eleven will follow him wherever he goes, and the original priestess of our coven will take back control.

I took a step closer to Bodey as another question popped into my head. *Didn't that cause problems with your original priestess?* If an alpha got displaced, there would be bitterness.

He winked. *Witches aren't like wolves. The priestess was honored to have them join us. She's learned a great deal from Dina and all the others.*

Jack caught up to us, matching our pace. His eyes were on me as he glanced at my feet. He chuckled. "That's why you're not struggling like Stella."

"Sneakers are smart." I shrugged, and Bodey grinned.

Are we sure no humans will stumble across us? I asked Bodey.

The witches spelled the area to repel humans for miles. Bodey glanced at me. *No one will come close until they take down the spells.*

Theo and Zeke turned and saw me. They tensed, and then both of them marched toward us.

"What the *fuck* is she doing here?" Zeke rasped. "I didn't grant her permission to be here. She needs to go. *Now*."

I hadn't considered how Theo and Zeke would react to my presence. I'd been so consumed by Bodey that I'd forgotten it might be an issue.

"You have no say over her anymore," Bodey responded, his hand moving possessively to my waist as he lifted his chin.

The buzzing sensation between us increased, and my head spun. I stumbled, falling into him and sending a jolt of electricity up my spine.

"What did you *do* to her?" Zeke pointed a finger at Bodey. "Did you drug her?"

CHAPTER TWENTY-NINE

THE HATRED in Zeke's tone had the little girl in me wanting to bury my face in Bodey's muscular chest. His arms were already around me protectively, and it'd be so easy and nice to fold completely into him.

Instead, I straightened and stared Zeke in the eye as he continued to march toward us.

By the time he was standing in front of us, my body had adjusted to the sizzle, which was a good thing. I wouldn't be stepping away from my mate.

"He didn't *drug* me." I enunciated every word to ensure there was no misunderstanding and to prove I wasn't under any sort of influence...well, other than heightened hormones that made me want to strip Bodey naked in front of everyone and take him for the world to see.

But then they'd see him naked, which had my wolf growling.

I took it back. I was under the influence of horniness that couldn't be satiated.

Lucas and Jack flanked Bodey while Samuel, Miles, and Stella came to my side, the six of us standing strong together. The advisers' parents also hurried toward us.

I lifted my chin. "I'm still not used to the connection between Bodey and me."

Eyes widening, Theo sniffed and gasped. "You mated with *him*? You're supposed to be *mine*."

Bodey snarled and stepped toward him, releasing his arm from my waist. "She *never* was or will be yours."

I caught his hand, not wanting this situation to implode. We were here for Samuel, not to announce our mateship.

Zeke's neck corded, and his face turned red. He glared at Bodey's and my connected hands.

"Wait." Janet lifted a hand as she moved in front of Bodey. "What do you mean, your connection? How would that throw you off balance?" Her gaze flicked between Bodey and me.

I lifted our hands. "Whenever we touch." My face flamed. I had no clue why she'd asked. The question felt oddly intrusive. Everyone here must have experienced the same thing with their mates. "Maybe it's because I haven't been able to pack link before, but whenever we touch, the sparks inside me catch me off guard."

"Sparks?" She glanced at Michael. "That doesn't happen when we touch."

Stella inched forward so she could look around Samuel at me and asked, "Wait, that happens to you, too? I thought Miles and I were odd since no one else had experienced that. I assume it happens because we're fated mates. We felt it the first time we touched, too, before we mated."

My heart stopped, and Bodey's fingers tightened on mine.

"That's not possible." Bodey turned to me. "We didn't feel this until after we forged our bond last night."

The air sizzled between us, sparking with the electricity.

"Her magic is still being freed," Dina said from behind us. She appeared beside Jack, her eyes locking with ours. "You completed the mate bond—and the exchange of blood for the claiming ritual—must have unblocked her magic. You couldn't feel it until after you bonded, but you two are fated mates."

Bodey touched my face, the zap coursing between us at the touch. He linked, *I always felt like you were the one I was waiting for, and I was right.*

My pulse pounded in my ears. Knowing I was his fated confirmed everything we felt for each other. We'd felt like we were perfect for each other because we were. The best part was we'd *chosen* to be together before learning this.

Knowing that Bodey had waited for me since he was a little boy made me fall for him even harder. The ironic part was that I'd envied the woman he was determined to be with, and it'd been me all along.

Jack whistled. "Well, I want to see how Zeke spins this since they're fated and already bonded." He snapped his fingers. "Maybe he thinks he can go back in time and cockblock Bodey."

"Man..." Lucas shook his head. "Just shut it."

"Listen to your friend," Zeke snarled, then focused back on us. "*I* didn't approve your mate bond, and I don't accept this, so Callie will come home with *us*."

"Like hell she will." Bodey's body shook with anger. "We've completed the bond, she's my mate, and we don't need your approval. She's twenty-two and independent."

"Bullshit. She is *not* independent. She lives with her parents, can't hold down a job, and has been living with me for the past week." Zeke clenched his hands. "Therefore, you needed to get permission from her alpha. And I don't give it."

My stomach dropped. I couldn't believe what I was hearing. *Is that true?* Was that why Zeke had stopped me from leaving the pack all this time?

Old rules that no one follows anymore. Bodey snarled. *Which we'll throw out as soon as Samuel becomes king.*

Michael cleared his throat. "Technically, that's true, but their being fated mates overrides that, which you should know, Zeke." His face softened. "Why would you want to separate them, even if they weren't fated? They clearly care for each other."

"She's meant to be Theo's!" Zeke stomped, his nostrils flaring. "Theo has been talking to her, spending every evening with her at my house, and asked her to go to the dinner with him last night. Bodey pressured her into this mateship!"

Hurt coursed through our bond into my chest, fueling my anger. Zeke was trying to cause problems by making Bodey think I was interested in Theo. Evil, conniving prick. I stepped closer to Bodey, wanting to reassure him, as I spat, "Yes, Theo came to visit me every night, and we watched movies, but that was all.

We ate popcorn, laughed, and talked *like friends* do. And to clarify, Theo asked me to the coronation dinner, but he informed me that everyone had to bring a date. He assured me we were going as friends. I've made it *very* clear to Theo that I'm not interested in him beyond friendship."

"Why would Theo think he needed a date?" Bodey rasped, his anger mixing with mine.

Theo lifted his hands. "With the rift between me and you four, I wanted Callie at the dinner with me. She's my *best* friend."

The way Zeke sneered at his son had regret pooling inside me, but I'd done nothing wrong. I was speaking the truth, trying to shut Zeke down. I hadn't meant to make this harder on Theo.

"This argument is pointless, and we have more important things to attend to, like crowning our *king*." Dina stepped forward, the breeze lifting her hair around her face. "They're fated mates and have completed the bond. There's nothing Zeke can do about it. If we're worried about an attack, it's even more imperative that we get Samuel crowned."

Everyone seemed eager to listen to her, and I was all for turning our attention elsewhere. I wanted to celebrate Bodey's and my relationship, not defend it. Once again, Zeke wanted to taint something I held dear, but I refused to allow it to happen.

"Fine." Zeke nodded abruptly. "While the witches finish their preparations, I need to take a walk." His hands were tight fists. He spun on his heels and headed away from us.

"Aren't we supposed to stay here together to prevent people from noticing us?" Alicia pursed her lips from her spot across from Miles and next to Phil. Her wavy dark hair hit the middle of her back and almost blended in with the shade of her black dress.

"If he needs time to collect his thoughts and calm down, let him have it." Phil took his mate's hand.

Carl nodded. "I agree. And we need to check in with our pack members."

"I don't like him walking off." Bodey glared at Zeke's retreating figure.

He was walking faster now that he was farther away from us. Like he was running out of time.

"Don't stress too much," Dan said as he came over and patted Bodey on the shoulder. "He can't do a damn thing about your mate bond. Let him mope."

That was true. The only way to end a mateship was for one of the mates to die. Most of the time, the living mate wanted to follow suit, but like all things, eventually, they learned to live with the pain.

"Let's separate and disperse this negative energy," Dina commanded. She strolled to the river with the other witches, who were wearing the same dress she was but in black. They all bent down and set amethyst and red jasper crystals along the embankment.

Janet threw her arms around Bodey and me. She linked, *You don't know how happy this makes me!* She leaned back and touched Bodey's cheek. *I was rooting for the two of you after seeing how you took care of each other. There's no better match, and Fate agrees. Once Jasmine finds a mate, our family will be full, and grandbabies will be on the horizon!*

Grandbabies. I hadn't thought that far ahead, but there was no doubt I wanted babies with Bodey...

although I'd like for us to have some alone time before we went down that road.

Bodey laughed, his happiness warming my chest. "Don't worry. If I have my way, we'll have a bunch of babies. I don't plan on letting my mate stay clothed often."

My mouth dropped, and my head jerked toward him. But damn him, my body was already responding to his words. *Bodey! Your parents are right here!*

He waggled his brows. *I don't care. They'll be hearing a lot of moaning from our room soon.*

"I wish I could meet Jasmine today," I said. Talking about his sister should change the direction of this conversation.

Michael nodded. "We wanted her to attend, but after last night, we didn't dare risk it. Having too many people here could draw unwanted attention. Luckily, many packs are close by if there is an attack, and the witches' perimeter spells will alert us before it becomes an issue."

"She's been like a sister to me, and I hate that she's not here, too," Samuel said as he eased closer to me, his gaze on Theo, who was still several feet away, listening to our conversation.

"She'll be home soon." Janet forced a sad smile.

Samuel linked to all of us, *Zeke's up to something.*

When is he not? Bodey grimaced and tugged me closer to his side. *We'll figure it out after the coronation. We need to focus on you getting your ink and the crown.*

Unfortunately, I fear it'll take removing his pack as the reigning pack in Oregon to put him in his place, Michael replied, running a hand over the back of Janet's royal-blue halter-top dress.

My heart squeezed. Removing Zeke's pack would have horrible repercussions, and my family would get caught up in the drama. However, I had to focus on one problem at a time, and I was certain Bodey and I would have time to figure out how to help them. Maybe they'd be more open to switching packs once they met Bodey, but I doubted Pearl would willingly join a pack in which I was the alpha's mate.

Theo walked over to us. Bodey tucked me behind him and puffed out his chest.

"Callie, can I talk with you?" Theo asked and clasped his hands in front of him.

"No," Bodey snarled.

"Samuel." Janet took his arm and tugged him and Michael toward the witches. "We should make sure they don't need any help."

Though they were giving the three of us a moment alone, I noticed Jack perk up and nudge Lucas. Jack nodded toward us.

"I'm not here to cause problems." Theo lifted his hands, and the foul smell of sulfur was missing.

"Good." I nodded, moving back to Bodey's side. I refused to be protected from this inevitable conversation. "Whatever you have to say can be said in front of Bodey."

My mate smirked. *I love you.*

Huffing, Theo rubbed his hands together. "Fine." For a moment, there was silence, and then he said, "Even though I wanted Callie as my—"

Bodey bared his teeth and grabbed Theo's shirt. Theo's head jerked back.

I placed a hand on Bodey's arm. *He's not a threat.*

I'm yours. I have been since the day you saved me at Hells Canyon. Let's listen to what he has to say.

Letting out a long sigh, Bodey relaxed and released his grip.

Theo tried to smooth the wrinkles from his shirt. He glanced at me. "I assume I have you to thank for that."

I wanted to roll my eyes. "Is that all you wanted to say?"

"He'd better have more to say. If that was all, then he and I are going to have a huge fight." Bodey got into Theo's face and growled, "She is *mine.*"

A vein between Theo's eyes bulged, but he side-stepped to focus on me. "If he makes you happy, then congratulations are in order. I want you to be happy, even if it's not with me."

Some tension eased from Bodey's body, and my lungs moved more freely.

"We good, man?" Theo held out his hand.

Bodey paused but then shook it. "As long as you stop trying to claim her for yourself."

"She's hard to let go." Theo mashed his lips together. "But if you're what she wants, I'd be an ass not to back off."

Unable to stop myself, I hugged Theo. I never doubted he'd come around, and when he took over the adviser spot, his attitude would bridge the gap between our pack and the other advisers.

Don't push it, Bodey linked, jealousy coursing through our bond.

I laughed and backed away, then looped my arm through Bodey's and pulled him to my side. I smiled. "Thank you. Bodey makes me *extremely* happy." I turned to Bodey and got lost in my mate's eyes. I couldn't imagine feeling happier than I did right then.

Tenderness lightened his irises. "If you'll excuse us, I want to talk to my *mate* for a moment before the ceremony starts." Bodey led me away to one of the few trees near the river.

He pulled me to his chest, our bodies flush. He tucked a piece of my hair behind my ear and linked, *I can't believe I was so stupid. I should've known.*

Known what?

His palm pressed into my lower back. *That we're fated mates.*

My magic was suppressed. There was no way to know. My wolf was trapped, and there wasn't a way to forge our connection until we mated.

He kissed my forehead and linked, *We'll find out who did this to you and why.*

The world spun. Finding out who'd hidden my wolf and why I'd been taken from my biological parents hadn't crossed my mind. Now that he'd mentioned it, I *needed* those answers. If a witch had blocked my magic, she must have altered my memories, too. "I'd really like that."

"Then it will be our priority," he whispered, tilting my face upward.

The thrum of our bond had me falling against him, and I wrapped my arms around his neck. "But first, Samuel."

Our chests rubbed together, and I forgot where we were. Something inside me tugged toward him and reveled in the way his body pressed against mine.

He growled. *You're making me forget why we're*

here. There's nowhere I want to be except in our bed with you.

Our bed.

The words rang between us. The fact we were one in all ways was still surreal, and we now shared a bedroom. *I can't wait until we get back.*

He kissed me, but when I tried to deepen the kiss, he pulled away. I chased his lips, and he chuckled.

As much as I want to ruin your lipstick, I have a secret I've never shared with anyone. He leaned back, a devilish smirk on his face.

I wasn't sure where this was heading. *Which is?*

Stella scares me. He winked. *If I mess up your makeup...*

I slid my hand between us and brushed his crotch. He hissed as his hips pressed into me.

I smiled sweetly. *You were saying?*

Footsteps pounded toward us, and Stella said, "Nope. If you ruin her makeup, you're on Jack duty all weekend. You know he'll be partying hard after the coronation."

Babe, I want to touch you all weekend instead of just now, he linked and took a large step away from me, detangling his limbs from my body. His eyes were wide as if having to deal with a drunken Jack was the worst thing in existence.

I'd lost to Jack. I wasn't sure how I felt about that.

"Don't get mad at me." Bodey gestured to Stella and said, "She's vicious."

The corners of her mouth tipped upward. "Don't you forget it." She flipped her hand and pulled me away from my mate, nodding toward the group that was flocking together once more. "Zeke's back."

"Oh." I hadn't noticed.

"That's what happens when you're ogling your mate." She arched a brow, but there was no judgment, just understanding.

"Fine." I gestured at her shoes. "I see you removed them." If she was going to give me hell, I'd give it right back.

"Yeah, I didn't realize we'd be out here. I thought it'd be more like the vineyard." She laughed. "From now on, I'm following your footwear lead."

As we reached the others, Jack smacked Lucas on the arm. "Look. She got those two to stop eye-fucking."

"Jack Landry," Destiny chastised, placing a hand on her stomach. "You do not speak like that in the presence of elders."

"Oh, damn." He winced. "I'm so sorry for doing that shit."

His mother glared at him, but when Taylor chuckled, Destiny's expression slipped as she fought a smile.

Zeke tugged on his black tie and wiped the sweat from his forehead. His face was a little red, but it didn't appear to be solely from anger.

He must've shifted or done something else to calm down.

"Let's move forward," he said as he lifted his chin. He wanted to pretend he was in charge of the situation.

Carl, Phil, Dan, and Michael scowled, but Dina picked up a small black cauldron and motioned for the other ten coven members to head to the water.

The ten stepped into the river, just enough for the water to cover their ankles. They winced from the cold but then schooled their expressions. Dina stepped to the river's edge, where the water ran under her feet, and gestured for Samuel. He took off his shoes and walked down the embankment through the small opening between the gems.

"Royal advisers, come and gather around," Dina commanded, her voice louder than normal.

Bodey squeezed my hand and slipped the car keys into my palm. He, along with Jack, Lucas, and Miles, went to stand behind Samuel. Zeke moved, but he glanced at me, his eyes glowing.

I shivered.

The rest of us stayed together, Stella on my right and Theo on my left. Zeke moved into place in the advisers' line on the side closest to our group.

Dina cupped the cauldron in her hands. "Once the ritual starts, it can't be stopped without dire consequences, which may include never being able to crown the king. If anyone wishes to bring up any concerns, now is the time."

Something hard settled in my chest, and my gaze went to Zeke. He was the likeliest person to contest Samuel's coronation. Bodey's tension swirled into me and merged with mine. It was odd that I could feel his emotions but more so that I could sense we were worried about the same thing.

When no one said a word, Dina nodded, and the unease within us ebbed.

"Samuel, please remove your jacket and shirt so we can watch the ink accept you." Dina gestured to the spot on the ground next to him.

Samuel obliged, and I could feel Bodey's unease. Knowing what this was about, I mashed my lips together. He didn't want me staring at another man's naked torso.

When Samuel was done, Dina continued, "Then the official proceedings shall now begin." She waved a hand toward the ten witches behind her and then at herself. "The ten coven leaders and the high priestess are taking part in the ceremony as proof that we will support the ruler moving forward. Our magic will mark the heir, thus giving that person the crown. The royal's acceptance of the ink is their vow to uphold the promise forged between wolves and witches centuries ago."

Footsteps shuffled against the grass, and I tensed. Someone was coming.

Everyone turned toward the noise except for Dina and Samuel, who remained staring at each other.

"It's Stevie," Theo said. "No need for alarm."

The ten witches lifted their arms, but a strange expression passed over all their faces. One gasped, "The perimeter isn't working."

Dina lifted the cauldron under her chin and continued, her words tense and loud, "In preparation for this ceremony, we spelled Samuel's skin to ease the suffering from the ink as it marks him. Additionally, herbs were administered to him to lessen the internal pain as well."

Stevie appeared, running toward us. Her dirty-blonde hair was braided but disheveled, strands flying everywhere, and her dark-brown eyes were wide and frantic. They locked on me as her pink pajama shirt blew behind her and her matching fleece bottoms dragged on the ground. She yelled, "The perimeter is down. There's about to be an attack!"

Something *was* wrong. She shouldn't be here. "What are you talking about—"

"The queen! She's attacking *right now*." Stevie reached us, her breathing ragged.

"How do you know that?" I swallowed, dreading the answer.

She averted her gaze to the ground. "Because I've been helping her."

CHAPTER THIRTY

IN THE FOLLOWING SILENCE, the world tilted under my feet. Stevie had been helping the queen? How? *Why?* None of this made sense.

Bitterness filled my mouth as anger stabbed my chest.

Dina continued, "The ritual includes the Snake River, which wields magic." She circled her hands, making the ink in the bowl. Her eyes continued to flicker around us as if she were seeking something. "To prepare, we went to the sacred site in each of the five states to gather the magic required for this ink."

"We don't have time for this." Stevie gestured to Dina. "We need to go."

"The ritual can't be stopped once it's started," Michael replied.

Baby, you need to leave, Bodey linked, then included his parents, along with other pack members I wasn't familiar with. *Everyone who can, go. We're under attack.*

I'm not leaving you. My gaze went to the ink, and I

stared, transfixed. It truly was a ritual...a rite of nature, magic, and our bodies.

Theo inched toward me, our arms brushing. He whispered, "We should get you out of here."

Bodey, we see wolves, a woman pack member linked. *A lot of them.*

The world froze. The parents around Stella and I tensed. Everyone had received the same message.

How is that possible? Janet asked. *No one knew where we were heading this morning except for the alpha advisers and Dina. We were so careful to tell only the alphas patrolling the area a short time before coming here.*

No one responded as a male linked, *We're under attack!*

"Providing the mark is my coven's promise to protect the new royal family." Dina waved a hand over the cauldron. "The royal's acceptance of it is their vow to protect us from our enemies in return. This is the natural balance between our species. And now the marking will begin." Dina threw the ink from the bowl in the air in front of her. "Goddess, mark the shifter who is to lead us until they depart from earth and move on to their next life."

The liquid hovered, suspended, as it rolled within itself. Then something shifted.

A warning buzzed in my neck and throat.

"Something's wrong," I whispered, unsure how I knew. A tether *yank*ed inside me.

"Yeah, we're under attack," Stella whispered. "Your sister must have told them the location."

"I didn't. I tracked Callie's phone to get here."

Stevie crossed her arms. "The queen called me thirty minutes ago to tell me things would be taken care of."

Howls echoed around us way too close, the sound of many wolves...more than had attacked us last night. We needed to get Samuel inked and out of here.

"You begged me not to come here." I remembered her pleading voice. This was too convenient.

Stevie winced. "Callie, I swear I knew nothing. I was scared the queen planned to disrupt the ceremony —that's why I followed up."

I wanted to believe her, but I couldn't, despite the missing scent of a lie.

I turned my attention back to the ink, which still hovered over Dina, and time stood still. I fidgeted, willing the ink to move. Salt-N-Pepa's song "Push It" started playing in my head. I was tempted to rush out there and blow the ink toward Samuel if it didn't get its act together.

The voice of the man from earlier popped into my head. *We're greatly outnumbered. You need to move and protect Samuel.*

My heart pounded. The spell wasn't complete, and worse, the advisers had to participate in the ritual. *I'll go fight,* I linked, hating to miss the moment, but it wouldn't last if the wolves got here and killed Samuel.

No, Bodey linked. *Don't run into battle.*

A familiar hand clutched my arm, and Theo murmured, "Come on."

"Yeah, we need to fight." I nodded, glad Theo was on the same page as me.

He tugged me toward the vehicles and growled, "We aren't fighting. I'm getting you and Stevie out of here."

I shook my head. "I'm not leaving Bodey and *running*."

"If you get hurt, everything will be for nothing." Stevie's bottom lip quivered. "I need you to leave with me."

"No!"

We're going to shift, Michael linked as he handed his keys to Janet and stripped off his jacket. He ran toward the sound of wolves. The other dads followed suit while the women stayed put. Michael continued, *The women need to go to the cars.*

Do not trust Theo or Stevie, but I agree you need to go with Mom, Stella, and the others. Bodey's words broke even through the link. His eyes were locked on me as he stood in place. *She might be the reason those scouts attacked you in Halfway. Go to my Jeep and leave. I'll let you know when to come back and get us.*

A sick feeling spread through my body. *I'm not leaving. I'm either here by your side or out there fighting to protect you and Samuel.* Actually, staying here might be better. If any wolves got past our pack, I could fight them off.

I glanced at the ink, which continued to swirl in the air as if it wouldn't accept anyone.

"What's the holdup?" Jack snarled. "Why isn't it moving?"

Dina's eyes narrowed. "I don't know."

Fate was a bitch.

As if she didn't appreciate my thought, the inky substance floated upward and formed a line as it inched across the sky.

The women surrounded me, watching the ink. I

didn't have to link with them to know that none of them wanted to leave their mates behind.

"Callie, this isn't up for debate." Theo yanked on my arm, causing me to lose my balance.

I caught myself and snarled, "I'm not going *anywhere* with you."

"Get your hands off her," Bodey growled, his gaze on me as his fear iced my veins. "Mom, get Callie out of here."

I dug my feet into the ground. "I'm not going anywhere, no matter what the three of you want."

Five wolves bounded out of the tree line toward us. More were coming, and Janet and the other women finally moved.

Janet took the keys from my hand and tossed them and hers at Stella. "Take our keys," she commanded. "We'll be behind you all in case we need to shift."

Stella nodded and herded the other women toward the vehicles.

I prepared to shift. I hadn't fought in wolf form before, but there was no time to learn like the present.

"What the *fuck*?" Jack gasped, and my attention flicked back to the guys.

The inky substance was floating over Samuel's head toward the advisers.

Lucas scratched his neck, his attention sliding from the ink to the wolves racing toward them. "I'm in agreement with Jack on this one."

"Do you know what's going on?" Miles's face turned to stone.

"No." Dina's eyes widened. "But we can't leave, or we won't have a ruler!"

"Maybe the ink knows Samuel isn't fit," Zeke dead-panned, though his body was tense.

The wolves were closing in; they'd be on them in seconds. I didn't have any time to lose. "I have to fight."

My skin tingled as my wolf surged forward, but Bodey linked, his horror bleeding straight into my heart, *Callie, go. Please. I can't stand the thought of something bad happening to you.*

I feel the same way about you.

"We're outnumbered, Callie," Theo rasped, tugging, but he released his grip on my arm and gasped. "You're sprouting fur."

"Holy shit!" Stevie exhaled. "How is that possible?"

My wolf whimpered and pulled back, even as I urged her forward.

What the hell was her problem? We'd just connected last night!

I searched harder for that connection as more wolves raced behind the first five. Every wolf homed in on Samuel, their bodies moving as quickly as possible.

Great. My second time shifting, and I was going to pass out.

Too bad. I refused to give up.

Callie! Bodey linked, and I could feel him racing toward me.

"The spell!" Dina shouted.

No! He was supposed to watch Samuel while the ink accepted him.

"Fuck the spell," Bodey snarled. "Fuck everything if she dies."

Agony stabbed into the back of my neck and upper shoulder, where the tingles had started. The pain was worse than anything I'd ever experienced. Blackness edged in around me.

"Shit," Theo rasped. "Callie, stay here. A wolf is about to attack you. Stevie, protect her. Don't let anything happen to her!"

"I'll protect her," Janet snarled. "*She* doesn't need to."

I agreed. I didn't trust Stevie to protect me. My heart panged even more.

I heard a wolf coming toward us. The worst part was that I couldn't see him, but I could hear paws racing toward me as others pounded toward the advisers.

"How is this possible?" Samuel gasped.

That was an excellent question. The wolves shouldn't be here. I lifted my head to see what was going on.

"Callie, it's going to be okay," Stevie assured me, her voice full of concern.

Even if I could, I wouldn't have answered her. I'd thought Pearl was a bitch, but nothing compared to Stevie's betrayal.

Bones cracked as snarls and the metallic stench of blood swirled around me, but I still couldn't see anything. I was blanketed in darkness.

I got on my hands and knees and tried to crawl toward the pull, but my limbs quit working.

"Callie," Janet rasped, her hands tugging at me. My body was dead weight, and she couldn't move me.

"Do *not* harm her," Zeke bellowed.

Torment assaulted me, taking over my body and senses. My magic coursed through me, reaching for the hurt as if inviting it to merge within me.

"Protect her!" Dina shouted. "The spell is in its final stages!"

Thank gods. It was about damn time.

"Bodey, Lucas, to the left!" Samuel yelled, his voice ragged. Then he grunted. "Guard her at all costs. Forget about me."

Something was off. I could hear it in Samuel's voice...feel it in the panic that slammed into me from Bodey. I couldn't focus on anything but the darkness and torture.

My wolf howled in suffering...and acceptance. Emotions collided as I gripped the earth underneath my hands.

"Someone help her!" Stevie shouted. "Something is wrong. I can't get it away from her!"

Panic churned into me from Bodey, and a flash of pain coursed through our fated-mate bond. My mate had been injured.

Bodey, I whimpered, unable to form words with my lips.

"Baby," Bodey rasped as his body dropped beside me. *I'm fine. I'm here. I need to carry you.*

A rough, warm hand clutched mine, and a strong buzzing sensation flared up my arm. I focused on the sweet agony from my fated mate touching my hand. If I was dying, at least his touch would be the last thing I felt...the best sensation in the world.

Snarls snapped around me as I clung to my mate and succumbed to the darkness.

ABOUT THE AUTHOR

Jen L. Grey is a *USA Today* Bestselling Author who writes Paranormal Romance, Urban Fantasy, and Fantasy genres.

Jen lives in Tennessee with her husband, two daughters, and two miniature Australian Shepherds. Before she began writing, she was an avid reader and enjoyed being involved in the indie community. Her love for books eventually led her to writing. For more information, please visit her website and sign up for her newsletter.

Check out her future projects and book signing events at her website.
www.jenlgrey.com

Blood Legacy

Rising Fate

The Royal Heir Trilogy

Wolves' Queen

Wolf Unleashed

Wolf's Claim

Bloodshed Academy Trilogy

Year One

Year Two

Year Three

The Half-Breed Prison Duology (Same World As Bloodshed Academy)

Hunted

Cursed

The Artifact Reaper Series

Reaper: The Beginning

Reaper of Earth

Reaper of Wings

Reaper of Flames

Reaper of Water

Stones of Amaria (Shared World)

Kingdom of Storms

Kingdom of Shadows

Kingdom of Ruins

Kingdom of Fire

The Pearson Prophecy

Dawning Ascent

Enlightened Ascent

Reigning Ascent

Stand Alones

Death's Angel

Rising Alpha

Made in United States
North Haven, CT
14 September 2023

41542646R00240